ASCALON

ELLEN L. EKSTROM

Whyte Rose & Violet, Scribes

Ascalon

ISBN: 978-0615990965

Published in the United States of America

Cover design: Whyte Rose & Violet Artists
Images courtesy of Susan Stewart and
AdobeStock

Whyte Rose & Violet, Scribes

www.whyteroseandviolet.net

To Stephen.

ASCALON

Prologue

The Wedding Breakfast

August 1205

PETRONELLE RAPPED ON the door and waited a moment. Leaning in just a bit, she hoped to hear laughter or conversation. Perhaps they were still asleep; after all, it was the morning after their wedding. When there was no response, Petronelle used the secret knocks only she and George knew.

Once, twice, thrice.

Still, there was no response. Only a dull echo in the stairwell of Ravenglass Tower repeating until there was silence. Testing the latch, Petronelle was surprised to find it free. She paused, tapping her fingers on the metal. If she entered would George's boot, hurled across the room, bid her a good morning as it did in times past? At least this morning there wouldn't be a mad dash on the other side of the door to hide whoever shared George's bed the night before and frantic, hoarse, whispering and giggling amidst the rustle of clothes behind the bed curtains.

Still, there was the boot she had to consider.

Petronelle leaned gently on the door, doing her best to raise the latch silently. It groaned from age and lack of oil. Then she peeked around the frame, carefully, just in case.

Joanna was alone and seated by the window. At the sound of Petronelle's footsteps and the rustle of her skirts, Joanna turned and smiled, looked away again.

"Good morning, Sister!" Petronelle greeted. "I may call you that, mayn't I?"

"Of course," Joanna replied.

Now Petronelle gestured towards the open window. "It looks to be a pleasant and warm day. I remember the view of Little Longdale was particularly excellent from here."

"Please." Joanna extended a hand to the window seat.

Petronelle crossed the bedchamber and settled onto the cushions, drawing knees to chin and wrapping arms around them. This was how she always sat when in George's enormous solar and that morning it felt natural for Petronelle to be with Joanna and watch the horizon change as the sun climbed into the sky and a new day broke. There'd been many mornings like this in the past, but those were with her quarrelsome older brother and not his bride. Rather than an angry exchange of insults and accusations, the cadence of a psalm echoed in the chamber. Petronelle listened to the whispered morning prayers Joanna offered, and was surprised. After everything she'd gone through, after all she suffered, she still had faith? She was ever a mystery, this Joanna.

They were night and day: Petronelle was fair of eyes and coloring and what some called spirited—her mother the dowager countess Maud called it selfishness and conceit. Joanna was dark of hair, her eyes were slate-colored, sometimes bluish, more often gray, and always bright yet guarded, as they were this morning. Had she not known it for a fact, Petronelle wouldn't have guessed Joanna a Welsh heiress, for she came to Skelwith Castle a skinny, elfin, girl in rags, following the great, golden, Earl of Grasmere, George Ascalon, like a stray dog.

She came unwillingly, Petronelle remembered. George had done a chivalrous thing and saved Joanna from the savagery of immolation and brought her to Skelwith "because I didn't know what else to do with her," he confessed later, "except that I wanted more than anything to kiss her, as wretched and as filthy as she was." Much to her brother's delight, he got that chance in the secret garden of the Golden Tower and a force of life came from those sweet kisses. To see his face when spoke of that time with Joanna! It was hard to believe, but George the great seducer, the charming flirt, was in love for all time. This was no easy seduction or light-o-loves to be forgotten. How it came about was worthy of a ballad. Now the elfin creature in rags was the Countess of Grasmere.

Despite the favor and title bestowed on Joanna Fletcher, the people in Grasmere and the castle too, took their time acknowledging her precedence and still called her 'the little whore' and 'the Witch of

Butcher's Lane.' They'd be sorry for it. When they discovered the new countess was the daughter of a Princess of Gwynedd and the Earl of Merioneth, George would have them bend the knee and beg her forgiveness or find themselves dancing at the end of a rope. Perhaps Joanna would mete out punishment herself. Petronelle would like to see that, for Joanna was more than her outward appearance. Ah, the moment she chided the proud Elinor Lucy and put her in her place, and later, when they returned victorious from Eskeleth, how she stared down Countess Maud! George found his equal in everything when he dragged Joanna out of that burning cottage . . .

> *O Lord, holy Father, almighty eternal God: who hast refreshed me with thy Word, I beseech that this sacrament of our salvation, which, unworthy sinner as I am, I will receive this day, may not come to me to judgment nor to condemnation for my deserts, but to the perfecting of body and soul to eternal life. Amen.*

Saying this, Joanna closed the missal in her lap and sighed.

"He went early?" Petronelle ventured after an unbearably awkward silence.

"It's what the earls of Grasmere do, or so he said," Joanna answered lightly. "And now we wait."

"The women of Ascalon get their strength from waiting—saints in heaven! After what he endured, he kept this?" said Petronelle, and she took George's tabard from Joanna's lap and held it to the light, fingering worn spots and frayed edges, blood stains turned brown and rust, the strips of red linen that formed a cross and now dangling by threads. There were new stains. His blood and Joanna's. "My poor brother," Petronelle sighed and crossed herself.

"He's somewhat whole, thanks to you. You proved yourself admirably. He was right to have you accompany him."

"I'm a spoiled girl used to getting what she wants no matter who suffers for it. God forgive me a thousand times for making it George."

Without diverting her glance from the horizon, Joanna smiled and said, "No, Sister. It was a dragon that suffered most of all. And then there was a sorceress, which I remember, you paid in kind for her unwanted attention to George."

How they laughed at this, these companions-at-arms and sisters by marriage, remembering the coppice of charred trees that looked like monstrous skeletons dancing; the sickly, pale, sunlight and sulfuric air in Eskeleth; the miraculous apple tree; the frightening Golden Tower; and the Three Challenges. Then, it was nothing humorous. In retrospect, the women knew they'd survived an ordeal from Hell and showed as much courage as the men, except for George, who showed amazing valor and strength and won every contest against all odds.

"T'was an Eve that threw the apple and drove a snake out of Eden!" Petronelle said, winking.

"And broke her fast with it," Joanna said wistfully, remembering how she fed George with apples from the great tree in the coppice. "I am grateful for those trials, for though my husband suffered much he did survive, we all survived, and they brought me here."

"And now you are a wife!" Petronelle teased and Joanna nodded, smiling. Petronelle leaned in and asked, "Was he gentle?"

"A perfect knight in so many ways. And a perfect night."

Petronelle began to reminisce about her wedding night and the solicitous advice that came with her sister-in-law's memories was ignored, for Joanna was no innocent nor virgin bride. Joanna spent months a prisoner of King John's men on the Welsh borderlands. She was sold from nobleman to soldier to fletcher and used like a whore and left for dead so many times.

Until her time with George, she was always used for another's pleasure and release, sometimes violently. Joanna never knew the excitement and sweetness of physical love that she discovered in George's bed and found she liked experimenting with love play, which made her husband's enthusiasm equal to hers . . .

". . . hate it when Roger must attend Court, for then we are apart for so many weeks. Tell me. Does my brother still snore?"

"He sounds like a . . . kitten," Joanna admitted, and they laughed again.

"Roger sounds like a hungry bear. He is a *hungry* bear at sunrise!"

"Are you with child?"

"I wish! But no matter; Roger says there's time enough, and I like nothing better than wishing him a good morning," Petronelle giggled, a pretty blush spreading across her cheeks. "He goes to London on the morrow to receive the titles promised to him."

"Petronelle Ascalon, now Mowbray, Countess of Myrce and Lady of Osterle and Kenning," Joanna said, leaning over to offer a kiss. "No one is your equal."

"Only you! No lady in the northwest is your equal. You'll sit in the place of honor at the high table for your wedding breakfast and you'll have a great household. I can't wait to see Elinor and my mother's faces when you enter the hall today, escorted by George's household guard!"

Again, Joanna was circumspect for she held dear the memory of another lady that men swore had no equal and on a momentous day: her mother, Elen, a princess of Gwynedd and the Countess of Merioneth. She held fast to the vision of Elen seated beside the Earl in the great hall of their manor house, especially on days when she was sad or lonely.

In her mind's eye, Joanna climbed the platform in the great hall where her parents sat in their great chairs of state. The soft wool of her new kirtle and *bliaut* whispered as she carried the hems to keep from tripping and scuffing her soft leather slippers. Joanna dropped the fabric so that it danced in folds around her as she knelt before Elen for a blessing. It was her fourteenth name day. How could she forget the smile on her mother's lips and in her eyes? That was the morning Joanna left for the convent in Towyn to begin her education. Months later the convent would be destroyed, and she would be taken by the English

King's men and used as a hostage in her father's quarrel with him. She'd never see her mother again.

The bards used to sing that Elen was the fairest of women in Gwynedd and remembering the way her mother often looked, Joanna knew this was so. Strands of gold ribbon and pearls were often laced through her mother's coal-black plaits, and her cheeks bloomed with rosy color. Her laughing eyes were the shade of the gray stones of the mountains Joanna's father, Rhodri, loved so well and he swore that she was the goddess Arianrhod come to life. Rhodri also swore that the crystal gray of Joanna's eyes was the same, that mother and daughter were one spirit and the goddess resided in both, that the daughter was equal to her mother.

Never once did Joanna imagine that she could be her mother's equal.

But if George were here, Joanna thought, *he would tell me I was equal to none.*

Had he not said just that hours before he slipped quietly away?

Instinctively, Joanna's hands gently caressed her belly, and she kept them so, thinking of the night. Surely there was a child already made from their love, for there had been the other times after the first at St. Bryde's, and she'd missed her courses. She was certain the way her breasts swelled and hurt was not due to George's enthusiastic attention, nor was her fatigue, and she smiled, remembering the hours of lovemaking.

There's no one like you, Joanna! I want no one. No other woman. I swear it . . .

". . . How you'll change this quiet, dull, place!" Petronelle was chattering and once again brought Joanna back to morning in the solar.

"That will depend on Countess Maud, I think."

"That will depend on *you*, Sister. George made it clear when he sent Mother to the lodge that there will be only one Countess of Grasmere holding court at Skelwith."

"I won't disappoint him."

You would never disappoint me.

George's words came to her as a breeze drifted through the window and felt his lips on her cheek. She smiled; since the three challenges at the Golden Tower of Eskeleth, which they now called the Trial, nothing surprised her. Nothing was strange. She was the happiest she'd been in her life. It was impossible to imagine what could spoil this.

Joanna rose and fetched the tabard from Petronelle, which she folded and placed under her bed pillow.

"He'll return," Petronelle said as she slid off the window seat.

Now Joanna threw the blankets and cover over the mattress and drew the curtains. "They'll expect to find blood," she sighed.

"But didn't you—?"

"Oh, yes, of course; but that was a while ago. When we were at St. Bryde's Abbey."

"But—oh. *Ohh!* Well, he's gone to be a contemplative. Most people don't expect monks to do much of anything," Petronelle answered with a shrug.

"And George Ascalon?"

They laughed at this.

"Come, Sister. My ladies are expecting me. I was told to dress in fine raiment for the wedding breakfast."

They walked arm and arm down the stairs of Ravenglass tower and at the landing took another flight of stairs leading to the left and up again to the bower, a large hall set apart for the countess. Joanna's ladies-in-waiting bowed when a guard opened the door and she stepped across the threshold.

"Oh!" Joanna whispered as she looked around and hoped no one could read the disappointment on her face.

Her private quarters were a suite of bare, cold, chambers, as inviting as a monastery cell. Someone at least had thought to set flowers in a bowl and freshen the air with sprigs of rosemary. Buds of lavender sent up their perfume from a tented bathtub placed near the fire pit in the center of the room. This luxury was thoughtful, inviting, and it was hers, Joanna mused.

No, she thought, smiling, it was impossible to imagine what could spoil this.

The doors broke open and Elinor Lucy marched in.

Nothing and no one could shake Joanna's self-confidence like Elinor Lucy, who was the wife of Skelwith Castle's chancellor, William Longleate, and who was once a rival for George's affection. Elinor spoiled the perfect morning when she came in uninvited and unannounced with two maids carrying a brightly-painted chest.

"Elinor? What's this?" Petronelle asked.

"The little countess is late for chapel and her wedding breakfast. Our Lord Earl instructed me to bring this Bride Gift, to let the little countess know she is not already forgotten," Elinor said.

Petronelle looked to Joanna first, then the embarrassed maids struggling with the chest, and then to Elinor. "What kind of remark is that, Elinor?" she demanded.

"Just what it is, my lady. A message from the earl to his little countess."

"Why by all that is holy would he entrust that to you?" Petronelle said. "And 'little countess?' That's very much an insult."

"I remember that was the name for every wench and whore George took a fancy to or took to his bed," Elinor replied, glancing at Joanna.

"Even you. His wife deserves better," Petronelle spat.

"Does she?"

"Oh, for God's sake! Put the chest down and let us see what's inside," Joanna snapped.

The chamber echoed with a thump and rattle as the chest was dropped.

"Goodness! Are there jewels and gold coins in there?" Joanna's lady-in-waiting Margaret quipped as she came forward to inspect the chest.

"It is heavy, Mistress Margaret," one of the girls said, rubbing her arms.

"Ah, then it must be a hoard of gold! They say a treasure was found in a cave near Chester from the days of the conquest and that King Harold hid it there himself," said Margaret gleefully. "What an honor that would be, to have such a bride gift."

"Wouldn't that be my luck? I could use it to purchase back my inheritance from the King," Joanna said.

"My lady countess, you once said you didn't expect much from the young Earl," Elinor commented when Joanna knelt to open the chest. She now glanced at each of the ladies, smirking. As far as Elinor knew, George Ascalon never spent silver on a lady except to pay her for the night's labor. This little mouse would be lucky to get a penny. No doubt the chest was full of George's personal effects for her safekeeping while he played the penitent. She was good at that, this little Fletcher whore. The ever-obedient puppy brought to heel, following the great, golden, George dutifully, hoping for a kind word, a crumb of affection or respect.

Or, Elinor thought, *perhaps I see myself in her and inflict my open wounds on her?*

The women gasped when Joanna threw back the lid to reveal four dresses made of expensive cloth, each of them decorated at the neck, forearms, sleeve cuffs and skirt hems with bands of cloth embroidered with metallic threads and jewels in contrasting yet harmonious tones. Each complimented Joanna's coloring and eyes: a soft yet vibrant rose, the darkest lapis, a luminous pale green that shimmered with gold when the light struck it, and a rich shade of wine. Under the layer of clothing were casks of jewels and ornaments.

"Quite a bit more than the nothing our countess usually expects, wouldn't you say, Elinor?" Petronelle jibed.

"Much more," Joanna said. She lovingly caressed the fabrics and glanced at Petronelle, smiling back.

"It seems my brother pays close attention to his lady, for each of these colors are perfectly suited to her," said Petronelle to Elinor, who quietly fumed, a smile frozen on her lips. "Elinor? Is something wrong? You look pale. Perhaps you should go lie down."

"The morning has been too warm," Elinor replied.

"Or perhaps the attention has been taken from you?" Margaret added.

"You ought to know your place!"

"Beside the countess, I think!"

Elinor raised a hand as if to strike Margaret and Joanna blocked it. Elinor slowly lowered hers, clenching it in a fist that disappeared, trembling, into the folds of her dress.

"Enough!" Joanna ordered. "Listen to yourselves! If being countess is like minding a gaggle of geese, then I'd rather go back to Butcher's Lane!" She turned to Elinor and stared daggers into her, knowing the woman was ready to say something altogether unkind. "Go on, Elinor; we all know what you're going to say."

"Not a thing, my lady," said Elinor.

The hour that followed was quiet as Joanna was bathed. Then the dressed were spread out on the bed and an animated discussion started among the women about which of the beautiful dresses Joanna should wear.

"Where's the coronet?" Petronelle suddenly spoke up. She'd been supervising the selection of ornaments and was now pointing towards where it usually sat on the smooth top of a velvet pillow on a bedside table. "The Countess of Grasmere's coronet always sits there. Where has it gone?"

"Perhaps the dowager countess still has it?" Elinor replied. "One of you," she said, snapping her fingers at the ladies, "go fetch it back from Countess Maud."

"Elinor, I think it should be you," Joanna said.

"My lady? I think she would not welcome me."

"Do you think that? Perhaps it is because you tried to seduce her husband not so long ago," Petronelle spoke up.

"That is long past," Joanna chided. "Knowing my father-in-law, well, it is conjecture, is it not? He is a man of the cloth now, isn't he?"

"My thanks, Lady Countess." Elinor demurred.

"Still, we all know how quarrelsome Maud can be. It would be best done by you, Mistress Longleate, as she counts you among her friends and she's likely not to bite you," Joanna continued. "And she wouldn't dare keep the coronet from you since you and she both think it is yours by some right no one has been able to cipher."

"My lady, how can you—?"

"Elinor, do me this favor," Joanna said quietly and motioned to the door.

Expelling an exasperated sigh, Elinor left quietly save for the whispering of her skirts on the floor and the slam of a door.

Joanna closed eyes and crossed herself. The room was quiet. Then she turned to look at the women and smiling, said, "How I came away from that unscathed is by the grace of Our Blessed Mother Mary!"

"Oh Joan," Petronelle giggled, using her familiar name; "You can be unkind."

"I may still have to lick some wounds," Joanna replied, and then, "Ladies! Will you help me dress?"

A flurry of activity made Joanna ready to greet the castle household as its new mistress.

The wedding breakfast was as important as the marriage ceremony itself, for the bride would be presented to the family and household and her husband would present her with 'morning gifts,' or 'bride gifts' that signified to others how well she pleased him and if the bedding had been successful. That George was content with his bride was evident by these expensive dresses, jewels, and ornaments. Still, this knowledge was of no comfort to Joanna and she steeled herself for a hostile reception. No one was more surprised than she when the doors to the great hall were opened and she stepped over the threshold. Everyone in the great hall stood and applauded; some cheered.

"Hail and long life, Joanna of Wales!"

"Hail to the Princess of Merioneth!"

"Praise to the Lady of the Golden Tower!"

"God save you, our good countess of Grasmere!"

Joanna was led to the high table and seated. The precious stones on her wine-colored dress and her necklace sparkled with rich color in the sunlight, which was reflected in her slate-colored, crystalline eyes. Because she had no coronet, the usual veil was dispensed with and her hair was coiled and braided with ribbons and jewels, which made some of the women gasp at this lack of modesty and respect for her married status.

Joanna looked out over the hall and barely glanced at the guests, for to do so would have made her nervous. She didn't want to know what they were thinking. She wanted only to get through the morning, the day, and count the hours until George was home.

The great chair to her right was conspicuously empty and eyes darted towards it as family members and retainers approached one at a time to offer courtesy to Joanna and to take their places.

"Will you not sit with me, my lord?" Joanna invited Aubrey Ascalon as he came forward. "As my husband is not able to be with us, it is certainly your prerogative."

"But not my right, Lady. Let me sit there," Aubrey said, gesturing to another place at her left.

"Be at ease, then," Joanna assented and smiled timidly at her father-in-law, who was now lord abbot of St. Cuthbert's in Grasmere. He'd relinquished his titles and rights to his son George when he entered the monastery, and judging from the looks cast around the hall, was still an oddity in a world where titles, lands, and nobility were all that a man could ask for. To give them up was unthinkable.

Courtiers, vassals, ealdormen, and clerics of Grasmere now approached Skelwith's high table in turn to pay respect to Joanna, who nodded and smiled and quietly said her thanks to each. Last to arrive were Elinor and Will Longleate. Elinor took her time walking to her place, deliberately bringing attention to herself in a form-fitting *bliaut* of bright yellow silk. Her slow gait exaggerated the roll of her hips and taut bottom, and the low neckline of her dress did nothing to hide her breasts. The sunlight cascading through the high, narrow, windows cast shadows on them and outlined their round shapes and nipples. The fabric clung to her thighs and stomach and shimmered as her movements made them quiver.

Petronelle let loose a high-pitched giggle. "God's life!" She shrugged at Aubrey, now glaring at her, saying, "Why bother getting dressed if you choose to have it all on display?"

"Quiet, Daughter; you have no reason to look for a quarrel," he replied.

"*She* does!"

"Master Longleate, was my coronet found?" Joanna greeted, extending her hand for a kiss. "Lady Elinor left the tower to find my coronet and returns in quite a remarkable gown."

Will frowned sideways at his wife, who remained aloof and quiet, with a smile on his lips so forced it would make his face crack to do otherwise. "Alas no, my lady countess. Perhaps it was mislaid when the dowager countess was removed to the lodge. We will find it, I assure you." Now he smiled broadly as guests snickered and started in with rude comments. "I can tell you for certain though, she isn't hiding it in her gown."

When the laughter died down, Joanna replied, "We all do see, Will. Trust me in that. And you are both welcome. The earl would not have it otherwise."

Elinor barely looked at her and bowed before Aubrey. Her movements were like the steps of an exotic dance. She knelt and smiled up at Aubrey, taking advantage of the angle and making sure he could see all that he wanted.

In a loud and clear voice Elinor said, "Skelwith and all of Grasmere is grateful our true Lord Earl thinks enough of us that he comes to our table once more, since the young earl George is indisposed."

"Is it your table, Elinor? When did my husband gift these cups and bowls to you?" Joanna remarked and that brought laughter. Then, more quietly, "The Earl of Grasmere is not indisposed; he is honoring a pledge to God. I do not apologize for him but only speak the truth. Who in this hall would gainsay that? Tell me. I did not think a single guest would. My father-in-law looks quite embarrassed by your attention, and I am embarrassed for you."

The beauty of Elinor's leaf-colored eyes darkened. She said nothing and glared back at Joanna, taking an empty seat at the end of the high table.

"You're doing well," Aubrey murmured to Joanna. "But then, this is nothing new to a princess of Gwynedd and heiress of Merioneth; to a girl fighting for her living in Butcher's Lane."

"I barely remembered what such a life as this was like before George pulled me out of that burning cottage. It comes back at times, as now; I am ashamed because I enjoy others' discomfort when they do not accord respect where it is due." Joanna remarked. "And, I do it because I know I can do it and no one will say differently, no one, save the King."

Aubrey took Joanna's hand and kissed it. "I pray for your happiness, Joanna. I hope George returns to take his place with you before the winter," he said.

"As do I, sir."

"Call me Father."

"As do I. Father."

"You are both needed. It's been years since Grasmere has had the support of its people."

"Would that be true if George had not gone away to atone for the sins of Constantinople and those of his family? If he had died at Eskeleth?" she wondered and looked at him sadly.

"Well, certainly if he had died. But then, they would say it was all his fault and say it was for sinning."

"Exactly."

"Why this gloominess? You are Countess of Grasmere now, the greatest lady of Cumbria."

Joanna would have answered but for the trumpets that sounded the first course. She beckoned the Master Cook and his household forward, and then did something unexpected: she stood for the chaplain's benediction. The hall echoed with the scraping of benches and stools as family members and guests rose. When all was quiet, Joanna bade the chaplain begin. No one moved or spoke until the *Amen* rumbled through the hall and she gave the chaplain a silver penny with her whispered thanks. Then with a graceful nod, Joanna invited her guests to be at ease. As she settled in, Joanna noticed Elinor's flirtatious smiles and comments directed at Aubrey, how she sent sweetmeats and compliments to him up the table. She would have to speak with Elinor about her conduct, as much as she loathed the it. *Little good will it do*, Joanna mused.

Midway through the wedding breakfast, a troupe of mummers came into the hall to great acclaim and applause. Juggling and acrobatics were the first of many entertainments, followed by a troubadour who sang the praises of 'The Princess of the Far-Off Mists.' All eyes fell on Joanna, who was clearly the subject of the ballad, especially the tale of The Golden Knight's lovemaking, which brought blushes and smiles to many ladies' faces including Joanna's, who avoided the attention by focusing on her wedding ring.

The master of the troupe then called for silence and several mummers in fantastical garb and paint ranged themselves before the high table.

"My Lords and Ladies!" the master cried out. "I bid you stay a while and see what unfolds, for we bring you a tale not so old, but quite new, and still a riddle to a few. We give you . . . The Trial of Eskeleth!"

To the somber beat of a tambor and with a harp's three note song, a golden tower made of parchment and gilded wood was wheeled in. It was followed by a great dragon—two men who wore a costume of painted leather squares that resembled a lizard's scales—which brought squeals of joy from the children and a soft rippling of applause and commentary in appreciation from the adults. One of the two mummers would roar while the other tossed bright red, yellow and orange ribbons from its throat: fire. This artifice brought more applause and gasps of wonder. The Dragon slithered and slid to the delight of its audience and then curled up like a dog to sleep under an apple tree made of broomsticks and silk, its tail coiled around the base of the tower. The master now sang a strange lullaby of angels and devils and the purity of man's heart. He bowed when done, a smattering of applause and some coin tossed from guests as he crept away.

Now cheers and applause greeted 'George' and 'Joanna' when they entered on a 'horse' made of a cart and furs. The actress Joanna was a bit too old and buxom, and her dainty mannerisms and timidity during the battles that followed were laughable. The guests cheered on the protagonists as together they battled the Lion of St. Mark, Goliath, and finally, the Dragon, which did not disappoint in its death throws. At the end of the last battle, a mysterious woman appeared from a theatrical use of light and smoke and stood in the center of the hall. She was tall, lithe, fair of hair and well-proportioned. Her arrival inspired whistles and lascivious comments from the men, for like Salome, she was dressed in layers of translucent veils. One brazen fellow at the knights' table offered her a silver penny if she'd stand in better light so he could admire the color of her nipples and the thatch of hair between her legs.

The Seductress danced around the embracing victors, who now exchanged ardent kisses. The actor George moaned, 'Joanna, my love, my angel, my savior! The debt is paid!'

"Not in full, my Lord of Grasmere! There is one debt unpaid!" the Seductress cried and started flinging gold buttons to the guests, who laughed and grabbed for the trinkets as if they were currency.

The Seductress tried to separate the lovers with gyrations and sinuous movements. Hips swayed, and hands glided over breasts, around to buttocks, and in between legs. She was urged on by the men in the hall as veils were cast aside one by one to cheering and applause with each new step in the dance. The actor George finally released the actress Joanna and took the Seductress in his arms, entirely under her spell.

The Seductress swayed and bowed, arched her back while in George's arms, twisted her body in acrobatic, impossible, contortions while she sang in a tongue that was foreign but musical. Then she glanced over and gave Joanna a sideways smile, telling and mocking. Her eyes seemed to glow like colored glass in a window and turn from bright blue to the yellow flickering of a candle flame.

Joanna's heart was in her throat now and she rose slowly with hands gripping the table for support.

No! Impossible! It can't be...

"What is it?" Aubrey whispered.

Joanna said nothing as the Seductress continued to captivate her audience with her dancing and singing.

Impossible, Joanna thought.

"Joanna, explain to me," Aubrey insisted.

Joanna shrugged him off and raised a hand for silence. With the other hand she summoned knights forward.

All eyes were on Joanna now as she said quietly to the woman, "You mock me; you mock my husband! You think our trials were amusements? Do you think to make light of our pain?" Now she addressed the four knights approaching. "Take this sorceress away. Lock her in the small tower and keep watch until I decide what to do with her."

"I've done nothing!" the woman protested as the knights surrounded her. "I beg your mercy, Lady!"

"What mercy did you show my husband, Lady of Eskeleth? Twice you tried to kill him and us. Not again, I say! Away with her," Joanna said.

"Joanna!" Petronelle gasped, seizing her arm. "Joanna, what are you doing? What wrong has this girl done?"

"Mercy!"

The shouts came from the troupe and the guests when it was obvious to all what was happening. "Mercy for her!"

Joanna first glared at Petronelle, then Aubrey, looking down the table at her family and friends. Why were they staring at her as if she had committed the offense? Surely Petronelle would not take Richildis' side in any quarrel, yet her sister-in-law was close to weeping. She now turned to the mummers clustered together a safe distance from the table, poised to escape, and then to the dancer.

The girl was not Richildis.

Standing captive between two knights was a Slavic girl whose tears streaked her perfect, pale, cheeks, black lines of kohl trailing from smudged sloe eyes. The linen veil stuck to her body with sweat and she shivered as much from cold as fright. A wig of false blonde hair made of sheep's wool was askew on her head. One of the knights removed his cloak and draped it over her shoulders.

"Mercy, Lady?" the girl implored.

Joanna acknowledged her request after a moment passed, eyes darting to the girl's, and then with a shameful flood of color in her cheeks, to the linen tablecloth and a wine stain that looked curiously like a heart. She traced the stain with a finger before saying, "I believe the fault is not yours."

"Yes, my Lady! I thank you. I was only doing as bid, I swear it!"

Joanna now looked at the master, who stepped forward cautiously, hands extended in supplication. "She speaks truly, Lady Countess. As were we all—we were paid good coin to do as bid."

"I ask your pardon then, mistress," Joanna apologized. She motioned towards Will Longleate and they spoke in whispers. Will bowed quickly and left the hall by a door in the screen, returning quickly with two purses that he gave to Joanna. She, in turn, passed one to the girl saying, "For your entertainment and pains, with our thanks. Go to the kitchens for a meal." To the master she gave the other said to him and his troupe, "Good sir, and you players, go with her and take your reward, too. Our meat and mead are yours."

Joanna then swept out of the hall, her women following, the blood pounding in her ears and her heart racing. Every pair of eyes in the great hall followed her.

I did not see Richildis; it was not Richildis.

Joanna's fear was in syncopation with her footfall as she climbed the stairs to the Lady Tower.

✠

JOANNA PAID NO attention to her women's pleas and refused to unlock the bedchamber door. Their knocks and frantic queries as to her wellbeing were ignored as she cowered behind bed curtains that were pulled tight and allowed no light or air. Clutched against her breasts was a crucifix she'd taken from the *prie-dieu* as soon as she entered. There was dampness on her palm and fingers; no doubt the sharp edges of the oak carving cut into her flesh. Drops of blood were a small price to pay for solace.

Why?

Why had she seen the sorceress?

The frightening dreams had gone away weeks ago and calm had settled where fear and anxiety once took hold of her heart. Although she hadn't witnessed the death, Joanna heard from the others that it was Petronelle who killed Richildis when she sought revenge on George for his father's misdeeds and for what she thought was George's slight of her.

The strange gray place with the sickly sky, the dull shine of the Golden Tower and the stench of sulfur and charcoal were as real now as they were months before. This wasn't her bedchamber in the Lady Chamber. Joanna found herself on the floor near the fire pit in George's chamber at Gawthorp manor. She was curled up like a dog on an old blanket over the straw and across the room, she heard the pants and sighs of lovemaking. Peering up, she saw George and Richildis in his bed. Before she could protest, Joanna was standing out in the courtyard of the manor. The sun was shining off the button from his tunic that Richildis held in her palm for all to see. The button throbbed like a beating heart as its glow intensified and then slowly dulled from bright yellow to the darkest red until it was drops of blood falling from Richildis' hand. Unlike the morning at Gawthorp, Richildis approached Joanna and pressed the bloody hand against Joanna's stomach and in doing so she transformed slowly into the scaly beast George defeated at Eskeleth. When the beast pounced and Joanna could see the slimy, red, dark, interior of its mouth with its sharp teeth, she was jolted out of the nightmare.

She bolted from the bed and unlocked the door.

"*Petra!*"

Joanna's scream brought her women and Petronelle back to the landing where Joanna was immediately caught in her sister-in-law's arms and brought into the bedchamber. She crumpled onto the floor near the hearth and convulsed as if taken by some illness, sobbing uncontrollably.

"She's gone mad," one of the ladies murmured.

"Get the physic and shut your mouth!" Petronelle barked at her. "If you only knew! Stupid cow! The rest of you, go!" She then motioned to Margaret.

"Not you, Meg; stay. The countess will have need of you."

The morning was warm, yet Joanna shivered and trembled and complained about the cold overtaking her. Margaret banked up the dying fire in the hearth and wrapped Joanna in a fur-lined cloak, then sat her down on a cushioned bench before the fire. Petronelle knelt before Joanna and took her hands, rubbing them gently to bring warmth back. Margaret fetched some wine.

"I saw her. It *was* Richildis!" Joanna whispered.

"I saw her too," whispered Petronelle in reply.

Joanna raised her eyes to Petronelle's and in her glance was both fear and relief. "What can this mean?" she asked.

"I wish I knew," said Petronelle. "But if one might hazard a guess, it's meant to harm and we both know who has that gift."

✠

WHAT A DAY it had been. Joanna was glad to bid farewell to the last of the guests and have privacy. She walked alone up the stairs and across the bridge from the donjon to The Lady Tower where a hot bath and solitude waited.

Joanna paused on the bridge to watch the last of the sunlight fade into the orange and purple horizon and took in the view of Little Longdale and the Vale of Grasmere.

Her home.

Their home, she thought, thinking how it would be with George standing here. He'd slouch a little, leaning against the rail. One arm would be around her waist and with the opposite hand he'd brush the hair off her face or tease her about the plaits that never stayed tidy. Then he'd pull her close and they'd watch the sunset in silence.

Those evenings would come quickly, she hoped.

Just as she turned to go across, she saw two women leave Ravenglass Tower.

They were in angry conversation as they approached, whispering and sniping at one another. Joanna was ready to greet them when the smaller woman's hood fell back, and Joanna saw that it was Maud Ascalon, George's stepmother. The other, Elinor, gasped when she realized they were discovered. Joanna raised her chin and stood a little taller and considered the women. They were frozen in fear until Joanna raised her brows and tilted her head questioningly, waiting. Finally, both women curtseyed and when Maud rose, a circlet of gold fell from her cloak and rolled and spun like a child's top until Joanna rescued it from spinning off the bridge and into the moat.

"Ah! You've found it," Joanna said. "My thanks." The awkward moment dragged on while Joanna studied the coronet and the women silently fretted. Finally, she held it out to them, saying: "Take it. You both obviously claim it as your right. But I tell you truly in the name of our Holy Mother and Saints Margaret and Anne to keep in mind that I alone now have the right, and my crown is here."

Joanna held up her hand to display her wedding band and betrothal ring.

The coronet was offered a moment longer and then Joanna drew back. "Neither of you want this? No? I'm glad we've settled this," she said and set the coronet on her head. Elinor and Maud made another obeisance. The chill Joanna felt was unmistakable as she walked past them into Ravenglass Tower, and it was in no part due to the sun going down. That icy hold on her spine whenever Elinor was in her presence didn't thaw, not even a month later when she woke and was sick, and for many mornings after, and her body began to swell and change with pregnancy. What should have been the greatest joy for George and her, and sweetest of victories over Elinor Lucy and her aspirations, made Joanna fearful for the child and herself as the months passed and the baby grew. She wrote to George as soon as she discovered she was with child:

> The excitement of knowing you and I created this child from our love, and that you will have an heir, is clouded by the shadow of Elinor Lucy, who watches with interest, as if she wishes harm to come to us and that her jealousy and bitterness over what she does not have will be rewarded somehow. I pray that will not happen, my love! If it is at possible, I pray also that you return to Skelwith and take your place as is your right; but more importantly, that you come home to me, and to our child.

CHAPTER 1

March 1206

A TRIO OF BUTTERFLIES flitted in a shaft of sunlight and distracted Joanna from her needlework. She watched them make patterns against the window for the longest time and would have enjoyed this diversion but for the jangle of breaking glass. Joanna started out of her daydream and found herself in the here and now of a Saturday in the company of her ladies-in-waiting. She glanced around the bower and saw her cousin Rhosyn, the youngest and newest of the ladies, with a half-grown dog and the remnants of a bouquet in her arms. The shards of a broken bowl lay on the floor.

"S-s-orry, my lady countess!" the girl apologized. "I was bringing in fresh flowers and the dog was underfoot,"

Joanna waved over one of the servants to clean up the mess. She then patted the footstool before her and invited Rhosyn to sit.

"George is like me—he never knows how to behave."

"Pardon, my lady? The Earl of Grasmere?"

"No; the dog. He was a gift from the Earl of Grasmere."

"Well, not the only gift from him . . ." Margaret said and looked first at Joanna and then Petronelle, who winked back.

"*Ohhh!*" Rhosyn gasped when she finally understood the jest. "Holy Mother forgive me," she murmured several minutes later, head down. "I shall have to do penance for my unholy thoughts!"

"You will not. You did me good service, Rhosyn," Joanna said. "I would have been content to watch those butterflies all day, for their dancing reminds me of how joyous life is, and how their movements are like my child's—he dances, leaps, and soars and kicks his poor mother from sunrise to sunset."

"That was never my brother," said Petronelle. "He was a sullen, quiet, boy."

"Was?" asked Joanna and they laughed together.

Joanna now showed Rhosyn the little gown she'd been sewing. "What do this think, Rhosyn? You were taught English Work by the nuns at Wilton. Is this comparable? If the truth be told, I've never liked needlework; but now I have good reason to appreciate its merits."

"But Lady, it's said there's no finer work to be found in Cumbria than yours. That alone," here Rhosyn pointed to a banner Joanna had sewn and embroidered almost a year ago, "is said to be a marvel."

"It is that," Margaret commented, taking a few stitches, and then gazing up at the magnificent work above them.

"No; the marvel is that we survived, and we have that to remind us of God's grace and our good fortune."

"Amen! It was God's will and not ours," Petronelle whispered.

One by the one the ladies glanced up from their work to study the banner hanging on the north wall of the bower. It showed in exquisite detail two lovers holding hands beneath a flowering tree, a great sword glowing with fire struck between them. Luminous thread and jewel tones and precious gold caught the sun and made the unusual silk-like fabric shimmer. The name 'ASCALON' was embroidered in gold along the borders and separated by crosses.

"Surely it is the reminder of a deadly folly. The dowager countess has said that repeatedly."

The statement came from the far side of the bower where three women sat alone. An elder woman dressed in widow's garb, a young lady-in-waiting that looked colorless and nondescript given the third woman in the trio, Elinor Lucy, who was dressed like a queen and holding her own court. It was Elinor who spoke.

Joanna ignored the comment and took up her needle to finish a row of stitches on the gown's neckline, little posies set in discs.

"If Elinor knew how that banner came to be she would show something of charity," Petronelle said low to Margaret. Petronelle glanced at Elinor, who chose that moment to look at her. *Or perhaps not.*

"This is a great day for the house of Ascalon and the Earls of Grasmere," Elinor continued. "Never in its history has there been so much cause for pride and we owe this to the accomplishments of its Earl."

Petronelle frowned and was about to speak, but Joanna reached out and took her hand, shaking her head. It would be a long day and now was not the time to find quarrels.

"Mistress Longleate speaks truly," Joanna said, smiling all around. "Great sacrifices have indeed been made for Ascalon and Grasmere, and see what it has given us. Let's finish here—"

As she said this, a volley of horns announced a cavalcade entering Skelwith Castle.

"And not too soon," Petronelle added. She clapped her hands and said, "Be lively, girls; as quick as you may. We shall have all of Cumbria at Skelwith's gates within the hour and no one to greet them."

"Lord, how I wish George was here," Joanna said speaking her thoughts aloud as she gathered up needlework. "He knows how to deal with all these princes, prelates, and self-important glee-men."

"George knows how to start quarrels with princes, prelates and self-important glee-men. Fortunately for Father, George isn't here, so he won't have to spend all afternoon and evening making the usual apologies. Lord, I miss do him!" Petronelle said.

"Indeed," Joanna said and sighing loudly, looked around guiltily as if she had to be seen doing something. A servant appeared in the doorway and before he could announce his business she asked, "Has my father-in-law arrived?"

"No, my lady. It is Bertrand de Jumieges, the Bishop of Eden, and he comes with a great household," he answered.

Joanna thought her face must surely have gone the color of milk by the looks she received from her ladies and how silent the bower became as she rose slowly and beckoned to Margaret. "My hair needs attention," she said. "I'm sure someone would remark if I didn't bind it up."

She stood still as Margaret wrapped her head in a linen barbette, gathered her beribboned plaits in a crespinette, and gently placed a yellow-gold coif of velvet upon her head. When Petronelle reached for the coronet, Elinor moved quicker and almost knocked Petronelle off her feet as she grabbed the heavy gold ornament from its cushion and placed it none too gently on Joanna's head. Joanna bit her lip rather than cry out from the sudden and unexpected pressure.

Stepping back, Elinor's eyes slid first to Petronelle, who fumed at her taking precedence, to the other women, who looked embarrassed.

"Well done, Mistress Longleate," Joanna said when she caught her breath; "I hope I measure up to your standard."

She almost looks the part, Elinor thought and though her words were secret, her icy demeanor and face told Joanna all she wanted to know.

"Perfect, darling sister!" Petronelle whispered, offering a kiss.

Lord, Joanna thought, *how many months has it been since I wed George Ascalon and was made Countess of*

Grasmere? Why does it still feel so foreign and unwanted?
The answer, she knew, was Elinor now paying such obsequious attention to her and the women of the bower smiling and whispering comments they thought she couldn't hear. Comments such as how she looked like a true noblewoman, even a queen.

If only George were here!

But he wasn't.

Joanna reached for her mantle and Margaret was there to help. "It's cold this morning and there's still snow on the ground," she said.

"Thank you, Meg," Joanna murmured as Margaret wrapped her in the costly garment of ivory wool trimmed with the silkiest of red fox hair. "I believe His Grace of Eden will approve," Joanna said as she glanced in a mirror one of the ladies held. "Let's be on our way. Mistress Longleate, not with the others. Walk with me."

Elinor nodded, smiled smugly at being singled out, and strode from the back of the column of ladies to walk beside Joanna as she led her women out of the bower. When they were on the bridge to the donjon, Joanna paused, a hand on her lower back. The ladies tarried a respectful distance except for Elinor who asked, "Is it the child?"

Joanna shook her head and held up a hand to stay Elinor's solicitous attention. "Your kindness gives you much credit," she began. "Especially today of all days."

"I could not do otherwise," Elinor replied and again, Joanna's hand stayed her.

"Ah, but you could. And you have."

"Why this scolding, my lady? Have I not shown you every courtesy?"

"We know that's not true. Must I remind you of my wedding breakfast? The entertainment was insulting and demeaning. You mocked my husband's achievements and the perils we endured."

"Do you accuse—"

"I do, Elinor. You knew what happened in Arkengarthdale because George shared our trials with his inner circle of friends, of which Will and you are privy."

"It was meant to be an honor," Elinor said quietly. Studying Joanna's pale complexion and the frown that gradually set on her mouth, she added, "After so long a time, my lady? That still troubles you? Perhaps you have taken a trifle too much to heart?"

"Sometimes it takes a good deal of pondering to find the truth. Of late your actions have made some things clear to me."

"I hope they are my respect and loyalty to you—"

"Enough. You pepper what sounds like praise with barbs and insults. I say no more. I would there be peace between us and will have it so, Elinor."

"It is as you say, Lady Countess!"

"You and I know it is not! We've never spoken except in anger about certain things."

"It does no good to bring up those painful memories, my lady," replied Elinor as she joined Joanna at the rail.

Side by side they stood and looked out over a horizon tinged with the colors of early spring—the appearance bright greens and blues, the purple and silver hills of Cumbria under drifts of snow, a bright blue sky. The Earl of Grasmere's favorite colors, Elinor noted. The colors of Joanna's kirtle and surcote.

"You will not belittle me out of jealousy and spite in the presence of my household or anyone, for that matter, because you harbor a childish resentment of my marriage to the Earl of Grasmere. Join our circle and not keep your own court. You know how it looks."

"I hardly know how to respond to that, my lady," Elinor protested, her face burning, and her hands clenched so that they stayed put. Striking this upstart little concubine would only make matters worse for Will and herself.

"Now of a sudden, you're at a loss for words? If you knew what befell us all those months ago, truly knew, and what we must face now, you would not be so envious. Nor would you heed the words of my mother-in-law Countess Maud. If you remember, it was she who sent the earl on that journey without knowing its danger. Or perhaps she wanted him dead, knowing the family's secrets."

Joanna now glanced over at Elinor. Her demeanor and look were undecipherable.

"I hardly know how to respond to that," Elinor repeated.

"I do prefer your silence, Elinor. A nod or a bow will content me."

Elinor dropped her chin and raised it slowly.

"Not so difficult, is it? If you will not in your heart feel friendship or loyalty for me, at least in the presence of my women and in this castle, make a show of respect for my place here. Do this for Grasmere. If you will not, then I will be forced to send you elsewhere where you cannot do harm."

The two women studied one another and then Elinor made an obeisance, a deep bend of the knee so that her dress melted into liquid folds around them. Joanna watched the angry rise and fall of Elinor's chest and how she trembled. With an imperceptible movement of her hand, she bade her adversary rise. Elinor kept her gaze downward and stepped aside as Joanna continued across the bridge and down to the inner ward.

CHAPTER 2

THE ENTIRE HOUSEHOLD was on the steps of the donjon as the first of many cavalcades rode past the gatehouse and barbican. Joanna stood a few steps from the ground, her ladies arranged around her with Petronelle at her right hand. They watched as knights and noblemen on horseback with their retinues, brightly-painted carriages and baggage trains swept past, the pageantry causing more excitement and comment.

There was to be a week of celebrations at Skelwith Castle, for the new Bishop of Carlisle was returning home after his recent consecration and installation. Nobility from the farthest corners of and closest towns in northern England continued to arrive for the celebrations in his honor.

Petronelle glanced at Joanna, who looked as if she would burst into tears at any moment. "You've captured the attention of everyone here, Joan," she said, using a pet name for Joanna reserved for family and friends. "See how they all admire you!"

Joanna offered a weak smile in response and bowed her head, sighing.

"What is it, Sister?"

"I was expecting the Bishop of Carlisle, not a prelate so close to our borders and one I hardly know."

"So? He will be here."

A volley of trumpets announcing the next cavalcade muffled Joanna's reply. The largest, and most elaborate of the carriages thus far barely squeezed through the barbican and great portal leading into the bailey, led by a smaller but no less ostentatious carriage.

"This must be Eden and his courtiers," said Joanna.

"My God, look at that!" Petronelle giggled. "Those banners have more gold in them than I've seen in a crown. The King's spy, perhaps? Ah! Certainly this gentleman!"

She pointed at the man disembarking from the carriage before Eden's. He was tall, thin like a heron and had a long, beaky nose protruding from a pale, shaven, face. Narrow blue eyes and full red lips completed his looks along with raven-black hair.

Joanna put a hand to her mouth to suppress a cry. She recognized this man. Sometimes his face came to her in her dreams in memories of days past. Times that were hard and frightening.

"Will," Joanna summoned Will Longleate closer. "Do you know this gentleman?"

"Lord Eustace des Jumieges, a new man. He's the baron of Eden and newly-struck knight. He is recently married to Agnes Strong, an heiress living in Great Langdale."

"Kin to the Bishop?"

"His cousin."

"I heard he saved the King in a hunting accident," Elinor commented.

"There is that," Will said, "or the tale of it."

"Another king's man come to make his name and trouble?" Joanna queried.

"Surely that. I don't doubt he thinks to add Grasmere to his patch in Eden."

"Will!" Elinor chided. "He'd never! And you knew he was coming today?"

"I heard a rumor."

"Well, if he's Agnes Strong's husband, perhaps he comes to pay homage to George by way of Father?" Petronelle said. "The Strongs have sworn fealty to Grasmere. They would stop him."

"If he has the King's ear and confidence, he may do as he likes," Elinor replied.

"George will stop him!"

"As to that, we will see."

"Whose loyalty do you have Elinor?" Petronelle asked.

"Enough! Both of you!" Joanna cried. Her outburst startled those closest to her and they grew quiet, watching the guests arrive and silently wondering what caused her anger.

The Bishop of Eden's carriage stopped at the foot of the stairs. Seconds later a prelate disembarked all, save Joanna, genuflected as he offered a sign of the cross from his gloved and bejeweled hand, and rose again with heads bowed.

Joanna noted his fine clothing and jewels. They looked familiar, as she had seen George wear that cross of hammered silver now hanging from the Bishop's reed-like neck. The tunic beneath his cloak looked suspiciously like the one Aubrey wore on the day of Petronelle's wedding.

Payment from Carlisle or stolen from Ascalon?

During this interlude, Eustace had insinuated himself on the party and glanced about like a child wanting praise for wearing his best robes, looking at everyone in turn with a disingenuous smile. But they all were fixed on his cousin the Bishop as he paused to greet each member of the court personally and bestow blessings. Eustace looked around for something of interest to stare at while he was forced to wait for his cousin and found the captivating wench standing in the place of honor among ladies of the court. Her belly was swollen with child and it only made her more attractive, given the roses in her cheeks and the glow of her skin. This must be the young countess, Eustace guessed. He envied the absent Earl of Grasmere, wondering too, just how exciting the night was that put her in this state. Such a pretty thing, this child-bride. Eustace continued to imagine all kinds of things that might have transpired and after raking his eyes over the Countess and receiving a cold stare, he assessed the ladies-in-waiting.

Now there was a pretty piece! The girl hovering near the Countess, a flame-haired chit younger than the others but well-endowed otherwise. He'd send for her later when the household was abed. Eustace stepped forward and smiled warmly at the girl, would have introduced himself but for the scowl on his cousin's face as he removed his gloves and handed them to Eustace as if he was a mere squire. It was a warning not to be taken lightly, but Eustace had ignored his cousin's warnings before.

The ladies now bobbed up and down in curtseys to Bertrand, who extended his hand for kisses. It was such a delight to watch their movements and the enticing views offered as the women and girls tried to move as gracefully and modestly as they could in their restrictive gowns. Only the Countess remained standing.

Eustace pushed a courtier and a clerk out of the way to stand beside Bertrand and said, "Lady Joanna, will you not kneel for a blessing?"

"Eustace," the bishop sighed, the voice and tone of one used to scolding.

"You would honor the King, would you not? The Bishop of Eden comes in the name of the King."

Joanna looked up at the bishop and smiled, saying, "My lord of Eden, good reverend father, we greet you well in the name of Grasmere and Ascalon. I am afraid you shall have to give this sinful daughter a blessing where she stands; I fear if I should kneel I may never rise again," she replied lightly, and the ladies giggled at her humor. Even Elinor managed to smile.

Eustace assessed her with narrowed eyes. "Did you not hear me? I asked why you do not honor the King's emissary, Lady?" he snapped acerbically.

"Indeed I did, and certain I do, Sir; the child I carry is of another opinion. He grows by the minute and soon I'm sure I'll not be able to walk at all but must need depend on him to carry me. But you are neither King, clergyman, nor God, Sir Eustace, and I am certain if they were here, I would be forgiven for this seeming lack of respect for their offices and they would wonder why it makes such a difference to you. Wouldn't you say, my lord bishop?"

The response was given with such innocence and such a charming smile that Bertrand erupted with laughter at his cousin's expense. While he called over his chancellor and clerks to share the jest, Joanna noticed the man lingering at the gatehouse.

Tall, powerfully built some would say, the bearing and carriage of a knight, yet clothed in a monastic's plain habit and cowl. He hung back in the shadows so as not to be seen, but there was no mistaking him for someone of less importance than who he was— George Ascalon, the present Earl of Grasmere.

While she engaged in light conversation with Bertrand and his party, Joanna raised her left hand to her breast and with the other hand touched the ring on her left hand. In response, George lifted the cross around his neck to his lips and kissed it.

"He greets you well," Petronelle whispered.

Joanna made no reply and feigned interest Bertrand's praise of the renovations to buildings along the curtain of the inner ward and the stonework of the new chapel.

"My lord, will you come this way; we have refreshment ready. And I wonder if you might be interested in how we have decorated the great hall with new hangings and paintings," Joanna suggested. She took the arm Bertrand offered and before they climbed the steps of the donjon she turned in hopes of seeing another glimpse of her husband.

He was gone.

Joanna extended a hand towards the great hall she and her guests now entered. The long, rectangular room was divided by two columns of pillars, a fire pit in the middle, the decorations evocative of a time past. The wooden pillars were carved and burnished gold in places with Saxon knot work—intricate, twisting coils in the shape of swans and later vines, symbols of creation and love. The walls had been scoured and painted white, their edges and borders decorated in bright colors. There were scenes depicting lords and ladies in a garden and at a tournament. On the screen behind the chairs of state were portraits of the three archangels: Raphael, Michael, and Gabriel. The windows were high and arched and glazed with glass. In one corner hung a richly embroidered cloth that divided space in the hall. A great number of gems and gold thread adorned the latticed design of roses and crosses on a rich blue ground. One could see a prayer desk and devotional panel, a cushioned bench behind it. A private space for the countess. The floors had been scrubbed and were covered with sweet-smelling rushes.

"It's not what I expected," Eustace sniffed.

"I'm not surprised," Petronelle said and stared daggers into him.

Bertrand paused to look around. "You're right, Eustace. This is not how I remember Skelwith's hall," he said. "It was damp, dark, and as bare as the poorest of monasteries when last I visited."

"It was. I wanted to bring light and joy into all the rooms," Joanna replied, "beginning here. It is a home. My—our home. I hope my husband will be pleased to see the changes when he returns."

"And how could the young Earl refuse you?" Eustace interjected and stepped forward to lightly touch Joanna's face. "Such beauty here. George Ascalon is to be envied."

Joanna glanced down, feeling her face burn. She was seven months gone with child and the man was flirting with her! A sideways glance at Petronelle and Margaret gave her confidence, knowing by their somber faces that they disapproved of Eustace's attention just as much as she did.

"You're too forward and familiar, Eustace," Bertrand scolded.

"Only praising our hostess, Cousin. Earl George would not complain."

"Don't be too sure," Bertrand replied and jerked his chin for Eustace to step back, throwing his cousin a withering look.

"Will you take refreshment?" Joanna offered and led Bertrand to the high table and bade him sit in the Earl of Grasmere's chair of state. She sat to his left in her own smaller chair. Eustace hovered while Elinor, Petronelle, and Margaret took cushioned benches below them, and Rhosyn acted as cupbearer.

A troubadour appeared as if out the air, his lute in hand. When all were comfortable, Joanna nodded to the musician, and he began to pick out a melancholy song.

"I know this song!" Bertrand exclaimed. "Was this not written by our late King Richard?"

"It was."

He savored the wine and leaned forward, closing his eyes, listening to the troubadour as he sang the lament of a man betrayed by family and companions at arms. "He composed this ballad while imprisoned," Bertrand ruminated.

"What we lost in paying his ransom!" Eustace grumbled.

Bertrand raised his hand for silence and said, "Lady Joanna, this is an interesting choice for such a day of celebration, for what do we sacrifice when we give ourselves entirely to Mother Church and are made princes without kingdoms and have the cure of so many souls?"

"Humility?" jibed Elinor. Her glance slid toward Joanna.

"I know that I am a prisoner of frailty and pride, and only the Lord will break the fetters," Joanna answered.

"*You*, my lady?" Bertrand queried.

"Did Ascalon not raise me up when I had been brought so low?"

Petronelle nodded in agreement. "He is proud of you, my lady, and were he here today, I know he would sing your praises."

"Thank you, Sister," Joanna replied.

"Earl George is not here?" Eustace asked. The tone was mocking and false.

"I'm sure you know he is not and will not be for some time," Joanna replied.

"Why today of all days? God and the Abbot would forgive him such a minor transgression."

"He made a promise and has no desire to repeat the mistakes of others. Tell me you know nothing of the earl's journey to Arkengarthdale where he championed Wulfstan of Eskeleth. How he vanquished Wulfstan's enemy and restored prosperity to a land long wasted. That was a debt repaid and a promise redeemed."

Eustace took a sip of wine and shrugged. "Some say it was all in his imagination and that none of it happened, that it was the invention of bards paid to tell of the great deeds of Ascalon so that we should look past or forget his misdeeds in Constantinople. It is said there he betrayed his men to save his own neck. Or that he'd gone mad."

"Lies!" Petronelle cried, on her feet and standing before him with clenched fists. When Joanna and Margaret both tried to silence her, Petronelle waved them off, saying, "I was there, sir! I watched the battles! I saw the demons, and I heard the voices of Hell! I saw the ghosts of fallen men. These my brother confronted and vanquished, as did our lady countess here. Do you say that it was our imagination or that we have gone mad?"

"Perhaps you contrived the fable to protect Grasmere's reputation. After all, both father and son have dishonored the name of Ascalon in one way or another, especially where it concerns alliances, lands, and titles." Eustace countered.

No one replied. In fact, everyone but Eustace looked embarrassed, though he failed to see it. He waited for a response, and looked to Joanna first, who was staring at her swollen belly and then at the pretty lass offering more wine. He smiled at the girl, and she blushed and smiled back.

"If that is what you think it may be—a fable, or allegory—it should be of little consequence to the King and to you. Why do you make Ascalon matters yours?" Joanna demanded but she gave him no time to respond and said, "My husband is at the abbey where he does penance. There he can be no threat to the King if he is a threat at all."

"Your assurance will make his grace the King content, Lady Joanna," Bertrand spoke up. "Forgive my cousin Eustace; he speaks out of turn and does not speak for the King. Isn't that so, Cousin?"

"Why dance around it when we all know why I'm here?" Eustace asked. "The King wants assurances and answers. I've been asked to see that he receives both from Grasmere."

"Isn't my father's consecration enough, Sir Eustace? We all know the King purchased him!" Petronelle snapped.

"Lady Petronelle, we both know that isn't true; Father Aubrey has shown a deep and loving faith and spirituality borne of these northern lands—"

"Oh, be silent, you fool!" she hissed at Bertrand. "When wasn't a bishop consecrated to suit the crown? Well?"

Bertrand didn't have an answer.

"My lady, you ought not to meddle where it doesn't concern you," Eustace warned.

"Doesn't it, Sir Eustace?"

"God in heaven!" Joanna sighed.

While Petronelle and Eustace argued, and Bertrand tried his best to silence them, Joanna kept her head bowed as she thought out what was transpiring. She knew why George had appeared so suddenly and was afraid for him. Touching her wedding ring, she thought, *Be swift, my love. Wherever you are, be swift and wary!*

CHAPTER 3

GEORGE WAS FAR into Skelwith Wood and on his way
to Grasmere when he heard the Abbey bells ring the
hour. Instinctively he picked up the pace and knew
he'd be late for *Nones*. It would be another sin to
confess, another mark against him and perhaps
discipline meted out, but a chance to see his beloved
Joanna again was worth any punishment. Smiling to
himself as he strode the wald path, George
remembered every movement, every vision from that
morning and thought back to the night they first met
when he'd dragged her from that burning cottage in
Butcher's Lane and suffered her ire after saving her
from immolation...

"Alms!"

The cry made George stop and look about. Once
more he heard the disembodied shout and the hair on
his skin prickled, a chill ran through him to his bones.
He waited, studying the trees. George expected bark,
leaves, and branches to turn into dragons, or ghosts
in bloodied armor to materialize from the
overhanging clouds and charge him as they did in the
forest not so long ago. His beautiful and warm Joanna
he expected to appear out of nothing and slowly
transform into the tall, imperious, and seductive

witch, Richildis, as mists swirled and danced upon the ground. And then the beast, the devil itself...

Jesu Maria! How long would this harrying plague his thoughts and sleep?

"Alms!"

"Who's there? Show yourself!" George called.

"Alms, I beg of you!"

George relaxed when a peasant crept out of the wood. The fellow looked about cautiously before he approached.

"*Benedicte*," George greeted the man. "Are you from hereabouts?"

"That's not your concern, Brother," the man said. "A coin is all I ask. Two, if you have enough to spare."

George's hand moved to where his sword would have hung in its scabbard and felt the smooth wooden prayer beads on his cincture instead, the empty scrip beside it. "I have no coin," George apologized. "But come with me to the Abbey; I'll see that you get some food—if it's work you need, our chapel needs repairs. Do you know stonework?"

A knife was swiftly out from under the peasant's tunic, and before the blade could wound him, George made a defensive move and disarmed the man, pinning him down on a muddy patch of forest floor.

"I haven't always been a monk!" George hissed as he pressed the peasant's blade close to his throat. "Do *not* test me today!"

He allowed the man his footing and shoved him in the opposite direction of Grasmere, watched as he disappeared back into the woods. A stupid decision, letting an outlaw free, but that was the Sheriff of

Cumbria's problem for now. He'd send word to let Sheriff Stephen Black know there were outlaws living in the wood again and worry about the problem when he returned to Skelwith as earl.

George started off again, this time taking the more-traveled path into Grasmere. Here he was bound to encounter tradesmen trundling along in carts to the market square or to the shops on Little Watling Street, the third street of that name, 'Watling,' which led all the way south to London, and ran through the town in good part to George's ancestors. There was a chance, too, that he'd meet up with the nuns from Saint Eadthryth, who would be delivering the linens for the abbey, or new-spun woolen thread from their sheep kept near Rowan. As luck would have it, George discovered neither on the path, but a gentleman sitting on a fallen tree trunk, struggling with his boot.

"Good morrow, sir," the gentleman called out as George approached.

"God give you peace," George replied as he started to pass by.

"You wouldn't have a lace, would you?" the gentleman asked. He held up a broken length of what looked like string. From what George could see, his boot was falling open and the sides flopped down. It would be impossible to walk in a boot like that. The gentleman now tried his best to lace the impossibly short string through the eyelets of the boot. When he stood up, the soft leather of the boot, which reached mid-calf, fell onto the instep and toes.

"I suppose they wear their shoes like that in France," George commented, smiling. The gentleman looked frustrated and seemed not to appreciate the jest. He took a few steps then sat down again.

"If you had a length of string, say, from the tips of my fingers to my elbow, it would do until I got to Chapel Stile or even Ellerwater."

"You could stop by Jack the cobbler's in Grasmere and he'd fix you up."

"He could, but I have no money."

George again reached for his scrip and remembered he had no coin. He studied the man's boots and then looked down at his own. "I tell you what. Let me give you mine. I don't have far to go, and my feet know these roads better than yours - I know where the stones are."

"Truly sir?" the gentleman asked, amazed.

"Come then, let me sit to take these off."

The gentleman shifted over and watched as George removed his boots and passed them over as if it was an extraordinary feat. He pulled the boots on and tried them out with a few steps.

"It's as if they were made for me. I thank you—what is your name, sir? Your family?" the gentleman asked.

"I'm no one important. Take the boots and may you have good use of them," George replied.

The gentleman smiled and he bowed his thanks. As he set off down the path, he paused and then spun around, taking a wineskin from his cloak.

"It's only fair that since you gave me your boots, I must share a drink with you. The morning is cold, is it not? Perhaps you have some ways to go?"

"Not so very far, but I will be glad to share your wine," George replied. "How strange that in one morning I encounter a beggar thief who would take my money and my life and a gentleman who only takes my boots, but offers wine in payment."

The jest was appreciated this time. The gentleman smiled and offered the skin. George had tasted the best of wines in England, France and the Holy Land and Byzantium, but this was an incredible vintage. The wine had subtle notes of fruit and spice, perhaps sandal, and a smokiness to it. If stars could inhabit wine, George was sure to have tasted them in this skin: tingling and bright.

"Why do you wait, sir?"

"Pardon?" George asked, wiping his mouth after taking a second drink.

"Why do you stay at the abbey? Have you not atoned for the sins of others?"

George was immediately on guard and leaped up and away from him, wishing he had a sword or a weapon in case this man also meant him harm. The gentleman laughed and shook his head, raised a hand to stay George's anger and fear.

"Do you not recall the words in scripture,
'Blessed are you, O God, with every pure blessing;
let all your chosen ones bless you.
Let them bless you forever.
Blessed are you because you have made me glad.
It has not turned out as I expected,

but you have dealt with us according to your great
mercy.

 Blessed are you because you had compassion
 on two only children.'

"I know this prayer. Tobit and the Angel. What's
that to do with me? I was taught that this is about
God's providential care for the righteous, the rewards
given for righteousness, prayer, and almsgiving; it is
about angels guiding and—Jesu! My head! How it
pounds! Not again! No more!"

George had his head in his hands as if they would
stop the pain that suddenly overwhelmed him. The
gentleman removed them and stood over George.

"It has not turned out as you expected, George
Ascalon. What does the dragonslayer do when the
dragon is dead? He listens for a truer calling from
God."

In that moment, George watched as he
transformed: his face radiated a soft, pale, blue light
and his features became exquisite and symmetrical,
like those in the gold and enameled ikons George
remembered from Constantinople. Even his simple
traveling clothes transformed into the robes of a
Byzantine nobleman. Upon his brow was a circlet of
gold and there was a star glowing in its center. His
eyes were as blue as the star.

"You haven't seen the last of me, nor of my
companions. You'll have need of us, that's for
certain."

The sun started to shoot bright rays through the
trees and blinded George. When he moved his hand
away from shielding his eyes, the man was gone.

Just another headache and the strange lights that come with it, he thought, *another daydream brought by pain.* When he reached the abbey, George would ask the Hospitaller to mix a posset.

Skirting past the shops and marketplace of Grasmere, George made his way to the abbey where he slipped through the gate and sprinted to the church. He whispered a prayer that the door on the north side close to the hospital and herb gardens might be unattended. *Deo gracias!* It was. He'd have to thank Brother Thomas with a silver penny. George managed to slip into the quire and take a stall before anyone could notice.

Anyone but the Bishop of Carlisle.

Flanked by the Abbot and the Prior, the Bishop indulged in the sin of pride for a moment so that he might turn slightly to exchange glances with George and then resumed his meditation on the serene face of the Christ high on the wall before him. The bishop tried not smile. In the face of Christ, he saw a disobedient member of the community and his ever obedient and beloved son.

George looked away first. He was glad when the Abbot offered the final collect and he could go back to work, was passing the cloister garden when he heard the call.

"George!"

He tucked his hands further into his sleeves and gripped his wrists. Turning, George made sure his father didn't have to call a second time and stepped to one side and waited, head lowered and face thankfully obscured by hood and cowl.

Aubrey Ascalon, the new Bishop of Carlisle, was still flanked by the Abbot and Prior. When the episcopal ring was offered to kiss, George glanced at it and then at his father. He did nothing. Aubrey's hand went into the folds of his cope.

"How are you, Geordie?" Aubrey queried smiling and using a family pet name. "You're thinner, and you look tired."

"I never knew the life of a contemplative could be so arduous," George replied. "No time for sport."

"You should come with us to Skelwith for the celebrations. Sleep in your own bed for a night or two. I've spoken with the Abbot here,"

"My Lord Bishop, I made a promise to you," George began.

"Father will suffice."

"As you and I discussed—"

"I know what we've said. That should not prevent you from joining our family and friends. Besides, you've taken no vows. You're not professed. You are a guest and in fact, you may leave whenever you wish."

"I have no desire to attend; the time alone will do me good."

Aubrey extended his hand as if to caress George's face and made the sign of the cross instead. "We'll leave it at that. If you change your mind, I would be pleased. I need not say how well it would please your wife, and your mother and sister. It is a great day for Ascalon." He nodded at the others and turned to leave. The Abbot remained and took a defensive stance against George, who was bigger and taller than he.

"May I have a word with you, George? Bishop Aubrey? Please stay, Bishop," the Abbot said. "I wish to know something of the earl's intentions." He paused, smiling, and then said to George, "What exactly do you want while you stay with us? The Obedientiary says you are avoiding the offices and keeping to yourself of late, wandering off in your own direction."

"I believe it is in God's direction I wander," George answered lightly.

"Others might say it is the direction opposite to that of the Holy Mother Church," said the Abbot. "And the King. Wouldn't you agree, Prior Martin?"

George glanced at the rugged-faced, imposing, cleric standing between himself and Warennes. This was a man he imagined would stand beside him in a shield wall or on the battlements of a castle and hoped he would do so now, so to speak. But Prior Martin found more interest in a cat ambling through yarrow and rosemary in the cloister garden than the conversation. George now turned his attention on Abbot Warennes, a young man not much older than himself. He had the look of a smug, self-important, son of privilege as would befit the godson, and some said, the illegitimate son of the King, someone who was used to getting what he wanted not because of his own diligence or work, but because of his connections. Stocky, ruddy, with the look of the Plantagenets and Angevins. Oh yes, godson or no, he was the King's bastard. Still, he was no match for George and George knew it; what a pity Alan Warennes, this puffed-up cleric, hadn't a clue.

He smiled disingenuously at the abbot.

"What others say is what they say. I keep my own counsel," George said.

"Especially where it concerns the King?"

"I keep my own counsel, sir."

Warennes cocked his head to one side and folded his arms across his chest in the universal stance of confrontation. Even so, he took a backward step, perhaps an arm's length from George. "Tell me; why did you come here?" he demanded. "Our community has seen no benefice from Grasmere since your arrival."

"Abbot Warennes, this is not the place nor the time," Prior Martin interrupted.

"No, let him speak, Prior Martin; we would hear his complaints," Aubrey spoke up.

George turned to the Abbot, brows raised.

"When a nobleman seeks a place in a community such as ours, it is the custom to offer a gift to sustain the house and assist the community in almsgiving. What do you contribute? You have kept to yourself, my lord earl, contribute little except a sensation of discord whenever you do move yourself to join us," Warennes chided.

"I am here to seek God's love and forgiveness. I am here to restore my soul after I championed my father in Arkengarthdale."

"That?" Warennes scoffed now. "That's a tale made of nothing, and nothing more than an excuse to foment discord and rebellion against the Crown! You plot against the King!"

"There are witnesses to the events who can disprove that rumor," George answered quietly. "Father, surely you've told them of the quest?"

"Abbot Warennes, George, this is no time for debate," Prior Martin said. "Have done."

"Let him speak," George insisted. "Well, Abbot? How do you know of a plot? I know of no conspiracy that I've contrived."

"Would you be so foolish as to make it public? It is said that you have used this so-called quest to build support from the other barons for your petition for Merioneth on behalf of your handfasted woman!"

"My marriage was Christian and in this abbey church," George countered.

"My son speaks the truth, Alan," Aubrey said. "I performed the marriage."

"But it was not sanctioned by the King. Every nobleman must ask leave of the King to marry and so his marriage is no better than keeping his woman in *More Danico!*"

George sighed. "The twenty pounds offered for my bed and board wasn't enough? I'll give you twenty more if you'd just shut up, Warennes, and stop insulting my wife. Sometimes I think a rock has more sense than you."

"And who is insulting now, earl George?" Warennes said.

As he had growled at the peasant from the wood, now George snapped at Warennes, "Do not test me today!"

"This stubbornness and self-importance will not give you Merioneth. It will only make your hold on

Grasmere tenuous and threaten your father's episcopacy. We can agree on that, I'm sure."

"Until his grace the King acknowledges the wrongs his chancellor, advisors, and intimates have done to the good people of Merioneth, until he makes such an acknowledgment to my *Christian* wife, and when my father realizes he is yet another pawn on the King's chessboard to be used and taken, we shall not agree on much."

George's tone was cordial, but the message and meaning were a challenge all the same. A gauntlet had been thrown down.

"That is treasonous!" Warennes gasped.

"I voice a reasonable concern of a son for his father. I ask my father to decide; either serve the Church, as his vocation and calling require, or serve the King. He cannot serve both. Christ has said this," George explained. "Obedience to God before a temporal king."

"And a son's obedience is owed to his father," Warennes said. "A father who now serves both God and King."

"No man in the northwest of England would dispute how well I have been obedient, nor would he think more owed. You are new hereabouts, Abbot Warennes. You do not know half of the story." George said, and then, "By your leave? I have work to do."

"You have it, my lord earl," Warennes replied after a chilly silence during which Aubrey and Prior Martin stared at the ground. "I'm sorry you will not share in this great day for Ascalon."

After receipt of a blessing, George was free.

A great day for Ascalon?

His father was yet another man elevated in the church at the expense of his family. Leaving his loved ones in the dead of night to take up the Cloth, elected Lord Abbot soon afterward, running the Abbey of St. Cuthbert's as efficiently as the best of royal courts. Now an episcopacy was settled on him. How long would it be before Archbishop, then Pope? More to the point, how much was paid to secure this post and what was the form of payment? How long would it take him to crawl into King John's bed and become a spy or traitor to his brethren at the expense of his soul?

Then there was the business in Yorkshire in the remote shire of Arkengarthdale and what was now being called 'The Trial of Eskeleth.' George was used to make good on a blood debt in payment for the stolen maidenhead of a noblewoman Aubrey had taken by force. . .

"George!"

Now what?

Head down, George hurried to the largest of the guest houses lined up against the walls by the foregate and ignored the footsteps behind him, the jangle of jewelry and whisper of heavy silk. Once inside the house, George ignored his father standing on the wrong side of the door while he gathered pens, quill pens, brushes, paints, and new vellum to continue the day's work. He sat before the desk and prayed for his father to go somewhere else, then looked up.

Aubrey was still there, leaning against the door.

"A conversation with you is never finished, is it?" George said.

Aubrey motioned for permission to take the chair next to the bed. George nodded and his father eased down carefully and slowly, owed more to the garments he wore than age. His jewel-encrusted vestments rippled in brilliant, light-catching folds on the packed-earth floor. The unexpected movement woke a kitten under the stool. Before it could escape Aubrey caught it in his hands and began stroking its silky back so that in time it was purring contentedly.

How easy it is for him, George thought. *Everyone loves him and looks past the warts. Even cats.*

"I had hoped the anger you brought home from the Levant would have died out by now," Aubrey said. "That's the true reason why you came here, is it not? To heal and ask God's forgiveness, to find your way again? You didn't need to come here after Eskeleth. You redeemed us there."

"That would have been easy enough had some things not happened. Why bring it up when now there are different quarrels between us?" George asked.

"You'll have to be specific."

"It isn't hard to cipher the why and how. After denying my wife's petition for the lands and title of Merioneth, the king ignores the election of Philip Mortimer, her only ally, as Bishop of Carlisle and hands it to you with conditions. You've been commanded to ignore her concerns. Don't deny it; I have knowledge of certain conversations. Now you're the king's man. His eyes and ears in the northwest.

He's put himself in the middle of a family quarrel and one to which a better king and man would close his eyes, but he won't, because we know he hopes to scoop up the coin and lands that fall when we kill one another."

"The marriage of nobility in the realm is his concern."

"It hasn't been of much interest to him where it concerns some of the barons. Grasmere is nothing compared to others."

"They are not married to a Welsh heiress who is a princess in her own right. The daughter of an attainted rebel. A girl married to a baron who is whispered to be a traitor for his actions and words. It matters a great deal."

"You've changed your opinion since the wedding day."

"I haven't. I am concerned about Joanna but afraid for you."

"Then stand with me and help me claim Merioneth for Joanna. It is hers by right."

"And yours by right of marriage?"

"That may be how our grandsires claimed Grasmere, but I assure you Grasmere is enough for me. I would willingly become my lady's vassal and expect nothing more from her than the love and devotion a wife owes her husband," George said quietly.

"You're beginning to believe those romances of the *chevaliers* you pen for your sweetheart," Aubrey sighed, waving a hand towards the stack of illuminated pages on the table.

"She has suffered much because of the faults of others; I wish to make her happy."

"Laudable, but—"

"And I will be a faithful husband."

George knew the comment was unnecessary, but he wanted to inflict a wound on this, the great day for Ascalon. He'd drawn first blood for Aubrey moved the cat off his lap and started to fidget with a ring on one of his fingers: a wedding band. *He still wore it?*

"Don't pick quarrels with the Abbot, George. Play the game he wants. No, no, now you listen to me! Yes, he has a turnip for a mind, and yes, he's a conceited fool and uses his connections to the King to get his way; what man would not if he had no talents to commend him? But know this: he is the most dangerous man to cross right now. Play his game. It's only for a little while longer, isn't it?" Aubrey said quietly. "Who knows? Perhaps word will find its way to the ears of those who can help you most. That flea in John Lackland's ear may very well be Warennes. Honor is admirable; living to old age would be preferable."

"It is not honor that binds me. It is disdain for and rejection of the same corruption and evil I witnessed in Constantinople. It was all for naught, that crusade."

George took a quill and began to copy out the last verses of the last verses of *The Song of Songs*. He worked quickly, the Latin set to parchment in neat, italic, script. He was almost done and would be finished with the work that evening; took a moment to massage a cramp in his hand and was startled that

Aubrey was still there, watching him. George set aside the page carefully, and then, "Thank you for your concern, Father. Someday I will come around to your way of thinking, but not today."

"This new quest will be your undoing, George," Aubrey said.

"How difficult can this be compared to what I faced in Constantinople and at Eskeleth?"

Aubrey had an argument for that but decided to leave it for another time. He came to smooth the wrinkled fabric of their relationship, not tear it to shreds. "Come and sit at the high table with us, Geordie. It is your table."

George started sharpening a new quill on a whetstone, the movements angry. "But for how long? What will happen when you've lost your patience with the King as others have, and do or preach something to upset him? Will you be struck down in your cathedral as Thomas Becket was? Will I have a fall while hunting in the weald? Drink questionable wine?"

"Once more, will you attend today?"

George shook his head.

"I shall give your regards to your sister and mother."

"To my sister."

The rustle of fabric and the hollow thud of the door closing made George relax. He waited and as soon as he was sure Aubrey wouldn't return took up the half-completed page to begin again.

CHAPTER 4

HOURS WENT BY as George worked. The sounds of life in the abbey—the lowing of a calf, or bark from a dog, the industry of the monks—kept rhythm as George copied down the last of the text. Then he set to illustrate the margins of the page. A fluid line became the branch of a tree; quick, curved strokes were roses and leaves. Soon there were two lovers in a passionate embrace under a canopy of clouds and apple trees. Now to add colors. Ah! The colors! But where was Matthew with the pigments? He'd been sent to the apothecary in Grasmere hours ago; nothing could be done until the colors were mixed and the gold-leaf applied. George put away his work and reached for a little box that contained Joanna's letters. He chose one and read it for the sixth or seventh time; he couldn't remember. The parchment was almost as soft as wool from folding and handling. Her story of domestic life and how she first felt her womb quicken with their child made him smile again.

Soon, my love, soon. Soon God will speak!

The door creaking open made him pause, and instinctively George reached for something to use as a weapon when he heard the footfall. A candlestick would do. The steps were now tentative and George whipped around on the bench and reached for the young novice standing over him, hands about the poor fellow's throat in a heartbeat.

"*Benedicte!* Be easy, Brother! It's only me," the boy croaked and successfully unloosed George's grip.

"What do you want, Brother Timon?" George grumbled and avoided the boy's scrutiny—the look he'd grown used to: a stare of concern and pity, mostly pity. That was quickly replaced by a toothy smile. Timon's face was bright and rosy; he had the naïve countenance of one who was in love with his vocation as it happened with those who first entered the church. He saw only goodness everywhere in life, even if a knife lay against his neck or his house burned around him.

"I've been to the apothecary in Grasmere and have the colors you wanted," Timon answered.

"Matthew didn't go?"

Timon shook his head. "Brother Matthew asked if I would go in his stead. He asks your forgiveness and says he did not shirk his duty intentionally."

"Why would I think that? I'm not the abbot or prior."

"We were all given leave to celebrate Father Abbot's, that is, Bishop Aubrey's, consecration. Our labors were put aside for the today. It's a small sin, isn't it?"

"That would depend on the sinner."

"I do my best to live a Godly life, Brother, Timon said, crossing himself.

"It was meant as a jest, Timon, though I could have used the colors earlier."

George's comment was ignored by Timon, who dug in the scrip at his waist for some coins and placed them on the desk. "Master Wulfnoth gives his compliments," Timon said. "He would not take your money this time for you did him good service that he hopes you will remember."

"Did I? I don't recall."

"Here is the verdigris and lac, and here's smalt, ultramarine, woad," Timon chattered as he took a parcel from his leather bag and unwrapped it and placed before George each of the items bound within the parchment square with a reverence given to the Host. "Finally, the beaten gold. See how fine it is, Brother; very thin as to be transparent."

"You did well, Timon," George said. "Go on now to Skelwith and enjoy the celebration."

"But I did go, Brother!" Timon laughed. "On my way to Grasmere. Matthew and Thomas both said to accompany them and take a cup of ale. And I did, but I did not forget the task given to me. Ah! I see how this miracle is performed, for it is truly that!"

He became silent as George started to apply gold leaf to the page before him, movements patient and painstaking as flakes were daubed onto the parchment and smoothed with a liquid substance, spread as if they were paint. Soon the exterior of the letter 'Q' glowed and a golden vine wrapped around the page of text.

"Your absence was marked by many," Timon now commented.

"I'm sure Father Abbot will hold me accountable for that sin of intentional omission. What do you think?"

"The penance will be small—oh! You were speaking of the illuminations," Timothy said and accepted the unfinished page George offered for his inspection. "Truly amazing work, Brother! But *The Song of Songs*? Is that text not sinful? Is it not forbidden?"

"Why should it be? Did God not put the words in the poet's thoughts to be set to paper?" countered George, taking back the page. "Would you like to see how the paints are made?" He began preparing new pigments, taking a mortar and pestle from a shelve behind them and carefully measuring grains, powders, and liquids in shallow pots. A conical bowl was set atop one pot filled with lapis-colored powder and George carefully poured a liquid into the cone so that drops rolled down. Counting them, George waited until he had enough and mixed the two ingredients into a vibrant paint.

Noting Timon's interest, George asked, "Would you like to be my assistant?"

"I would. Father Abbot suggested I work on the Gospel Book for the Abbey and I should learn," Timon's voice faltered.

"But?"

"I could not assist with this." His finger jabbed towards the pages.

"What, *The Song of Songs*?"

"It glorifies . . . carnal love."

"It is carnal love that makes us whole."

"Surely not! It is an abomination! What makes us whole is our pure love for Christ."

"That, too—Brother Timon, you blush like a virgin! Are you a virgin?"

"I'm a novice."

George shrugged and dipped a new brush in readied pigment to color the wings of bluebirds. Quick, short, flicks of the brush and there were feathers. Another dab of gold and it looked as if the sun shone upon the wings.

"Let me posit this. If carnal love between a man and a woman is an abomination, as you call it, why did God give us the desire and ability?"

"Our Lord went out into the desert for forty days to test himself against the devil and to resist temptation."

"Temptation from what?"

"Brother!"

"From what? Drink? Food? Women? Dice?"

"All manner of temptations I think!"

"That isn't the answer I was seeking. Perhaps you've never made love to a woman. I tell you, one doesn't feel complete until you've shared such an experience with someone you love. To take her in your arms and feel her heart beat, hear her voice, her laughter, feel the warmth of her skin on yours. The giving and receiving of love. The divine moment when all the senses come together as one and knowing it is shared. That is God's gift," George said, and paused, smiling to himself. The image of Joanna sleeping with a hand tucked under a cheek and her dark curls spilling over her shoulders and breasts came to mind.

How she tugged at the blankets and took them all before snuggling close. These happy memories were also a gift and one that sustained him over the weeks since his arrival at the Abbey.

"You've known the world." Timon challenged.

"I've bedded girls if that's what you mean. Speak plainly."

"I suppose such experience gives one a better understanding of a man's sins when they come to you for confession."

George laughed. "No one would seek me out to be shrived! The sins I carry are legion and heavy."

"You are like our new Bishop. He came to the church after a dissolute life."

"Where did you hear that?"

"Truth be told, he leads it still," Timon whispered conspiratorially and crossed himself for added measure. "There is talk of his love for the young Countess of Grasmere, the Lady Joanna. I saw her this afternoon. All the gentlemen paid court and I swear all were in love with her, and how could they not be? Her dark beauty, grace, and warmth commend her. Praise be to God that the Earl of Grasmere saved her from an immoral and self-indulgent living before taking holy orders himself and now, to be consecrated Bishop of Carlisle!"

George suppressed a laugh. "Timon, do you know of whom you speak? If people knew the truth, they'd know it was she who saved the Earl."

"A camp follower and whore? The leman of a fletcher from Butcher's Lane?" Timothy scoffed.

The comment was insulting and George had heard the slanders many times before. Today, however, he would not brook them. *Bear with one another; forgive each other . . . The Lord has forgiven you; now you must do the same*, George prayed. Still, the calm wouldn't wash over him, and George asked God to send this idiot brother about his business.

Timon was prattling on about the red kirtle he'd seen the countess wear on market day and how everyone complimented the beautiful young woman. George knew the dress. It was a perfect color for her.

"Do you go to Grasmere Market to hear the gossip?" George asked of a sudden. He laughed and then paraphrased from Paul's second epistle to the church at Corinth: "I fear that when the Lord comes again, He will find you during quarreling, jealousy, anger, selfishness, slander, gossip, conceit and disorder. How are we to be an example to sinners behaving like that?"

"When everyone says the same thing, it could hardly be gossip."

George considered this for a moment. "Where is your charity, Brother?" he finally said.

"I do pray for her soul, and for the souls of all sinners, especially fallen women, for we must show the love our Lord showed to the woman caught in adultery."

"You assume a great deal there, Brother."

"It is no assumption. The Countess of Grasmere has not repudiated a sinful life, but benefits from it! Father Abbot has said as much."

"Has he?" George held his pen in midair, inspecting his work.

"If you came to mass, you would have heard this."

"The Abbot has preached about the Countess of Grasmere."

"Did I not just tell you?"

George put aside the pen and wiped his hands on a cloth. "Her life, whatever it might have been, is a matter between God and herself. The abbot should look to his own faults; however many are counted against him."

"Surely you do not condone her actions!"

"What might those be?"

"It's been said—"

"—I know she left a man who beat her, used her as no person should be used, and found God's grace and love in seeking peace and being a helpmate and friend to others," George interrupted. "She now has an exemplary life as far as I can tell. You've heard of her bravery and valor during the Trial of Eskeleth?"

"Father Abbot says that's a minstrel's ballad devised to cover the lady's sins, that it never happened."

"He wasn't there to see her bravery."

"And you were?"

George hesitated before he answered. "It was told to me by Aubrey Ascalon."

"He would say that, wouldn't he? It's said the child she carries is the Bishop's, that her husband was executed in Constantinople—the true reason for the tale of Eskeleth. To hide his sins, as well. Hah! That explains why the Bishop paid her such attention today. Well, we were born to sin, and the Lord forgives. Why else would He smile upon Aubrey Ascalon, who is no worthier to be consecrated Bishop of Carlisle than you or me, and The Countess little more than Jezebel?"

George was on his feet, the precious pages and tools of his work scattered as the desk nearly toppled over when he came around to take Timon by the cowl. "For a man who has put aside all worldly cares and things, you show a curious preoccupation with the Countess of Grasmere and our new bishop."

"What is that to you, Brother?" Timon sputtered, trying to break free. "Abbot Warennes says the fallen look to us for the path to salvation, that we must be guarded against false idols."

"If I were you, I'd attend to the close study of scripture and shut my ears to the opinions of men like the abbot who seek adoration and power. Open your eyes, Brother! Since he arrived, Warennes sought a most worldly life and spends too much time and energy on pointing out the faults of others, especially those of Aubrey Ascalon and his family."

"I've witnessed your quarrels with the Abbot. You've always got a bone to pick with him. I will pray for you, Brother, and hope you come to recognize his goodness and holiness lacking in our so-called benefactors, the Ascalons."

Timon was about to leave, but George yanked him close, tightening his hold on the brother's cowl.

"You don't know who I am, do you?" George growled.

"Let go of me! What do you think you're doing? I'll call for the abbot. I said, let me go!"

"Do you know who I am?"

"Let go of me!"

"I am George Ascalon, Earl of Grasmere. I don't need the Abbot's spy and bedmate watching me from the shadows and you may tell him that!"

"I'll pray for you!"

"Pray for the Abbot."

Timon wrested free and escaped, the door to the cell banging against the wall and its clamor bringing silent but curious monks out into the close. Each, in turn, stared at George and before returning to their cells put a finger to their lips. They were not surprised in the least. Discord and disorder seemed to follow George Ascalon.

✠

THE SIZZLE AND STENCH of tallow warned George that his work was done for the night. He glanced over at the lump of wax that was once a candle and then at the moon shining through the narrow window. George pushed the lump closer as he bound the last of the pages between the leather covers and buckled the work closed. There! After months of work, it was done.

His whole body ached from sitting at the desk, and his stomach growled. Too late for supper; he'd have to pay the porter for bread and stew if there were any to be had. George stretched and yawned just as the abbey bells called the brothers to Compline. The scuffing echoes of sandals on the pavement lengthened and faded. He waited until the last of the sounds died before gathering up his personal belongings in a saddle bag, placing the illuminated book between linen shirts and woolen hose to protect it. The door creaked as he knew it would and George didn't bother to push it shut as he walked to the guest house stable and thought he'd made a perfect escape when a man came from the cloisters.

"Do you go to do God's work, Brother?"

The cresset lamp in Prior Martin's hand swayed back and forth like a thurible, smoking curling up into the night sky and the flames lighting the path as they danced back and forth, a barrier between himself and George.

"I go to Grasmere," answered George, adding, "For good." *Why lie? They'd all know by morning.*

Prior Martin slowly brought the lantern down and pointed it towards the stable. "You go with my permission," he said.

"Brother Prior, is that you? Hasten! We are late for Compline—what do you do there? Who is that with you? Brother Prior?"

Warennes' calls prompted them to move quickly in the shadows and as soon as they were in the stable George closed the door and waited a moment before he went to a stall furthest from the doors. A gray stallion snorted its pleasure to see him, especially when George took an apple from his pocket and offered the fruit.

"You're an unhappy man, George Ascalon," said the Prior.

"You've always known that," George said as he knelt to unlock a chest. The Prior offered the light so that a saddle cloth barded with the Ascalon colors and device and a saddle could be taken out. Together they fitted the horse and again waiting, listening, they went out into the yard with George leading the horse.

"I cannot offer advice, for you will not take it," the Prior said. "But you will take care?"

"No one I love will come to harm and I will protect the abbey as best I can in exchange for the kindness you showed me. I swear by the love I bear my wife and lord father."

The Prior smiled. "Bishop Aubrey will be glad to hear that you love him."

"He knows it. He knows that I disagree with him; that is all."

"We part as friends. Let me give you a blessing."

"Gladly, for I'll have need of it, Brother Prior."

Raising his right hand, the Prior placed it gently on George's head and said, "The Lord bless you and keep you; the Lord make his face to shine upon you, and be gracious to you; the Lord lift up his countenance upon you, and give you peace."

George swung up into the saddle. He turned the horse about with gentle pressure from his leg and offering a salute, he rode off, the chanting of voices at Compline in his ears.

He was at Skelwith Castle by the time that holy office concluded.

CHAPTER 5

THE SKY WAS the color of pitch and the air held the tang of tilled earth, just like the last time George rode for Skelwith Castle in the dead of night. Then, Joanna was riding with him and he remembered how warm it was with her little body snuggled against his, her arms around his waist. She had whined and quarreled while George managed to keep his patience with her. Even now the scent of scorched wool and filth came to memory, the imprint of a sooty hand on his tunic. The fear in those crystalline eyes as she pleaded with him as the cottage in Butcher's Lane burned and toppled around them while they argued. He laughed aloud now, remembering how quickly the fear turned to defiance and anger as he dragged Joanna Fletcher away from that life. Petronelle said he'd finally met his soul mate and equal. How right she'd been.

George kicked the horse into a gallop, eager now to be home than ever before, to be in Joanna's arms.

There was no need for the sentries to send up lights to announce his homecoming this time around; at that late hour, the approach up to the drawbridge was bright with lamps hanging from trees and torches lining the path. From the activity in both wards, it was certain the first night of celebrations for Aubrey was finally ending. Stable boys and grooms were busy bringing horses or driving carts, wagons, and carriages as George rode through the gatehouse and outer ward past the chapel and household buildings into the greater ward. No one paid him attention; he was another person among many in a disorganized, busy, place. Even the groom that took the reins of George's horse failed to recognize the lord of the castle.

He slipped unnoticed into the great hall and looked around for Joanna, who was conspicuously absent, wandered through the little circles of guests and bypassed servants still carrying trays of wafers and cups of mead. No one looked familiar; these guests were courtiers from the south. He recognized no one from Grasmere. A cleric took a second glance at him as George walked by and it was just as well he'd kept his cowl and hood up. All the better to see others' misdeeds: an over-dressed courtier had a pretty red-haired girl on his lap and she didn't seem to mind being kissed and groped beneath her clothes. There was no mistaking Alan Warennes sneaking away with a gentleman of someone's household. That was no surprise; the perfumed peacocks tended to go their own way. His father Aubrey was laughing with another cleric and filling their cups. And who were these knights?

"Good evening Brother, Ascalon welcomes you. Do you require anything—my lord! Earl George!"

William Longleate's happy exclamation when he approached George was met by a shake of the head and finger to the lips. Crooking a finger, George summoned him to a corner at the northern end of the hall behind the screen.

"Why this secrecy, my lord?" Will laughed.

"I don't want anyone to know I'm here; not yet," George responded, and clasping the other man's arms said, "Will, it's good to see you."

"And you! Pardon, but are you well? You're thinner and pale,"

"The life of a nobleman suits me best. I'll revive once I have the good food of Skelwith in my belly and can work the land with my tenants, perhaps oversee the building of a new bower for my Countess."

"If you would allow my help I would be glad of it," Will offered.

"Of course! Thank you for looking after everything and everyone, especially Joanna."

"I could not do otherwise for you, my lord. Are you home for good, then?"

"I am."

"This is good news. I'll see that your rooms in Ravenglass Tower are prepared,"

"Don't bother. I have other plans for the night." Saying this, George winked and took one of the torches from a sconce and then pushed aside one of the tapestries against the southern wall, found the door and passage to the Lady Tower.

"I never knew—!" Will said.

"Now you'll forget seeing it. I'll see you in the morning?"

Will bowed away as George stepped into the narrow corridor and closed the door behind him. He expected the musty, staleness of an enclosed space and was surprised by gusts of fresh, clean air and the flickering of torches along the way. Perhaps Joanna had discovered the secret route to her tower and made use of it now?

The passage was L-shaped and led to a casement that brought one up to another floor, another L-shaped corridor, and then a landing with two casements and third and fourth landings. One set of stairs led to Joanna's chambers in the Lady Tower, the other to the roof and another bridge connecting the tower to the ramparts of the donjon. When George arrived at the second landing, he was surprised by a cloaked figure stepping out of the shadows.

"My lord bishop, I knew you would not resist this invitation," purred Elinor Lucy as she threw back the hood and unloosed the brooch to her cloak, revealing a lithe, perfumed, and naked body. As soon as George came full into the light she gasped and pulled the cloak around her.

"Elinor. I remember the last time we met by chance in a stairwell," George commented. "Who were you expecting to meet? Not me, I hope."

"No one, my lord!"

"No one?"

Elinor tugged on the cloak, pulling it even closer and tried to move around George, who took her arm. "I beg of you, sir, let me go,"

"Who?"

"You mistook me, my lord,"

"Which Bishop?"

"What do you mean?"

"Tell me now, and who, Elinor."

He knew by the way Elinor refused to meet his gaze and how she strained. Not much good would be done if he pressed the question further. George let go of her and she fled, her shadow like a black fog creeping along the angles and expanse of the passageway. The creak of a door opening and closing let him know she was gone.

Another short flight of steps led to the third landing, another corridor, where, at the end of a passage, an iron-framed door gave entrance to the chancellor's quarters. If George's suspicion held true, Elinor had waited for Aubrey to invite him to her bedchamber there. George was nearly to the landing when for the second time that evening a cloaked figure blocked his path.

"Good evening, Father," George sighed and leaned against the wall with arms folded across his chest and a leg extended to keep him from going any further. "It's good we meet because I want you to stay clear of Elinor Lucy. God knows what designs she has on you that will be our ruin."

The person came closer, movements slow and plodding as if hindered by wounds or fetters. The tell-tale ring of metal against stone, the clank of chain, made the last close to the truth.

"You say well, George." The voice was almost a whisper, rasping, and cold. After moments of labored breathing, "But whose ruin is it really?"

"Christ on the Cross!" George swore. Facing him was the specter of a Crusader, as gray as the stones surrounding them, as transparent as the open window above the landing. Before George could dodge out of the way, the specter was on him offering a kiss of peace full on the mouth from lips as cold as ice.

George grabbed for him and seized nothing. He found himself teetering on the edge of the stairs and fell, crashing into the wall as he tried to regain his steps. Then he felt the stab of a sword, something so cold it burned. Looking down he saw the Crusader's translucent gauntlet and the clean blade of his own sword, Ascalon, coming out of his mid-section. Where was the blood? The entrails? Now he glanced around and found himself on the wharf at Constantinople with knights of his own vanguard fighting one another tooth and claw. The sensation of cold and heat was excruciating. The scream he heard surely must have come from the men in combat on the wharf, but it was his own guttural cry for mercy as he fell into the bay.

☒

JOANNA HEARD THE CRY in her dream. It was the wailing of an infant and as she turned slowly to discern from where the cries came, she first caught the scent of exotic perfumes, then spices, and then the smoke and fire, the stench of burning flesh. What should have been a bright, clear, morning in a Mediterranean port with an already warm sun speckling red-tiled roofs on pale stone buildings was a nightmare of smoke, fire, and blood.

Joanna panicked, not knowing where to run. The infant's wailing rose in timbre until it was the unmistakable death scream of a man. She found herself moving effortlessly as if floating through the teams of fighting knights to the quayside, arriving in time to see George falling into the water, another bloodied corpse floating midst the cogs, galleys, and hulks.

"*George! No!*" Joanna screamed.

". . . . My lady? Joanna? Joanna! Wake up! Please!" Margaret was calling, a gentle hand on her shoulder as she was roused from the nightmare.

Joanna sat up in bed, soaked in sweat and panting for breath. She placed a hand on her belly and felt the child kicking. *Thanks be to the Virgin Mother!*

"It was another bad dream, my lady," Margaret consoled. "I'm told that they come more frequently as your time comes near. Shall I sleep beside you, Countess Joanna? Perhaps someone being close will ease your night terrors?"

That's what they were, Joanna thought. She shook her head and settled back into the featherbeds and pillows while Margaret tucked the covers around her as if it was swaddling and forced a smile of thanks.

"Ah! The lamp's gone out," Margaret remarked as she prepared to leave. She pointed to the glass cup suspended over the bed from the curtain railing. With speed and ease, she lowered the lamp and re-lit the wick so that a pale golden glow filled the enclosure of the bedcurtains.

"Sleep now, my lady," Margaret whispered as she tip-toed from the room.

The gentle swaying of the lamp and its shadows lulled Joanna back to sleep, where this time she heard not cries of distress in her dream, but the cheers of the people of Skelwith Castle as George returned from his 'exile.'

He rode his favorite gray stallion, Argent, which was barded with Joanna's colors of red and silver, and his colors of deep blue-green and gold in a patchwork. The children of Grasmere ran after him tossing flowers and waving Ascalon pennants. A knight followed George and carried the banner Joanna had sewn at Eskeleth, the mystical threads and colors glowed like halos and blocked out the hot summer sun as George pulled up rein at the steps where Joanna waited, holding the hand of a little boy much in coloring like his father.

Swinging down from the saddle, George took the boy up into his arms and made him laugh. After a quick hug and kiss, he set the child back on his feet. George took Joanna in his arms and offered a passionate kiss of greeting, his lips warm, urgent and sending waves of desire through her. Now came the quickening breath, familiar roiling and ache, the sensation of heat that nearly brought her to climax, and just as it had happened so many times before, she woke to find herself alone and disappointed.

"Sweet Jesu! How—?"

Joanna had turned gently so as not to disturb the babe finally asleep in her womb and sought to take George's pillow; she found George himself, leaning on an elbow and smiling down at her.

How long he'd been there, Joanna didn't know, but he smelled of cold air and horse and she supposed he only just arrived.

"This is what I missed most of all," he murmured and then leaned down for a kiss.

Joanna felt moisture on her cheek and assumed it was sweat or tears but when she swiped it away, found blood staining her fingers.

"George!" she exclaimed softly. "Your face is bleeding!"

"That? I shared a skin of Grasmere's good wine with Will ere I came up and it got the best of me. I stumbled on the stairs," George lied, kissing her again. "I'll live."

By her arched brows and how her delectable mouth formed the shape of an 'o,' George knew she believed him.

"Here now! What're you doing?" Joanna asked as he started to undress.

"Coming to bed so I can greet my wife in the manner I've been dreaming about for months."

"Not until I've cleaned that wound."

"It's just a scratch!"

Joanna pulled him under the bed lamp to see for herself. Just so, it was a small gash along the right cheekbone, which she dabbed at with the cowl of his discarded habit.

"Well?" George sighed after a while.

"You'll live."

"What did I say?"

She let him go so he could finish pulling off his clothes and watched, smiling softly. The months as a contemplative hadn't softened his body, for he was still lean and muscular. Joanna knew all the scars on his body. There was the claw from the lion of St. Mark on his shoulder. The stripe across his breast was the Archangel's fiery sword. The jagged line down the inside of his right thigh was received during the last battle in the abbey, a wound given by Richildis.

"Well?" George asked again, but this time in a more suggestive tone.

Joanna tossed aside the blankets. "Come to bed," she replied and pulled him into an embrace.

"Our son is happy to have his father with us," Joanna giggled between kisses and as George pressed as close as he could, her swollen belly quivering as the child within kicked. He ran a hand lovingly over her skin and felt the movement.

"Is it possible to sleep with such activity?" George asked in wonder.

"When one wants to sleep, yes," said Joanna as their kisses grew hot and George willingly followed her lead.

CHAPTER 6

"IT'S ALMOST MORNING," Joanna yawned hours later. George lifted his head from her breast and pushed aside the curtain. Just so, the horizon was beginning to turn, and in the next chamber, he could hear the women of Joanna's household stirring from their beds.

"How is it with you?" George asked as he turned to look at her. "Our babe is safe?"

Joanna laughed. "Are you still so worried? Our love play was gentle enough, and I swear it was beneficial for both child and mother!"

"I hope the mother was satisfied?"

"Marvelously so," she purred.

"If my wife is contented, I could not be otherwise. Besides, it does a man good to hear that's he's appreciated in bed." George now pressed an ear against her belly, trying to hear the child. "How many weeks? Soon, I hope?"

"He'll let us know. I have no doubt of that, given how he lets me know of everything else."

They both laughed as Joanna's belly shook and rolled and the tiny impression of a foot appeared when George placed a gentle hand on the velvety roundness of his wife's body.

"Go to sleep, my boy! Your mother needs her rest," he whispered.

"My heart, what if the babe is a little girl?"

"May she have her mother's beauty and wit. We'll make her such a great marriage that—"

"—Ah no! Let her be given an education and a taste of its gifts before we send her off to be a brood mare for some foul-smelling, bad-tempered, old man with no teeth or sense of humor! One who flops up and down on top of her like a fish out of water!" Joanna scolded and then playfully smacked him with a pillow.

"Holy God on the Cross! Hopefully she won't have her mother's sharp tongue!"

"It will be the best weapon she has in the realms of men."

"Only if, when she's a wife, she knows how to use it properly."

"Is this what you mean?"

Joanna flicked his earlobe with the tip of her tongue, and then tickled his neck, and finally the inside of his mouth. Her hands glided over his torso, pausing every now and then to pay attention to those places she knew would rouse him.

"Woman, you will kill me for sure!" George moaned but made no attempt to escape as their love play began again.

Their reunion continued until the bells rang ten of the clock. George was the first to rise, shoving back the heavy bed curtains and squinting in the morning light pouring into the bedchamber. Joanna claimed his pillow and settled against the bolster to watch him amble about the room.

"Jesu! I don't remember this chamber being so bright," George said as he partially shuttered one of the eastern windows and turned to smile at his wife and then look at his surroundings, the puzzled glance of one who was trying to remember them as they looked before. "You've made it . . . warm!" he laughed, nodding approvingly at the brightly painted columns decorated with climbing roses and gold leaf powdering. Where once a tabernacle of the Virgin took pride of place in the room, the little shelf and its doors were now painted blue with gold stars and a vase of flowers filled the niche, alongside one of George's wooden knights from his childhood. Embroidered hangings, surely Joanna's work, decorated one wall: an orchard of apple trees on one, angels soaring through clouds on another, a third, the Archangel Michael with his fiery sword and wings worked in gold and silver thread and holding the Sword of Ascalon in the other hand. The bed George already knew was comfortable and inviting and was spread with coverlets decorated in Joanna's needlework. Even the prayer desk and book cupboard were painted cheerfully. Fur skins and heavy mats of reeds covered the floors instead of rushes.

George came back to the bed, saying, "I would never have guessed this used to be my stepmother's chamber."

"Forgive me, but it was as sterile and uninviting as a nun's cell."

"Surely you'd expect no less from Maud?" George remarked, pulling on his small clothes and breeches.

"Are those from Eskeleth? From Arkengarthdale?" Joanna demanded of a sudden, her brow creasing as she leaned forward with the covers hitched around her to get a better look.

He glanced down and nodded. "How could you tell?"

"I remember the blood stain," Joanna answered, and George looked where her finger was following the rusty-brown stripe of a battle wound on the inside of his right thigh.

"Let's burn them," George said, and he stripped them off with his small clothes and exchanged them for the monastic habit he'd worn for months. When his face popped through the cowl's wide opening, Joanna reached across the bed and pulled him close for a kiss.

"I'd not complain if you burned that, too," she said.

"In good time; let me go to Ravenglass for my own things."

"In good time," she teased, letting the bedclothes drop so that her charms were visible, her skin glowing in the morning sun, and she had more freedom of movement to entice him.

"I have a gift for you if you would pause a moment in your seduction," George chuckled and moved away. He managed to slip out of her arms and reached into the satchel he'd brought, presenting *The Song of Songs* to her.

"This is beautiful!" Joanna exclaimed. Her delight was obvious from the way she carefully turned the leaves and gasped at the illuminations and fine calligraphy. "Where did you find it? Tell me,"

"When I ought to have been at my labors for the community, I locked myself up in the guest house and made this. If I could not have you in my bed every night, or in my sight by day, this sustained me. For what is love between two people but a holy gift of God?"

"With great delight I sat in his shadow,

"and his fruit was sweet to my taste.

"He brought me to the banqueting house, "and his intention toward me was love," Joanna read aloud.

"Ah, and have we not feasted?" he laughed seductively.

Again, they feasted.

✠

IT WAS GOING on midday when the servants began to call for Joanna and then knock at the door.

"Make them go away," George groaned and then laughed, diving under the covers. "Don't they know we've been separated for seven, long, celibate, months? Tell them your attention is for your lord and husband,"

"Who I will say is asleep—shush! You are home now, and we can look forward to this evening,"

"After the last of the unwanted guests has gone home or passed out in a corner of the great hall," George grumbled. "Gesu, it'll be morning by that time."

"It may be. But such is our lot as hosts," Joanna said as she grabbed her robe and pushed herself gently off the bed.

"I will look forward to much of your undivided attention!"

"*Shh!*"

Six anxious faces greeted Joanna when she unlocked the door: her ladies-in-waiting Rhosyn, Isabel, and Margaret; Emma, George and Petronelle's ancient nurse; Petronelle, and the redoubtable Elinor Lucy. Were they not so concerned it would have been laughable, given their open mouths and wide eyes when Joanna appeared with the robe barely covering her nakedness. She stepped aside to let her women in.

"Is everything all right, my lady?" Margaret asked, her eyes immediately falling on Joanna's swollen belly.

Joanna held a finger to her lips and with the other hand gestured towards the bed. "Quietly, please; the Earl still sleeps." Gasps of delight and surprise answered her and she added, "Yes, he is home, thanks be to God. Isabel, go to the Master Cook and see that he has a breakfast ready when my husband wakes."

"At once, my lady!"

"Quietly. . ." Joanna laughed softly.

All the women set to their work except Elinor, who stood by the hearth and stared first at George's cloak dropped on the bench there, and then to the bed behind the frame of curtains. She picked up the cloak and ran a hand over its soft velour weave, inhaled its scent and closed her eyes, remembering George's leave-taking for Crusade, how they made love and promises. Then the bitter homecoming and how they made violent, quick, hot, love on the stairwell as if to punish one another for promises broken. He'd come home a disgrace and brought with him Joanna Fletcher, the little whore of Butcher's Lane, to whom he gave attention and regard quite unlike that he'd given other women, including herself. What were promises to the earls of Grasmere? How long before George Ascalon broke Joanna's heart? Tears blurred her vision and spilled onto the fine cloak.

"Wife? What do you do there?"

Will Longleate had entered the chamber and stopped when he saw her idle, frowned when he noticed how she held the cloak against her breast, and how Elinor's face colored pink with shame. His anger rose when he saw the tears.

"What's done is done! God almighty on the throne, Wife! Be glad for what you have, though I am sorry it's not enough!" Will hissed as grabbed the cloak from her and tossed it on to a bench.

"Master Longleate, is something amiss?" Joanna asked. Will turned about and bowed saying, "My lady, the Bishop and his household invite you to come hawking. Knowing your love of falconry, he's brought with him the most beautiful of birds; you'll have your pick of gyrfalcons and peregrines."

"Which bishop?" George asked from behind the curtains. A moment passed, and he appeared in his monastic garb, yawning, and rubbing his eyes, ignoring the bowing and scraping that started up.

"Your father, The Bishop of Carlisle, my lord."

"Of course. Unless it was roasted and basted in butter I doubt if Eden would give a second thought to a falcon, so it must be my father, eh, Petra?" George said, winking at his sister.

"Brother, that tongue of yours will land you in trouble," Petronelle commented, and then kissing his cheek, added, "but in truth, I'd be concerned if it didn't! Welcome home! It's good you're here. We've all missed you."

"We'll talk later, Sister," George said, playfully tugging on a braid as he had done when they were children. Then he turned to Joanna and kissed her hand. "I'll see you soon." Lingering over her hand, he whispered, "Dress for your hawking party." The voice was suggestive and mysterious.

As soon as he was gone, a washing basin was carried in and set before the fire. Elinor stood apart and glared as Joanna was stripped to be bathed by Margaret. Rhosyn and Petronelle took her hands to secure Joanna's footing in the basin; they anchored her and shared her laughter and conversation as soap was lathered over the heavy breasts and pear-shaped roundness of her belly that seemed to swallow up the usually diminutive girl. Elinor noticed the red marks on Joanna's throat and along her shoulders and breasts. Love bites, no doubt! Indeed, she had a flush of color that ran the length of her and the tell-tale scent of lovemaking was soon masked and cooled down by the rosemary soap.

"That babe is coming soon, mark me," said Emma as she brought fresh body linens from a chest and laid them on the bed. "When they're as stubborn as this little prince, it only takes a little attention from his father to help him along!"

The women laughed at her reference and someone noticed that Joanna was carrying the child lower than the day before, which started an animated conversation about the mysteries and realities of childbirth.

"Shall it be another Christ Child, I wonder?"

Elinor's acerbic question, spoken under the breath but loud enough to hear, made everyone turn and stare. Joanna was the only one who did not seem to mind, but the sudden flush to her face and how she clenched her fists gave clues to her anger. For the longest time, all that could be heard was the rise and fall of water as Margaret and Rhosyn continued to bathe her.

Then, "If being here is so onerous Mistress Longleate, take your leave. Otherwise, help me dress," Joanna said calmly.

They stared each other down for a moment, Elinor's eyes once again flickering over the voluptuous body of the younger woman. The bile of jealousy and anger rose in her throat and it took some control for Elinor to move as if she didn't care and Joanna Ascalon was nothing to her.

She turned her back on Joanna and moved to the chests, noisily throwing back the lids. Elinor crouched in place to rummage through dresses, none of which would fit Joanna in her state. Her eyes lit, and she smiled when she found one. Of course, the pale rose kirtle cut of velvet, envied by Joanna's ladies, and one of the four gowns George gave to his bride. Joanna was perfection in this color, and the cut displayed her curves to their best advantage, but now when swollen from pregnancy and sallow from the morning sickness that continued to plague her even at this late time? What a sight she'd be!

The kirtle was yanked from the bottom of the chest and tossed on the bed. A pearl-colored shift of silk was next. Good choices these, a few of the ladies murmured, but voices were hushed as Elinor bunched up the costly fabric and dragged it over Joanna's head, pulled and tugged it laboriously over Joanna's arms and swollen body so that red marks appeared where the fabric creased. Just as quickly Elinor started pulling the heavier kirtle over Joanna's breasts and belly with more force until it was feared the seams would tear. Joanna was swaddled tightly in the garments and was helpless against Elinor's attention especially when she started to lace up the gown at its sides.

"The cords will go no farther, my lady," Elinor grunted as she continued to drag on the laces and pull them tight until the side seams were joined – and then burst apart. Joanna cried out in pain and let a sleeve rent when she reached up and struck Elinor across the face. Elinor bowed, regal and composed, and glided out of the bedchamber, but not as composed as Joanna.

"Help me, one of you," Joanna said as she struggled for breath and surreptitiously massaged her stinging hand. Margaret and Rhosyn stepped in to loosen the cords and rip the seams to free Joanna of both kirtle and shift.

"We can repair these for after the babe is born," Rhosyn commented.

"My lady should make Elinor do the work," Petronelle suggested as she went to look at the dresses hanging from pegs in an alcove. Pulling back the curtain, the sun fell upon a rainbow of colors. A kirtle of pale rose was selected, and a shift of gold-embroidered celery green found. Both were of soft wool and more giving. Petronelle found a great length of silk ribbon to replace the thick laces and threaded the soft fabric through eyelets loosely to allow more freedom of movement and so that the shift beneath showed through.

"Perfect."

George, freshly bathed and sporting new clothes, was leaning against the door frame. He came in now and in his hands was a small painted coffer of wood tied with a ribbon that matched Joanna's pink kirtle. "Ladies, if you would?" George motioned towards the door.

"What's this?" Joanna asked when they were alone, and George held out the painted wooden box.

"Another wedding gift—belated, of course," George said.

"Ah, I do like being a bride!" she giggled. "But what else could you give me that I do not already have?"

He gestured that she should open it and smiled as she untied the ribbon warily, watching his face, then the box, as if something might spring from it when opened. What she found was a brooch-shaped cross decorated with Anglo-Saxon vine work and studded with a garnet stone at its center.

"How beautiful this is," Joanna sighed as she kissed him and then turned so that he could place it around her neck. They stood at the looking glass, Joanna's fingers tracing the vine work, rubbing across the smooth, large garnet while George kissed her neck. "Have you been to Canterbury? Crosses such as these are found there."

"There's a secret to this cross and it has an interesting history. That story will be yet another Morning Gift." George said, placing her arm on his.

"God's life—riddles!" Joanna sighed playfully.

"Heed what I say now. Go off with the others and tell them the fields around the Abbey are perfect for sport. Slip away and meet me at the Abbey Church."

"You want to make love in a church, George?" she gasped, eyes wide.

"No, why would you–? No! I have to show you something and explain all this mystery."

"I would know this mystery, George."

"You will. I promise."

"*You've* been the mystery since returning," she said lightly, patting his face.

"Only because there is much to keep safe."

George's comment was cryptic, and Joanna glanced up at him for an indication of what he meant as she went down to the great hall and he took the stairs back to Ravenglass Tower. He merely smiled as they parted ways, for the time being, a finger to his lips.

CHAPTER 7

"MY LADY, YOU spoke truly when you suggested the abbey fields for hawking," said Eustace des Jumieges as the party from Skelwith Castle watched birds swoop, circle, and dive for their quarry. A patter of applause rewarded Aubrey's gyrfalcon for its success in capturing a sparrow.

"My lord of Carlisle, will you make a wager in this next round?" the Bishop of Eden called. "The winner to give his earnings to the poor box of a cathedral. What say you?"

"And that would be the cathedral in Eden, my brother?" Aubrey laughed. "Add shirts and caps and I'll take those odds!"

One of the squires removed his cap and began collecting silver pennies from the guests who were eager to participate in this friendly wager. They laughed and took cups of wine from stewards, debating the contest as birds were hooded and made ready. Joanna stood apart from them, watching and encouraging her favorites, but not participating.

"You will not go hawking, Countess Joanna?" Prior Martin asked, joining her.

"No; I feel out of sorts. Ah! I ask your forgiveness, Brother Prior. Pardon me for the presumption of using the field today. It is but a fallow field most of the time, and a shorter distance to the castle than where we usually ride," Joanna said. "I couldn't go as far as the weald and I didn't want to spoil their amusement."

"It is of no moment, Lady. Worry not."

"The Bishops will give their winnings to the poor. What if Ascalon gave the birds' quarry to the abbey for pots of stew for our hungry brothers, and the lay servants?"

"As you say, Lady," Prior Martin said, bowing.

"Ah, but I am tired. I should go back to the castle. But first, I would like to give tribute to our Virgin Mother. Would you walk with me to the church?"

"My pleasure," he said, bowing again.

She waved off her ladies, strolling slowly with Prior Martin across the field and towards the gate that led into the Abbey.

"Earl George arrived safely I take it?" Prior Martin queried when they were a distance from the others.

"Yes."

"Abbot Warennes is glad to see him gone. But he undoubtedly weeps for the loss of another twenty pounds."

"That sounds suspiciously like disloyalty on your part."

"You know where my loyalty lies."

They walked in silence now and Brothers at their work in the gardens bowed respectfully when they saw her and waited silently until she passed before taking up spades and rakes again. Prior Martin paused when they arrived at the church.

"Will you not join me in prayer?" Joanna asked.

"I would not intrude on private devotions."

"It is no intrusion."

"Even so,"

"You will dine with us tonight?"

"It would be my pleasure. God keep you."

"And you," replied Joanna as she pushed aside the curtain blocking the opened door and stepped inside to a dusky church. One window high above the quire was all that allowed light and it wasn't much. Movement in the choir stalls assured her that George had arrived and after an awkward and hasty reverence before Christ on the Cross, she used the votive candlelight to guide her where he stood near the shrine of the Virgin and Child.

"You didn't waste time, my lord!" Joanna said brightly as she approached him. "I bid you keep your promise and tell me what this great mystery is."

"Tell *me*."

Abbot Warennes smiled as he stepped into the light, raised his hands in question and then folded them into the sleeves of his habit.

"My lord abbot!"

Joanna moved away as he came closer. The smile was frozen on his lips as he looked straight at her, though his eyes were dead.

"I'm sorry—I was expecting to meet my husband. Is he here?" Joanna's words were sweet and even in tone, even though she'd betrayed her surprise.

"What are you doing here? I thought you were hawking with the others."

"The Earl asked me to meet him here, and so—"

"You make an assignation in a church?" Warennes hissed.

"You mistake our purpose."

"I can think only of one purpose for a husband and wife long parted from one another!"

"This is the church of his ancestors. We come to give thanks for his return and to ask the Holy Mother's protection when it comes time for our child to be born."

Joanna now looked around Warenne's shoulder towards the door, her brows knit together. "He did promise to be here,"

"I thought he was with you. He slipped away without permission during the night. He has penance to pay."

Joanna stepped forward and unloosed the purse hanging from her girdle. Money she was going to wager on the falcons. "This should be sufficient. It's yours if you want it." The purse was offered and it was only a moment before Warennes took it, hefting its weight in his palm. "It's a goodly amount, sir. And were you to ask, we would be glad to offer more."

"That isn't what I want!" hissed Warennes. "By the time your child is born the Earl will have come to terms, mark me. And you would do well to encourage him to make it so."

He stared at her silently, raking his eyes over her body and resting at the quivering belly. The child in her womb was kicking. Joanna immediately placed her hand over it protectively and glared back at Warennes.

"What would you have me do, Abbot Warennes? Tell me," she said. "He is temporal lord of this abbey, the castle, and the lands hereabouts for miles. Give me the terms."

"Do you expect me to bargain with a whore from Butcher's Lane? You should think again. Good day, Mistress."

"I am the Countess of Grasmere and your lady! You will remember that!" Joanna called after him when Warennes pushed past her.

The door slammed. Alone in the church now, Joanna turned at every noise, every shadow. Even the scuff of her shoes on the pavement gave her a start.

A dull ache in her back that had plagued her for hours now felt sharper, almost like a burning that traveled down into her buttocks and thighs and made her catch her breath. Joanna massaged her lower back and sat down, breathing deep and slow, waiting for the pain to subside. Surely it was too early for the child to come?

She closed her eyes and whispered a prayer to the Virgin Mary that the pain would go and that her baby would be safe. While she prayed, Joanna saw Abbot Warennes as he was moments ago. Close and sneering, his face red with anger, his breathing labored. Then the face became marked with leprous sores that bled. The skin was torn away in places and the muscles of his cheeks and neck exposed. Joanna opened her eyes and gasped.

The candleflames now whipped back and forth and the shadows suddenly became the spectral knights of Eskeleth. Each appeared out of the stone pillars dividing the nave; like smoke they arrived and stood silently, encircling her. Their swords stood before them at rest. Joanna was ready to escape when they raised their hands to stop her. She stepped back when a candle flame slowly grew in brightness and size, the pale orange turned to blue that gave off stars and shards of color. It swirled and spun until it was the shape of a woman. Joanna could make out a blue robe and mantle, a white veil and wimple covering her black hair. Her face was serene and she smiled tenderly. She wore a necklace of diamonds and carried a golden book, upon her brow was a silver crown sparkling with stars.

Joanna managed to kneel in the presence of this spirit or saint, she didn't know which. She knew by the loving, gentle, smile that she was in the presence of the Holy.

"Lord Jesus, protect me! Holy Mother of God, protect me! Saints Anne, Michael, Margaret, shield me!" Joanna whispered, unable to take her sight from the exquisitely beautiful woman who continued to smile.

"They will and shall. As will I," said the woman in a soft, husky, voice much like that of Joanna's mother. The woman barely touched the pavement as she glided towards Joanna and raised her up. The touch was warm and of flesh and blood. She kissed Joanna's brow and left her holding a *marguerite*, a daisy. "You have much to give, Joan ferch Rhodri, daughter of Elen and beloved of Grasmere! Expect more mystery; expect more favor."

She was gone, fading into a bar of stained-glass light that poured down from a window above the chancel and into the circle of knights. They too, dissolved as the sun shone brighter through the windows.

Joanna was still staring at the flower in her palm when George at last swept in, spurs ringing on the pavement, the groan and creak of harness and leather. When George smiled and reached for her, Joanna went to him and clung tightly.

"Sweetheart! What's this?"

"The abbot was here. You didn't tell me what a frightening man he is. There is more the Devil than God about him. He wants matters between you settled before our baby is born. What are they? George?"

He sighed and answered, "I've been commanded by the King to give up the entitlement of Grasmere to the Abbey, for by his word against my father's it is not mine to hold."

Joanna made an exasperated sigh. "Ascalon has held Grasmere and Skelwith Castle for nearly two hundred years! Why now?"

"Like so many castles and lands in England, it is a matter of the King's interpretation of a diploma."

"A poorly-executed transaction by your father?"

"You know my father too well."

"Well then, produce a diploma or deed."

"If it could be that simple, my love. There is no charter. No deed except this."

George took the cross suspended on its chain around Joanna's neck. "And this is the cause of the dispute," he said, sliding fingertips across the smooth garnet at its center and the gold vines surrounding the stone and each arm of the cross.

"I want no part of this if it brings you torment," Joanna swore, then she tugged at and broke the chain and would have flung the cross into the chancel but for George's hand on hers.

"This belonged to my father's ancestor, a man who lived here before the Conquest."

Joanna now looked at the cross in a different light, marveling. "Truly? As ancient as that?"

"Perhaps older. My father has always called it the deed to Grasmere and patent for our title. Come with me; let me show you what I've discovered."

George walked a well-worn path of paving stones to where a shrine dedicated Virgin and Child was set apart from those of other saints in the church. Kneeling, he took the dagger from his belt and used it to pry a stone loose in the pavement at the Virgin's feet. He pushed the stone aside, and then took a candle to show Joanna the ladder leading down to what looked like a crypt.

"It's down there," George whispered, the candlelight wavering as he sought to illuminate the passage. "A sepulcher and a coffer lie in this chamber, set far back into the vault out of sight as if they were placed so to protect them."

Joanna knelt and leaning on George for support peered down into the black, musty, hole, catching glimpses of a stone sepulcher and statues of saints against the walls.

"I think we and Father are the only ones living who know about this," George said as he replaced the stone and scuffed his boot along the edges of the stone, pushing dirt about to hide his disturbance.

"But what is it exactly?"

"Hidden treasure, family documents."

"Why leave them?"

"They're safe from our enemies."

"Would it not be better to have them close?"

"What do you mean?"

"I fear Eustace des Jumieges and Warennes; they conspire against you."

George laughed nervously. She was intuitive and observant, his wife, and though he loved her for these qualities, he feared for her safety, knowing what she said might be true.

"What are they to Ascalon? Did I not slay a dragon, best Saint Michael, and Goliath?"

"Yes, but will you have God on your side ever again?" she asked quietly as she touched his cheek and kissed him.

"If you are with me again, yes."

"I will be," she replied releasing him from a quick and tension-riddled embrace.

"Not that way," George said when Joanna started back towards the narthex and great doors. "There's a door in the Sacristy that leads to passageways: one to the Cloister and Chapter House and one to the gates into town, another to the Abbot's Lodging."

"Gesu, another mystery?"

"No; I have no desire to see Father until this evening. He'll want explanations and I'm not in a mood to offer any."

"Ah, George," she sighed and followed him. "Sometimes all people want to hear is the truth."

✠

"JOANNA, YOU LOOK so pale! Are you well?"

A motherly pat on the cheek and a hand on the forehead came with Petronelle's inquiry. Upon entering the bedchamber, she'd found Joanna listless and sitting beside the window with a Gospel book in hand.

"The babe will not leave me alone," Joanna replied with a feeble laugh.

"And his father?"

"I'll fear the day when he does not."

"Well, you have guests for supper waiting below: two bishops, their households and practically all of Grasmere," said Petronelle as she started looking at dresses and opening jewel casks.

"Stop it! Please, no more; I'm not a poppet," Joanna meekly protested as she rose. "What I wear would suffice for the Lord were I to stand before Him."

"God be praised with all His Saints! My sweet Joan has come back to me!"

Smiling, Joanna looked in one of the casks and chose the most audacious coronet to set upon on her veiled hair: one glittering with diamonds and teardrop-shaped pearls. "I didn't say I wouldn't want to impress our guests," she said as she placed it.

Her ladies were waiting on the landing and just as Joanna arrived with Petronelle, George came from Ravenglass. Without greeting he placed Joanna's hand on his arm and looked straight ahead as they processed quietly to the great hall. No playful banter between them, no adoring glances. Not even a chaste peck on the cheek. Petronelle glanced at her brother and sister-in-law and wondered what was wrong.

All heads turned when the doors were pushed back and after a moment of silence, cheers and applause greeted George and Joanna as they processed to the high table. Aubrey and Eden bowed as George and Joanna took the places of honor. Eden had been sitting at George's place and he quickly moved out of the way, as did Eustace and Abbot Warennes, both looking ill. Father and son barely acknowledged one another.

"Welcome home, my lord earl," Eden said with a polite nod. "This must be a surprise for your vassals and retainers, given your happy reception."

"No one could have been more surprised than my lady countess," George said, turning to kiss Joanna's hand. His gesture brought more applause.

"How well loved you are, my lord!" Eustace chuckled and raised his cup in tribute.

"More so than the last earl," Aubrey commented, also raising his cup. "But then, I never had to battle demons."

"You left that charge to your son," George replied as he washed his hands in the basin of rosewater brought forward.

"But who was it that taught you to battle dragons?" Eden laughed.

"My wife," said George. "She was and is my second. Her bravery is formidable and amazing to behold. I'm very careful not to make her angry. God and the Saints help any man who should try."

"Even the king?" Aubrey said into his cup.

Eustace guffawed. "A woman against the King?" he asked.

"Eustace, I'm sure that's why you came," Aubrey said. "A woman alone in a castle is easiest to cajole or giving in to honeyed promises. You weren't expecting George to be here and now will have nothing to report to the King, and worse for you, I suppose, wait even longer for Great Langdale." He looked at Eden, who winked conspiratorially, and then at Eustace, concluding with "But how good it was that our King sent you as his emissary. If that's what you are."

"His Grace laments that he could not be present for your investiture as Bishop of Carlisle, matters of state as they are. He is making a progress north and will honor the Bishop when he arrives soon. I hear he is at Lincoln now."

"Putting down another revolt or denying an heiress' right to her lands?" George whispered to Joanna and they laughed together.

"What, sir?" Eustace asked. "The music,"

"I said, I lament our king must always be concerned with matters of state and not enjoy his ease; that he cannot trust another man to deal with castles and land."

"Ah!" Eustace chuckled, nodding. "Perhaps he'd trust a diplomatic man like yourself?"

"It would be John's fortune and Grasmere's loss if a man like George were interested," Joanna replied.

"You'd deny a royal summons or appointment, Earl George?" said Eustace, surprised. "Even if it meant that your wife's title and lands were restored to her?"

"If it meant I was the King's hostage for one purpose or another, such as titles and lands," George answered.

"His Grace the King is known for fair dealing," Eustace said. "All he requires is loyalty and obedience, just as you require the same from your vassals."

"Then explain to me how suddenly one man benefits, and another is stripped of a living based on this loyalty and obedience?" George countered. "Take Warennes, as an example." George pointed towards the Abbot, who was scolding one of the servants for spilling wine on his robes. "He'd benefit from my being thrown into an oubliette."

"George, keep it up and you will be," Aubrey murmured across Joanna.

George and Aubrey exchanged withering glances and moved apart when the porter brought the first course of dishes.

"My lady, that jewel around your neck; it looks ancient," Eustace commented.

"This?" Joanna brushed aside a veil to allow a better view of the cross.

"Treasure your husband brought from the Holy Land?" Eustace asked. He dipped the chunk of bread he gestured with into the sauce before them and licked it off while staring at Joanna's breasts just as hungrily.

"A belated morning gift from George," said Joanna as she smiled at George and fingered the cross. Aubrey exhaled a sound of surprise, almost like a kitten purring, when Joanna held the cross out for Eustace's scrutiny.

"Bishop Aubrey seems quite taken by it," Eustace laughed now. "Or is it the obvious charms of the lady who improves its beauty?"

"Too bad for my father that I won her love ere he ever had a chance," George replied. "For once luck was on my side."

"Scratching at that scab even now?" Aubrey grumbled.

"It's a constant irritation, like your new loyalty and position."

"You don't wear pettiness well, Geordie. Forgive and forget."

"Be silent, both of you!" Joanna exclaimed; "By'er Lady, even though this babe is not yet born, I have not one, but two little boys to scold! Now enough! No, not another word!"

Eustace was going to remark but thought better of it. He instead raised his cup to the Countess of Grasmere. Ah, what he'd give to *parle* with her!

"You are full of wit and purpose, Lady," Eustace said when tempers cooled.

"What woman is not, sir?" Joanna retorted.

"Plenty. You remind me of a princess I met not long ago. Your beauty and your wit reminded me of her."

"How clever you are, sir, in your wooing. I thank you for the compliment, but it falls on deaf ears," she said and offered a disingenuous smile before reaching over to take George's hand and kiss it. Her action prompted him to say, "What's this?" and Joanna then leaned over and kissed him full on the mouth, which brought applause and laughter from the guests.

"How they enjoy the simplest of entertainments," Joanna sighed. "It's as if they'd never seen two people very much in love."

"It is a rare gift."

"Have you never been in love?"

Eustace raised his cup and drank, then set it down carefully before speaking again, as if the answer was in the cup. "Once I was in love with a great lady. You remind me of her; in fact, I think we have met before."

"Have we?" Joanna asked, incredulous at the very idea. This man was as oily as fish and just as slippery. He was handsome in a way, but not enough to make her blush or flirt like the other women in the room, especially her cousin Rhosyn.

"I was traveling through the west of England and met a lady quite like you. A twelve-month past, or maybe more,"

"I doubt if it was me, sir."

Eustace again raised his cup to her and winked. Joanna suddenly felt a chill. He did remind her of someone.

✠

AFTER THE REST of the meal was spent in silence, Joanna bade servants to move the tables so that the guests might linger to play at counters and listen to a minstrel hired to entertain them with ballads. Some took to dancing. George moved through the hall to greet and reacquaint himself with vassals and villagers, take the gauge of the King's emissaries watching him as closely as he watched them. Joanna sat with her women and watched the dancing, particularly enjoying George and Petronelle as they led couples in a carol. Aubrey came up and bowed, gesturing permission to sit with her.

"Only if you promise to behave, Father!" Joanna teased.

"On the heads of my children, whom I love beyond measure, and my daughter-in-law as much," Aubrey swore lightly.

"Have a care; we wouldn't want to lend credence to the gossip."

"And what is that?"

"That you are the father of my child and we are lovers."

Aubrey looked stricken, his smile faded, and his skin turned gray. "What foolish, idle, talk!" he sighed as he took the cup Joanna offered and drank, handing it back.

"I'm surprised you didn't know since it was your abbot who preached the lie last week and has done nothing to stop the chatter. In fact, I think he enjoys my discomfort."

"Now I understand George's anger."

"You would have been proud of me, Father; I sat with my eyes on the carvings of angels and saints decorating the pulpit and said nothing, nor did I blush. And the little earl I carry decided to sleep during the homily."

"As did most of the congregation?"

"Obviously not, since the gossip has spread."

"You sat and listened to this diatribe?"

"It wasn't as if I had a choice, did I? Had I protested by walking out, that would have added more gossip to the midden heap."

"This isn't fair."

"Father, I've grown accustomed to what is fair in life, and what is not. Someday I will tell you of my parents and what the King has done to us. Perhaps then you'll understand George's zeal for restoring my inheritance."

"I'll make amends to you, Joanna. It isn't fair. You've had much turmoil in your life and to add this? Well, with what's to come, it isn't fair. I shall offer tomorrow's mass in your name and the child's. God will see the right of it."

What was to come, Joanna wondered?

CHAPTER 8

"YOU WILL TELL me all George, else I shall throw this into the moat."

Joanna's demand came with resistance to more kisses and coupling. Alone within the closure of the bed, the curtains pulled for privacy and the lamp above the bed casting golden shadows on their bodies, George softly laughed as she pulled the sheet up and dragged the cross around from the back of her neck where it had fallen during their lovemaking. The cross glowed and George moved closer so that he could take it in his fingers.

"Ah no, love!" George said. "I only want the cross for now."

"Right you are, sir! For now that's all you'll have until you tell me."

"And then you'll give me what I want," he said, leaning in for a kiss. She put her fingers against his lips and tried her best not to smile.

"What did I just say?"

"You deny a dying man?"

"You're not dying, George Ascalon."

"I'm dying of long-denied desire and mean to make up for lost hours,"

"Perhaps you're going moon mad—hey there! Now stop!" Joanna laughed as he pulled back the sheet and began to tickle her. "You win! You win!"

George gave her a passionate kiss, then drew her into his arms by pulling gently on the chain that suspended the cross around her neck. He held the cross in his open palm.

"I would I'd never found it," George said softly. "When my father and I spoke for the first time after my return from Constantinople, he said that buried under a stone at the foot of the statue of the Virgin and Child in the abbey church was the deed to my inheritance. One night when no one was about, I pried loose some stones and discovered the entrance to a crypt. On top of the ledge by the ladder, I found this cross wrapped in a rag. I expected a charter sealed with red wax, not this pretty thing, nor the crypt below.

"When I demanded an explanation from Father, he told me it was a pledge from an ancient king to our ancestors and it gave us Grasmere."

"What was the pledge?"

"I can only guess that Grasmere was ours for serving the King. Father hinted at that, though he won't say more—but there is more to this pretty cross. And now that Eustace des Jumieges knows and shows a keen interest, he sends spies around or may do the work himself. Ah no; I don't expect he'll dirty his hands."

"He was interested in where it lies," Joanna sniffed as she pulled a bed robe across her naked shoulders.

"You have a high opinion of your charms," George teased.

"Well, when I've given birth to this son of yours, all of my charms will go away."

"A pity," he answered and nuzzled her neck, moving towards a breast.

"Well, you've kept your part of the bargain," Joanna said as she slid into his arms. After a long, lingering kiss, she pulled away, frowning.

"Now what?"

"George, I think we should keep it safe. I have a place in the bower."

"Then I wouldn't be able to admire it—or your charms."

"Take a good look while you still have a chance," she replied.

George replied that he would be more than happy for the opportunity, and when at last they fell to sleep, he had the cross clutched in his palm, his head on Joanna's breast.

✠

GEORGE WAITED IN the abbey chapel, mystified by the summons he'd received from his father. *Perhaps,* he thought, *Father has come to his senses and will renounce his allegiance to the King and serve God.* If that were the case, he hoped it would not go so badly for Aubrey as it did for that great English saint, Thomas Becket of Canterbury.

Of all the abbey buildings, this chapel was his favorite place. The scents of stone, earth, beeswax, and incense brought a contentment he'd never known before. The smiling Virgin Mother and Child, and the serene militant and peaceful saints that decorated the walls, were more family to him than his own except for Joanna ferch Rhodri, daughter of Elen, his Welsh princess and wife, his exquisite lover, and soon to be the mother of his son.

George relaxed into the recess of the stone bench along the wall, waiting. The more he relaxed, the more his head drooped on to his chest and the hand on his sword fell away. He was almost asleep when he heard the footsteps and the door opening. The footsteps stopped, and George waited, then rose. He put a hand on the pommel of his sword, just in case, and walked toward the sound now filling the chapel: the sound of wind and bells.

The door to the cloister suddenly burst open and an incredible and blinding golden light flooded the nave. As bright and painful as the light was, George was drawn towards it and didn't look away. The more he looked, the more he saw the white, shadowy, figures of men lined up in battle formation - a vanguard. As George approached he was blocked by a knight made of flesh and blood and as real in appearance as himself.

His tabard of white and gold emitted a light brighter than the moon, and even the sun. His hair was black and glossy and fell to his shoulders; his eyes were the brightest blue. The knight saluted George with a raised sword and George returned the compliment, taking the sword of Ascalon from its scabbard and raising it with a flourish. Whether it was the play of light or his imagination, George gasped when the blade started to glow gold, then lavender and then gold to pink, the words etched into the fuller bright and visible:

Caste we awei the werkis of derknessis, and be we clothid in the armeris of liyt.

The knight bowed again, and two great wings tipped with blue, pink, and gold feathers rose from behind him and fanned out. George knew it. This was the angel he met on the road to Grasmere.

"Why do you persist?" George angrily wanted to know. Have I not proved myself? May I not have peace?"

"Are you fit for more contests, George of Grasmere?" it asked in a low, melodious voice. When George took a defensive stance suitable for battle, the angel laughed. "No, my lord! Not with me. Never will you fight those battles again. Those ahead of you are much worse, even so."

"If what you say is true,"

"You have no reason to doubt the Father. Or his Son. I come as their messenger."

"Why?"

"Your deeds in Constantinople. What Christ asked of you, you accomplished." The Angel now smiled.

"I don't understand—"

"*Ascalon!*"

The shout came from Abbot Warennes who strode through the chapel at an angry pace towards George. Alarmed that Warennes would see the messenger, George moved toward the chancel. The Angel, however, had melted into the stone pillars, a finger to its lips, a smile on its face and became just another decoration in the limestone.

"Our conversation wasn't finished," Warennes growled.

"I had no desire to break my fast arguing with you about what is not yours," George replied.

"You tend to walk away whenever you hear something that displeases."

"I'm looked for at the castle, so if you don't mind, Abbot?" George attempted to get around him but Warennes moved to the right and blocked his path. Trying to move around him made the dagger and sword on his belt clang like bells.

"You come armed into my church?" Warennes said.

"God's house, not yours," George replied. He climbed the chancel steps and laid the weapons upon the altar. Turning to face Warennes with arms outstretched in question, George said, "What is it you want?"

"Skelwith and Grasmere," said Warennes. "You knew. You didn't have to ask."

"But isn't that what Eustace wants?"

"Eustace des Jumieges? You're not serious!"

"That's the only reason he would come to Grasmere. He's been promised something by the King, just as you have. You both can't have what is mine."

"You know I can!"

"Did my father strike a deal with you, like that with Wulfstan of Eskeleth? Shall I champion the Holy Mother Church in payment of a sin?" George asked, stepping down from the chancel and approaching Warennes so that they were facing to face. "Unless that is the reason, you'll never have rights to what is mine. I am here to make sure that doesn't happen. Be content with your abbey, Warennes. Who knows? Perhaps the King will give you an episcopacy like he did my father."

"You say well, George Ascalon."

"What? Who's there?" Warennes looked around for the source of the voice. "Jesus protect me!" Warennes cried, and then to George, "You bring the devil into my church!"

The angel and two knights appeared out of the light and stood silently, blocking the entrance to the cloisters so that their shadows were thrown across the flagstone floor.

Warennes seized the great, jeweled, cross on a chain around his neck, holding it up as he rambled off verses of prayer, jumbling them into nonsense: "O Lamb of God, who takest away the sins of the world, have mercy upon us ... for on the night he was betrayed, Jesus took bread and broke it, gave it to his disciples and said, 'take. Eat. This is my body which is given up for thee. Lord Jesus Christ, son of the living God, having mercy upon me a sinner! Forgive me my sins and transgressions, I beg of thee, O Father! I beseech..."

One of the knights glided forward-his spurred boots barely touching the ground-and took Warennes by the throat. Soon the Abbot was gasping and sputtering for breath, clawing at his throat, which became scarred with bloody scratch marks as he fought. The more he thrashed and struggled, the darker his face became until it was purple. The Abbot foamed like a mad dog and growled as he tried to work himself free. He went limp and was dropped to the pavement. The Angel raised a hand and pointed to the door and then was gone, as were the knights. Rather than follow, George ran to the altar and grabbed his sword, but it was like white-hot steel and burned so that he screamed in agony.

". . . *George!* George, wake up! What is it?"

Joanna was shaking him gently, bending over him as he thrashed. Soon he wept and grabbed Joanna, mumbling and muttering nonsense about knights and angels.

"Only another night terror, my love; only a nightmare," Joanna whispered as she kissed his sweating brow and felt his chest for the rapid and frightening beating of his heart. "Come,"

George clung to her and wept, and she rocked him as she would a babe. He at last drifted off to sleep towards dawn. Joanna dressed quickly and slipped out of Ravenglass Tower to hear Mass and to pray for her husband's tortured mind and soul.

It was as if nothing had happened in the night when she found George waiting for her in the bower later in the morning. He looked no worse for his fright, but he immediately noticed the shadows under her eyes, that purple bruising of fatigue.

"Our babe kept you awake for most of the night, didn't he?" George after they greeted one another.

"In truth, it was my lover that had me awake," she replied, taking her basket of needlework from a chest and settling on a cushioned bench. Joanna unpacked what looked to be a tiny shirt but when unfolded

127 - ELLEN L. EKSTROM

carefully was a christening gown with delicate faggoting and minuscule gems decorating the border around the long, full, hem. Her flosses, beads, and gemstones arranged on the table beside her, Joanna began her day's work. "You tossed and turned and rambled on about nothing and everything," she said after a time.

He moved away slowly and scuffed his soft shoes against the floorboards as he paced and finally stopped before the banner, glancing up at it and fingering the gold braiding she'd recently put around the hems. "Tomorrow is the last day of festivities, thanks be to God. I don't know what more Grasmere and Skelwith can do to celebrate the Bishop of Carlisle," he said.

Joanna took a few stitches, paused, and then picked them out, starting on the embroidered edge of the christening gown again. "Did you mean what you said the night before last?"

"What did I say?"

"That I was your second and my bravery was formidable."

"Every word, my love!"

"That contents me. I'll be your second in the battles to come," Joanna said, smiling up at him. His look was quizzical, and she added, "Your father said there are more battles to come and I can only guess it's the question of titles and lands, though I still do not understand why there's a question."

"Put it out of your mind, love. It will be made right."

George stood behind Joanna, placing his hands on her shoulders. For some time, he stood thus, watching her work magic with silk thread and a silver needle.

"I remember they told me how you made a cloak of dragon scales and embroidered that banner. I thought I dreamt such things until I saw them for myself," George said, kissing the top of her head.

"They're nothing compared to your labors," she answered. Again, they were silent and contented to be in the other's company.

George marveled at his contentment and happiness. Had there ever been a time before Joanna that he could say this honestly? Even with the present political intrigues, he had something his father never had: a good marriage and a loving wife to stand by him. Hopefully, there'd be sons to inherit and plenty of them to stand with their parents against the King and his followers.

After a time, Joanna sighed happily and held up the finished gown. "Our child will be wrapped in the cloak for his Christening and then he will wear this little shift."

"It will be another day of celebration for Ascalon," George replied.

"But first,"

Joanna held out her hand for George's arm and she raised herself up. She walked to the far end of the bower and pushed back the curtain separating an alcove from the rest of the chamber. Taking a key from her girdle, Joanna unlocked a door behind another curtain and led George into a small room with an arrow-slit of a window high on a wall, under which stood an altar with a tabernacle holding the blessed sacraments of wine and bread and devotional panels of the Virgin and Child, the Archangels, and Saint Margaret of Antioch, who rose out of the belly of a dragon. A prayer desk and cushioned bench stood before it. There was another door, which led into the treasury. After showing George this, Joanna slid her hand under the cloth draping the prayer desk and touched the carved side. A little drawer slid out. She took the cross from around her neck and placed it reverently into the drawer, pushing it shut and draping the embroidered woolen cloth over it again and then turning to George, saying, "I was told that the household treasury was the provenance of the lady and so I had Will Longleate supervise this addition as well as this lady chapel. He doesn't know about the prayer desk and I alone hold the key. I suppose this is the least I can do for Ascalon?"

George said nothing, brushing off a tear from his cheek and swallowing the lump that had risen in his throat. There were so many things to be grateful for, and not to be taken lightly.

✠

ONLY AN HOUR or two left, Joanna thought, watching the guests dance and make merry. *Then I shall have George to myself and we can prepare for our child's birth.*

What a day it had been: George took almost all of the prizes in the tourneys. Others reaped rewards, too: the Abbey of St. Cuthbert's was given a relic of its saint brought from the holy island at Lindisfarne, several gold-inlaid chalices, and a new chasuble and cope. A pair of gray stallions for George and Joanna were making themselves at home in the stables. Aubrey had outdone himself in gifts and gratitude. Joanna only wondered what favor he would ask in return for this generosity. As much as she was warming to him and appreciating his kindness, there was something about him that she couldn't put a definition to, and she found it difficult to forgive a man who deserted his family for God and left a son ill-equipped to take on battles with the nobility of England.

George was able to slay a dragon and several demons, but the King of England?

The child had kicked all day and now that he was quiet, the backache Joanna suffered was getting worse. Old Emma said that in the final weeks the entrance to the womb would stretch to make it easier for the baby's delivery and with the stretching came pains that came and went. Tonight they were bothersome and Joanna decided to retire early. George was dancing with Petronelle and other ladies of the court; she wouldn't be missed.

"Rhosyn, Margaret, I'm tired and will go to bed. Rhosyn, go before me to the lady tower." Joanna said and for once allowed Margaret to help her to her feet. Her ankles were swelling and it seemed as if she'd become a pig's bladder that children batted about in a game—all round with no legs or arms. She couldn't see her feet.

"My lady?"

One of the household knights had approached and looked concerned.

"Sir Thomas, it's nothing; I'm near my time. I'm weary and will go to bed. You'll tell my husband for me?" Joanna said kindly.

"They're looking for Earl George," Thomas replied and pointed to a pair of knights all begrimed from a hard-ridden journey standing at the entrance of the hall.

"Bring them forward," Joanna sighed and dropped wearily back onto her cushions. The knights came quickly when Thomas beckoned them. "Sirs, you are welcome to Grasmere's table," Joanna greeted. "Our meat and mead are yours."

They bowed respectfully and one of them cast a glance at and nodded to his companion, who looked familiar to Joanna and who knelt at her feet.

"Sir?" she asked.

"We seek the Earl of Grasmere," he said.

"He's just there, dancing," Joanna replied. She studied his weathered and tanned face and then clasped her hands together and smiled. "I know you!" Joanna said brightly; "You're the Sheriff of Cumbria. You saved my life."

"My lady, it was Earl George, if I remember."

"But you took his side in the quarrel and I remember that well. Let me call George for you, Sir."

It took a moment to capture George's attention and he came over, red-cheeked and breathless from his exercise. "Why, Stephen Black! It's been some time, hasn't it, Lord Sheriff?" he greeted.

"My Lord, may we speak in private?" the Sheriff asked, glancing around at the people drawn to their audience. "My news is not good."

"This way," George said, waving towards the screen behind the high table. When Joanna followed, the Sheriff held up his hand in warning.

"My wife will hear our conversation," George said.

"As you say."

Once they were alone, George looked to the Sheriff.

"The abbot of Saint Cuthbert's was found dead this afternoon."

"Rest his soul," George said, crossing himself and Joanna echoed the sentiment and did the same. "I'll gladly pay for his burial service. And masses for his soul,"

"And the Bishop of Eden and a novice – a boy called Timon."

"What??"

"My lord, you are accused of their murders."

"No! That cannot be!" Joanna exclaimed, taking George's arm protectively.

"My lady hear me out," said the Sheriff calmly and glanced at George, waiting for his response.

"We'll talk. Tell me more of this," said George. "Come."

George summoned a torchbearer and gestured at Stephen Black, inviting his guest to follow.

CHAPTER 9

RHOSYN HUMMED A tune she'd heard that evening while she plumped the bolster pillows and slid the warming pan under the bed cover and blankets. There'd be fewer nights like this if Eustace des Jumieges kept his word. Rhosyn would have ladies-in-waiting and pretty gowns and jewels. Of course, if her father hadn't sided with Rhodri of Merioneth in his quarrel with the Cymric princes and the King of England, she'd already have what she wanted. Why, if matters turned out as she hoped and as Eustace promised, she could pay her father's ransom and she would be a princess in every way and not just in name. She was nigh on halfway to her goal. The handsome baron Eustace had paid her compliment twice that evening and called her a charming beauty. And here she was, serving as the Countess' maid of honor! What stories she'd tell when she met the baron later.

His invitation came as no surprise since Eustace had partnered her in three carols and shared cups of wine, and Rhosyn wasted no time in accepting it. Margaret scolded her for that.

"He's married to the heiress of Ambleside, you stupid girl! If you give him what he wants he's not bound to return the favor!"

"How do you know?" Rhosyn sniffed. "It's not as if he'd ask someone like you. Noblemen often take lovers, and they in turn often do well for themselves. Look at my cousin Joanna—a disgraced princess, her father attainted for treason, and rumor has it she'd lived as a harlot in a bawdy house until she met Earl George. At least I'm still a Cymric princess,"

"In name only, Girl!"

"Still, a princess. And if Joanna could be raised so high, why not me?"

The conversation didn't end well with Margaret threatening to tell Joanna and have Rhosyn dismissed or worse, demoted to the kitchens. The girl didn't care. Rhosyn's fantasies of being crowned Queen of England in the great abbey church of Westminster were on her mind while she performed her duties, especially those concerning Eustace. Would he take her to bed that night? She'd never been but she certainly hoped so! He'd promised to be gentle and would teach her how a man and woman lie together. She was so consumed by what she would say and do that she didn't hear the footsteps on the stairs and the door open.

"With what evidence do you bring this charge against me?" Earl George was saying as he entered, Joanna and two knights with him. He snapped his fingers at Rhosyn, wanting her away and Joanna nodded, gesturing to the wardrobe. Rhosyn picked up the clothes she'd laid out and hurried off, going where bid, but keeping the curtain open just enough for light and to see and hear. She'd never seen Joanna look so pale and George so angry.

"You were seen and heard quarreling with the Abbot," one of the knights answered George.

An anxious rap on the door announced Aubrey, who swept in, going straight for his son. "You left the hall so suddenly, George—What's amiss?" he wanted to know. "Good evening, Sheriff Black."

"My lord bishop this doesn't concern you, but the young Earl," the Sheriff said.

"Then let me remind you we are on Ascalon land, and as Earl of Grasmere, it is George who bestows justice!"

"And if George is the suspect?" the Sheriff countered.

"That is slander, sir!"

"Father, your abbot is dead, and I've been accused of the crime," George interrupted.

"How did he die?"

"Not just the abbot, my lord," Stephen Black said. "Bertrand des Jumieges, the novice Timon, are also dead. They and the abbot were found together with their throats cut from ear to ear."

"God in heaven ~!"

"Father, sit and be silent."

"I will not! This is slander and false!"

"Father, for God's sake,"

"As I was saying," the Sheriff said, talking over their quarrel to silence George and Aubrey, "Earl George was seen and heard violently quarreling with the abbot only days before."

"And every day while I was in residence, as any number of the community will testify if asked," George admitted. "If you mean the conversation we had several days ago, it was nothing more than an exchange of opinions. My father was present."

Aubrey nodded.

"A quarrel in which treasonous accusations were made by the earl against the king," the Sheriff interjected.

"Words said in anger, nothing more," George answered.

"Where were you during the night?"

"It wasn't me; I can tell you. I was in my wife's bed and wasn't about to leave it to murder a man I barely knew nor cared for and for no reason. Nor would I harm a bishop, especially one as gentle and foolish as Eden. You have the wrong man, Sheriff."

"But my lord, you were seen in the church earlier quarreling with Abbot Warennes. Will you deny that?"

"I am in the church every day."

"And so you were in the church with him?"

"I was."

"You did quarrel?"

"When did we not?"

"And what was this quarrel about, my lord?"

"I left the abbey without consent."

"Isn't that a crime in itself?" asked one of the knights.

"Come now, man!" George chided; "You know the news hereabouts; you know that directly after my marriage to Joanna I took up residence at the abbey to do penance for the many sins of Ascalon. There were more than a hundred witnesses to my vow, including the Countess and my father."

"What he says is true," Aubrey spoke up. "And as Earl George has said, there were many quarrels with Alan Warennes. He was usually the first to pick a fight. Warennes, that is."

The Sheriff's eyes slid to Joanna and back to George. Both looked calm. Not even a hair quivered on the countess' brow. George raised his chin a bit higher and then brows arched, questioningly.

"Do you deny quarreling with the abbot about the entitlement of Grasmere? Did you not, my lord earl, argue with the abbot concerning the rightful heirs of Grasmere?" the Sheriff insisted. "Earl George? What say you?"

"He constantly argued that Grasmere and Skelwith were not mine and were to revert to the Crown. These were his assertions. I quietly told him where he could put them. You accuse the wrong man. Keep in mind, Stephen, that any inquiry should come from no one but the King and I doubt if His Grace would know of this unfortunate death so quickly to order an inquest."

"He would trouble himself. The abbot was his kinsman."

"So it has been alleged. But when has John ever cared about anyone but himself?"

"That is treasonous, my lord!"

"I mean no harm to the King, Stephen. You can tell him that."

George and Stephen Black stared each other down, and it was the sheriff who blinked. "I'll take your word, my lord," the Sheriff said.

"Before you go, Stephen, may I have your assurance that you make this inquiry out of respect for the rule of law in England and not because you have been promised something?"

"I do what I am told, my lord, and what the law requires." He bowed and was gone. Aubrey was about to speak but George raised a hand, listening at the footsteps on the stairs and it was a moment before he waved off his father.

"George, how many times—" Aubrey began, but George waved him off again.

"Father, I've done nothing wrong. Save your breath to cool your broth."

"It will matter little to the King whether you're innocent or not. With Warennes dead he'll find an excuse to take Grasmere."

"Another excuse."

"What?"

"Another excuse to take something else that belongs to us, rather, to Joanna."

"I haven't forgotten that, George. If anything, it was a foolish undertaking," Aubrey said.

"And if Eskeleth had been Mother's? The entirety of Arkengarthdale? What would you have done?"

Aubrey was silent a moment, toying with the cross suspended on a heavy chain around his neck. "I would have done what I've done," he said quietly.

Joanna busied herself with the brush and comb on her dressing table, moving about hairpins like they were soldiers in a battle plan. She didn't dare look at Aubrey or George.

"Leave us, Father," George snapped. "Now, if you please."

Aubrey was ready to argue but Joanna nodded and gestured towards the door. He looked at his son and then left.

"What are we going to do?" Joanna asked.

George shrugged. "As much as I despised the idiot, murdering Alan Warennes wouldn't have been worth the trouble it's going to cause."

"I had a nightmare last night – the Archangel Michael came to me in the chapel at the abbey with two knights. Warennes came in,"

"And he was killed,"

"Yes."

"What if, George, that it wasn't a dream? Do you remember that day in the market in Grasmere?"

"Before we went to Eskeleth?"

"You remember, then."

"Of course I do."

"It wasn't a dream."

He was out the door, slamming it as he went. "God's holy life!" Joanna swore.

Moments later, while Joanna paced the bower, Rhosyn came from the antechamber. "Are you well, Cousin?" she asked.

Joanna blinked, looked at the girl, and frowned as if surprised by her presence. "Tired, that's all. Thank you. The banquet was overlong and tiresome. Perhaps we shall have some quiet now." She groaned as she sat on a bench before the looking glass.

"You looked beautiful tonight, my lady," Rhosyn said as she unbound Joanna's hair and started to brush it out. "I heard some of the men's praises. You've stolen some hearts, I think!"

"Thank you." The comment was dull and flat.

"Is it true, Lady, that you fought a dragon with Earl George?"

"I fight them even now,"

"Pardon?"

"Nothing."

Rhosyn moved away and scooped up a night shift of pale ivory and a bed robe made of soft wool in ruby red. "Earl George always says how beautiful you look in this color."

Joanna waved her off, saying, "You may go; if you see Margaret or Petronelle, tell them they are needed here. They most likely are in the bower." As Rhosyn slipped away, Joanna called her back. "Cousin, I regard you as a friend. May I be sure of your friendship?"

"Of course!"

"Then you will say nothing of what you heard?"

"What I heard, Lady?"

"Come, Rhosyn! How could you not? My lord was angry and shouted at his Father and Sheriff Black."

"Your secrets are mine."

"Thank you."

When Rhosyn still stood before her, Joanna dismissed her with a tired wave. The girl curtseyed and rather than go to the bower as bid, she hurried down the staircase and out to the inner bailey to the great hall, on the lookout for servants or other guests, pausing and holding her breath when she heard footsteps or conversation. When she was certain it was safe, Rhosyn continued to the western end of the hall to the guest rooms and tried a door, finding it unlocked as had been promised.

The door opened into a bedchamber that was as fine as that of the Earl and Countess' rooms. A pair of heavily embroidered curtains separated the room, giving privacy to the half where there stood a large bed on chests. As soon as the door closed, Eustace came around the curtain and smiled.

"Not the shy little violet I supposed," Eustace greeted in a teasing, smooth, voice. He came forward and kissed her brow.

"I would have been here earlier, my lord."

"I was beginning to give up all hope."

"Forgive me, I was attending to the countess' night livery when Earl George, the Countess, and others came to the bedchamber in lady tower."

"The bedchamber? Their conversation must have been important and secret to have chosen such a place,"

Eustace was now kissing her cheeks and gently stroking her face.

"Indeed, sir! I was dismissed while they quarreled," Rhosyn said trying to contain her excitement in his intimate attention.

"And yet you know they quarreled?"

"I hid in the Countess' wardrobe."

"Clever by half! So . . . what did you hear?" Eustace asked as he started to nuzzle her neck.

"The conversation was private, my lord."

"You can tell me. Are we not friends?"

"I made a promise to the Countess to keep her secrets."

"What if I were to promise to keep your secrets that are the Countess' secrets?" Eustace suggested as he turned Rhosyn in his arms so that they were facing each other. He cupped her face and kissed her lightly. "I would not expose either the Countess or you, my sweeting."

Rhosyn started to relax and she closed her eyes while Eustace's kisses trailed from neck to her shoulders. She sighed happily, saying, "The news wasn't good. Abbot Warennes, a novice, and the Bishop of Eden were found dead and Earl George was accused of the murders."

"That doesn't surprise me; Warennes and the Earl have been enemies since the day Warennes came here from London."

"I fear for the Earl and Countess," Rhosyn said.

"I will be their champion," Eustace said huskily as he moved closer, his lips almost touching hers. "I will be yours–and more, should you desire it."

Her mother told her something of how it was with men and how to win favor by giving them what they wanted. Queens and princesses practiced the art of womanly persuasion. Rhosyn was told it should be no different for her, the daughter of a Cymric prince with fealty to King John of England. With this in mind, Rhosyn offered Eustace a kiss that indicated she was more than willing to accept his terms.

✠

"THERE YOU ARE!" Margaret snapped when Rhosyn entered the lady tower the next morning. "Where've you been? The Countess is in a bad mood and has no patience this morning. Go on; find something she can wear!"

Rhosyn curtseyed again and avoided the stares of the other women hurrying as they had never before in getting Joanna bathed and dressed. The Countess was nowhere in sight; perhaps in the private chapel off the bower.

"You stink of sex," said Ancient Emma in passing. "Rolling about in a squire's bed all night?"

"What if I was?" Rhosyn snapped. "What if it was a great lord's bed?"

"The lord and lady won't take kindly to having a lady-in-waiting swollen up with a brat, especially a so-called princess of Wales," Ancient Emma sniffed back.

"No one spoke so ill of my cousin when she came to Skelwith."

"That shows how little you know! Ah, there's always one girl who sets herself above the others, though in this household there's been two."

"You're unkind," Rhosyn said.

"I only mean to warn you, girl. The countess is a good and kind lady and that my lord George chose her for his wife says a great deal, for there is no better a man in all of England as far as I'm concerned, and you will not darken their names!"

"I'm only doing what my lady mother and father asks of me," Rhosyn answered, her voice tinged with innocence and hurt.

"Rut about like a whore for whatever scraps off his table he'll throw at you? You're not the first nor the last to believe a man's lies. Stop what you're doing and think of the harm you might cause!"

Rhosyn nodded and swallowed the lump in her throat, fought back tears. She'd have to tell Eustace that evening when he sent for her and she was certain he would. He would protect her from these jealous crones and bitches. After all, when she left his bed that morning, didn't he say to be wary of the Ascalons?

Joanna entered now and the women all curtseyed, Rhosyn being the first to show respect. Lord, the countess looked ill, as if close to death. Her complexion was gray and the circles under her eyes were more purplish-blue than the day before. If this was what it meant to be with child, Rhosyn wanted no part of it. She stared Rhosyn up and down.

"I called for you in the night, Cousin."

"I wasn't feeling well, Lady. I was worried about contagion – making you ill."

"That's considerate, but of little use. I'm not feeling well at all. Help me to bed," Joanna said quietly.

"Is the baby coming? Shall I send for George?" Petronelle asked, going to her side. She began to rub Joanna's back gently as she had seen midwives do with women giving birth.

Joanna shook her head in response as she lay down, slowly easing into the pillows and featherbeds as if she was as fragile as Venetian blown glass and would break. From under a pillow, she took a string of pearls to which a jewel-studded cross was attached next to a larger pearl – her prayer beads. The beads slipped through her fingers one at a time as her lips moved in silent prayer. If one looked close, as Rhosyn did now, tear drops dotted Joanna's lashes and slid down to stain the pillow.

"Come, let us be about our work and let the countess rest," Rhosyn suggested to the others. For once, no one argued with her.

So, matters are as bad as Eustace guessed, Rhosyn thought as she tip-toed out of the lady tower bedchamber and quietly closed the door.

CHAPTER 10

"MY LORD, SHE'LL listen to no one," Margaret said to George when he arrived in the tower later that day. "She says nothing, refused to eat or drink; I'm of a mind to send for a priest, as is the Lady Petronelle."

"Perhaps it's fatigue. The last week has been difficult for all of us and with the babe," George shrugged and looked past Margaret to the curtain-enclosed bed.

"Oh George, don't be so foolish, it's something to do with the last night of the fetes," Petronelle snapped in passing. "You'll tell me soon enough, I hope?"

"Nothing to do with you, Sister," George replied. "And none of your business."

"I'll speak with George alone," Joanna called from behind the curtains. The three looked at one another in amazement and George gestured for Margaret and Petronelle to leave. As soon as the door closed, Joanna pulled aside the bed curtains. He was shocked by her appearance: Joanna's face was pale, but her eyes were rimmed-red and her cheeks blotchy. Her usually bright eyes were dull.

"Sweetheart!" George cried, pulling her gently into his arms. "Whatever our quarrel is with the Sheriff, we will prevail - don't we always win our battles?"

"No, it isn't that," Joanna said, starting to sob again.

"The babe?"

"I remembered him! I know who he is!"

"What is it? Who do you remember?"

"Eustace des Jumieges," Joanna gasped now. "When the King's men entered the convent and took me, he was one of the nobles. The king gave me to Eustace . . .!"

Joanna started to wail, and George hugged her tighter. Nothing more needed to be explained. When she fell into an exhausted sleep, George called the ladies back into the bedchamber and saw that Joanna was made comfortable. He would visit again within an hour.

Out in the stairwell, he found Will and took him aside. "Is Eustace des Jumieges still about?" he asked.

"No my lord, he left Skelwith last night."

"He is not allowed here ever again."

"My lord? He is one of your vassals."

"It makes no difference. Call everyone for a council, except him. The Sheriff's summons will need a response."

Within hours, George's vassals in Grasmere obeyed his summons and a great council was convened. The men seated on either side of the table and at the ends were silent when George finished his account of the Sheriff's news and the summons.

"Three churchmen found dead in a church," said Will. "That's not news."

"But one was a bishop, Will," replied a knight.

"A Bishop newly consecrated," another spoke up.

"Still, a bishop. We don't want another Becket, do we?"

"The abbey might. Think of the pilgrims and the pence."

The laughter that followed was strained and nervous.

"But why?" asked Will. "Perhaps there were thieves about."

"I came across a fellow in the wood by Grasmere when I returned from Skelwith on the morning of my father's return," George offered in a manner of one mentioning a cat crossing the lane - it was nothing of import.

"Why didn't you say something?" Will said. "Sheriff Black would have no cause to accuse you, my lord."

George looked down the table at him. "He still doesn't, Will, and it really doesn't make a difference. Does it?"

The men at council nodded in agreement.

✠

THE NEWS CAME after a fortnight had passed, a letter from Lincoln where the King was staying during a northern progress, in his own hand and stamped with the great seal of England. The messenger was nearly dead for riding so hard, and as for the horse, the dogs in the kennel would be feasting for days.

"Trial by combat?" Joanna exclaimed.

The seal waved back and forth as George held the letter over her and she stared up at him incredulously.

"The King has summoned me to appear before a court of peers in Carlisle. If I refused to confess my crime, the King will have me prove my innocence by combat with his champion, Sir Falkes deBrent. God will prove the right of any accusation and crime against me if I perish or exonerate me if I prevail."

"Monstrous!" Joanna said. "But George, if you can defeat an archangel and a dragon, what is a mortal man to you—"

"There's more and it's worse news. The chief justice for this court of peers will be my father."

"Oh God, no! This cannot be!" Joanna cried and snatched the letter away from George to read for herself. There it was in hastily-scrawled penmanship: *It is our will that Aubrey, Bishop of Carlisle, and known well in those parts of England in his diocese, sit as adjudicator and preside at our pleasure.*

"I knew John would use him to get at me!"

"You've already shown that you can win in combat, George," Joanna said, taking his hands. George pulled away.

"But we know I won't prevail, don't we? John will see to that!"

"What will you do?" Joanna asked.

"Nothing," said George, folding up the letter and tossing it on the floor to be sniffed at by Joanna's little dog. Disinterested, he got out of the way as George stomped across the bower and poured a glass of wine, drinking it quickly, and then poured another.

"Don't you think you should do something?"

"Anything I do will be judged. If I respond too quickly, it will be seen that I am guilty and eager to defend myself. If I respond with a letter and question the King's summons, I will offend the King. If I show up to honor the summons, somehow the contest will go against me and I will be killed."

"If you do nothing, they will come for you. This is a way for the King to end the negotiations for Merioneth. If you are a prisoner of the King or dead, he'll take what he wants."

"Joanna, please."

"I have the right to know if I'm to be a widow," she snapped, "or if I should prepare myself for marriage to one of John's liegemen. Grasmere would be a ripe plum for picking, as would I. Our son will be the King's ward and you know what happens to royal wards. Remember what happened to Prince Arthur of Brittany after the old Henry's death. Remember what happened to me when my father was tried and accused of treason. At least God saved him when he escaped and fled, never mind what happened to me—"

"Joanna! Enough."

"Who's to say that Eustace won't come for me again and use me as he did before? I'd rather die. I'll take my life and my babe's!"

George immediately went to her and cradled her in his arms, stroking her hair and kissing her forehead.

"That would be a punishment for me, my love. I know it's selfish to say, but the King would be glad of your end. How much better for us if we were to live and make him miserable!"

At this Joanna laughed.

"I'm sorry!" Joanna apologized, clinging even tighter. "I'm not myself . . . and the baby . . . the worry now,"

"Hush! I wish I had a tenth of your courage and strength," he said.

"You still think I'm strong?" Joanna whimpered, wiping her eyes with a sleeve.

"Have I not said so many times?" he asked.

"What kind of wife am I to say what you must do when I've been witness to your courage and your valor?"

"One that loves her husband. And I am a most fortunate man, my love."

Another night passed, and then a day, and George made up his mind to honor the summons. Joanna watched George ride through the gates of Skelwith and wondered if she would ever see him again.

✠

JOANNA TOOK SOLACE in prayer. Mornings began in Skelwith's chapel to offer prayers for George, the entire household compelled to pray with her. As soon as the service was done, the others filed out silently, but Joanna stayed behind usually with Margaret, Petronelle, and Rhosyn in attendance and standing back a respectful distance as Joanna finished her prayers and spoke to the chaplain. She composed letters to her father-in-law in Carlisle requesting that he recuse himself from the proceedings, which she knew were contrived and false. She also wrote to the constable of the castle there, inquiring of George's whereabouts and safety. The letters were always returned unanswered. She turned to reading and needlework to soothe her nerves and kept to the Lady Tower despite the official duties expected of her.

Then came a development in early May which was unexpected but welcome.

"My lady! My lady, come and see!"

The shout from below stairs made Joanna push herself slowly off the cushioned bench and reach for Margaret's arm, hoping it was one of the ladies with news of George. It pained her to move, but Joanna kept a brave face and smiled at her ladies. Lord, but the child in her belly grew. Breathing was becoming as difficult as moving about to do ordinary things. And the child was taking his time.

One of the ladies burst into the chamber, pointing behind her, excited, and unable to speak. The footsteps on the stairs to the bower were slow and heavy, and there was a jangle of spurs. Joanna's heart was in her throat as she focused on the door, waiting, imagining how he would look: bearded, no doubt, with new scars from blows received during combat, perhaps thinner. Or worse, from days of imprisonment. The King was known for his cruelty. Her father used to say that there wasn't a crueler, more hated, king in England since the Bastard conquered England almost two centuries ago. John Lackland was blood kin to that Norman stock and he'd see that his champion spared no quarter for George Ascalon.

The footsteps paused, and Joanna assumed he was on the landing. They started again and just as she was going to the door, it opened.

"Roger!" Petronelle cried when the knight entered and swept low in greeting. Joanna dismissed her women so that Petronelle and Roger could enjoy a more private reunion and she went into the small chamber hidden behind the wardrobe at the end of the bower. She resisted the urge to weep and stared out the small window at the hills above Grasmere until there was a knock on the door and Roger Mowbray entered and knelt before her.

"Welcome to Skelwith, my friend," Joanna greeted as she wiped her eyes. "You've been greatly missed."

"And I have missed your company, lady," Roger answered, kissing her hand. "I also bear greetings from Adam of Gawthorp, who offers you this kiss."

Roger bussed Joanna's lips with his own.

"My lord, is that all he offers?" she teased. "You must have succeeded in making him a gentleman!"

"You'll see for yourself tomorrow when he joins us. We shall all be together again."

"You haven't heard. George was summoned to Carlisle by the King."

"Don't tell me George is being honored!" Roger laughed.

"He is to undertake a trial by combat to prove his innocence for a charge of murder."

"George? No, I don't believe it! Who was it he supposedly murdered?" Roger exclaimed.

"The Abbot at Saint Cuthbert's, Alan Warennes, a fellow named Timon, and Bertrand des Jumieges, the newly-made Bishop of Eden."

"There's no such bishopric!"

"Not until a few months past there wasn't. The mystery is why, and why they were together, and those three."

"No. Why would George do something like that unless his life was threatened?" asked Roger.

"He didn't do it."

"Who is this abbot and this newly-made prince of the church?"

"The abbot was the King's favorite. Some say one of his bastards or a godson, but it matters little. The King will have his vengeance. As for the Bishop, he was recently come from Normandy, from the Avranchin, Avranches, I think. I knew him only for a moment, but he seemed a Godly man. What his kinship to Warennes was, and his cousin Eustace, I cannot say. And the novice. Perhaps in the wrong place at the wrong time? I don't know. More to the point, George had no reason to kill either," Joanna explained sadly.

"No reason at all, my lady. He foreswore killing."

"George was with me all night," Joanna said.

Roger's big, handsome, face grew dark and his usually bright and merry eyes more so. He set back on his heels and then grunted as he rose to stand, then helped Joanna to her feet.

"When did he go?" Roger asked, leading her back into the bower.

"It's been over a month."

"That long? That isn't good. That's not good at all! Carlisle is not that far north; we can send a man to learn George's whereabouts," Roger said as if to himself. In a louder voice, "How in God's name did he manage to get himself stuck in this mess?"

"Sit with us and I'll tell you what happened," Joanna suggested and waited for Petronelle and him to seat themselves on the cushioned settle across from her to begin. The candle had burned down to the quarter hour mark by the time she finished her story.

"He took no seconds?" Roger asked.

"He was not allowed, my love," said Petronelle.

"When Adam arrives tomorrow we'll go to Carlisle and sort this out."

"You put your life and honor in peril if you do," Joanna spoke up. "George is already in danger."

"Pah!" Roger scoffed. "We've faced worse."

"But the king, Roger?"

"What will John do? Drop one of his damn books on my head?"

"Something terrible, I think," Petronelle said.

They sat in silence now, keeping their own counsel for the moment. Petronelle had tucked her hands beneath her chin and stared at the shadows on the floor, sighing loudly ever so often before saying, "I wish I knew what to do for George. It's not like before when we rode to Arkengarthdale."

"It's a shame that the king never saw me in the wood when I cut down those robbers," Joanna giggled of a sudden.

"My lady, were you not so heavy with child I'd take you with us, for you've proved yourself with a sword," Roger replied and offered a devilish wink.

"I am exactly what you need now," Joanna replied. "A woman heavy with child is frightening to behold when she's angry and I have never been angrier than I am now. Help me up, sir, and if I can walk across the bower to pour cups of wine, perhaps that will convince you how right it would be to take me along. There is nothing I'd rather do than go to Carlisle."

"My lady Joanna, though your wrath would be worse than your husband's, I have no desire to anger him by putting your life and the life of his child in peril. Let Adam and me go on your behalf."

"No."

The objection was quiet and forceful and enough to persuade Roger to take Joanna to Carlisle.

✠

THE COUNTESS' PARTY made ready for its departure three days later. While it assembled in the greater bailey, Joanna called the captain of the guard, her steward, and clerks, to the great hall. The reason for her departure from Skelwith was known by all; they knew she would make a formal announcement. What intrigued Ascalon's household retainers was the presence of Elinor Lucy among them.

"Gentlemen and ladies, we greet you well and are glad to see you," Joanna began. "You know the reason for this summons and had I any other choice, I would stay to await the birth of George Ascalon's son and heir. I cannot. I ask you to watch over Skelwith with the good care and love you showed my father-in-law and his wife Maud, and my husband, short as his time here has been."

Joanna paused and pressed a hand to her belly while the child moved and kicked. She smiled faintly wondering if the babe knew his mother's voice already or knew who his father was. Now she smiled more broadly and said, "My lady Elinor, would you come forward?"

Elinor glanced about and hid her smile, sweeping forward and knowing all eyes were on her. She curtseyed and rose as if the movements were for a dance. Joanna smiled knowing how much her rival was enjoying this moment.

"Lady, we entrust to you the care of this castle, with your husband, our good and loyal friend William Longleate. You shall be chatelaine in our absence. When next you see my husband and me, we hope to find our home such as it is now, and if so, we will reward you for your labors handsomely."

Joanna signed for Rhosyn and Margaret to attend her, and with their aid, she rose and walked slowly out of the hall to join her cavalcade. As soon as they were gone, Elinor glanced at the skeptical courtiers staring at her, and smiled primly, saying, "You will be glad of this."

CHAPTER 11

THE AFTERNOON WAS unseasonably cold and Elinor stood on the palisade walk wrapped in a woolen cloak to watch Joanna and her party ride out on yet another fool's quest. Standing beside her was the dowager countess Maud, George's stepmother and Petronelle's mother by blood.

"Do you think they'll succeed like the last time?" Elinor asked.

"I wouldn't know," Maud replied; "I don't have the gift of foresight. Do you, Lady Longleate?"

"If I did, I could have prevented Joanna Fletcher from coming to Grasmere," Elinor said and looked a last time at the little party disappearing into the horizon.

"If God is on their side again, you will have nothing to claim."

"What claim do I have?"

"Come, girl! Everyone from Carlisle to Lincoln knows what goes on in your head!" chided Maud and she placed a hand on the plain gold cross she wore at her breast. "God will have the right of things again and we will have Countess Joanna to thank for that. Whatever George's faults, he chose a worthy mate after all. She risks all doing this." Maud turned to Elinor now. "Would you risk your life and the life of your unborn child to rescue him?"

"My lady, you do me much wrong—"

"I only speak the truth, which is what God compels me to do no matter how injurious my words."

Elinor was glad Maud couldn't see her rolling her eyes. For the last hour, the old woman prattled on and on. She wished Maud would stop talking about angels and saints, and how they would defeat the magic of the Old Ways, how Jesus of Nazareth and God would be victorious in the End Days.

"Peace have done!" Elinor sighed. "God has been of little help to Ascalon. George wouldn't be in Carlisle and undoubtedly chained up in a prison cell now if God lifted had lifted a mighty finger."

"Foolish though that quest might have been, I think it took the Almighty a while to cipher who was the best man to wager on - Aubrey or George. Who do you think saved Aubrey's bastard?"

"Careful there, my lady! Sacrilege will get you in trouble."

"It is you who should be careful, Elinor." After a moment, she added, "Come with me to the chapel."

"Why should God listen now? I have more faith in the wind and rain. I know those will come."

Maud now crossed herself and whispered a prayer. She knew Elinor still held to the Old Ways and had been known to practice its arts. She would be burned as a witch if she wasn't careful and Maud was certain Aubrey, Bishop of Carlisle, wouldn't raise a jeweled finger to help her, even if the rumors of their being lovers were true.

"It is God who brings the wind and rain and gave his Son the ability to calm them," Maud said.

"You tire me. We talk and talk . . ."

"Perhaps you ought to listen. I'm going in to dine."

"Come with me to the great hall. With the Earl and Countess gone, there is no one to gainsay your being there. The cook will be glad of something to do."

"George has his spites and I have no desire to walk so far home at nightfall. I'll go home to the lodge."

The lodge was an ancient hall from the days before the Conquest that Aubrey modernized with wall hearths, chimney pots, and glazed windows. The thatched roof was replaced with slates from the Cumbrian hills and the walls replaced with stone. It was comfortable, luxurious even, for the time, and had its residents been anyone other than Maud Ascalon, it would have been furnished as befitting their places in society, but Maud kept the lodge as barren and simple as a convent. And as cold. The servant let the fire die in the hall. Elinor wrapped her cloak tighter and took a seat beside the wall hearth where a barely visible flame grew from the logs.

Always atoning for others' sins, Elinor thought derisively as she watched Maud collect her prayer beads and a psalter and sat across from her.

"I've told you what I think ought to be done about Skelwith and how to go about it. You do agree with me, my lady?" Elinor said.

"No."

"George has an untenable position. Any man would agree to the terms."

"Is George any man?"

Elinor sighed and cast her an icy stare. "You sound almost endearing. Have you finally grown to love him?"

"He is Aubrey's son and I still love his father."

"Love all the same."

"I have confessed my sins of envy and hatred. I've made my peace. So long as George breathes, he is Earl of Grasmere. His wife will give him an heir, and she is a Welsh princess. There's nothing you can do."

"Done without the King's consent! The daughter of an attainted lord and traitor. He'll be made to put her aside and then take an English noblewoman."

Maud reached for the flask of wine and poured a cup before saying, "Why don't you say yourself, though how you shall put aside Will Longleate?"

"It can be done," Elinor insisted. She self-consciously touched the jewel around her neck and squeezed it so that it looked like it glowed brighter, the ruby color a bright spot in the gray dimness of the hall.

"You are too confident, Elinor. As I said before: I would be careful were I you."

Thank goodness you're not! Elinor thought as she curtseyed and then said she'd find out when supper would be ready.

Off the kitchens were two guest chambers and it was to the largest of these rooms Elinor went, locking the door behind her. There was nothing unusual about this; Maud had given Elinor the room when Joanna banished her. Besides, it was far enough away from the hall and bower that Maud and Elinor wouldn't disturb one another.

There was only a slit of a window high in the northern wall but there was enough sunlight to illuminate the room. Still, Elinor lit a candle and placed it in the center of a small table up against the wall and below the window. From a cupboard she took a bowl, two flasks—one of wine and another filled with water—a key, using the key to unlock a chest. Throwing back the lid released a musty scent of juniper into the room. Hidden under folded robes and shawls was a little clay jar stopped with wax.

She began whispering in the tongue of her ancestors, the people of Wales, who lived on the island of Britain before Alfred the Great, before Danelaw, before the Normans. The wax stopper was broken, and the contents poured carefully into the bowl then mixed with water and wine. An earthy, sensual, scent almost like sandal but more bitter, rose in a thin smoke.

Elinor continued to whisper, her voice becoming more passionate. Suddenly a pale red flame appeared and the jewel around her neck glowed and pulsed. She screamed as the jewel began to melt and drip onto her breasts. She screamed in pain, then swooned and fell. When she woke, Richildis of Eskeleth was standing over her.

CHAPTER 12

RICHILDIS STARED DOWN at the woman sprawled on the floor and it was some time before she extended her hand to help Elinor to her feet. Elinor flinched at the icy grasp but managed to hide her revulsion. *God forgive me, but I must do this*, she thought as she looked at the woman whose gilt beauty remained untouched by the limbo of the afterlife. This was no apparition, but a flesh-and-bone creature.

"Twice now you've called me back," Richildis said coolly. "I have only so much time left. When will you give up?"

"George is a captive of the King and his little whore has gone to save him," Elinor replied.

"Do you wish to save or destroy him?"

"Destroy her."

"You might have done that any number of times, Elinor. A shove over the bridge or palisade, poison in her favorite dish."

"And if I failed? I would have been hanged or worse."

"Witches are burned."

Richildis at last moved and took the bench at the foot of the bed and Elinor watched in fascination as she did this extraordinarily normal thing. The woman moved and spoke as if she'd never been dead. If Elinor knew all the truth about Richildis of Eskeleth, she would have known that death had never been an obstacle for her. Only men.

"Do you think it would be worth the trouble and the risk?" Richildis asked.

"A debt repaid."

"Ah!"

"Why do you laugh?"

"Because I used to think the same until I witnessed George in battle. His strength, his prowess, how he uses his wits and his love. There's no match for him, not one born with the Gift. The lady Joanna has it too."

"Impossible! If that were true, Richildis, how do they escape the Church's punishment?"

"Unlike you, they keep it to themselves and they do not use it for selfish gain. As far as I can tell, they do not call upon it. Perhaps they do not know of it. Their faith alone is formidable in that they have weakness and strength. They stumble and fall. How else could George have survived the Trial of Eskeleth? Protected by the Christian God. That itself is powerful magic some say is not magic at all, but truth and life."

"What?" Elinor approached now, her fear gone. "Are you saying you cannot succeed?"

"No. I'm thirsty; do you have some wine?"

Elinor, thinking this was part of the Richildis' plan, quickly poured a cup of wine and offered it and then watched as she drank. How disappointed she was in this innocuous, normal, action. Richildis knew this, and smiled, running her tongue along her lips to savor the tang and sweetness.

"Gascony. Good. George always keeps a good cellar, though his father has always been more partial to wine than his son. George appreciates nothing simpler than ale. I suppose it's the Saxon influence that still runs in his veins." She now smiled at Elinor. "I have always wondered why George cast you aside. Now I know."

"What?" Elinor forced herself to stay where she was for fear of what Richildis might do if struck.

"You're selfish, ambitious—the perfect wife for a nobleman. Still, it is something in the Ascalon blood. See who his father is; a man that cast aside my beloved aunt after he got her with child. More, please," Richildis held out her cup and Elinor poured. "Do you know why her disgrace enflames me?" Elinor was about to speak, but Richildis continued. "She was a mother to me when my own died in childbirth. I had no woman to raise me and teach me other than my aunt. She had no dowry, no inheritance, because my father lost it all in one intrigue or another. He killed his brother to obtain Eskeleth and Arkengarthdale. Did you know? That didn't help matters. But then we received a letter from Grasmere. We thought we'd been saved when the Earl of Grasmere, Aubrey Ascalon, paid court to my aunt. He spoke of an alliance that would join our great houses and our great spread of worthless lands to his rich lands. How wrong we were. Once he came to my father's court he seduced her. My father Wulfstan was ready to declare the marriage when Aubrey saw the chancellor's daughter and fell in love with her. You know her, Elinor. Countess Maud. He took her to his bed in no time and promised marriage. When confronted with his change of heart, Aubrey used my aunt's devotion to the Old Ways as an excuse to cast her off. He left her carrying his child. You know the rest."

"You know what I have suffered," Elinor said, taking Richildis' cup and drinking from it. "You will help me a second time?"

Richildis stood and touched Elinor's face. This time the hand was warm. She leaned over and kissed Elinor, who was surprised by how loving it was, and how it aroused her. "My sister, I will help you," Richildis answered.

"In all things?"

"Whatever you like, but you must agree to pay the blood fee. Are you willing?"

"The last price was too steep, Lady Richildis."

"I think you will agree that what you want is worth any coin. See,"

Richildis turned her right palm upward and a speck of green and gold light grew into first a flame and then a revolving sphere. Elinor felt sleepy, watching the sphere turn and spin, as if she'd taken a draught of poppy juice and when she was startled awake by what sounded like thunder, George was standing before her. He smiled and said, "Is this not what you've been thinking? Is this not what you want?"

Elinor reached for him hungrily and said yes.

✠

ELINOR WOKE AS the moon was rising and sat up, looking around. Where was George? Could it have been a dream? She saw that she was naked and she felt damp and sore, sticky between her legs. No, it couldn't have been a dream, Elinor thought, smiling and remembering. She slid out of bed, dressing quickly and tying back her hair. She left the guest chamber and went out to the hall where Maud was still sitting in the chair by the hearth, a string of prayer beads still sliding through her hands as she mouthed the prayers and responses. As Elinor took her cloak, Maud said, "You missed supper and Vespers. I shall pray for your soul."

Now Elinor turned, her green eyes like glass and the scowl familiar. "And who will pray for you? You agreed to this and you made her a guest even knowing who and what she is. Your soul is in peril. I think, Countess, that you would be glad of the outcome. I think you will be glad to have taken a risk."

"No. I would be glad to see Aubrey's son the abbot of a monastery in Jerusalem and my daughter countess of Grasmere. I would be glad to have my grandchildren her heirs. The Mowbrays are an old and noble family. This would restore their fortunes and secure ours."

"That won't happen," Elinor said. "You know it and yet you say your prayers hoping that God will smile on you and yours. God will never smile on you again, Maud!"

The door slammed as Elinor left and Maud sighed, holding the beads tighter and repeating the response she'd just said, staring the prayers over again.

Outside, Elinor picked up her hems and walked quickly up the hill past George's 'Hiding Place' to Skelwith. The guards recognized her and knew she'd come from the Lodge, allowing her entry. She paused while they opened the gates and raised the barbican. Silver pennies, Elinor knew, were well spent in getting what she wanted.

Will was coming from the treasury as Elinor passed through the gates. He waited for her and then took her arm none too gently when she was close. "At the Lodge again? Will you never learn, Elinor?" Will grumbled.

"The Countess appointed me chatelaine of the household while she is away on her Fool's Errand. I am the dowager's chief lady-in-waiting. I was seeing to business." Elinor snapped.

"Yes, and if you hadn't insulted the young countess, you would now be her chief lady-in-waiting as befits your marriage and family. It's not too late to admit you were wrong."

"Do you expect me to throw myself at her feet and beg to be taken back?"

"I can speak to George."

"Your word against the little whore that shares his bed—"

The strike was quick and forceful so that blood trickled from Elinor's lips. She touched her face and wiped the blood, never taking her eyes from his. "Never speak of the Countess like that again! She has been a boon to Grasmere and it is the Count's good fortune to have a wife like her!" Will scolded, his voice loud and echoing into the bailey. Guards and servants pretended not to hear and went about their business but interested all the same that Will

Longleate had at last put his imperious, unpopular, wife in her place.

"Who knows when she'll seduce you?" Elinor fired back. "Perhaps she already has. I've seen the way you look at her."

"Say anything more and I'll strike you again, Elinor!"

"You will regret your anger, my love." Elinor swept past him. As she went, she threw a glance at one of the guards staring at them, who immediately cast his eyes downward as he flushed red. "This is none of your business! Do you hear?"

"Yes, my—"

"Not a word. Do you hear?"

The guard nodded and stepped out of her way as she mounted the donjon steps.

Servants scattered out of her way as she strode across the hall to the great tower staircase. With head high and eyes forward, Elinor ignored everyone she encountered, even her spies from Joanna's household. One of the ladies approached, but she held up a hand to silence the woman and pushed her aside. The rest of her path to the steward's apartments in the great tower was unencumbered by people in her way. When arrived in the corridor she was relieved to only find Will's guard outside her bedchamber.

Elinor relaxed as soon as she locked the door and immediately undressed to bathe. She was still tingling from her encounter with George and relived every moment as the clothing dropped to the floor.

"No!" Elinor gasped as she discovered the blood. Her monthly course had started. She realized that there had been no lovemaking with George, no erotic encounter, the most exquisite and memorable of her life. Richildis had played her for a fool.

✠

"YOU TRICKED ME!" Elinor hissed when she summoned Richildis a week later. "Why did you do it? What have I ever done to you that warranted such cruel behavior?"

Richildis stared at her with cool disregard, a look that warned others to be careful where they tread. Unfortunately, Elinor wasn't one that paid attention to such clues.

"What do you want now, Elinor?" Richildis sighed.

"I shouldn't have to tell you. I want her dead! I want Joanna in a grave!"

"Do what other Christians do; pray to your God and maybe He'll listen to you. I am weary of your complaints despite all that I've done."

Ready with a barb, Elinor merely stamped her foot like a child when Richildis left the room, and then threw a jug against the door. The shards rained down onto the flagstones and brought a nervous servant into her bedchamber. "Clean that up!" she ordered and sat watching him sweep up the mess she'd made while smoldering with anger. If Richildis wasn't going to help her, what could she do, or who might she ask? She could always send a letter to the King or petition for an audience with him. He was coming north to deal with George. Yes, that would be the best solution. She slipped into bed and sighed happily as she worked out a plan. Stretching the length and width of the bed in contentment, she started to fall asleep. Elinor was used to sleeping alone; she preferred it. There was no snoring, talking, or constant movement and having the blankets taken away on cold nights. There were no demands on her body. It was the way of things for people like her, nobility that saw marriage not as the melding of two souls for all time, but for begetting heirs and property, and so she was immediately suspicious when she woke and found Will sitting on the bed and watching her sleep. He was dressed only in a pair of breeches.

Will Longleate was one of those men whose physical attributes couldn't compete with those of men like Aubrey and George Ascalon, but the fair eyes and hair from his Nordic ancestors made him attractive, and his years as a knight kept him lean and muscular. Elinor was well-acquainted with his body and that is why when she saw the scar over his right breast from a sword in a long-ago battle, she knew it was Will and couldn't be one of Richildis' stratagems or apparitions. An intimate knowledge of the person was required for Richildis' dark art to take effect; as far as Elinor knew, she never had cause to see or know Will. When he leaned over to kiss her, she placed her hand on his chest and felt the smooth, ridged scar of skin unevenly knit together, just to be sure.

"Do you remember where you got this wound?" Elinor asked between kisses.

Will chuckled. "Why do you ask? It was fighting against Welsh raiders. I took a sword there trying to keep Griffud Rhys from escaping. I won the fight and a good ransom, which gave me the means to marry the most beautiful lady in Cheshire."

"That would be me, I guess?"

"You guess right, my love."

She was surprised by the passionate kiss he now offered. It was warm and urgent, the beginning of an even more surprising coupling and night. Hours later, still wrapped in Will's arms, she panted for breath and patted away the sweat dripping between her breasts and down her stomach, pulled a sheet around her midsection to calm the itch and rash from his beard grizzle.

"I must thank that little Slavic maid; I confess that I was jealous when I found out about her and you, but she's taught you some things I would have never guessed you capable of. I might even thank her. What do you say?"

Will still had his head and neck against her, his body relaxed.

"Will? God's me, have you fallen asleep already? Come along, Will. Will!" Elinor laughed.

She gently pushed him off and when he fell onto his back, Elinor saw that he was dead. Mouth agape, lips blue, and eyes staring into nowhere. She resisted the urge to scream and scrambled off the bed and into a robe, throwing the covers over his body.

Men died in their beds, didn't they?

She'd heard that lovemaking sometimes killed men whose humors were weak, that their dispositions couldn't take the excitement. Will, she thought, was strong in everything, but he was getting on in years, almost fifty.   That had to be the reason, Elinor thought.

Why then, did she know that Richildis had moved him aside to make room for George Ascalon?

Elinor crossed herself and whispered a prayer.

CHAPTER 13

THE CITY OF Carlisle was an ancient Roman settle-
ment to the north of Grasmere in the Westmoreland.
The Ascalon party's journey from Skelwith Castle
would have been short had Joanna not complained of
increasing backaches and nausea. Roger gave the
order to stop at a manor outside Penrith when Joanna
demanded to rest.

"Are we still on Grasmere land?" Alan Middleton
wanted to know, glancing about at the wooded
approach to the walls and gate of the great hall.

"This is in the Bishop of Carlisle's holding, I
think," Petronelle responded. "His tenants and
freeholders won't refuse his daughter-in-law and
daughter, would they?"

"The sooner we arrive in Carlisle, the better, I only
need a half hour at most to rest. *Holy Mother!*" Joanna
gasped as a pain shot through her.

"My lady!" Adam exclaimed and nearly shoved
Roger's horse aside to get to Joanna. "Forgive me;
please forgive me! This is my fault."

"I hardly think you're the father of my child,
Adam," Joanna jested weakly. "Here, take the dog. I
fear I'm scaring him,"

"No, I meant that I shouldn't have insisted on
going immediately to Carlisle when I arrived at

Skelwith, but it would have been my good fortune. . ."

"We were going anyway—oh, *fokken!*"

"That's enough; Adam, stop flirting with the Countess and help her off the horse," Roger ordered as he slid out of the saddle and reached for Joanna. Adam and Roger both lifted her and gently set her on her feet. Almost immediately Joanna doubled-up in pain. They hobbled to the gate and Adam pushed it open so that Roger could lead Joanna through. Petronelle met them at the doors of the manor, trying her best to contain her fear.

"Open! I come in the name of the Earl of Grasmere! Open!" Roger bellowed as he set to the doors.

"God help me!" Joanna cried and stared down at water pouring from her womb and soaking her skirts.

The woman who answered his pounding looked around Roger to Joanna, leaning against Adam Middleton. She glanced at the puddle at Joanna's feet.

"Her time's come, if I'm not mistaken," the woman said without greetings and stepped aside. "You did well to stop. Come, sir, bring your lady wife in."

"She's not my woman. She's the Countess of Grasmere and Princess of Gwynedd, Lady Joanna Ascalon of Merioneth. Where's a chamber for her?" Roger demanded.

"This way."

Joanna was led to a bower in the south of the Great Hall next to a chapel. Once settled the men were sent away and Joanna was left with the hostess and Petronelle, stripped to her shift and encouraged to walk about.

"Do you come for the faire?" their hostess asked. "Grasmere's a good way from here."

"Yes," Joanna said quickly looking to Petronelle. "The Three Maries Faire, is it? God's wounds! It's like a hundred knives stabbing my back—white-hot steel from the forge!" Joanna gasped and paused until the wave subsided.

"If you can talk you have time still, my lady," the Hostess replied kindly and patted her cheek. "Your first?"

Joanna nodded frantically when a wave hit her again. Petronelle rubbed her back and whispered encouragement.

"Who shall we thank for this kindness, Good Wife?" Petronelle asked.

"I am Aethel, a widow. My meat and ale are yours. And you are—?"

"Petronelle Mowbray, lady of Osterle and Kenning and sister-in-law to the Countess here, Mistress Aethel. That great rude bear of a man is my husband, Lord Roger Mowbray. The boy is our friend, Adam Middleton of Gawthorp."

Joanna let out a scream and that ended the conversation for now.

Downstairs, Roger and Adam heard the wail.

"It's begun," Adam gulped, looking up at the ceiling. "I remember my mother's birthing pains, only the babe died."

"We'll not be hearing memories that black, Adam," Roger warned.

"We—she's lucky we came here," Adam said.

"Hunh," Roger grunted. "If a manger was good enough for the Holy Mother to birth her Son . . . we should leave the women to their work and go on to Carlisle. There's nothing we can do here."

"You go, my lord. I'll stay with the women. This is George Ascalon and the Lady Joanna's son. May the saints and angels protect her and the child," replied Adam and crossed himself.

"Still carrying that candle for Joanna?"

Adam ignored him and looked around the well-furnished hall and for signs of ownership like a family device or banner. None of the usual things—banners, flags, shields—hung over the chairs of state. In a corner was a stool and a loom, a shelf of books, and a devotional panel of the Virgin and Child before which a candle burned. An illuminated Bible of exquisite work and certainly great cost was open to a page, more than likely the daily reading from the Holy Office. The smells of supper cooking drifted in from a kitchen somewhere near. The building was timber-and-stone, whitewashed like some churches he'd seen, and the plate and furniture were dear. Some of it was carved like that in Skelwith Castle with the old Saxon designs. Whoever their hostess was, she was certainly wealthy.

Another scream made Roger jump. He was ready to leave when their hostess appeared. "Is she well?" he asked, somewhat embarrassed.

"For a first birth, yes. We'll see in time," she replied. "Do you want some ale and bread?"

"Please," Roger almost begged. The woman smiled and disappeared again, bringing with her a comely maid who carried a tray with refreshments. Roger gulped down a cup of ale when Joanna's next scream echoed through the house, followed by her wailing. Aethel sat beside him and patted his hand.

"This is what all women suffer but we are fortunate to forget the pain once the child is delivered. Women are strong and redoubtable. Frail lilies we are not."

"You have experience in this, no doubt," Roger said. "Mistress,"

"Mistress Aethel, I am the widow of Thegn Siward, who is a vassal to the Bishop of Carlisle."

"Thegn? Do they still use that title?"

"Hereabouts. Yes. A good and honorable title, my lord."

"You'll have no argument from me. This far north the old ways are still lived and revered."

"Some, but not all," Adam spoke up.

"As it should be, sir. I'll return to the lady Joanna. You take your rest. There's nothing you can do."

"As I said to Adam here. I'd sooner be on the road to Carlisle."

"Wait a while, sir. You may be needed," Aethel replied, patting his shoulder as she went.

"How long, do you think?" Adam ventured.

Roger shrugged. "You never know. Leastwise, I don't know."

"I remember my mam,"

"That's enough of that, Adam Middleton." Roger poured another cup and nodded, drinking again and soon oblivious to the labor of childbirth as he snored, helped along by a drunken fog.

✠

"JOANNA DEAREST TAKE some watered wine," Petronelle encouraged, holding the cup to her lips.

"No, I can't; I'll only wretch again and this room is starting to smell," she replied, trying to get comfortable on the bed. "Let me walk again, please."

Petronelle helped her rise and supported her with an arm as Joanna walked slowly to a window. She pulled back the shutter to Petronelle's horror. "You'll damage the baby!" she said.

"No, I will have sunlight and fresh air. It's never harmed a calf or a lamb born in a field. When my son finally decides to greet the world, we have blankets if he's cold. The rules of monks and priests and holy physics who have never birthed a child mean nothing to me."

"What if she's a girl?"

"Don't spoil it, Petra. Here now, where's George?"

"George? God's me, is the delirium setting in? He's in Carlisle."

"No, silly goose girl!" Joanna tried to laugh. "The dog!"

"Ah, downstairs somewhere. Your screams scared him almost to death."

"Poor sweeting; I should have left him at Skelwith."

A knock on the door and Aethel came in with a maid carrying a birthing chair, which was set under the window by Joanna's instructions. Aethel smiled and took a quick assessment of her young guest. The shift was stained with all kinds of fluids and matter, her hair like a bird's nest, her face red and tear-stained from the exertion and her eyes puffy and ringed purple by fatigue. Still, Joanna's beauty shone through and she managed a smile when asked how she fared. A day had passed since the first pains. It wasn't uncommon for childbirth to last this long.

"Let's clean you up, Mistress," Aethel said as another two maids brought in a tub of steaming, fragrant water. Petronelle began to protest but Joanna shook her head and gladly allowed the maids to wash every inch of her with the perfumed water. Her hair was combed and plaited and she was slipped into a fresh linen shift that smelled of rosemary. Joanna began to relax and move more easily and it was then the horrific pain shot up her back and sides, around to her front and then she felt the pressure as if something dropped or fell in her body. Something was caught between her legs. A moment then, more pain and the urge to push whatever it was away from her.

She was led to the birthing chair and sat with shift hiked up to her waist. Two maids crouched at her feet while Aethel made a quick examination. "Now you must push—bear down with all the energy you can muster and push. That's it, my lady!"

Joanna gritted her teeth and pushed with her entire body. Her arms and legs shook with the effort.

A wave of pain came over her and she began sobbing. "God help him if he ever touches me again! Damn all men! I've failed him! George will never forgive me!" she wailed and pushed again and for the first time in hours she felt relief.

"What do you mean?" Petronelle laughed, kissing her cheek. "You've just given George a son! A little man but healthy all the same and so beautiful!"

Joanna looked down and saw one of the maids holding a baby that was the color of chalk and covered in what looked like animal fat. His color improved when Aethel cleared his mouth and the boy wailed louder than his mother.

"Now you must push again for the afterbirth and then we'll put your son to suck and you can rest. There's nothing like it, to lie abed with your babe beside you and taking from his mother. This won't be as hard—what's this? My lady, push! Push now!" Aethel instructed.

Again, there was the incredible pressure of something moving quickly and stopping between her legs. Doing as she was told, Joanna bore down harder than before, though she thought the effort would tear her apart. Moments later, another baby entered the world, smaller than the first, but just as perfect in form, covered in the same white grease, but bleating almost immediately: a little girl. Joanna fell back soaked in sweat and exhausted, shaking from the exertion.

"A girl, a precious little angel, this one!" Aethel cooed and showed her to Joanna, who smiled weakly and felt back against the chair, closed her eyes, and dozed.

"My lady? Countess Joanna, can you hear me?"

The woman's voice came in and out of hearing as if Joanna was under water. She mumbled a protest; all she wanted now was to sleep. She felt someone taking her arms and then an arm went around her waist as she was lifted gently off the birthing chair. Cold air from the window chilled and soothed as the soiled shift was removed and someone was washing her. Another shift was pulled over her head and shoulders, this one was warm and incredibly soft against her skin. She felt the downy featherbed and inhaled the scent of the clean sheets, the pillows, as she was helped to lie down.

Slowly Joanna relaxed and listened to the sounds of the women as they continued to wash her. One of the children bleated angrily over the sound of pouring water and gentle laughter. Someone gave her a posset to drink and then she felt the warmth of her babies as they were put to her breasts. A tingling sensation overwhelmed Joanna and she felt the babies' soft mouths and nips as they took to suck. Before she fell to sleep, Joanna smiled her thanks to Mistress Aethel and Petronelle. She felt the sting of warm tears and whispered a prayer of thanks when another woman appeared at her bedside.

"Thank you, Lady!" Joanna whispered.

"You've told me that already," laughed Mistress Aethel as she gave Joanna watered wine to drink while the children sucked.

"There's another," Joanna said, weakly gesturing behind her.

"There's only you, Lady Petronelle, my girl, and me, and the babes. Sleep now, my lady."

Joanna frowned and kept looking at Aethel, who moment by moment her appearance changed until standing at the side of bed was not the kindly midwife but the saintly woman who had given her the *marguerite* in the abbey chapel.

"Ascalon is secure," the lady said in her warm, low, voice and as she said this, two other women stood on either side of her. They were as ethereal as she and both sang a lullaby while a comforting, soothing light came through the bedchamber window. "Ascalon is secure. Sleep, my girl. Go to sleep."

Joanna felt the pressure of someone sitting on the bed, but she was so exhausted she couldn't open her eyes. The scent of wildflowers and incense filled the room and she felt a loving, comforting embrace. Joanna fell to sleep in the lady's arms.

CHAPTER 14

"WHAT WILL YOU call them?"

Joanna looked up from admiring the babies nursing yet again and smiled at Petronelle, who was bending over them, touching their little faces in awe.

"Leof and Nara," Joanna replied, kissing the tops of their heads. "For now. Their father may have something else in mind."

"Pray not Osprey or Torold, or any name from the house of Ascalon. I think Joan and George would be perfect," Petronelle said, straightening up and now tucking the shawl around Joanna's shoulders.

"I hope they'll see their father soon," Joanna sighed, disengaging Leof, who after a pat managed to belch up wind and go limp, ready to sleep. Nara refused to let go and after a whimper Joanna let her have her way. "I have a feeling you'll wrap your Papa around your finger as I did mine, sweeting!" she laughed. "I will find a wet nurse, though, for you two shall wear me out if you keep sucking every hour."

She relaxed into the bolster and enjoyed the gurgling sounds Nara made, the warmth of the child against her skin. Leof was now sleeping next to her and twitched every so often and it made both her and Petronelle laugh, wondering what dream prompted his activity.

"It's been three days. They will need Christening. Perhaps Mistress Aethel can tell us of a church nearby," Joanna said.

"Why not my father? We can have them done in the cathedral at Carlisle."

"A favor for a favor, then. We'll let him baptize only if he tells us what he knows about George."

"Now that's unfair, Joanna."

"You would think the same if it was Roger in his place. Aubrey's silence is unnerving. We should leave for Carlisle by week's end. Roger and Adam will be there by now."

"Hopefully they've found my brother and he is safe and well. I instructed them to go directly to Father's. We will be given rooms in his palace and Father will know what is happening."

"Will he side with us, I wonder?"

"Listen to us! Talking in intrigues and politics as if we were purchasing silk cloth at the market," Petronelle said and she crossed herself.

Joanna was going to say that any wife would speak so but became silent when Mistress Aethel came into the bedchamber with fruit, cheese, fragrant rosemary butter and a fresh loaf of bread that still steamed and smelled like heaven to Joanna. At last, something other than pottage or gruel.

As if she'd known Joanna's thought, Aethel said, "A little feast for the mother. Those two will suck you dry and take your energy, but how they'll smile and charm you while they do it!" Mistress Aethel chuckled. "And you'll let them because there's naught in this world more perfect than the love of a mother for her babes." She turned to the amused Petronelle and placed a hand on her stomach, which made the girl yelp. "You'll know yourself soon enough! I can see the signs!"

"How can you—? You're a witch!" Petronelle exclaimed.

"Petra! She's nothing of the sort!" Joanna scolded. "She's wise in the ways of life, isn't that right?"

"Six babes of my own and a midwife to many more," Mistress Aethel said as she plumped the pillows behind Joanna and then cooed at the children.

"Mistress, we thank you for the kindness you've shown, but we must go to Carlisle and find my husband," Joanna said more seriously now.

"In two days' time, my lady. I wouldn't travel before that. Let your milk finish coming in and the children will have enough to keep them happy and you should have more strength."

"I'm strong enough now," Joanna protested. "If I were a farmer's wife or a peasant,"

"But you're not," said Petronelle.

Aethel nodded. "Aye, my lady. Few have the benefit of a few days' rest."

"Very well," Joanna sighed.

"Oh, you do have a pretty pair of rosebuds!" Aethel crowed. "You are blessed, Lady."

The widow chucked each of the children under the chin and then gave Joanna a kiss on the brow. When she scuffed out of the chamber Petronelle, with her hands still on her stomach, glanced over at

Joanna, a look of puzzlement spreading over her flushed face.

"How did she know?" Petronelle whispered.

Joanna shrugged. "Some women just know these things, and then reaching for her hand and smiling, asked, "It's true then, Petra?"

"Yes; though I've not told Roger," Petronelle said, smiling and then the two women embraced and giggled.

"We will have to keep you safe from harm in Carlisle so that when we return to Skelwith you can prepare in comfort for your child," Joanna said.

Petronelle nodded and after a moment said, "Joanna, perhaps we should return home now."

"We've come this far."

Again, Petronelle paused before speaking. "I know you're right; I would walk barefoot to Jerusalem for Roger."

"Then we will go to Carlisle."

✠

AS SOON AS Joanna felt strong enough, they set off in a small *charrette* pulled by a strong Welsh pony, both of which were loaned by Mistress Aethel.

"Return them when you are able," the good wife said after exchanging embraces and kisses with the women. "I will know you are safe."

"Would you take a gift in payment of your kindness?" Joanna asked.

"Nay, Lady. Truly nothing. I have all I need and my husband, rest his soul, left me comfortable."

"Please take him," Joanna insisted, and handed over the puppy. "You'll need a watchdog being so far afield." Joanna now gave her a silver penny. "Add it to the poor box in my name."

"Do that yourself, I beg of you, when you've found your husband," Aethel said and pressed the coin back into Joanna's hand. "Now. On your way. I shall pray for you."

"And I you."

More kisses and embraces were shared and finally Petronelle climbed onto the driver's bench and saw to it that Joanna and the babies were settled comfortably for the short journey. She snapped the reigns gently and they set off.

The self-assurance and control of the situation that Joanna exhibited days before were starting to dissolve but she kept a brave face as the walls of Carlisle rose on the horizon late in the afternoon.

What am I doing, Joanna thought as she stared out the window at the countryside. Roger, Adam and their men were enough to help George if he needed them, and if they weren't, what could she do? She was putting her children and Petronelle at risk. Joanna knew the King's cruelty. She was still regretting her decision when they entered Carlisle at dusk just as the watch changed.

Joanna craned her neck out the carriage window to look at their surroundings. With the sun going down every building on the street looked like the same gray rectangular shape.

"That must be it," Petronelle pointed towards a great townhouse flying the Ascalon colors that stood hard by the cathedral. She snapped the reins and they were moving again.

Carlisle was not as big and sprawling as York or even London, but it was an orderly maze of streets and parks attached to noble townhouses and palaces, and like her larger counterparts, filled with buildings so close it was like riding through dark tunnels until the street ended at a patch of grass or open square and the light was better. Fortunately, the streets were nearly deserted as night fell, lights starting to flicker in windows, which made it easier for the women to reach their destination. Petronelle drove the *charrette* through the covered passage and into the courtyard of the Episcopal Palace and stopped when a liveried servant approached them holding a lamp high.

"Are you lost, girl?" the man asked kindly.

"I am Petronelle Ascalon, wife of Roger Mowbray who is earl of Myrce, and lord of Osterle and Kenning. I am the daughter of Bishop Aubrey. I have with me his daughter-in-law, the Countess of Grasmere and her two children."

The servant held the lamp higher to illuminate Petronelle's scowling face and then pointed towards the stables. "Go there."

"Girl!" Petronelle swore under her breath as she glared at the man before leading the *charrette* away. A cleric and servant were waiting in the inner ward.

"Welcome. You are?" the cleric greeted as Joanna and Petronelle disembarked.

"Joanna Ascalon, Countess of Grasmere. Here is my sister-in-law, Petronelle, Countess of Myrce."

"My lady of Grasmere, this is a surprise," the cleric said in a more obsequious voice and with a deeper bow. "The Bishop will be delighted to see both of you—all of you," he smiled now at the infants asleep in a basket that Joanna took from the *charrette*, "as you come unexpectedly."

"My brother was summoned to Carlisle by the King," Petronelle snapped. "Tell me you didn't know about that."

"I didn't," the cleric protested innocently and gestured towards the stairs into the palace. At that time of day petitioners and clerks were absent and palace eerily quiet. An occasional cough, a door closing or opening echoed, as did their footsteps as they walked through corridors and up stairwells of a palace that was austere in its furnishings and decoration. The cleric stopped at a pair of doors at the end of one staircase. "Wait here, if you please," he said and disappeared behind the doors and then reappeared moments later. "Bishop Aubrey is at his leisure and will see you."

"I should hope so!" Petronelle said under her breath.

The audience chamber they entered was like the rest of the episcopal palace: sparsely-decorated and suitable for a monk. At the north end, there was a fire in the wall hearth and a table set with cups and a flask of wine, a great chair called a *cathedra*, the bishop's throne, which would normally be in the cathedral in front of the rood screen or in the sanctuary, but it looked in need of repair as it was half decorated with gilding and paint. Benches were pushed up under the windows. A great crucifix carved of oak hung on a wall.

Aubrey was standing at the fire with his back to the door and as soon as he heard the footsteps, he turned.

"Petra!" he said, striding across the room to embrace her. "When Brother Matthew said my daughter was requesting an audience I could hardly think what he meant. But here you are, my girl."

"Don't you know, Father? We've come for George," Petronelle answered.

Nara woke and started to wail. "May I put the basket down somewhere?" Joanna asked when Aubrey turned sharply, a look of surprise across his face. She glanced around and chose one of the benches.

"Your grandchildren, Father," Petronelle said, bringing him forward.

"Here are Leof and Nara, my lord. Leof is but a few minutes older than Nara, who has decided to be the most vocal," Joanna said and stepped back, gesturing towards the children.

"Like her aunt in that respect!" laughed Aubrey as he peeked down at the babies. Nara stopped her howling and shoved a fist in her mouth while Leof yawned and was content to go back to sleep. Aubrey said a prayer and made the sign of the cross over each and continued to marvel at the little ones, putting an arm around Joanna and offering a hug. "As beautiful as their mother. Joanna, I'm glad you're well. But how little they are! How long ago?"

"A fortnight."

"And you are out? But your churching!"

"We got as far as Penrith when my pains started. I didn't want to be alone with the children and wait to hear news of George. You'll give me absolution for this little sin, won't you? Roger, Adam, and their escort should have arrived by now. I sent them ahead. I assume they're here?"

"I haven't seen them, Child."

"What about George? Where is he?" Joanna asked fearfully.

"Why, I don't know. Why would he be in Carlisle?"

"He was summoned here to answer for the death of Abbot Warennes," Petronelle explained.

"But George pled his innocence! I was there when the Sheriff came to Skelwith and I heard the conversation," Aubrey said.

"That's as may be, and I'm certain Sheriff Black believed George, but a warrant was signed by the King commanding George to appear for a trial by combat in Carlisle or suffer death," Joanna said.

"Father, we've come to champion George in any way we can," Petronelle said. "Surely you will help us?"

"Of course. You were right to come here."

"If he's anywhere, he's in the castle. You'll take us there?"

"Of course, of course. Not tonight, though. I will need to make inquiries."

"Why not tonight?" Joanna demanded. "A letter from you would release him. Carlisle is your city."

"It is the King's city. As is every town, village, and city in the kingdom," he answered quietly. Joanna stepped back, trying to hide her disappointment and anger as she studied Aubrey's gray, pale, face.

Something is not right, she thought.

Aubrey's mood suddenly shifted and he was all smiles again. "There are rooms enough for you girls and the babies. I'll have Matthew prepare chambers close together. Now. Let me see these little ones," said Aubrey as he picked up both sleeping infants and held them in his arms, smiling broadly. "If I'm not mistaken, and my memory hasn't failed, they both take after their father, for the Ascalon fairness is very pronounced! See how this little one pouts; I remember that look on George's face."

"Oh Father, they're little lumps right now," Petronelle laughed.

"Petra!" Joanna giggled. "Father is right; Leof does look like George, especially when asleep. And George still pouts."

"Go you ladies in. We'll speak in the morning and I'll send word to the castle," Aubrey said. He gestured to a clerk, who led them out. Taking a last glance at her father-in-law before leaving, Joanna knew he wouldn't keep his word, especially when Aubrey refused to meet her gaze and looked away.

CHAPTER 15

THE SUITE OF rooms at the top of the Bishop's palace was spacious and comfortably furnished unlike the others in the palace residence. Joanna and Petronelle lacked for nothing and yet Joanna felt she was under house arrest, for Aubrey had forbidden them to leave the palace grounds and stay in their chambers unless escorted to church for mass.

"This reminds me of the Golden Tower of Eskeleth," Joanna said to Petronelle while they dined one night, a week into their stay in Carlisle.

"How? It doesn't stink of Sulphur and decay and there's no annoying harp song," Petronelle said and waving her hand about, added, "and there's lots of color. Many pretty things."

"We're guests, yet we are not guests."

"Father is making sure of our safety."

"He doesn't want us going to the castle."

Petronelle glanced at her and noticed for the first time how ill she looked. The babies were keeping her up all night and the worry over George was making her irritable and anxious. She was losing weight too quickly.

"You're not well, Joanna—"

"Of course I'm not!" Joanna shouted back. "My husband is probably locked in a cell in the castle and

I have no idea where he is, or if, God forbid, he is dead! Of course I'm not!"

"Joanna,"

"Go about your business whatever it is, and leave me alone!"

Petronelle crept away to her own chamber.

After mass the next morning, Joanna stayed behind to speak to the priest. He smiled at her as he gathered up sacred vessels and linens, saying, "My lady?"

"Father William, I wonder if you could answer a question," Joanna began.

"Of course, if I am able."

"To begin with, I am the Bishop's daughter-in-law, Joanna Ascalon, late of Merioneth and Princess of Gwynedd."

"Yes, my lady."

"My father-in-law. I wonder if he has been in correspondence with the governor of the castle."

"Not that I'm aware."

"Surely he's given you instruction?"

"You know my husband the Earl of Grasmere is being held there."

"As to that, I know not. I'm sorry."

"But are you not the Bishop's confessor, and secretary?"

"Yes,"

"Then you would know if he promised—" Joanna caught Father William's frown of puzzlement and whispered an apology before genuflecting to the presence of Christ at the altar and hurried away. Her abrupt and noisy entry into the suite of apartments set the babies to wailing and Petronelle let loose a shriek. Joanna kicked open an empty trunk and started piling clothes and shoes into it, rushing about. She suddenly stopped and turned to Petronelle, "Get your things together and I'll take care of the babies. It was a mistake to come here. We must go home."

"What?!"

"It doesn't make sense that your father has been so silent and is ignorant of George's whereabouts when he was there in the room, in my bedchamber in the lady tower, when the charges against George were first made," Joanna said as she picked up speed and started putting the children's swaddling and shirts, their napkins and caps, into another, smaller, trunk. "Petra, we're safer at Skelwith."

"But we're already here!" Petronelle exclaimed. "And what about Roger and Adam? We should get word to them!"

"Where will we send word?" Joanna asked quietly but forcefully. "We don't know where they are. Or even if they arrived in Carlisle."

"What do we tell Father?"

"Nothing. We leave now."

Petronelle sighed and did as she was told with much grumbling under her breath. Within the hour they were packed and hurrying out of the palace. No one thought to ask what they were doing and by the time Aubrey realized they were gone, Joanna, Petronelle, and the children were on the road south.

✠

"THEY WERE HERE and then they were gone."

Roger stared at Aubrey skeptically, then at the clerk standing at the bishop's right.

"They were here," Roger repeated.

"Must I repeat myself, my lord earl?" Aubrey said acerbically.

"They were here, and then they were gone. It makes no sense, Bishop. We agreed to meet here."

"You allowed two women to travel alone south?" Adam queried.

"Master Middleton, you of all people know these are no ordinary women. Did they not defend themselves in the Forest of Kentmere? At Eskeleth in the three trials? At the abbey in Keld? George spoke proudly and often of their abilities," Aubrey said.

"I agree with Adam. You should not have let them go, not with the King riding north," Roger replied.

Aubrey paled and signed for a cup of wine, which the clerk passed to him. "How do you know this?"

"We went to the castle. While playing at dice and cards with the household guard it was easy enough to get information," Adam said.

"The girls are safe," Aubrey said somewhat forcefully. "I don't doubt they're on their way home. There are two convents on the road where they could ask for lodging."

"Now that we think we know where Petronelle and Joanna are, where is your son, Bishop?"

"How should I know?"

"If you know about the King,"

"I think you'd better ride south. It's for your own good," Aubrey said, his voice now calm but forceful.

"No," Roger replied, his hand on his sword pommel. "I think we'll stay in Carlisle and make some inquiries at the castle now that we've made the acquaintance of its guards, to say nothing of the knights."

"You put my son in peril!" Aubrey shouted at them as they turned to leave.

Roger paused and spun around. "So you do know what's going on."

"Just go!"

The men bowed and left the audience chamber.

Out in the street, Roger glanced up and down and then started pacing. "Do you believe anything the Bishop said?" Adam wanted to know.

"Aubrey Ascalon deserted his family for the church and offered his son in his place to answer a blood feud. The man has no honor. Of course I don't believe him! I'm more interested in knowing what else he's sacrificed for the King."

"I'm of a mind to go to the castle and look around. They know us, so. . ."

Roger nodded and headed north towards the keep and the russet-colored piles of stone being used to construct the outer curtain wall. It was easy enough to circumvent the masons and builders; to them, they were just another pair of knights. It wasn't until they were past the inner curtain and going up the steps of the keep when a soldier stopped them and asked their business.

"I come on behalf of the Sheriff of Cumbria, Master Black. I have the King's warrant to take one of your prisoners with me back to Great Longdale. He is a lord of the realm and must needs be brought to justice in his own county."

"Let's see this warrant," the soldier said, reaching for Roger's scrip.

"Can you read?"

"All I need to see is the King's seal. That's good enough."

"Then let me show you."

Roger pulled a scroll neatly bound with a red ribbon and a thick wax disk dangling from it. The sentry grunted and nodded when he saw it. "That way. The small tower at the end of the bailey. Down the stairs, two flights, at the end of the hall. You'll see the door. Tell the guard your business."

"The King is beholden to you, sir," Adam remarked, offering a silver penny.

"Now that's something to remember to my grandchildren - the King of England beholden to the likes of me!" the sentry laughed as they walked away in the direction he pointed.

"I didn't know you had a letter from the King," Adam whispered.

Roger shrugged and nodded in greeting to the sentry standing at the entrance, holding up the scroll. A guard sitting at a table blocked the entrance to the first stairwell. Ahead of Roger and Adam were citizens of Carlisle with baskets of food and clothing for prisoners. Two pennies gained entrance into the jail cells. When it was Roger's turn, he placed a gold *dinar* on the table and held up the scroll. The guard nodded and looked at the coin, then Roger.

"Take it," Roger coaxed. "Perhaps you have something else for us?"

Another coin was placed carefully.

A key was taken from a leather scrip on the guard's sword belt and passed with a finger across the table. For added measure, Roger discreetly placed another gold coin on the table and tossed down two pennies.

Just as the sentry directed, they went down two flights of stairs and found themselves in a long, dark, corridor with a door at the end. Roger took the torch out of the sconce and walked carefully, watching the rats, that seemed to appear out of the walls and floor, scurry across their path. Another guard was leaning against the wall by the door and he came to attention when he saw the two men.

"We've come to relieve you of your duty," Roger said as he held up the scroll. "The lord earl is coming with us to Grasmere for his trial. The King has no desire to come this far north."

A coin exchanged hands and the door was opened. George was sitting at a table under the arrow slit which served as a window, his back to them as they entered. He turned as they approached. Roger saw the quill pen in his fist and knew George meant to use it as a weapon.

"Come, my lord, we're taking you home," Roger greeted, adding loudly, "by signed order and warrant of the King."

"What?" George asked, incredulous.

"Let's get your things," Adam said, picking up George's cloak and satchel. "I don't suppose your sword is anywhere nearby?"

"They took it,"

"My lord earl's sword," Roger said to the guard. "It is a precious thing and has been in his family since before the Conquest. Do you have it?"

The guard looked puzzled and then went out, returning moments later with another guard. "He says there's a sword," the man said to the other.

"The Sword of Ascalon," George offered.

"That ratty thing?" the second laughed. "Wait a moment." His boots were heard on the stairs, disappearing, then a jangle of keys, a thud and echo of a chest being opened and closed, and then the footsteps again. The guard was holding George's sword belt and the sword of Ascalon, which he would have passed on to George had Adam not intercepted him.

"I'll take that. Where were you schooled? You don't give a prisoner a weapon!"

"Come, sir, we'd better be on the road soon. The magistrate and the King wait at Skelwith Castle," Roger said as he bound George's wrists and led him away.

This was too easy, Roger thought as they rode out of Carlisle an hour later.

CHAPTER 16

EUSTACE DES JUMIEGES pounded his fist on the table and screamed, "Where did they go? Tell me!" The hour since his arrival in Carlisle had been tense. He'd expected to take his quarry to the King and found the Earl of Grasmere had gone missing. The captain of the castle guard swallowed hard and dared to look at the angry man across from him. "No one saw where they went, my lord. They said they had orders from the King,"

"The King? I am the only one who has orders from the King and they are to keep him here until the King arrives! Would you like to be the one to tell His Grace that the Earl of Grasmere escaped under your watch?"

The captain of the guard and his lieutenant glanced at one another and then looked to Eustace, shaking their heads.

"Get out – wait! Go to the episcopal palace and send for the Bishop. I want him here within the hour."

"Yes, my lord," they said in unison.

Eustace threw his cup at them, hitting the door as it closed. A servant dunked but still received a spray of wine. He used the towel on his shoulder to wipe the sweet, sticky, German vintage off his face and out of his hair. "Shall I prepare some refreshment for when the Bishop arrives?" he dared to ask.

"No. We're not going to make him comfortable."

Aubrey arrived at the castle without a guard and a clerk as the bells rang the hour. Eustace was still pacing the great hall and keeping the servants nervous when Aubrey entered. Eustace turned when he heard the servant and glared at the Bishop. Aubrey wasn't holding out his hand for the kiss of peace and it was just as well.

"What do you want, Eustace?" Aubrey greeted without the usual cordialities. He tossed his gloves on a table and reached for a cup to pour himself some wine before a servant could do it. Aubrey waved the servant off, saying low, "Take yourself out of here, boy, and your companion. You're safer away, trust me."

Eustace and Aubrey were alone now; Aubrey at one end of the hall perched on a window seat, Eustace in the great chair of state on the plinth.

"Where is the governor?" Aubrey asked, glancing about between sips of wine.

"Gone to meet the King. He approaches Carlisle."

"I knew nothing of his progress north."

"Now you do, my lord. You'll be privy to more information once you tell me where your son has fled."

"George is gone?" Aubrey said with mock surprise. He was an excellent mummer so that Eustace couldn't have known he was lying. The fingers of his left hand were crossed beneath the folds of his cloak.

"Two men saying they had a writ from the King took him earlier in the day. Did you know about this?"

"No, no, no. Not in the least. If they had the King's writ . . . Sir Eustace, is my son safe?"

"That will depend on whether the so-called agents were truly from the King. If they were not, George hasn't a chance in Hell of surviving when the King does find out what happened."

"Do you know what happened?" Aubrey asked him.

"What do you think, Bishop? Why would I call you here if I did?" Eustace sneered. "What are you hiding?"

"I hide nothing. If I knew where my son had gone, I would not share that information with you. I have more love for my son than you give me credit for."

Eustace walked over to Aubrey's window seat and shoved himself down beside him. "I credit you for being shrewd and politic. It is how you got this far," Eustace said in a quiet, controlled, voice that even though calm, was threatening. "Aubrey, you made a bargain with the King for your episcopacy. Are you willing to go back on your word? A traitor is a traitor even if he wears purple and scarlet robes."

"I will not betray my son or take away his inheritance."

"Aubrey, you promised the King that you would give the King a secure foothold here in the north and would give him Grasmere in return for the episcopacy."

"No! That wasn't the agreement! *I* was to give him that security by holding the diocese of Carlisle. My son would have fallen in line as long as he was allowed to keep his lands and title and his wife given her inheritance in kind. I will not betray George! I've done enough to hurt him already!"

"You won't have to worry about that if you're not around," Eustace said. Pulling a knife from his sleeve he drew its blade across Aubrey's throat and watched him slump over as the blood pulsed from his neck and then oozed to a trickle. With his free hand he pushed Aubrey's body on to the floor. Eustace now sighed and stepped over the corpse to reach the door, which he opened and waved a guard over. "See that the garrison is ready to ride. We're going to Grasmere in the morning," he instructed.

The guard bowed.

"Find someone to clear away the mess in the hall. Make sure he's discreet."

Again the guard bowed and looked over Eustace's shoulder into the chamber where Aubrey's body lay in a grotesque halo of blood behind its head, a stream of it slowly wending towards the door.

✠

GEORGE WAS SILENT for most of the ride south and it wasn't until they passed Hartsop and were resting in a cave nearby that he finally spoke.

"Thank you both," he said.

Roger offered some dried beef and ale. "It was Joanna's idea to find you.

"That doesn't surprise me," George laughed softly. "My sweet, amazing, Joan!"

"You look well."

"Well enough; I was treated more as a guest than a prisoner. They didn't want to turn over damaged goods to John for the trial by combat," George said. "Besides, I paid enough in silver to keep the guards on my side. Tell me, why was the trial moved to Skelwith?"

"It wasn't," Roger answered matter-of-factly and took another drink of ale from the skin Adam was passing around.

"What about the King's warrant?" Adam asked.

Roger pulled the scroll out of his scrip. "Thank the saints and angels the guards couldn't read or know what the King's seal looked like." Roger handed over the scroll to George. "This is Joanna Ascalon's letter to her husband informing him of the birth of their son and daughter. Oh, you owe me three gold *denarii* and eight silver pennies."

"I have a son? *And* a daughter?" George laughed. He tore at the scroll and hungrily read the news. "She's named them Leof and Nara! God be praised they're all well! I have a son and a daughter! My poor Joan! So little yet carrying such a precious and great load."

"They're a handsome pair, my lord," Adam said.

"You've seen them?"

"Yes; we were there when she gave birth. Well, not there exactly. We stopped at Penrith at the manor of a widow called Aethel because Joanna's pains came upon her quickly and too early. We went ahead to Carlisle while Joanna, Petronelle, and the babies rested," Adam gushed happily. George, however, was not amused.

"You left them in Penrith?" George hissed, his voice rising.

"No, no, my lord! They went to Carlisle and met with your father, then returned to Skelwith," Adam replied, looking first to the scowling Roger and then to George, still unamused. "As far as I know. *Ow!* God's life!"

Roger smacked Adam on the side of the head. "We could have done without your sharing that bit, Adam Middleton!" he scolded.

"He was bound to learn!" Adam whined, rubbing the spot.

George shoved himself to his feet. Without another word, he grabbed his sword and made for the horses tethered outside. Adam and Roger scrambled to keep up and soon they were riding hard and by morning they'd reached the northern marches of Grasmere.

On the road from Keld Roger shouted at George, pointing east. The lily and leopard banners of the King and twenty-five knights and their squires. They were riding to Skelwith.

"Adam, go ahead of us and raise the alarm. I left a hundred knights to protect the castle; I'm certain we can defeat a quarter of that," George instructed. "Go around to the south entrance. There's a door in the curtain wall that's hidden by shrubs and bracken, to the southwest. Here," George pulled the medallion of the earls of Grasmere out from under his shirt and passed it to Adam. "That will get you in."

"As you will, my lord," Adam said, saluting George with his sword before riding off.

George and Roger watched until he disappeared from the horizon and then followed, using a path known only to natives of the area that bypassed the Roman road and Ermine Street from the south. The King's men were still on the horizon by the time they reached the castle. A peasant who lived in one of the lean-tos against the curtain wall put down the reed basket he was weaving as they approached and immediately bent the knee upon recognizing George.

"Robin Weaver, did you see a lad go through the door?" George asked.

"Aye, my lord."

George tossed him a penny. "See that no one else goes through," he continued, gesturing toward the dozen sheds and lean-tos that housed laborers making repairs to the castle and its curtains. "Make sure they hold their tongues." The weaver glanced about and then nodded, returning to his work.

Following Adam's lead, they pushed aside shrubbery and bracken obscuring a door the same color as the castle stones and tried the latch. It opened after applying some force and the men went through.

"Clever Adam!" George whispered. "He's lit the torches. Roger, watch your step now; we have to go down some ways and then up."

The passage went down into a dank tunnel that reeked of offal and horses, of old hay and rotten food. The air became wholesome when they saw a sliver of light shining down from the tunnel's ceiling. Roger

found a ladder off to one side and placed it so that
George could lead the way. George felt around above
him and then threw open a trap door and climbed
into a corner at the back of the stable. Both men
paused to get their bearings and would have
continued to the donjon had it not been for an
unfamiliar soldier waiting in the shadows, holding a
dagger to Adam's throat. The man was taken by
surprise and coughed up blood as soon as George
thrust his blade into the man's exposed chest.

"Drag him into a stall and throw some hay over
him," George said, peering out the stable entrance
into the yard.

"Whose man is this?" Roger wondered, nudging
the body with a boot toe.

"I don't recognize the badge. Maybe Scottish or
Welsh mercenaries come over the border? In any case,
let's hope there's not more," Adam replied as he took
the dead man's arms and dragged the body into a stall
furthest from the entrance. Roger started scuffing dirt
and straw over the trail of blood, being careful to stay
out of the stable doorway.

George motioned for Roger and Adam to follow
him and they crept along the perimeter of the yard,
going towards the donjon. One of the stable boys
recognized George and was ready to hail a greeting
when Roger seized him, a finger to his lips, and his
hand over the boy's mouth.

"I'll make you a squire if you do as you're told,"
George whispered.

The boy nodded eagerly.

"I just killed a soldier in the stables. Whose man is he?"

"Lord Eustace."

"Do you know how many there are?"

"A score, I trow."

"That many? Look you, here is what we're about, but I'll need your help."

The boy nodded and listened carefully. Moments later and on George's signal, he ran to the donjon steps and shouted, "My lady! My lady! Come quick! So many! So many there are!" As expected Eustace's soldiers came out of the hall and George, Roger and Adam skewered them or slit their throats. While they dispatched the soldiers, the boy rang the alarm and the Ascalon household guard appeared and met battle with more of Eustace's men. Though every blow or swing was countered, they fell and soon Ascalon's numbers were decimated. George found himself cornered until one of his household guards threw an ax and the man fell, the ubiquitous, dead-eyed, stare of shock permanently etched on his grizzled face and mouth agape to show brown, broken, teeth.

There was movement to George's right and he turned quickly expecting another of Eustace's soldiers but saw a hideous creature coming at him with a bloodied club. He'd fought this one before - the knight with the putrid, decaying skin sagging from his bones, the skin oozing with sores and writhing with worms. They'd met in the market square of Grasmere.

George rolled out of the way as the club came down and smashed the leg of a knight already dead, blood and bone spraying him. The creature attacked again, this time with a massive ax with a head the size of a man's, the handle made of an animal rib. Again, George moved out of the way, leaping and spiraling as the weapon came at him. Vapor came from the creature's foul mouth as he labored for breath; it stank of decay and the Sulphur of Hell. The stench made George nauseous, worse still when the vapor became a fog and he was blinded by it. He heard the battles around him, the shouts of Roger and Adam, but he was at a loss to see where safety was. Everywhere he looked was sallow mist and shapes of men fighting. The creature raised his arm to attack and George had a clearing to stab and roll. He screamed when the creature fell on top of him and was trapped by mounds of putrid flesh that transformed into snakes writhing across his chest and wrapping themselves around his neck. Suddenly, the world around him went black. The dizzy sensation of floating above the ground came upon him; George watched as the creature was attacked by knights and dragged off of his lifeless body. The blackness faded to gray, and then a blinding white, and George was standing in the great hall of Skelwith, but not the hall Joanna had furnished. It was the barren, sterile, hall of his childhood after his father deserted the family, after he'd gone to crusade. Roger and Adam were off to one side near the screen, on the carpeted plinth where his chair of state stood. In pride of place was not his father, nor his stepmother, but Elinor.

"Welcome home, my lord."

"Get up from that chair," George ordered.

"It is my castle, so it is my right."

"Lady, what is done is done. You have a fine husband, a fine living, and titles. Be content."

"If I have learned anything from living at Skelwith is that contentment is only a word. Sometimes it is spoken in peace treaties."

"Is that what this is, Elinor?" George asked.

"You would hope so. No. Prove yourself." Elinor nodded towards musician's gallery above them. A cloaked woman came from the shadows and with deliberate motion, she slid the hood of her cloak back and revealed her identity. The blonde beauty and lithe, voluptuous body were unmistakable. Richildis smiled down at George.

"Ah," George laughed; "a parley I'm familiar with. More quests, more challenges."

Extending her hand, Richildis chanted a prayer and extending a hand, filled the hall with a thick, gray mist, almost like sheared fleece, but transparent. The ground quaked and rippled so that all save Richildis had to struggle for footing. Out of fissures came her knights, the same as those George fought at the abbey of St. Bryde's in Keld. They rose as if from graves and with swords, axes, and spears at the ready, attacked. Adam was the first of the defenders to draw what he thought would be first blood, crowing in delight at his prowess and then screaming for help as more of the knights came at him.

George and Roger found themselves back to back as they fought, each battling across the hall in opposite directions. Swords sliced, and knights became clouds that evaporated and then materialized again as knights that were stronger and more vicious. The battle continued for what seemed like forever and when it looked as if both George and Roger would drop from exhaustion, Richildis raised her hand. "Enough!" she shouted.

The knights slowly disappeared and in their places were Eustace des Jumieges and his men. Eustace approached George and held out his hand for his sword but he refused to relinquish it.

"Your sword, sir," Eustace said.

"When I and my sons are dead, and not before," George replied.

"Stop it!" Richildis shouted when Eustace reached for a dagger and was ready to lodge it in George's breast. "We said this would be honorable," she continued. Eustace shrugged and taking a few steps back took the cudgel one of his soldiers carried in his belt and struck George soundly on the head. Roger and Adam made ready to go to his aid when he fell but were held back.

"Take the earl to his quarters in Ravenglass Tower," Eustace ordered. "Mowbray can go to his wife's quarters. Find Mowbray's wife and see that she's locked up with him. The boy put in a cell."

✠

GEORGE CAME TO hours later. He felt the side of his head to make certain his skull wasn't cracked, and winced, then sat up. It took a while for his vision to clear, but there was no mistaking the woman sitting by the bed. Elinor greeted him with a smile and then waved over Rhosyn, who carried a tray laden with food and drink.

"You must thank me for Eustace keeping his temper and not killing you," Elinor said, offering a cup of wine.

"Get out," George said. He refused the cup. "God knows what you put in it."

"You'd be dead if we wanted you so. No one wants to poison you, George. You're no use to me in a shroud," Elinor said and drank from George's cup, wiping her lip with the middle finger slowly in a seductive manner, and then raising the hand to show George as if to say, 'See?' To Rhosyn she said, "Tell Eustace that Earl George is awake." The girl's eyes slid to George and then to Elinor and back again. "What keeps you, girl? Do as you're told," Elinor ordered.

George interrupted. "I have nothing to say. Tell him not to bother."

Rhosyn waited at the door, hearing this.

"I said, go!" Elinor shouted at her.

"But,"

"A change of loyalties, Rhosyn? Eustace and the King won't be pleased," Elinor snapped.

George looked at the girl, who turned shamefaced red and glanced away, biting her lip and fighting tears.

"Your cousin my wife knows what it is like to do the bidding of those who are her enemies if only to stay alive," George said gently. "Or those one believes will keep their promises no matter how false."

"Forgive me, sir!" Rhosyn cried and then in a gush, "He said he was your friend and that you were joined with fools wanting to kill the King, that you were intent on taking the kingdom for yourself and he was only saving the King—"

"Shut up and do as you're told!"

"I have never wanted the King dead, Rhosyn."

"I beg you and my lady to forgive me!"

"Enough! Go and find Eustace before I beat you within an inch of your life and give you to the garrison for sport!" Elinor shrieked at her.

"You promised not to harm him! Eustace promised not to harm either of them!" Rhosyn cried, turning on Elinor.

"That's not your concern!"

"Rhosyn, you aren't helping Ascalon. Just go," George said. "We'll talk of forgiveness later."

"Yes, my lord. I'm sorry!" Rhosyn offered a curtseyed before leaving.

Elinor turned to George with a smug, annoying, smile spread across her lips.

"No negotiations until you bring my wife and children to me," George said preemptively. "No parley. None of your tricks." He was firm, his voice controlled and forceful and the smile was gone from her lips.

George slowly swung his legs over the bed and moaned softly from the exertion and the pain. He looked down to see if there were any wounds other than those to his head and was satisfied he was somewhat whole after the battle. Next he staggered to the window, throwing out the shutter. The moon was full and a cool wind was blowing through the dale. Candlelight flickered in the hamlets and villages leading to Grasmere. Below, in the greater ward, his guard was on watch. One of them looked up and saluted. George barely raised his hand in acknowledgment.

"Eustace, Lord of Ambleside, my lord," said a page when the door opened. George turned and leaned against the casement for support.

George raised a hand when Eustace started to speak saying, "No words with you on any matter until you release my wife and bring her to me with my children."

"Reasonable. Lady Elinor, see that it is done," Eustace said.

"That wasn't the agreement, my lord!" Elinor argued.

"Any bargain made with Elinor Lucy is bound to get you into trouble or give you a thousand regrets," said George to Eustace.

"Lady Elinor, do not make me ask a second time," Eustace said.

Sighing loudly, Elinor made one of her dramatic exits. A moment of silence passed and then George said, "What are you about, Eustace?"

"Seeking justice for the King."

"I didn't kill Alan Warennes. I had nothing to do with it."

"But you did marry a Princess of Gwynedd without the King's consent. His Grace was in negotiations with the Welsh princes of Gwynedd for the borderlands of Merioneth when you married the lady Joanna, daughter of one of Rhodri's sons. Your actions are treasonous."

"Let me defend myself before a jury of my peers. The King's late father, Henry, gave his barons that right. Our good King John could do no less."

"The King will do what the King will do. Don't think yourself greater than him, or worthy of treatment befitting a prince."

"I am no greater than any of the barons. But I do hold the rights to the earldom of Grasmere by right of birth and gift of William the Conqueror. He gave Grasmere back to my ancestors when they agreed not to rebel against the Normans," George said. He moved slowly towards the great chair by the hearth, every move watched carefully by Eustace, and eased himself down on to the cushion. Settled now, George looked at Eustace and managed a weak and disingenuous smile. "How did you come to your living, Eustace? Were you not the son of a tailor in Chepeside? I heard it said you purchased your title with the blood of your late first wife, Judith, married yet another heiress who fell upon misfortune and then you found your way up here where no one knows you or your past to woo and ingratiate yourself to Anne Swope of Ambleside to take her lands and titles by marriage."

"Not so different than what you did."

"No, you're wrong. I had no knowledge of Joanna's parentage when I dragged her out of the burning cottage in Butcher's Lane. Unlike my father, and you, I don't prey upon landed women for what I can get. I don't murder my lovers and I wouldn't murder my wife."

Eustace was noticeably offended by George's remarks. His face turned red and his trembling hands moved into his sleeves where they couldn't be seen.

"I know what you did to my wife."

George's salvo was delivered in a quiet, unemotional tone that put Eustace over the edge. Just as he lunged for George, the door opened and Elinor entered, stepping aside for Joanna. Joanna rushing into George's arms prevented an altercation and Eustace and Elinor watched as the couple embraced.

"Earl George," Eustace began.

"Leave us!" George ordered.

"Certainly. We'll wait below."

"George! Thank our angels and saints you're alive!" Joanna said between kisses. "I couldn't sleep imagining the worst,"

"All will be well," he answered, hugging her tightly.

"Forgive me for going to Carlisle–I thought I could help."

"I am pleased you love me enough to take such a risk," George said. "I'm the bigger fool, my love. I should have stayed here and not honored the warrant. We had enough arms and men."

"They've been paid off! They're sworn for the King, and for Eustace."

"Not all. Come, see."

George brought her to the window where the one knight keeping watch had become a dozen and they all saluted when the couple showed themselves. "We'll think of a plan to thwart the traitors and their leaders."

The knock at the door made them jump and George crossed the chamber, taking a candlestick as a weapon. He waved at Joanna, signaling her to hide behind the bed curtains. Once she was out of sight he moved towards the door.

"Who's there?" he called.

"Margaret, my lord, with Anna, the wet nurse, and your son and daughter."

George opened the door just a bit, and then threw it open and watched in amazement as a train of servants entered carrying chests and cradles, followed by the women and children. With quiet efficiency, the women set the cradles down and placed the children in each, while the chests were thrown open to reveal swaddling bands, napkins, shirts and caps. He stared down at the sleeping children now tucked in for the longest time, and then looked to Joanna.

"My lady, we can put up a screen to give you and the earl privacy, should you wish it," Margaret suggested as two servants entered with carved panels of oak wood that were hinged and painted and set side by side to make a screen that divided the chamber in two.

"Yes, that would be best, since we don't know how long this room will be our only home," Joanna replied quietly.

"My lady, I heard Elinor talking to a servant. They do mean to keep you here, but in some comfort," Margaret said. "I will wait upon you and Anna will care for the children. There'll be another maid, soon, I think."

"Very well, Meg."

"I'll send for food and drink then?"

"Yes, please."

Margaret disappeared behind the screen and then the quiet close of the door let them know she'd gone. Anna's voice was calm and soft as she instructed servants to organize the children's clothing. It seemed to Joanna that nothing had really changed, except that George was with her and they were prisoners in their own home. Joanna looped her arm through one of George's and looked up at him. He was still staring at the sleeping babies.

"All right then?" Joanna asked.

"I suppose," he answered, and looking down at her, smiled and gestured towards their children. "How do you tell them apart?"

"Well, Nara is on the left; she has the pale blue blanket and the lace cap. Leof is on the right with the purple blanket and plain cap." Joanna knelt before the cradles and brought George with her. "You'll soon discover that they are two very different people. Nara will let you know if she approves of you, or doesn't, and Leof is just about satisfied with everything."

"And you? Are you satisfied?"

Joanna cupped his face in her hands and kissed him gently. "You are here. Our children are safe."

"For now."

"Eustace des Jumieges would not dare harm us."

"But the king,"

"I am afraid of him. What shall we do when he arrives?" Joanna asked. "Elinor said he was marching west from Lincoln with an army."

"I can summon my vassals – those who are still loyal to Ascalon. We can negotiate a peace. It all depends, however, on what we're willing to concede," George said.

"He'll ask for Merioneth first."

"Why give him anything?"

"We'll pay with our lives. And the children will be his hostages," Joanna whispered. "You know the stories of Prince Arthur of Brittany's son and how the King dealt with him after King Richard died."

George nodded. "We'll all go. There's a way out of the tower. We could go at night and seek help. Your women are sworn to you?"

"Of course," Joanna said, adding, "But what about Petronelle?"

After a time, George said, "We cannot stay, Joanna. We must go tonight."

✠

NEWS OF THE Ascalons' escape reached Elinor and Eustace more than an hour after the small party crept down the hidden staircase behind the great hall screen and went by stealth into Grasmere. There they secured horses and a carriage and were soon out of reach.

"Surely you have the skill to find them!" Elinor shouted at Richildis when they met in the lodge hall. My lady, tell her it needs to be done!"

Countess Maud was in her chair by the hearth stitching a new shirt and by the way she concentrated on the needlework seemed not to pay attention, though her eyes continually went to Richildis and occasionally her fingers sought the comfort of the crucifix she wore on the girdle at her waist.

"If they are gone, they are gone," Maud sighed, taking another stitch carefully and drawing the floss slowly. "Isn't that what you wanted, Elinor?"

"Yes, Mistress Longleate, hasn't this worked to your satisfaction?" Richildis asked.

"I promised the king I would bring Ascalon to his knees if he gave me Grasmere in return!" Elinor shouted. "What will the king give me now if I cannot deliver George Ascalon to him?"

"What you deserve," Maud answered, looking up and smiled. "Nothing."

Elinor turned on her. "You've changed your mind about George."

"You're wrong, Elinor. I told you what I wanted. I have a daughter who deserves Grasmere. She is of my blood and the blood of Aubrey, Bishop of Carlisle. She has every right to the title and lands."

"She has Myrce, Osterle, and Kenning. What do I have?"

"More to the point is what do *you* deserve?" Richildis queried. "I have quarrels enough with George Ascalon and his father. Do not expect my help for whatever you plot with the King. He will break his promise to you, be sure. Isn't that true, Maud?"

Richildis glanced at Maud, who was whispering a prayer, a hand on the crucifix. They glanced at one another and Maud was the first to look away.

"Why did you of all people summon me here?" Richildis demanded quietly of her.

"I hoped that you would turn towards good and

the light that is Christ. I pray for your soul and that your gift of healing would be put to better purpose. But most of all, that your heart would turn to the Lord our God, and help my daughter. I mean, my children. I raised George from infancy and he's as good as mine," she answered.

"No!" Elinor shrieked.

"Oh be silent, you cow!" Richildis hissed and shaking her head at the furious woman pacing back and forth, took her cloak and left the hall. She went out into a cloudy, mild, morning. The moon was giving way to the sunrise, now a breathtaking wash of orange and pink along the Cumbrian hills. Nature held no interest for Richildis, however. She went to the stables and saddled a horse, riding it hard out of Skelwith and over Ascalon lands eastward to the wild country of which she was familiar.

CHAPTER 17

"IT'S JUST THERE, beyond the wood. Do you see? If you look between the trees. . ."

George pulled up rein and looked at the timber and thatch manor set on a hill in the shadow of the mountain, surrounded by a forest. The wooden palisade with its sharpened logs looked no more defensible than a freehold in a Cumbrian valley. Still, it was on a hill and set high enough that one could easily watch invaders approaching.

Perhaps they were being watched now.

"We'll be safe there?" George asked Joanna.

"My father's ancestors of Aberffraw have held Castell Idris since before the Saxons invaded this island," Joanna answered. "My uncle will welcome us."

"When will we be in Merioneth?"

"We've been riding through it for three hours."

They'd been riding hard and fast for three hours and a fortnight. Only now did George feel secure and know that they were safe from King John's soldiers especially when they went off the main road and started the climb up to Castell Idris. English knights could never make this climb, not even with hardy ponies. They paused in the heat of the summer afternoon at a freehold outside the approach to the castle.

"Good day, Lady. Who is the master here?" Joanna spoke in Welsh to an elderly woman drawing water from a well. Startled, the woman nearly spilled her bucket and retreated a few steps from the strangers on horseback that had suddenly appeared. She glanced past them and saw the women in the cart, then looked at Joanna who nodded and smiled in greeting.

"Dafydd ap Cynan, my lady," said the woman, nodding back.

"The son of Cristina?" Joanna asked.

"She of blessed memory," the woman said.

"May God assoil here. I am Joanna ferch Rhodri, he that is an uncle of Prince Llywelyn ap Iowerth. We seek the help of Dafydd," Joanna continued. "He will know me. He is my uncle. Will you send a man to Castell Idris and let him know that Joanna is here, and she brings her husband, George Ascalon, the Earl of Grasmere? Tell him also that his kinswoman by marriage, the lady Rhosyn, is also here." Joanna pointed to the cloaked figure sitting in the back of the cart.

The woman put down her bucket and turned to leave, but George called her back and pressed a silver coin into her palm. "For your pains, Good Wife," he said, and Joanna translated.

"Thank you all the same; for Rhodri's girl I would do this for thanks alone."

They watched her struggle up the hill and slip through the gate, kept watch as an hour passed, and the heat became unbearable, took shade under trees by a blacksmith's forge until she at last reappeared with two of Dafydd's guards and another man, perhaps a member of the Aberffraw court from his bearing and dress. George put an arm around Joanna as they approached, their eyes set on her. "Here is the lady and her man," the woman said to the courtier when they were within hailing distance. "See? She has the look of Rhodri's wife."

"So she does," he replied, nodding. Turning to the couple before him, the courtier bowed and said, "Lady Joanna, welcome home. I am Ioan ap Bleddyn. Dafydd's counselor."

"Here is George Ascalon, the Earl of Grasmere and my husband, sir. My cousin Rhosyn is with the women in the cart."

"You are all welcome. Come with me."

They followed their guide up to the manor, which, once past the palisade, was a busy cluster of buildings as in any castle in England and one that was amid expansion. Walls of stone and the first floor of a massive keep were in progress. The workers and household members paid no attention to the visitors as they cleared up for the day and went to their lean-tos and huts along the perimeter of the walls. Sentries climbed up to the walkways and came from the towers set into the walls at their corners, taking positions for the coming night. The wealth and importance of their host was apparent in the state of the buildings and the industry, the fine dress of courtiers and soldiers.

"The prince is waiting in the hall," said Ioan and he waved at a guard at the end of a covered walkway that led from the stairs they'd just climbed, then he turned to George. "You will leave any weapons you have."

The Sword of Ascalon and George's dagger were reluctantly given to a servant who disappeared with them into a room off the hall.

A cloud of smoke billowed and caught them by surprise as the great carved doors were thrown back, though not as surprising as the sound of a bard's song that greeted them. George and Joanna, their women and the children, were led to a tapestry-covered plinth where a tall, thin, man with raven-black hair and large blue eyes sat on a carved, high-backed, bench with a pretty young woman beside him. She might have been his sister or daughter. The carved eagles of Aberffraw spread their wings along the oaken back. Once they were before the plinth, George and Joanna bowed to their host. Dafydd ap Cynan crooked his head, smiling, then crooked it back again, folding his hands before him. Finally, he slapped his thighs and bellowed a laugh.

"My God! One moment I thought I was seeing my young brother Rhodri, and the next my cousin Elen! Child! It's you, Joan, isn't it? Where have you been? Welcome! Welcome! You are welcome!" Dafydd exclaimed. He beckoned to Joanna, who, after a worried glance at George, came forward and knelt before him. Dafydd raised her up with a hand and gave her kiss on the brow. He now crooked fingers at George, who wished he hadn't given up his sword and dagger. The man looked as if he could befriend you one moment and slit your throat the next the way his eyes shone and were so wide as if he was touched by madness. "Earl George, you are welcome; you are all welcome."

"We are grateful for your hospitality," George said.

"You're far from home, Earl George. Cumbria is some long ways off."

"We fled from the King of England's men, my lord," George finally said.

"Which ones?" Dafydd asked, brows raised. George could have sworn by the smile starting on his mouth that the prince thought it amusing.

"The so-called lord of Ambleside, Eustace des Jumieges."

"Oh. That one," sighed Dafydd. "A preening, pretty, Norman, that one. He's been poking about my borderlands with the foul excuse that he speaks for the Bishop of Eden and wants a rapprochement of some sort between Cymru and the western marches of England to solidify his hold on some shire and towns that were gifted to the Bishop and him. Do you know anything about it?"

"No." George paused, locking glances with Dafydd. "But the Bishop of Eden is dead now. I try to stay out of that kind of trouble."

"Hah! Well, come have a cup of ale with me and we'll talk. My wife will see to your lady's needs and those of your children. Two at once! Hah! You must tell me your secret!"

Dafydd bounded out of his chair and walked over to a table that was laden with food and drink, waving George over. His consort rose more slowly and was assisted down from the plinth by her lady-in-waiting. She looked to be a full nine months gone with child.

"We are grateful to you, Lady," Joanna said, curtseying.

"I am Angharad. I could do no less, Countess. My husband speaks often and fondly of his beloved kinsmen Rhodri and Elen."

"And unkindly of my father's foolishness?" Joanna queried.

"That, too. But more of the King of England's treatment of you. When you were taken from the nuns at Towyn, my husband sent men into England looking for you, for it was his desire that you live as his ward after Rhodri's disgrace and your mother's murder."

"Not as a hostage?"

"Lady Joanna, you know our people. We do not punish women for their fathers and husbands' mistakes."

"Our people's ways have changed since I last lived in Merioneth," Joanna responded as she followed Angharad to the women's bower. Angharad made no response, but Joanna saw the hard set of her mouth and a chilling coldness reflected in her already dark eyes.

✠

A WAR COUNCIL was summoned as soon as Dafydd heard George's story. The Cymric princes arrived at Castell Idris and met in the great hall. George sat beside Dafydd at the high table set on the plinth and listened as the lords greeted one another in their native tongue, wondered what was being said about him. Finally, it was George's turn to speak. He stood and came around the table to stand in the center of the hall.

"I thank you, princes of Wales, kinsmen to my wife, Joan ferch Rhodri, the daughter of Elen of Gwynedd." George waited while a scribe translated, and the hall grew silent after it hummed with approval at the mention of Joanna's mother, a much-beloved woman in Gwynedd. "You know that Rhodri ap Cynan, after much consideration, accepted a freehold in Merioneth offered by John of England for swearing fealty to him and was named an English earl as a boon. It had been agreed that the English would stop raiding your borderlands if Rhodri would serve the king. He was later betrayed by that same king when he refused to betray you, princes of Wales, when the agreement lost its importance in the King's eyes. Rhodri refused to betray you, I say, again.

"When he renounced his English title, the threats to his safety and those of his wife and daughter were many. He fled Wales to find support and no sooner had he left his wife in the care of her cousin, Elen was raped by the King's soldiers and murdered. Her daughter, my wife Joanna, was living at a convent in Towyn at this time and was taken by force and made a hostage, first, and then a slave, and it was in that dishonorable state I found her in Grasmere. I made her my wife and my own love, and I made a promise to her on our wedding night that I would help her reclaim Merioneth."

George paused to regain composure after this emotional monologue and to form his next argument.

The men in the room were silent, waiting. He turned to Dafydd. "My lord," Then to the assembly. "Princes. I am here to ask for your help in claiming Joanna ferch Rhodri's inheritance, and to ask for your men and arms in helping me take back my lands in Cumbria, stolen by the lord of Ambleside, one Eustace des Jumieges – the puffed up Norman as Prince Dafydd so rightly calls him. He is aided by a lady of the court that was once a friend to Ascalon, the traitress Elinor, Lady Longleate. This is being done in the name of the King and in retaliation for my wife demanding what is hers by birthright. And there is more. I need your help to clear my name of a false accusation of murder made by these toadies. It is said I murdered the Bishop of Eden and his lover, the abbot Alan Warennes, and a novice of the abbey."

The murmuring in the hall grew louder, like angry bees.

"What if you did?" one prince spoke up. "What's that to us?"

"In fact of matter, I didn't. But I see I need force to persuade my betters of my innocence. If the King's puppet is so willing to take my lands bordering your own, what will stop him from encouraging the English King to dishonor the agreement he's made with your great prince Llywelyn? What will stop the King from taking your lands and murdering your wives? Taking your daughters as slaves?"

Again, George waited as his words were translated and the room again started to hum with voices but this time not as cordial or in agreement. A small, wizen, man with enormous, sloe, eyes that shone against his black hair and pale, withered, skin, stood and looked around at his countrymen.

"I am Mirthyn of Towyn, Earl George. We know this story of the lady Joanna ferch Rhodri. It is as much our dishonor as the fair lady's," he said. "We remember that night when the soldiers came and burned the convent to the ground and slaughter all the women."

"Then why have you done nothing to help her?" George asked.

"Earl George, take heed," Dafydd warned, shaking his head.

"It is a reasonable question, is it not?" George said.

"We have quarrels enough with the English despite my kinsman Llywelyn's treaty with them."

"We quarrel among ourselves," Mirthyn admitted. "My only question is this, Earl George. What is our reward for giving you our men and arms and riding with you?"

George didn't hesitate. "My wife has agreed that every prince who brings his banners to Ascalon shall each have a freehold in Merioneth without condition."

The exclamations were loud and disbelieving. George continued: "I cannot speak your tongue but let me guess that you don't believe me and think me a fool."

"For suggesting this to the lady Joanna, but not in your choice of wives," Dafydd laughed and others joined in, including George. "What magic do you work that makes your lady wife so agreeable?"

"She taught me how I should love her."

Again there was laughter, this time with applause and the stamping of feet. When it was quiet, Mirthyn spoke again. "How do we know you'll keep your pledge?"

"My name and my deeds are my pledges," George answered.

"So we're heard from Englishmen before you," Mirthyn scoffed. "What's to stop *you* from taking our lands and women?"

"The princes of Cymru and their men!" someone shouted and there was raucous agreement from others.

Dafydd held his hand up for silence. "Who among us has not heard of The Trial of Eskeleth?" he asked, looking around.

"A bard's fantasy!" Mirthyn said. "The days of deeds and magic are over."

"They're not," George replied. "Not if the magic belongs to our Lord of the Kingdom of Heaven."

"Do you claim to be the Champion of Arkengarthdale?" asked another prince.

"I do. I am."

"*You* are the knight who slew the dragon?" the man asked incredulously. His comment was followed by murmuring and deferential nods at George.

"You have the Sword of Ascalon," Mirthyn said derisively. He glanced around, smiling at the princes, sure he'd caught this Englishman in a lie.

"If I may?" George asked, turning to Dafydd, who nodded. "Boy, bring me my sword," he said then to a page. The boy ran quickly to the side chamber and returned moments later with George's sword, which he handed over with a reverent bow.

The sword rang like a bell as George pulled it slowly from its scabbard. He held it pommel and crossguard first to Dafydd, who smiled as he inspected the weapon and then returned it to its owner. Every man in the room strained to get a look at this famous weapon that had vanquished a dragon, and some said the Devil himself.

"An ordinary weapon," Mirthyn scoffed. "Any of our Cymric smiths could fashion that." He came forward and studied the sword's workmanship.

"It was made for my father on the occasion of his taking crusade."

"As I said," Mirthyn replied.

"You slew a dragon with it?" someone asked.

"It saw me through three challenges; the so-called dragon was the last," answered George.

"How? Did it shoot ice?" someone asked.

"Is it poisoned?" another questioned.

"I heard a sorceress enchanted you and gave you the strength to vanquish the Devil," said one prince.

"I don't know about that," George said and shrugged.

"Yet you fought and won," Mirthyn said.

"It was the Lord's doing; I am certain of that."

"When a Cymric prince fights, he is the strength and the power behind his sword."

"I won't argue with you on that; it's true for Englishmen. As I said before, my deeds are my pledges and what I have spoken is true. Any man who brings his banners to Grasmere shall be rewarded."

As he said this, the sword began to emit a saffron-colored light that sparkled as if dew drops or rain danced in the beams. It could have been the play of the torchlight in the room, but enough of the men knew it wasn't and gasps now filled the sudden silence.

Dafydd watched the light pulse and then slowly fade as George replaced the sword in its scabbard. He said, "Your argument is sound, but we will need time to consider what you ask. Our meat and mead are yours while you are at Castell Idris, forever how long our councils take."

If George had any other convincing arguments, he swallowed them with the strong ale Dafydd offered. The question died on his lips: How long would he have to wait?

CHAPTER 18

DAFYDD AP CYNAN spared nothing for the comfort of his guests and Joanna was relieved that she and the children would not have to ride for another day or two. She was exhausted and sore and whenever she closed her eyes the desire to sleep overwhelmed her. As the guests of honor at Dafydd's table that night, she summoned all her strength to stay awake. Angharad was pleasant and conversed mostly about the mysteries of childbirth, to which Joanna did her best to respond, answering questions and allaying fears, but she wanted more than anything than to sleep. She was relieved when Angharad said she was retiring for the night. It gave her an excuse to leave.

"I know you're a long way from home, Lady Joanna," Angharad said as they said good night; "but I would think it a boon to have you here when my child is born."

"Then we shall pray that the men take their time in negotiating terms," Joanna artfully lied. "God give you sweet rest, my lady." Alone in the bedchamber with Margaret, Joanna said, "We will pray that we leave here on the morrow and go straight back to England!"

"My lady?" Margaret asked.

"You heard me. I want to go back. Something is not right. I feel no safer here than in Grasmere."

"Earl George is a persuasive man, my lady," Margaret said as she undressed Joanna. "He will make the Welsh princes see the right of your claims and then you will be secure."

"Let us pray," Joanna sighed.

She was glad for the furs and the soft sheets as she sank down into the pillows and mattress, glad for the song Margaret was humming as she put away things and lit the night lamp. Lovely Margaret! Always the first to see the good in any situation and loyal in the bargain. If George had not been with them, she'd have invited Margaret to keep her company, but tonight as tired as she was, she needed George.

"Shall I stay until Earl George comes up to bed, Lady?" Margaret asked cheerily.

"If you would," Joanna yawned. She leaned over the bed to look at the sleeping children. "I will never stop gazing on them in wonder, Meg."

"That's as it should be."

"Do you know what?"

"My lady?"

"I have no care for Merioneth."

"What?"

"I meant what I said. I will go tomorrow morning and ride back home, to Skelwith Castle, if I could convince George that Grasmere is more important to us."

"Merioneth is your home!"

"Now that I am here, and I have seen it, I have no care for it. My mother was murdered for lands and sheep. I think sheep."

"Surely a castle!"

"There was something of stones called a castle, though it was little more than a bower and hall. I fancied it to be more than it truly was."

"By your leave, it means a great deal to the earl."

"He has done this because he wishes to make me happy. I would be happy at Grasmere."

"I won't argue with that."

"You think me a selfish, spoiled, woman."

"Only tired, my lady."

Joanna reached now for Margaret's hand and kissed it. She fell asleep moments later with Margaret's motherly kiss on her brow.

✠

"HUNTING. YOU'RE GOING hunting?"

George looked behind him to see his wife standing with arms crossed against her breasts, the bed robe carelessly draped over her body. Early morning sunlight showed her to exquisite advantage and if he had more time he'd change that scowl to a contented smile; her lovely body was even more enticing since the births of Leof and Nara. But there was no time. Dafydd made the invitation the night before, after Joanna and the children were settled in their chambers and the Cymric princes kept George up with their questions about The Trial of Eskeleth pried out him with ale. He was still exhausted from their escape from England and would have liked to stay with Joanna and the children, but his host insisted, saying it would be a perfect time to talk man to man.

"George?" she asked, this time more quietly. A sure sign that she was angry.

George finished securing his sword and *seax*, took the bow and quiver of arrows from the servant waiting at his side. "Your kinsmen thought I'd like venison to take back to England."

"Between the two there's nothing different."

"It will give us time to discuss our plans."

"And what are they? It's been a week and you talk and talk, and nothing gets accomplished, while the children, the women, and I sit waiting."

"Go back to bed, sweetheart; it's early yet."

"I'm wide awake. Your stomping about made certain of that."

"I won't argue with you, Joanna. I think this is the best way to getting what we want," George said as he strode across the chamber and gave her a quick kiss before leaving. He wasn't certain, having no knowledge of the Cymric tongue, but there was no mistaking the colorful name Joanna shouted after him.

George forgot their quarrel as soon as he was on a sturdy Welsh pony and riding into the forest surrounding Castell Idris. It had been a long while since he'd ridden for sport, though he wasn't expecting such a small mount; he was accustomed to his fine stable of horses at Skelwith. The ponies, one of the squires said, were better at climbing the wild hills and going into the forests. Now side by side with Dafydd, George started to relax and enjoyed the easy banter of equals, of exchanging tales of war and wenching, stories that became more outlandish as the day grew long and the ale skins that were passed around drained.

At the foot of the mountain called Eyri, one of Dafydd's squires called a halt; the advance men spotted quarry: a fine eight-point stag, sleek and noble with an exquisite, glossy, red pelt.

"That would make a fine bed robe for your countess, eh, Earl George?" Dafydd jested.

"I'd need more than fur to get back into her bed given her foul humor this morning."

"Then we'll give her a feast and a bed robe! Come!"

Dafydd kicked spurs into his pony and started the climb, followed by his men. George struggled to keep up, unused to the pony and the terrain and fell back behind the squires. The party halted and took positions behind rocks and trees while the stag grazed unaware. The sound of the wind in the trees and birdsong covered the men as they prepared and moved in for the kill.

Suddenly arrows started flying. Not wanting to miss his chance to show the Cymric princes his mettle and prowess, George was knocking an arrow to take a shot when he felt the wash and heard the whirring of an arrow coming at him.

For a moment he thought it was an accident or a dangerous joke, that one of the men was teasing, or the archer was drunk, when another arrow flew towards him, and another. George wheeled the pony around in a full circle and rode for the protection of a copse. There he took cover behind a fir and waited. When the arrows kept flying in his direction, George drew his sword. He bobbed and wove out of the way of arrows and charged Mirthyn, slicing the man's bow in two.

"Hey! You show bad manners, Englishman!" Mirthyn said, laughing.

"I suppose courtly manners gives one leave to kill a guest!" George bellowed. "What the Hell did you think you were doing?"

"Be at ease," Dafydd spoke up as he joined them, literally coming between what looked to be a deadly confrontation. "Earl George at your ease! Mirthyn's sight has always been poor. Why look, my lord; your pony is the same color as the stag."

"I don't see anyone riding the stag."

"It was a mistake to welcome him," Mirthyn sneered. "Didn't I say, Lord Dafydd?"

"That's enough," Dafydd answered. He shot an angry glare at Mirthyn and the other princes coming to find out what the quarrel was. There was no mistaking the look between Dafydd and Mirthyn. George knew it; it was the look shared by men when their plans were foiled. George walked back to his pony but looked behind him as he went, just to be sure he wasn't chased by an arrow or dagger.

"You mustn't take insult by it," Dafydd said later in passing when George was on his way to his rooms.

"How should I, then? Were you my guest, I would be certain to keep the arrows and knives locked up," George scoffed as he edged by Dafydd, who gently took his arm.

"It's to be expected when you come to our land and ask our princes and lords for help. To many, you're another greedy English lord."

"I assure you I am not. What I have said and pledged is true, Prince Dafydd."

"Accept my apology and let us be friends. We are kinsmen by marriage, are we not?"

George glanced at the hand Dafydd was offering and then solemnly nodded, taking it. The grasp was firm and unyielding. It was as if Dafydd wanted to wrestle. George maintained his grip until Dafydd finally let go and smiled at his guest. If George had looked down he would have seen Dafydd flexing his palm and fingers to rid them of pain. He didn't see Joanna watching from the landing until he turned to go up the stairs.

"No venison?" she asked cheerfully.

"An eight-point stag. We shall take a fine red pelt and some excellent meat back to England," he replied.

"Soon, I hope?"

"Soon."

But how soon, George wondered as he sat beside Dafydd at the high table that night. Had George not grown to manhood in Jerusalem and Constantinople, he'd never have believed his father's warning that men could speak with both sides of their mouths. Here in the great hall, the princes were hale and hearty, clapping each other and him on the back for a good day's hunt and pledging their arms and horses to George for his quest. Recounting the day's adventures but leaving out the ambush in the forest. *Only hours before . . .* George thought. He looked down the table at Joanna, who was uninterested in her meal and seemed to be nodding in agreement or responding to the lady Angharad out of politeness.

Soon, George whispered, looking at Joanna, who smiled as if she heard him at the end of the table.

"Earl George," Dafydd was saying to him now. He poured more ale into George's cup and clinked it with his own in a show of brotherhood. "The princes and I have a proposition for you. Will you join us now?"

Soon, Joanna mouthed, and blew a kiss as George reluctantly followed Dafydd to yet another council.

✠

CLEAR-HEADED BUT exhausted, George bade Dafydd and the princes a good night just as the cock crowed. God's life was it so early? he wondered, climbing up the stairs to his bedchamber. The question of hour had replaced his plans to take Grasmere back for only a moment. The princes had come to an agreement with him. The hours of negotiations, the days of hunting, falconing and going on raids, the nights spent feasting and drinking had paid off and to his benefit. All would be put in place in the morning.

The door was off the latch and George went in.

"All is well, George?" Joanna whispered in greeting.

"You're still up? Did you wait for me?"

"Yes and no; Leof is cutting teeth and keeping all of us awake," she said, coming to him for a kiss. "I did want to hear about this latest council, though."

"It was the last, thankfully."

"We're going home?" she exclaimed, and George put a finger to her lips, laughing softly.

"Quiet now, you don't want to wake the babes. Tomorrow for certain. I'll tell you more when we're on the road back into England. For now, I just want to lie in your arms and snore to the heavens."

"Ah, that would be the usual night for us?" Joanna teased.

"Naughty kitten!" George teased back and batted her gently with a pillow.

"I'll show you what naughty is like, my lord earl!" Joanna answered as she slipped out of her bed robe and under the covers.

"A very naughty kitten – I can't wait!"

George quickly undressed and was down to his small clothes when he noticed a figure in the corner near the garderobe. It was a woman by the folds of cloth and the veil shimmering ghost-like in the rays of moonlight. She moved soundlessly towards him. "Margaret? Is something amiss?" he called softly. "Anna? Who are you, lady?"

"Sweet Jesu!" Joanna cried as she grabbed the discarded bed robe and threw it back on.

The woman now came full into the light and stood by the window. She was dressed in a fine gown and wore, as he guessed, a silk veil, but atop that was a crown made of stars. Her smile was warm and welcoming, and it seemed to emanate from her large eyes.

"Madam? Is there aught I may do?" George asked, pulling his shirt back on. "I didn't see you there,"

"I have a message, George Ascalon," she whispered, but loud enough to hear. "Leave Wales now. Dafydd ap Cynan is not your ally, but the worst of enemies. They have no intention of giving Merioneth to Joanna, nor give you aid for Grasmere.

Go now, before he murders your wife, your children, and you. Go."

George was ready to argue with her but for a knock on the door. Glancing at the woman, he picked up his sword and listened at the door. The knocking became frantic.

"My Lord of Grasmere! Open!"

Rhosyn was outside. He opened the door the width of a finger and saw her with Angharad.

"What is it?" he asked. "What do you want?"

"Leave Cymru now," Angharad said.

A chill ran down George's neck and back.

"You say this; should I trust you enough to let you in?" he demanded.

"You waste time arguing and put your lives in peril."

He admitted Angharad and Rhosyn and bolted the door behind them.

"Please my lord," Rhosyn pled while George and Joanna hastily dressed. "We are all in danger – even the lady Angharad."

George looked to the lady and she nodded. "After you left the council, Dafydd and his close companions changed their minds. My husband has no intention of giving Lady Joanna her birthright. They plan to kill you in your bed," Angharad explained hurriedly. George was ready to speak but she raised her hands to stop him. "I pray you, listen! Your horses and cart are ready, and I have two men at arms sworn to protect you."

George glanced towards the window. The lady was gone, but something like a jewel sparkled on the sill. He went over and picked it up and his breath caught in his throat. It was one of the dragon scales from the Trial of Eskeleth.

"My lord? Why do you hesitate? You must go!" Angharad continued.

"Bundle up the children," Joanna ordered Margaret and Anna when they stumbled sleepy-eyed into the chamber. "We take only what is necessary."

"Earl George, you have to go!" Angharad pled.

"And when do they attack? Do you know?" George asked while he continued his preparations with Joanna and the women.

"When the bells for Prime ring."

George glanced at the hour candle on the bed table and nodded. "We have less than an hour. It will be enough time, do you think?"

"If you hurry, my lord," Angharad said.

But as soon as belongings were locked in chests and the children secured in their baskets, men's voices and the ring of steel echoed up from the hall. Footsteps crept on the stairs, occasionally, a plank would creak. George made for the door, sword in hand.

"Do you think your wife and children will survive if you're foolish enough to attack?"

The noblewoman was standing before him at the door, barring his exit.

"I won't run like a coward, not like—"

"Like before?" the woman asked, smiling sadly. "You weren't a coward then. You're not a coward now."

"My lord Grasmere? Is there something wrong? Why do you hesitate?" Rhosyn was tugging on his sleeve.

George looked over at her and then back at the noblewoman, who was gone. He was holding not one, but two, of the dragon scales. They glowed brightly in the early morning light streaming through the window.

"Going out that door is a sure way to die or be captured," Angharad warned.

"Well, is there another way out of here?" George asked, looking around.

"I'll show you," Angharad said. She silently motioned to the eastern wall of the chamber and instructed the George to push aside the chest up against it. She clicked a heel on the floor and a hatch sprang open, standing aside as first the women and children and then George crept through.

Once again, George and his family were fleeing for their lives in the dead of night.

CHAPTER 19

"WHEN YOU SAID we were riding to safe lands and allies, I knew this was what you meant," Joanna said to George as they approached the walled and gated town on the moor. She reached out and took his hand, squeezing it affectionately and then bestowing a kiss. Behind her the children were protesting the pause and she turned, saying, "Peace, little lambs! Your papa's brought us to safety, thanks be to God!"

A month had passed since their escape from Wales and they still were no closer to recovering Grasmere, nor were they safe from the King, whose assassins and spies were stationed on Watling Street, the main road connecting north and south, and Ermine Street, one of the busiest roads in England. Still, they were happy and sure of success. George led his party over the smaller, wooded paths that were usually the reserve of bandits and murderers, and through hamlets and villages as they traveled, to the wilds of northeastern Yorkshire, to this place that once he feared would be his doom. Now he hoped it would lead to his restoration.

The air was clear and bright with the scent and sight of wildflowers and The Golden Tower of Eskeleth shone brightly in the late afternoon sun. Outside the town walls, the coppice of grotesque trees with their blackened, twisted, branches and trunks were now flowering apple trees divided by a spring that flowed from an unknown source. The country around Eskeleth, the expanse of moor and low hillocks called Arkengarthdale, was dotted with a patchwork of farms and freeholds.

"How different it all is," Joanna murmured as if to herself, but George heard and nodded in agreement.

"That will make our task easier, my love," he said. "It hasn't been that long since we were last here, and Father once said that in Eskeleth memories were long. We have also an ally in my grandfather. He will be our champion."

"I never did thank him; not properly."

Joanna said nothing more, as she was thinking of the last time the house of Ascalon came to this remote place in search of help. Alliances were made and broken and the revenge for Aubrey Ascalon's treachery was almost deadly, paid for in full by his son, George. She glanced at the horizon towards the setting sun. The gilded walls of the castle and the town now glowed with an orange light, like fire. It wasn't ominous, or deadly, but comforting and welcoming.

George gave the signal to halt as they approached the town gates. Riding alone, he saluted the sentries who immediately crossed their pikes in a defensive stance, refusing admittance.

"Who approaches The Golden Tower?" one of them called.

"Your champion, George Ascalon, Earl of Grasmere," George called back.

"We have no champion but Wulfstan of Eskeleth,"
the sentry said.

"True; that's as may be, but he will tell you that George Ascalon redeemed a debt and saved you from death. I do not speak to brag of my deed, only to give the facts," George answered.

"We've had too many knights from the south looking to improve their fortunes," the sentry scoffed. "Get on,"

"Hold!" said another man, who by his clothing and armor was a knight. He came from the guardhouse and removed a glove as he approached George. "He is who he says he is. This is Osprey Cynefrid's grandson, George Ascalon of Grasmere, the son of Lady Fay. He is in truth and fact our savior. Welcome, Earl George!"

A sign of peace exchanged between George and the knight as they shook hands and then embraced.

"Now open the gates, damn you!" the knight shouted. The gates were opened, and the knight waved the Ascalon party forward.

They entered a town at the end of a market day, and what a difference from the previous visit, Joanna thought again. A few paused to gape at the strangers but most went about their work, whether it was carrying food into the great hall beyond the castle walls, or closing shop for the day, or lighting the many torches on the walls and in the three rings of baileys surrounding the Tower. Joanna craned her neck at the roof and saw the trees. The secret rooftop garden was still there. There too, was the chapel in which they prayed before the Three Challenges. A priest stood on the steps, smiling as the Ascalon party approached. "God save you, George Ascalon of Grasmere!" he called and made the sign of the cross.

When it became knowledge that George Ascalon had arrived and was entering the castle, feeble and then heartier cheers went up from the folk. Riding beside George, Joanna heard her name whispered and soon she was offered nosegays and children ran alongside them, shouting greetings. The happy tumult brought Stephen Langley, The Golden Tower's chancellor, to the steps of the donjon. At first, he was frowning and demanded to know of his knights what all the noise was about but seeing George he broke into a grin and then called behind him. Soon Osprey and Wulfstan joined Stephen on the landing.

Osprey approached with open arms as soon as George and Joanna dismounted, and they embraced and exchanged whispered greetings.

"Well, George, Earl of Grasmere, you return in better state than when you left," Wulfstan interrupted. "You and your companions fled like thieves in the night without offering thanks, and now you receive a warm welcome."

Wulfstan, Lord of Eskeleth and Arkengarthdale, looked healthier and more robust since their last meeting. Joanna avoided his smile and looked about and saw that everything and everyone looked normal for a noble household. The women were fashionably-dressed, as were the men. Servants and retainers wore their lords' devices on their surcotes and tabards. The knights were very much alive. And now the assembly, cheering only moments before, was quiet and looking uncomfortable as it waited for George's response to what was certainly a barbed comment.

George reached for Joanna's hand. They stood before Wulfstan and knelt to offer courtesy, waiting until given permission to rise. That took some time. Wulfstan finally motioned for them to stand and looked up at George. "Welcome back, my lord and lady. What does Grasmere ask of us?" he said.

"I offer an apology," George answered. "When last I came to this place, I repaid a pledge made by my father and honored his debt, my lord. As for our sudden departure, my companions only did what they felt was our right. To leave quietly because they feared for my life. I was ill, if you remember. The challenges took most of my life. We took nothing but what we came with. Oh. Save a cart, which we returned. And horses. I believe that is all."

There were a few snickers and laughs at this, but those were quickly silenced by Wulfstan's hand. "You must want something to come back," he asked. "Am I correct?"

There was no hesitation when George said, "Yes, my lord."

"It's no surprise to us. We knew a fortnight past that you were coming."

Wulfstan stared at him for another long, painful moment, and then silently invited them into The Golden Tower and to his private chambers.

George remembered the uncomfortable words exchanged in this solar not long ago and knew history would repeat itself. Stephen Langley, Osprey, and several courtiers joined them, taking seats around a fine table painted with symbols and decorations harking back to the ancient people of Nordic origin who populated the region. At the end of the table, Wulfstan took a seat before an illustration of a great serpent devouring itself and invited George to sit at the opposite end – where the great mystic tree, Yggdrasil, spread its gold paint branches and roots across the polished oak table top. Joanna sat to one side with the women and children.

"No, Lady Joanna, you will take a seat among your equals," Wulfstan said.

"Pardon, sir?" Joanna asked looking around at the councilors and courtiers, all of them grim-faced. Even her husband.

"Take a seat, Lady." Wulfstan gestured towards a seat at the middle, where Freyja the goddess of fertility looked out over the chamber, holding a child to her breast in one arm, and grasping a sword in her right hand. Glancing at George for only a second, Joanna took her place.

"We welcome the ancient and noble house of Ascalon back to Eskeleth," Wulfstan opened. He glanced over at the children sitting on Margaret and Anna's laps. They were quiet for once and smiled with toothless grins when they noticed the attention given to them. "Your children are beautiful," he said to Joanna. "That's no surprise, considering their parents."

"Thank you, sir," Joanna replied.

"Do you know what the people of Eskeleth call you, Lady?" Wulfstan said.

"I shouldn't like to think,"

"The Little Warrior. And now, have you come to be second to the Hero of Eskeleth?"

A thin thread of laughter circled the chamber and Joanna lowered her head in shame. Raising her eyes, she saw George's sympathetic smile.

"A favor for a favor is all we ask," Joanna said, shrugging.

"Ah, Ascalon's favors," Wulfstan scoffed. "I am reminded of the time when Aubrey Ascalon, now Bishop of Carlisle, came to us for a favor."

"We seek your help, Wulfstan. We've come to ask for your men and arms to aid us in reclaiming Grasmere," Joanna said without provocation. George was ready to silence her, but when she turned and smiled, he knew it would do no good. He nodded assent. "I am now Countess of Grasmere. My home has been taken from me by King John's man, Eustace des Jumieges, on his behalf. We are being punished for marrying. Just as my husband came to vanquish your enemy, we ask you to come to Grasmere and aid in the destruction of ours."

"Bolder she is!" Wulfstan laughed, looking to Stephen Langley and Osprey. "If I say no, should I be afraid to sleep at night?"

"Yes," Joanna replied. "Just ask my husband; my anger is more dangerous than his sword Ascalon."

Laughter circulated again and even George smiled at Joanna's wit. When it was quiet again, Stephen Langley leaned forward.

"The Ascalons get themselves into trouble with women and marriage, don't they?" Stephen asked Osprey. "Earl George, weren't you promised to a lord's daughter at one time and like your father, forsook that vow?"

"My father's errors were worse than mine. I made a pledge to another woman, true, but I took Crusade against my will, and it was she who married another in my absence when the rumor went out that I was dead or executed for treason. I took this lady, here, as my wife out of choice and necessity," George spoke up.

"Necessity? How?" Wulfstan said.

"It was necessary to marry Joan ferch Rhodri, the daughter of Elen because I could not live without her."

"Chivalrous," Wulfstan sniffed. "Chivalry doesn't win wars."

"It is most certainly the cause of conflict as well you know, especially where it concerns your sister and your daughter," said George, who raised his brows, waiting for a response.

Wulfstan shifted uncomfortably in his chair and looked at Osprey, then Stephen, who both looked away. "Your point is noted. We need not speak of the past again."

"Agreed."

"And so, Earl George?"

"Will Eskeleth help us?" said George.

"I will call a council meeting and we will put your request to a vote—"

"No, Father."

Heads turned as Richildis entered the chamber. Joanna stared daggers into her as she glided in as if carried on the air, so light and careful were her steps. Courtiers crowding the doorway parted to let her through. Richildis curtseyed to a horrified, angry, George and bowed slightly to a stone-faced Joanna before pausing before her father's chair. She knelt and kissed his hand, then rose.

"What is your objection, Daughter?" Wulfstan asked.

"I have no objection save to wonder how many hours will you spend discussing what needs to be done, when George has already spelled it out for you?"

"What?" Joanna gasped.

"I don't need you to champion Grasmere, lady, or sorceress, or whatever you are," George demanded.

Richildis turned to face him. "No, but who here understands your predicament more than I?"

"What do you want?"

"Earl George, I want nothing but equanimity."

"You?"

"Has it not been said a thousand times a thousand that a man or woman who sees the errors and hurts they've inflicted is worthy of forgiveness if their actions to amend their lives is genuine?"

"*If you forgive the sins of any, they are forgiven them; if you withhold forgiveness from any, it is withheld.*" George quoted from scripture.

"And which will you do, Earl George?" Richildis offered a smile and then turned to the assembly. "Hear me, all of you. I speak truly when I say that my kinsmen owe a debt to Ascalon and should help this earl reclaim Grasmere. Upon my life."

"Your life? Lady, I watched you die, and yet here you stand." George said.

"That you did, my lord. The power of the ancient ways and folk is equal to that of the Christian God and His Son, Jesus of Nazareth, called the Christ."

"I know that the Lord our God is good. What I saw and lived was nothing good. The comparison of your dark craft to the light of Christ is offensive and I'll hear nothing in its defense!"

"But you prevailed against evil. It was your strength and your faith that resurrected Eskeleth and Arkengarthdale. Is that not good?"

"Perhaps it was more to do with luck."

"Nonsense! You know otherwise. What if I were to promise you that my help will be as good and loving as anything from the Son of God?"

George shook his head. "No. I will not use evil to take my lands back."

"She doesn't speak of evil," Stephen spoke up.

"What is more evil?" Richildis asked. "The ancient ways or the King of England? We all know what he does to his enemies. We know what he will do to your wife and children if you give in to his demands even if you swear to be brothers."

"I cannot."

Richildis smiled and shook her head. Her eyes flickered amber in that moment. She turned to Joanna with browed raised. "My lady? Do you also deny this offer?"

"Forgive me if I do not trust you. You've given me no reason."

"The Knights of Eskeleth are Grasmere's if you want them. We can also call upon the fyrds of Arkengarthdale. The dales of Yorkshire know George Ascalon."

"What are you doing?" Joanna demanded. "You wanted to destroy us once not long ago. Now of sudden you wish to champion us?"

"The King of England and his men are greater and more powerful enemies than any I fought here in Arkengarthdale and they are close to home.," George said. "I understand well what the lady suggests. Unfortunately, I don't know what I may give her in return. I don't doubt for a moment she'll want something."

"I am dying," Richildis said and her statement drew a collective gasp around the chamber. "My father is also dying. There are only so many years a life has, no matter the prayers and the magic. We are the last of our people. We will help you reclaim Grasmere if you pledge fealty to my father Wulfstan and become the heir to Arkengarthdale."

"Grasmere is my home. Skelwith Castle is my home," George answered.

"What use are they if you cannot sit in the great hall at Skelwith or walk the lanes of Grasmere and Little Langdale, of other villages and towns in your holding?" Richildis wanted to know.

"I am a Christian knight, sworn to uphold the Christ, to obey the Gospels,"

"My lord, how will you betray your God by taking what is yours?" Wulfstan asked.

"What is mine? I've told you what is mine."

"As the son of the Lady Fay, Eskeleth and Arkengarthdale are yours."

"How do I know there's not another bastard son somewhere?"

"There isn't. I swear to you there isn't."

"No," George said.

"If you are so troubled, do you not have absolution and penance?" Wulfstan asked.

"I cannot."

George bowed and left the chamber, Joanna on his heels.

"It is as before, George Ascalon," Wulfstan called. "You will consider what is asked and you will come to my terms."

✠

HE REMEMBERED THE way to the roof garden and went there immediately after leaving. Wulfstan's pleas were echoing in the chambers and corridors as he fled. By the time he reached the garden, there was nothing but the sounds of nature: the birdsong at twilight, the bleating of lambs as sheep were brought from the high pastures, the rustle of wind through trees. Orange and yellow lights started to color the windows of the Golden Tower as the sun slipped past the horizon and night came on. George walked to the row of apple trees and leaned against the trunk of the largest, arms folded, brow creased in thought and fear. A servant silently appeared to light the lamps in the garden and made an obeisance to George before starting his work. By the time he was done, Joanna arrived.

"Are you angry with me?" she asked, keeping her distance.

George sighed and shook his head. "At my father. Always at my father."

"Didn't you agree that we should not speak of the past again?"

"It's easier said. I wish Petronelle was here. She always has an answer or convinces me of doing what is right." George now glanced at Joanna and felt his face burn in shame when he saw the look of hurt on her face. "I'm sorry; I always know you will side with me and whatever I might plan, but Petra isn't afraid to challenge me. She knows my weaknesses as well as my strengths."

"As will I, in years to come," Joanna said softly, taking his hands. "We have help now, George. We have the means to take back Grasmere."

"What you're asking me to do is commit heresy and to renounce my faith, for that is what will happen if I accept that creature's offer."

"You may be shriven; you can do penance. You've done it before."

"You of all people, ask me to do this."

He started to turn away, but Joanna gently pulled him back and took his face in his hands. "Where is my George? Where is Petra's brother? Please don't leave angry! Consider what I am about to suggest. We summon your vassals and we make our stand. If all looks lost, only then do we commit the Eskeleth knights and banners."

"*She* put you up to it, didn't she?" George scoffed.

"No; it was your grandfather. He said the armies of Eskeleth are as Christian and as mortal as you and me. Richildis had nothing to do with it. My love, what do you say?"

George glanced at the lamps dancing in the breeze like so many fireflies and was reminded of a night in Constantinople when he was forced to make a decision that would destroy his men. Then it was torchlight on a street near the harbor and he met in secret to devise a plan. Each of the men agreed to what George had devised, and in the morning . . .

"George? What do you say? It is a good plan and it will work. Your grandfather wouldn't put us in peril."

He looked down and saw Joanna's pale, anxious face. Her eyes were wide and dark as they were fixed on his.

"If it comes to that," George finally responded. "But I haven't made up my mind. If it comes of desperation or as a last resort when battle is finally met."

Joanna sighed with relief and pressed close for an embrace and kiss.

CHAPTER 20

WHILE THE VASSALS of Ascalon and Eskeleth mustered at The Golden Tower and plans were made, The King of England at last arrived at Skelwith Castle and like his father Henry, the second of that name, took bad news very badly. His rage could be heard throughout the castle and, as one of Ascalon's guards wagered, as far as Lake Windemere. He'd taken his spies' reports at face value and wasted a journey west from Lincoln to deal with the renegade baron George, Earl of Grasmere, only to discover he was gone. Eight silver pieces wasted on men who were no doubt in Grasmere's pay! No one dared to mention that if King John hadn't taken his time in arriving, he would have captured his quarry. Stopping to hunt and hawk, to judge tournaments, was all very well if he wasn't being threatened. Complaining about the incompetence of his kingdom's barons and railing about bad fortune to every nobleman that entertained him along the way north wouldn't win allies in this petty war of ambition and precedence he was willing to wage.

"*Commands?*" Maud scoffed when Elinor came to the lodge with the news that the King of England would dine at Skelwith that night.

"He is the king, my lady."

"A fool. No. My retirement and the precedence of George's wife gives me leave to stay away. I will not dine with him."

"He commands you," Elinor insisted.

"Let him command all he likes; let him call down the sun, moon, and stars upon me. John Lackland forgets who my father Osprey is and what people I come from!" Maud said. "I will stay here. Do what you like, Elinor; you will anyway and much good it will do you."

"Perhaps if you had won the King's confidence twenty-two years ago George would not be Earl of Grasmere now and Aubrey would still be in your bed. Think about that."

"That shouldn't concern you. Now go away, you stupid cow."

"I'm offering to help you, Maud! To help Petronelle!"

"Did you not hear me, Girl? Leave!"

The one thing Maud enjoyed about her relationship with Elinor Lucy was watching Elinor's angry, dramatic, departures. They never failed to please or entertain. Satisfied that she was gone, Maud rose from her place by the fire to a writing table nearby and from under the open Bible took a document—a letter she'd started writing the night before. Maud sat down to review her work.

✠

ELINOR PRETENDED NOTHING was amiss and had seen that a banquet was prepared as if it was a typical royal visit. It was in hindsight a good plan, as the wine, food, and company calmed King John so that his disappointment might be forgotten for the time being.

The laughter, conversation, and music from the great hall could be heard in the North Tower, where Roger and Petronelle waited for the summons, and when it came, they were escorted down by four of the King's men. The hall was silent as they entered. Petronelle's eyes immediately went to Elinor seated at the high table beside the King and to her left, Eustace des Jumieges.

Both Roger and Petronelle gave their courtesy to the King, who only waited a moment to let them rise.

"Thank you for your hospitality, my lady of Myrce," John greeted. "Elinor Lucy has seen that we are well provided for."

No doubt, Petronelle thought, and then smiling at the King, "Grasmere's meat and ale are yours, Your Grace. We are honored to host you and your companions." Here Petronelle glared at Eustace and Elinor. "Undoubtedly you'll know that Ascalon has hosted several Kings. Harold, the second of his name, before he met his untimely death, your Father, and your brother. Worthy men, all of them."

Elinor suppressed a gasp upon hearing Petronelle's thinly-disguised insult.

"My lady," John said to Petronelle, his eyes raking her body up and down while he smiled disingenuously. "We greet you as the lady of this house and representative of the noble family of Ascalon. We are sorry your brother and his wife aren't here to greet us."

Petronelle didn't respond but looked down at the floor.

"Where are they?" John asked.

Again, Petronelle didn't respond. Her eyes slid to Roger who warned with a barely perceptible shake of the head.

"Lady Petronelle, where is your brother?" John demanded quietly and when Elinor made ready to speak, he held his hand up for silence. "Your loyalty to your brother does you credit, but loyalty to your king comes first."

"I do not know," Petronelle said as she dared to look at him.

"What?"

"I do not know, Your Grace."

"Speak louder. Are you saying George is not here?"

"My lord, you know he isn't here," Roger interrupted. "Why do you persist?"

"Silence!"

"Your grace, George Ascalon is not here," Roger continued.

"You try my nerves and patience, Mowbray! If you want to keep your lands and livings, and your head, you'll shut your mouth! Now. Lady Petronelle? Where is your brother?"

Petronelle locked glances with John and said nothing.

"Well, Mowbray, your turn. Do you know where your brother-in-law is?" John demanded, leaning forward. "Well? Why aren't you answering?"

"My lord, you told me to shut my mouth."

John jerked his chin at one of the guards and the man struck Roger with so much force that he nearly fell. The blood from his mouth spattered Petronelle's gown and face.

"Answer me, you bastard!"

"Would that I did know; I would be with him."

"And under the same warrant and death sentence! Lady Petronelle I'm sure you're smarter than your husband. George has been gone since early spring, am I correct?"

"Yes, Your Grace."

"And here autumn is upon us and in all this time he's never once sent a letter? I hear you are close as brother and sister. Wouldn't you want to know that he is well? That your sister-in-law, whom I hear is as dear to you as a blood kinswoman, is well? Is she not with child?"

"Yes."

"Surely she must be delivered of her brat by now."

Petronelle looked at him with daggers. "The earl's son and heir, not a bastard brat."

"Like him. Well, that would make you the true heir to Grasmere, wouldn't it? Perhaps you and I could parley about entitlements. I know I would enjoy that."

Now it was Elinor's turn to stare daggers at the King.

John leaned forward, studying Petronelle carefully, a frown creasing his brow. "Lady, were you not with child? I heard a rumor,"

"I lost the child,"

"What? Speak up,"

"I said, I lost the child. Ask your men about it. They would know the reason why."

"Ah. Well, George will be sorry to hear it, you two being so very close as I understand it."

"What do you mean by that?" Roger snapped.

"Silence! Lady Petronelle, where is your brother? Tell now or else," John demanded.

"King John, I truly do not know of his whereabouts. He has always been secretive," Petronelle said.

"She speaks truly," Elinor added.

John held up his hand for silence, asking Petronelle, "Did he go to France? Italy? Denmark?"

"I cannot say,"

"Spain, perhaps?"

"I . . . I heard something during the spring," Petronelle said.

"George was seen at the court of Prince Dafydd ap Cynan," Elinor volunteered and smiled at Petronelle in smug satisfaction.

"Wales? Ha!" The King laughed, slapping the table. "Did he think to find support there? I tell you, if I cannot win the loyalty of the Welsh princes, George of Grasmere hasn't got a chance in Hell!"

"His wife the lady Joanna," Petronelle started but King John pounded the table with his fist.

"Enough! It is because of that little whore your brother is out of favor. But I think he would return if he knew that his dear sister and two of his friends needed his help. I hear George is fond of champion those in the greatest need," John said.

"Your grace," Petronelle implored, trying to keep back tears.

"I know what. He's gone back to the Holy Land."

"My lord,"

"I know; you cannot say. You should reconsider your loyalty, Lady Petronelle. You haven't got a champion."

Now Petronelle raised her chin defiantly. "My parents. I do not see my mother at your table. Perhaps it is because she thinks you as loathsome as your great, great, grandsire, William the Bastard. My father is in Carlisle praying for your soul and hoping for your quick death!"

"We'll speak with the dowager countess at our leisure and persuade her to change her mind," John replied, smiling. "Your father isn't praying for anyone unless it's from Purgatory. He's dead."

"What?" she gasped, and looked to Roger.

"We had a disagreement," Eustace spoke up and chuckled, looking to Elinor. She had gone gray and was staring at Petronelle. "Do not trouble yourself about his soul. The canons at the cathedral made certain he was buried in hallowed ground.

"You killed him?" Petronelle screamed. "In his cathedral like Thomas Becket?"

"In his audience hall, if you want to know. But dead is dead."

"I was hoping to make him Archbishop of Canterbury, or even my chancellor. No hope for that now," John sighed as he reached for the cup before him and motioned for a servant to pour. He motioned to his guards and they seized Petronelle and

Roger. "We will keep you in comfortable confinement until such a time as we decide what to do with you, or when George returns, and we can bargain with him for your lives," John said, and he started to laugh. "Comfortable confinement! John turned to Elinor. "My lady, which of the chambers would suit the lady Petronelle and her husband?"

Elinor pondered a moment and avoided Petronelle's hateful gaze. "That would be . . . yes, that would be the Lady Tower. The rooms are small and serviceable. I'm told they're cold most of the time."

"Then the Lady Tower it is." John motioned to the guards. "Take them. One of the servants will show you where the Lady Tower is, or Lady Petronelle will be more than happy to oblige. That is all."

They were led away under the watchful but wary eyes of Elinor Lucy, who, once they were gone, moved from the high table and curtseyed before the surprised King and left the chamber. John thumped on the table the cup he'd been drinking from and waved Eustace over. "Go after here," he hissed. The hall was empty of guests and only the King and a servant were at the table when Elinor was escorted back. "Get out!" John shouted at Eustace and the servant. To Elinor he said more softly, "Lady, join me here." When she sat beside him, he planted a kiss on her brow and then one more firmly on her lips.

"I swear you enjoyed that," he murmured seductively. "Am I right?"

"If you say so, my lord," she replied.

"Elinor, what did you expect me to do? By doing nothing I would have been seen to be weak against the earl and his allies and would you have your king look weak and foolish?"

Elinor's face was stony and a sure indication that any chance of bedding her that night would be difficult. Still, he always managed to get a woman to agree with him, even if it took force or coercion.

"It is a dangerous thing you do, my lord," Elinor replied as she dipped a crust of bread in the sauce on John's trencher. "But it is yours to do."

"I have enough troubles without small fish like Ascalon to stir things up."

"Since his return, George is popular with his vassals and tenants. The people do love him. The Lady of Myrce is as well-loved. You will get an argument from the dowager countess, Maud of Eskeleth, since she considers Petronelle the rightful heiress to Grasmere."

"Sympathy for a witch?" John laughed. "The stories my father told of the beautiful Maud and how she seduced Aubrey, making him leave his rightfully betrothed pregnant and alone..."

"You have it the other way around, my lord. Aubrey seduced first the lady Fay, who was the sister of Wulfstan of Eskeleth, and then he seduced Maud. Keeping both Maud and Petronelle here would cause all sorts of problems for the crown. You may wish to consider moving them to Eustace's manor in the south. No one knows who they are in Wessex, nor would they care."

"An excellent thought, Lady Elinor!"

"I only wish to keep the peace, your grace."

"Grasmere is fortunate to have you as an ally."

"I would think it is the King of England."

John raised his cup to her and smiled, was glad she smiled back and leaned forward to take another chunk of bread from his trencher, allowing him a view.

"Would you help me then, Lady Elinor?" John asked, skimming his fingers over the tops of her breasts.

"What do you require?"

John pulled her close and whispered what it was that would be required of her. Elinor was only too happy to agree. When later that evening Elinor recounted the conversation to Maud, the dowager countess sighed and picked up her prayer beads, starting to thread them between her fingers, the cool stones smooth against her skin. Elinor rolled her eyes as she took wine, saying, "That isn't the answer to everything, you know,"

"It has sustained me in worse times."

The silence following was pocked by the faint click of the beads knocking together. Every now and then Maud would finger a bead, and if one looked close enough they would see a tiny indentation where George and Petronelle had teethed and left their marks. 'The Children's Beads,' Maud called them, and they brought her solace – even remembering the solemn little boy who was George.

". . . and so, we'll send Petronelle and Roger south under guard tomorrow. That squire will go with them," Elinor said. "And so will you."

"What?"

"You heard me."

"This is my home!"

"There's going to be a war, Maud," Elinor sighed. "It will be too dangerous for you and Petronelle."

"And what about you?"

"I'll look after myself."

Maud nodded and smiled, saying, "First you plot with that woman of Eskeleth and now you change your loyalties when you fail to get what you think is owed. Do you think the King will keep his promise? Even if you sleep in his bed, he'll conveniently forget whatever it is that he promised, and you'll be given to his followers, passed around from noble to knight to stable hand, just as little Joanna was."

Elinor struck her soundly across the face. Maud did not flinch, however, and turned her head so that the other cheek was available.

"You are the last person who should scold another about loyalties, my lady!" Elinor said. She waited, her hand red and stinging from the blow, eager to strike this imperious woman again. When Maud refused to speak and kept her gaze on Elinor, the younger woman took a step back and clenched her fists at her side.

"What do you wait for, Girl?" Maud asked quietly. "There are many sorts of ways to kill me. I'm sure you know of one or two. Look around the room, there are tools enough to help you finish me off."

Elinor's gaze fell on the metal poker for the fire. She was close enough to reach it and with one blow Maud's fragile little head would crack like a walnut. Reaching, she was stopped by Maud.

"But you won't," said Maud. Rising, she kicked the poker down and grabbed it and its clatter woke the old tabby sleeping by the chair. The cat yowled but not as much as Elinor did when Maud struck her on the back. "Get out!" Maud hissed.

"Bitch! Just who is the sorceress, I wonder? You've played the dutiful and pious wife all these years! And what did you earn? Betrayed so many times by your husband because you were taught that men stray from their wives' beds and it was the way of things! He bedded me, he raped George's little love from York and he tried to seduce Joanna! He's paid for it."

"He takes his penance in service to God and the church," Maud replied, trying to control her angry trembling. "I've forgiven him his sins."

"He'll need your prayers even more now that he's dead."

A moment passed and then Maud shrieked. "No!"

"Eustace killed him."

"Get out! You liar! You whore! No!" Maud continued to scream and attacked her. Elinor fended her off but was gone, swearing vengeance.

Maud's shrieks and wails continued for most of the evening. When she had worn herself out, one of the servants crept into the hall and asked if she was better. Maud frowned and looked at the girl as if she was moon-mad. Was she alright? Of course she wasn't! The family was paying for Aubrey's sins and Aubrey— oh Lord, he had paid the blood debt, what more had he done to deserve such an ending?

Maud slumped on to the bench by the fire and mouthed prayers. The beads slipped through her fingers and every time the 'children's bead' passed, she took a labored breath and fought tears.

What have I done, oh Lord my God, she prayed.

CHAPTER 21

GEORGE IGNORED THE servant's outstretched hand bearing a letter and waved him aside, listening to the horns.

Three long blasts, and then two after the count of two. The signal he'd been waiting for.

He hurried up and onto the wall walk of the donjon's great tower battlements to see the arrival of three *fyrds* flying banners he recognized, relieved that his summons was honored.

"Richard Day of Oxen Fell and Geoffrey Cole of Winster. And William Arnulf of Elter Water! You have powerful allies, George," Osprey said, joining him on the wall walk. "Will it be enough?"

"Against the might of England? Probably not, but a *parle* with the King wouldn't be amiss with these barons beside me. I have a fool's hope that the King will be wise and listen, but then I remember when did the King ever listen to anyone save himself or his latest favorite?" George asked as he started down to the bailey. Just as he reached the stairs, he turned to face Osprey, a frown etched into his brow. "I wonder if I should accept Wulfstan's offer and just stay here. John won't come this far north and fears the northern lords, truth be told. I could give Skelwith to Petronelle; it would be her right as Aubrey's legitimate child."

"You are Aubrey's heir. The Archbishop of York saw to it."

"The Archbishop of York is out of favor, Grandfather."

"The episcopal bull is locked away somewhere, isn't it?" Osprey ventured. George threw him a wary glance and continued down the stairs. When he reached the yard, all three cohorts were arrayed across the bailey.

"You are welcome, sirs," George greeted the lords.

Richard Day spoke first. "How could we ignore your request? If the King picks a fight with the honorable house of Ascalon, he fights with us."

"As to honorable, I am still in doubt," George answered, smiling. "Even so, your presence will be rewarded, you may be certain of that."

"Last week some of the King's men were on my lands asking about you. They set several freeholds afire and threatened the people of Elter Water," William said.

"The sooner we leave, the better," said George. "Tomorrow then?"

The lords assented, and the day and night were spent preparing for the march to Grasmere. Joanna watched anxiously as men prepared for war. From her place in the great hall, she had a view of the comings and goings, the councils around a great table with maps spread and cups of wine holding down the curled ends. Occasionally, there would be an outburst or disagreement, then discussion and all would be quiet again as they came to an agreement.

Joanna looked up from her reading when Richildis approached with her ladies-in-waiting and was anxious, wondering what she could want. Being in her company was a little worse than Elinor Lucy's. Both women knew how they affected Joanna and surely enjoyed her discomfort. Margaret moved her stool closer to Joanna as if she could read her lady's thoughts and patted her shoulder.

Richildis offered a radiant smile and gestured to a bench opposite, to which Joanna responded with a nod of her chin.

"George will redeem Ascalon," Richildis said after they'd sat in silence for a quarter hour during which Joanna read the same passage at least twice and Richildis studied Joanna as a cat watched its prey.

"I hope that is the case, Lady," Joanna replied, not bothering to look up. "The king has the whole of England to call upon."

"But will they answer his call?"

Joanna slammed the book shut. "John will take lands and money, imprison wives and children, or worse, if they do not."

"We will pray that George succeeds. His victory will instill a hope for justice in England."

"Do you pray, Lady?" Joanna asked, now looking up, amused.

"Why do you think otherwise?"

"I didn't say,"

"You did."

"But you embrace the old ways."

"I did. I did embrace the old ways. Like Saul of Tarsus, let us say I had an awakening. The God of

Christ is as powerful as the magic of the old ways, for who was it that gave us the power but God?"

Joanna didn't know how to respond to that. Finally, "You are changed, Lady, since we first met. Have you changed your mind about George?"

"I've done penance."

"I was going to say . . . you know what I am thinking."

"It's not by magic but by intuition and history, Lady Joanna. Shall we say that I have learned from my mistakes and then say no more?"

"Your apology is accepted."

Richildis frowned and glanced at the younger woman, noticing a smile as she picked up a book and leafed through it, pausing to run a finger down the exquisitely-wrought lettering that was illuminated by bright colors and gold-leaf embellished angels and creatures.

"What do you read?" Richildis now asked.

"The Holy Gospels. The Gospel according to Luke."

"Ah."

"Do you know the Gospels?"

"The stories of Jesus of Nazareth?"

"The same. Do you know them?"

"Perhaps you will share them with me."

"We'll see."

They were silent again while Joanna read, and Margaret plied a needle, and Richildis studied her hands and the jewelry on her wrists, fingered the pendant around her neck. Finally, Richildis sighed and rose. Margaret and Joanna stood, waiting.

"Lady Joanna, you are my equal here. Be at ease." Richildis paused, smiling, and then, "I do have a request."

"Yes?" Joanna asked warily.

"I wish to accompany you to Grasmere."

"That is not my decision to make, Lady."

Richildis studied her and then smiled. "It is. Please speak to him tonight. It will be to your benefit if I come."

I remember the last time you came with us, Joanna thought.

"You have nothing to worry about, Joanna. George is yours body and soul. One can see that when you are together," Richildis said as she turned to leave. "You will speak with him?"

"If I remember," Joanna said under her breath.

✠

"I HAVE SOMETHING about which I must speak," Joanna said after George moved his bishop perilously close to her queen.

"Pay attention to the game; I'll have you in check soon enough."

"I remember the last game I played here," Joanna said brightly. "Adam Middleton demanded a kiss."

"I heard about that. Well? Make your move,"

"It's about Adam, and Petra and Roger, when I've said my peace."

George sighed and leaned back on his chair, then stretched and hooked his foot and ankle around hers. Across the chamber the children were being readied for bed and the sounds of laughter and infant prattle competed with the thunderstorm that broke over Eskeleth an hour before.

"What is it?" George finally asked.

"Richildis wants to accompany us back to Skelwith."

"No."

"My love listen to me,"

"Why do you ask, Joanna?"

"I ask because if we fail Adam, Petra and Roger will be in more danger than they are now. The king will see to their executions."

"Who's to say he wouldn't put them to death once he learned we were marching on Skelwith?" George said.

"I beg of you, my love,"

"She is no guarantee of our safety or success."

"George, she said something to me today while you were in war council. She said that the Christian God gave her the power she uses, and His power is greater."

"She will say whatever she will to win your affection. I say no. She stays here."

"Do I ask much of you? Am I a whining and irritable crab?"

"Tonight, yes."

"Do I not please you in so many ways?"

George's frown receded, and he offered a smile while drawing her close for a kiss. "In very many, many, ways, my heart," he now purred, getting close. "But do not ask this of me."

She sighed. "Yes, my lord."

Joanna now made her queen's move and said, "Checkmate," before rising and going to wish the children a good night. She went to bed when Wulfstan called for another war council and George made his excuses to leave. She was half-asleep when George finally came in hours later.

"Joanna?"

She shivered as the covers shifted but didn't move.

"We've never been angry before sleeping. Let's resolve our quarrel."

". . . not angry, but disappointed," Joanna said, her voice muffled by the blankets.

"That woman is evil. You know this. Do you expect her to change suddenly?"

"If it could happen to Saint Paul on the road to Damascus so many years ago, why not again? Why not now?"

"Oh, maybe that she is cleverer by half. What if I did invite her? What if things happened as they did before—with strange creatures, and phantoms, traps, plots? What would we do?"

Joanna sat up and quickly hitched the covers around her. She didn't miss that George smiled and noticed how she worked to cover herself. "We keep her under guard," Joanna said. "We bring a priest with us. The moment she tries something—stop staring! I mean business!"

"And so do I, as soon as we resolve our differences."

"I won't bargain with you, George. Not like that. Surely you understand how desperate we've become that we are here arguing about a woman who could help us,"

"A mortal enemy!"

"A woman who has found God and wants to make amends. Why must we argue when the answer is before us. We could be at home with Leof and Nara. You once said you'd be happy being a gentleman farmer. Has that dream faded? God's life, you are like every nobleman—"

George grabbed her by the shoulders and nearly shook her, saving fervently, "I am not like them! I would die in battle first before ever becoming like them! Those are hurtful words!"

"Spoken like a nobleman."

"When will you understand?"

"When I am home at Skelwith and when I am not afraid for our children!"

George swore under his breath and was gone.

CHAPTER 22

"IT SEEMS THAT all men ever do is march and march and then march to war. And then they march back. Those that survive."

Joanna glanced over to look at Margaret who ended her comment with a sigh. The woman was pushing a needle through linen, though what it would become, Joanna couldn't guess. Hopefully not a shroud. She said nothing to Margaret and resumed her vigil on nothing. The children held no interest that morning, nor did her Gospel book. George had been absent from her bed for three nights. She was ready to blame Wulfstan, for he'd held a nightly war council to discuss the reclaiming of Skelwith and Grasmere, but where did George go after the meetings ended? She studied the pretty serving girls and wondered. None of them seemed to avoid her nor smirk when in her company, nor carry that air of superiority some women took on when their lover was the lord of the manor and carrying on a dalliance right under the lady's nose. In fact, they barely looked in George's direction when he did come to the bower. Those moments were fleeting and business-like in nature. He'd poke his nose into the cradles and ask about the children, speak with Anna about their care and then turn to stare at her for the longest time as if he wanted to say something but couldn't. He'd leave without so much as a word for Joanna.

I will not back down, Joanna thought as she sat in the chapel one morning a week into the *impasse*. No one else came for Mass and so the service went quickly with prayers, a reading from scripture, the consecrated elements from the reserve held in the ambry. The priest seemed to be in a hurry anyway, and for once Joanna was glad to be done with the morning obligation.

"I remember the first time I entered this chapel," Joanna spoke up as she watched the priest clear the table of vessels. "We came to honor the pledge of Aubrey Ascalon. It was the night before the first trial. No one was here; the altar and vessels were covered in dust. But there was a flower that came to life of a sudden just when we left. We'd knelt at the rails here and prayed. And when we were gone, the flower had taken a new life of its own."

The priest nodded politely as he went about his work, though his movements belied his discomfort of having the young woman in his chapel.

"The Archangel Michael and the lion of Saint Mark, if I remember correctly," the priest said.

"Yes! That was the first trial. You were there?"

"We all were, Lady. We will be with you again, should you so desire," he answered.

Joanna opened the scrip at her girdle and took out a coin, placing it on the altar. "For the soul of my husband," she said.

"But, my lady, he hasn't died – has he?"

"Keep it. For when the time comes."

"May that not be for years."

Joanna nodded her thanks and slipped out of the chapel and walked through Eskeleth to the coppice where the battles had taken place. The pavilion was gone and where it once stood a chantry was being erected. The workers paid no notice to her when she sat by the spring under the shade of one of the apple trees. The sun was warm and soothing, and she closed her eyes, listening to nature, something that would have been impossible before. The workers' conversations drifted over, sometimes with laughter and Joanna smiled. That, too, would have been impossible before.

Over the cacophony that lulled her into napping, she picked up the sound of slow, careful, footsteps that stopped near her. Joanna kept her eyes closed, waiting. If it was George, he knew what he'd have to say.

"My lady?"

Osprey was standing over her. Joanna shielded her eyes from the sun and smiled up at him, saying, "Grandfather?"

"You are called for in the chapel." He held out a hand to aid and Joanna rose gracefully, looking up at him as she dusted offer her clothes, waiting.

"Have they left for Skelwith?" she wanted to know.

"Soon. Please, come with me."

"He knows he's wrong," she sighed.

"Please,"

"As you say."

Joanna dutifully followed Osprey, who winked at her and beckoned her hurry. The unfamiliar knights loitering near the chapel gate of the bailey came to attention when Joanna arrived and saluted her, then bowed their heads. Osprey pushed open the door for her and stood to one side.

George was standing with the noisome priest near the altar.

"Father; George," Joanna greeted. She nodded at the priest and offered a perfunctory curtsey to George, who kissed her lightly upon the lips when she stood.

"Am I to hear your confession?" she tartly wanted to know.

"The priest here has heard it, but I need your absolution."

"What have you done?"

George led the way to the baptismal font standing in a darkened corner at the back of the chapel. When George, Joanna and the priest were ranged around the font, an acolyte came from the sacristy with Richildis.

"If George Ascalon and you will not accept my help for who and what I was, perhaps he will accept that help from a Christian?" Richildis said. Removing her veil and mantle, Richildis stood in a white linen shift and waited as the priest offered prayers over the water being poured into the font. Finally, he took Richildis by the hand and led her to the font, saying: "The Lord vouchsafe to receive you into his holy household, and to keep and govern you always in the same, that you may have everlasting life."

"Amen," the others said together.

"Do you forsake the devil and all his works?" the priest now asked Richildis.

It was a moment before her response and Joanna felt the lump of disappointment in her throat, thinking that Richildis had played her for a fool.

"I forsake them," Richildis said.

"Do you forsake the vain pomp and glory of the world, with all the covetous desires of the same?"

"I forsake them."

"Do you forsake the carnal desires of the flesh, so that thou wilt not follow, nor be led by them?"

"I forsake them."

"Do you believe in God the Father almighty, Maker of heaven and earth?"

Again, there was a telling moment, but Richildis said at last, "I believe."

More prayers were offered and finally, the priest asked, "What do you desire?"

"Baptism."

"Will you be baptized?"

"I will."

Three times the priest poured water over Richildis' face and head saying, "Richildis, I baptize you in the name of the Father, and of the Son, and of the Holy Ghost."

During this sacrament, George watched Joanna's face and drew her close, putting an arm around her waist and kissing her hair. "I confess that I should never have doubted your advice," he whispered. "And that I love you!"

Joanna nodded, blushing, and avoided the priest's glance in their direction as he recited the communion prayers; the serene, smug, look Richildis wore as she was robed in fine garments and a fine crucifix wrought in enamel and gold was suspended from her neck.

"Well then," Joanna said after offering Richildis the kiss of peace. "So now we are sisters in Christ."

"And I shall do what a sister would, Joanna ferch Rhodri. I will protect you and see that no harm comes to you or children. Upon my life." The light of the candles reflected in Richildis' pale eyes and seemed to spark and turn amber and then red.

"And I, you. And since we are sisters, we will keep no secrets. Upon my life."

They exchanged another embrace and both turned to smile at George.

"You will tell me now why you are so eager to help us," George said.

"What is this?" Richildis said with a smirk. "Did you not agree with the countess to accept my help?"

"Yes. But you bowed so easily. It makes me suspicious. Conversion comes with a clear conscience and a pure heart."

"When we are at Skelwith, my lord. Then I will spill out my heart to you."

"Why not now? Let us know so that we may prepare ourselves for any eventuality."

"What do you mean?"

"Treachery is something I'm familiar with, Lady,"

"My lord, and you Richildis, enough," Osprey demanded.

"George, I beg you," Joanna whispered.

"My lords, ladies, will you pray with me?" the priest interrupted.

Joanna was the first to kneel at the altar, followed by George and Osprey, who were on either side of her, with Richildis a safe distance away. George turned in the middle of the *Nunc Dimittis* to adjust the cloak tugging at his throat and saw Richildis smiling serenely. Or what he thought was a serene smile. Cats always did look innocent before they pounced on their prey.

✠

IT WAS DECIDED that evening they would all leave the next day, with George and his army leading and the women and children behind them. The morning broke with a thunderstorm and when Joanna and the women came down to the yard a canopied wagon waited for them. The oiled sail cloth was painted and decorated with fanciful flowers and vines traced with gold. The servants were placing sliding shutters along the side panels to keep out the worst of the rain and cold. Once done, Stephen Langley beckoned Joanna to board first.

"Where will the Lady Richildis ride?" Joanna asked as she settled in, reaching for Nara. "This wagon is only large enough for my ladies and the children."

"Another wagon behind you, Lady."

"Ah," Joanna said, staring out the back at the ostentatious carriage drawing up behind them. She remembered it from their journey before. Richildis left the cover of the porch and swept into the carriage, her furs and hems untouched by the rain. A young girl closed the doors and stepped back, standing in the downpour, waiting.

"Why does she wait?" Joanna wondered aloud. "More to the fact, why will not Richildis allow her to ride? There's room enough." When no one responded, she knocked on the shutter and said, "Tell the girl she may ride with us."

Furs and woolen wraps were spread for the women and children, each tucked in and ready for the journey south. The carter was shouting commands to start when a panel slid back, and the young girl boarded. She took a place beside Margaret and Anna and brushed the hood off her face, wiping water from her eyes. Smiling at Joanna, she nodded in greeting. "Am I to thank you, Lady?" the girl said to her.

"And you are-?" Margaret demanded.

"Miriyam, goodwife."

"A Jewess! Why do you come along?"

"I am a companion to the Lady Richildis."

"Then ride in her carriage, Miriyam."

"Peace, Margaret; she is welcome," Joanna scolded. "Miriyam, would you like to hold Nara? She watches you with interest."

"May I please, Lady Joanna?" the girl asked with delight. Once the baby was in her arms, Nara grabbed hold of a stray lock of ebony hair dangling from Miriyam's cap and tried her best to bring it to her mouth. "Ah no, sweeting! That won't taste as good as your nurse's milk or a thumb!" Nara now began to pat the girl's face and squeal happily.

"See how's she taken to you, Miriyam!" Joanna said. "Nara is the most particular of my babes. I am blessed to have you on this journey home."

"Yes, you do have a way with children," Margaret complimented.

"I had a baby sister, but she was killed by knights," Miriyam said softly.

"May God assoil her," Joanna whispered and crossed herself, as did the other women following suit. "Your parents?"

"With my sister. I escaped. I was brought from York by Sir Aubrey when he found me hiding in the buttery. I suppose you know him since he is the Earl's father?"

Joanna looked at the shocked faces of her women and said, "Yes. This is how you came to Eskeleth to serve the lady Richildis?"

"Yes, my lady."

"He is a good man," Anna spoke up.

"Yes," the others echoed.

They rode in silence, listening to the wheels creak and groan as the caravan left Eskeleth, the ringing of mail coats and harness of their guard riding alongside, the patter of rain and the rumbling of thunder, the crack of lightning. Miriyam smiled down at Nara, who had fallen asleep and looked drowsy herself, caught the studied glance of Joanna and perked up.

"Miriyam, you look familiar," Joanna said.

"Mayhap we've seen one another in Grasmere, Lady."

"You've been to Grasmere?"

"Oh yes, when my mistress sought help from Sir Aubrey and received it from his son, Earl George. It was Earl George who saved my life."

"I know him to be very kind, my husband."

"I was ill, and he was the only person who saw my sickness for what it was - a plague. He gave me his room in the tavern hostelry and I stayed there for weeks while I mended and returned to Eskeleth whole."

"He never said a word," Joanna whispered under her breath. Then louder, "I know the Lady Richildis. Does she treat you well?"

"As can be expected. She's stopped pricking my finger for blood and for that I give thanks to God."

The women gasped and shuddered. Margaret and Anna shifted as if to move away from her, but Joanna reached out to take her hand. "There is something so familiar, Miriyam."

"I come from Carlisle, my lady. If you have been there, perhaps we've seen one another?"

"That could be so, but I doubt it," said Joanna, smiling. They rode in silence for a time and watching how Miriyam now played with Leof and made him laugh, she said, "I wonder if you would come to live with me at Skelwith. Anna would be glad of the help."

"Oh yes, Lady!" Anna said happily. "They're becoming a handful, these two!"

"It is for the Lady Richildis to decide," Miriyam answered and lowered her eyes.

"I will speak with her and then we'll see."

Joanna now leaned back into the cushions and shifted the furs, her eyes lighting on Miriyam every now and then and thinking that she'd seen the girl somewhere before.

CHAPTER 23

THE ARMY ARRIVED in Keld at dawn several weeks later and after a hastily called council, it was decided that the forces would be divided to take Skelwith unaware and after a day's rest they'd march to what they hoped would be certain victory. By nightfall, the camp was up and cookfires lit the field where they stayed. Beyond that was the forest of Keld and the abbey where George had vanquished Richildis upon his return home so many months ago. The battle was on his mind as he dined with Joanna in the command tent. Outside, the conversation of soldiers, music and laughter punctuated the stillness of the night.

"Tomorrow seemed such a long way off when we left Eskeleth," Joanna sighed, pushing away from the table. "It seems we have been gone from home for years."

"Soon, love," George responded. Joanna suddenly laughed. "What does my lady find so amusing?" George said softly, leaning down to kiss her neck.

"God's me, I just remembered the renegade crusaders that fell upon us! Stephen Langley ran screaming and Richildis sat in her carriage like a queen. Petronelle and I got us to safety but not before giving battle to the fools."

"That was when we met Adam Middleton of Gawthorp," George added.

"Sweet Adam," Joanna said, crossing herself. "I hope he is safe and whole."

"We'll rescue them."

George rose and took Joanna in his arms and they stood in a silent embrace, clinging to one another as they had so many times before during their journey. Joanna stayed with him that night and in the morning said goodbye. Joanna, the women, and children would go on by a different route to Grasmere and take sanctuary in the abbey. George's men had stripped the carriage of decoration so that it looked like a yeoman's transport. The women were dressed in simple homespun and the babies swaddled into straw baskets. As they rode off, Joanna turned back and raised a hand, blew a kiss, at George who stood at the roadside watching.

"It will be good to be home," Margaret said after a while.

"Is Skelwith a large castle?" Miriyam questioned.

"Not as large as Windsor, or Westminster," Margaret answered, "But large enough for the earls of Grasmere."

"You've been to Windsor and Westminster?" Joanna asked her, smiling. "You never said."

"I was in the service of our late queen Eleanor as a girl. I never saw the castles until she was released from prison after old Henry's death. I was only there a short while. And then I returned home to Grasmere to serve Countess Maud – just before Earl George returned home."

"I've never been to London," Joanna replied. "I had hoped to go there. My father went to London to seek support from the Queen and her followers when King John reneged on his promise to the Cymric princes. George talked me out of going."

"I think, Lady, that George could talk the Holy Mother down from Heaven," Margaret jested and after a few feigned exclamations of shock, the women all laughed.

"I wonder if he hasn't already?" Miriyam giggled, which brought on more laughter.

"Miriyam!" Joanna said in a teasing voice; "I thought by the look of you that you were a sober and good lady!"

"I am those things when I want to be," the girl said. The conversation then turned to the foul weather chasing them across the northwest of England and then sighs and murmurs of how good it would be home again.

"Do you think he's still there, Lady?" Miriyam asked Joanna. "Your father? Perhaps you may seek him out in London when Earl George has taken Grasmere."

"I'm certain he's dead, or he lives in exile."

"You shouldn't give up hope," the girl said, smiling. "I will pray for you if you'd like."

The smile was familiar and warm, Joanna thought. She took the girl's hand and found that it was the same. *Where have I seen her before*, she wondered?

"You are a blessing, Miriyam," Margaret said. "I should never have thought ill of you, and for my harsh words I beg your forgiveness."

"There is nothing you need to ask for. I am here for a reason." Miriyam then leaned over and gave Margaret a kiss on the brow, meeting Joanna's smile with her own.

The journey was slow and hampered by the weather, but uneventful. As soon as they were clear of the forest, the guard George assigned to the women surrounded the carriage as it navigated the muddy roads and paths westward. Joanna peered out from behind the shutter every now and then and saw the stalwart knights in a block formation, with eyes forward and jaws sternly set. As soon as the mere and town of Grasmere were within sight, the knights broke away, leaving only a solitary guard as the carriage lumbered through the town gates to arrive on a sodden but busy market day.

"We're home!" Anna exclaimed, and she was stopped from leaning out a window by Joanna.

"We mustn't draw attention to ourselves," Joanna warned. "The King probably has enough spies in town as a dog has fleas."

They had little to worry about; the arrival of yet another carriage or wagon into Grasmere caught no one's notice as townspeople transacted custom in the market square and tried to get home before the weather got any worse, though that seemed impossible from the continuing showers and the threads of lightning going from dark cloud to dark cloud. They went straight to the abbey and the carriage pulled up at the gate. The knight dismounted and rang the bell, spoke with the porter and then gestured to the carriage driver. Two raps on the door. It was safe to alight.

Margaret, Anna with the children and Miriyam disembarked, then Joanna. The knight offered his hand for assistance.

"My thanks, sir," Joanna said.

"My lady, you are more than welcome," George replied and winked at her from under his hood.

"George!" Joanna gasped. "Why aren't you with the army?"

"Did you think I'd let you go all that way without me?" George said. "Hurry now. Before anyone takes notice."

Brother Prior was waiting outside the abbot's lodgings for them. He nodded at George and then unlocked the door, escorting the women and children into the well-appointed and spacious house. Abbot Warennes had lived like a prince, it seemed, Joanna thought as she glanced around.

"Where is the lady Richildis?" she demanded suddenly.

The other women glanced about as they too realized she was missing.

"Who, my lady?" the Prior asked.

"She has gone on to Skelwith. It was a condition of her accompanying us," George explained. "The lady has offered to assist with strategy." His glance at Joanna told her the rest of the story.

"My lady, if you would?" the Prior beckoned, leading her into the audience chamber on the first floor. They were in another richly-decorated room that befit a royal prince with finely-carved chairs and benches and tapestries hung along the walls. The Prior led Joanna to the wall near the hearth and pushed a stone, revealing a gap in the masonry. Between the stones was a wooden panel. Pushing the panel aside, the Prior showed Joanna a staircase. "This leads into the church and into the sanctuary if any of the King's men come, or the King himself. We grant you the right of sanctuary."

"God bless you for your kindness and charity," Joanna answered.

"Joanna, I must leave now," George said quietly.

She turned to George. "I will take care of our little ones; you must promise to take care of yourself."

They stood silently, remembering every detail, even the smallest, of the other, from the way George's hair fell into his eyes, the blondish-red stubble of beard, the startling blue color of his eyes, to the heart-shaped birthmark on Joanna's neck, the symmetry of her face and the flawless perfection of her skin.

He kissed each of the children and then Joanna. "You'll know when we arrive. I'll come for you when it's done."

"I love you, George."

"My heart, I love you! And our son and daughter. God grant that the angels and saints protect you!"

"And you,"

He took his leave after passing the Prior a purse that looked heavy with coin. The door rattled shut and Joanna looked around again and saw the women already at work to make it a home for them. When she realized she could be in the house for days, even weeks, or that she would never leave, Joanna began to weep.

CHAPTER 24

JOHN LACKLAND, AS the King of England was called, was unaware of the army approaching the castle and decided that Skelwith was such a charming place with good forests for the hunt and hawking that he sent messages to London that he would stay until the errant Earl George came home or died, whichever came first. Besides, the company of Elinor Lucy, the Widow Longleate, was very pleasant. Very pleasant indeed!

The only disappointment (other than not catching George Ascalon unaware and taking him in chains to London) was the weather. The heavy rain that seemed to pour over Cumbria made it impossible to hunt or hawk. The weather was always contrary to his expectations. Too bad he couldn't have sway over it like he had in the Kingdom. John had to settle for entertaining himself with the ladies of the court and when he grew bored with them, a book from the library that traveled with him. Settled in a colorless, monastic chamber with his copy of Herodotus and wine, John put his feet up on a fur-lined cloak and warmed himself before the fire one of the servants was thoughtful enough to kindle. The patter of rain would have been soothing to most people, with its drone blocking out domestic noise, but John found it annoying until he couldn't read another word and slammed the book shut. He shouted for a servant. A boy appeared and fell to his knees before the King.

"Send for the Lady Elinor," John ordered.

The boy was gone and within moments Elinor entered the room, dressed elegantly and scented with an intoxicating perfume. John smiled. Excellent! She knew the game being played.

"Lady Longleate," John greeted.

"You sent for me, Your Grace?"

"I was wondering if, when this rain stops, you'd ride with me. Cumbria looks beautiful and I suppose there is good hunting and hawking in these parts? I can understand why George Ascalon treasures it."

"It may be days before the rain stops, Your Grace."

"More's the pity! What do you do for entertainment on days like this?"

Elinor knelt before the King and leaned forward. "What do you think?"

Gods! John loved a woman who didn't need coercion or money and was inventive. Lying in her arms spent and sweating hours later, the King wondered where she had learned her love play. Elinor lay with her back to him, the sheet barely covering her. He could see the violent rise and fall of her body as she caught her breath and started to relax, and there too, was the provocative curve of her hips and the top of her buttocks where they met the small of her back, peeking out from under the linen sheet. Most women would work quickly to cover themselves but not Elinor. Surely, she wanted more. John reached out when a lock of her hair slid off her shoulder and fell against her naked back. It gave him an excuse to touch her. Why was it that all desirable women felt like the finest silk and the slightest touch roused him?

"All's right with you, Lady?" John queried. His tone was less altruistic and more selfish. He wanted to hear that he'd pleased her.

"I am content," Elinor said, rolling like a cat so that she was on top of him. "I have the King as my lover and he has satisfied me like no other."

"I am pleased, Lady," John said, reaching up to kiss her. He moaned when she bit his lip and positioned her hips against him. "*You* please me right well! But it comes with a price, I suppose?"

"How can you say that, my lord!" Elinor pulled away, her eyes wide and the hair spilling over her shoulders so that it obscured her full, round, breasts, but gave an enticing view of her nipples. John swept aside the locks of hair and started to play with her, hoping it would make her more agreeable and less prone to conversation. John hated talkative women, especially in bed.

Elinor gently removed his fingers. "What can you mean? Isn't being the King's lover enough for a woman?" she asked.

"For some, it always comes with a demand of some kind, Elinor," John replied. Nothing angered him more than a woman who didn't make herself available to him, especially when the afternoon had been spent so marvelously as this one. He was the king! No lady would dare.

"Well, I've never heard that from a woman!" John scoffed.

"Those women aren't me. And haven't I been adventurous and inventive, my lord?"

He didn't like the conversation and he didn't want to use force to get her to pleasure him, but he was impatient and if he had to do some things, well, it would make his pleasure all the more. Still, John didn't like the way she was looking at him.

"Tell me what it is you want, Elinor." The sigh was more of a whine and he was pouting.

"Give me Skelwith and make me countess."

"To do that I would have to make you Ascalon's wife."

"No. If he's dead and his wife whore and brats are dead, you can give it to whomsoever you wish."

"What about his sister and her husband?"

"Dead."

"You would have me commit murder to give you a love token?"

"You were going to have them killed anyway. What difference does it make?"

It really didn't.

The bargain was still in negotiation later that afternoon when they were enjoying a supper by the fire. Dusk was looming, and the torches were lit. John's minstrel was singing a *virelai* from his French county of Mortain and Elinor was feeding John sweetmeats and kissing away the honey left on his lips. He was contented and happy, and sure the night would be as memorable as the afternoon, if not more exciting. He had some things in mind for which he was almost certain Elinor would be game. She wouldn't be put off as so many other women had . . .

The bedchamber door flew open and three of John's soldiers entered with the smell of rain and the damp on them, dripping as they halted near the hearth so that steam rose up and water sizzled as it slid from their cloaks and helmets.

"What?" John asked.

"There's an army approaching Skelwith," said one of the men.

"Do we know who they are?" John demanded.

"No one recognizes the colors," said one.

"But do we know who they are?" John growled. "The colors don't matter, you whoreson!"

"This could be the army you requested from the Bishop of Eden, your grace."

"Who is dead," muttered one knight to the others.

"And whose death we may thank for this trouble," Elinor said as Eustace breathlessly rushed in with his personal guard.

"Do we know who it is?" Eustace demanded.

"One might guess," Elinor said.

"What would yours be?" Eustace asked.

"Silence!" shouted John. He spun and turned on Eustace. "Well? I can blame this on you,"

"Your grace! I was only doing as bid!"

"Do we have enough men to defend?"

"Enough,"

"What do you cipher is enough?"

"Let's see. You Grace, if you would?"

Eustace stepped aside to let John lead the way out. With the soldiers following, John went up to the wall walk on Ravenglass Tower and searched the horizon. The rain was falling in sheets now and he was soaked through to the skin by the time he could make out the gray shapes of two columns of men marching behind a dozen or more knights.

"Hah! We have more than this army," Eustace laughed over a clap of thunder.

True, John's army at Skelwith was three times the size of the battalion marching towards them. John was never the warrior his legendary brother Richard had been, but he was a soldier nonetheless and gauged the situation as he continued to be pelted by the rain and wind. Finally, he nodded to himself and motioned to his soldiers.

"This won't be a battle," John scoffed as he went back down. Even so, he ordered the castle garrison to stand ready. Soon men were on the walls, crouched behind arrow slits and war machines rolled into place in the outer bailey. The household was ordered to prepare vats of oil and offal to be employed when and if the enemy reached the inner bailey. It wasn't likely.

Elinor was pacing the chamber when John returned with a squire. "Is it George?" she wondered, not looking at him and took another turn around the room.

"Why would you assume that, Lady?" John asked. He snapped his fingers at the squire. "To work, boy."

"Who else would be interested? This is his castle and birthright."

"Eustace wants it to expand his lands in exchange for fealty."

"You'd have a better chance at Ascalon's fealty. Still, it is George's, is it not?"

"Are you privy to information kept from me for some reason?" asked John while he stood for arming.

"Of course not, my lord. I was merely thinking that this would be one way of giving me what I want."

He grabbed her arm as she passed and pulled her to him. "And then you'll give me what I want, won't you, Elinor?" John said, kissing her violently.

"Haven't I already, Your Grace?"

She slid out of his arms and slinked across the room and out the door, rolling her hips to best advantage, making sure the King could enjoy the view.

CHAPTER 25

THE STORM RAGED on, soaking the monks of Saint Cuthbert's Abbey in the very little time it took to walk from the dormitory to the church for Vespers. Already waiting for the service and seated in a corner were Joanna and the children with her women. Brother Prior acknowledged the little party with a sidelong glance as he gave reverence to the presence of God at the altar. When he turned to intone the opening collect he noticed a good many people of Grasmere standing in the back. This was unusual for a mid-week service and he surmised it had to be due to the rumor of an army approaching. Grasmere had nothing to fear from it; the town should have been more concerned about the King taking up residence at Skelwith with an army. Still, Brother Prior didn't complain when the wooden bowl he used to collect alms at the end of a service was heavier than when the service began.

Joanna was queuing in line to give an offering and to greet the Prior when a soldier appeared at her side as if from candle and incense smoke and pressed a square of parchment in her hand saying, "All is well, Lady Countess." With that, he slipped away, mailed boots ringing on the flagstones.

Stepping to one side, Joanna gave Nara to Margaret and turned from the others to read the note. Just as she assumed, it was from George:

> *Stay where you are. You are under the protection of the Archbishop of York. This has been seen to. Know I am safe and anxious to return to you, my love. I will come when Skelwith is ours once more. Ever your servant, husband, and lover, George.*

Joanna returned to the queue, taking the fretful Nara from Margaret. "Now there, Daughter! Shall we be brave for your papa? Let's see a smile. There my girl!"

"Good news, I hope?" Margaret hinted, nodding towards the parchment still in Joanna's hand.

"Comfortable words. Come, let's go back to the Abbot's Lodging."

The rain had turned from downpour to mist and the women stepped carefully on the slick cobbles to make their way back to the house. Joanna paused for a moment when she saw the three soldiers standing outside the door.

"Do you know them?" Rhosyn asked. There was fear in her voice. The women now drew rank around Joanna and waited for her orders, if any.

"I don't know," Joanna admitted. She began walking toward the knights. "Peace be with you," she called to them.

"Lady Countess," one of them greeted and all three bent the knee as she finally approached. "We are here at the request of the Earl of Grasmere."

She glanced at each in turn, noting how similar but how different they appeared. "I thought I knew all of my husband's captains and knights,"

"Here is surety of our charge to see that no harm comes to you or the children, or your ladies."

The first knight took from his scrip the Cross of Ascalon, and then gave her his sword, which was tied with a white linen band upon which a red cross was embroidered. The second took a lily from his tabard and gave it to her, with the lantern he'd been holding. The third presented the banner of Ascalon, folded into a neat square and tied with ribbons in Ascalon's colors upon which he set a small alabaster jar.

"Where did you get this?" Joanna asked, picking up the cross. She'd hidden it in the bower months ago.

"One who loves you well led me to it."

"Ah, I do understand. Then you are welcome. Come inside for a cup of brandywine. You must be chilled to your bones."

"No lady," the third knight replied. "Our orders are to protect you and let no one enter."

"Then we shall bring refreshment to you—ah no, Sirs! I will have no argument. My lord will tell you that it does no good to quarrel with me!"

Once inside the house, Joanna started the brandywine herself and gathered apples, cheese, and bread in an oilcloth sack. The meal was brought to the knights.

"God give you peace and keep you," Joanna said as she offered the food and drink. Strangely, they did not respond, but stood with backs to the house, and staring out onto the night landscape. She could have sworn they turned to stone statues but for the rise and fall of their chests. Setting the sack and jug down, she quietly retreated, staring at them as she slowly closed the door.

The rain returned late into the night and woke Joanna. The plink-plink of drops falling against the glazed windows woke her. Try as she might, she struggled to find a comfortable place in the strange bed and tossed and turned. Leof was awake and cooing in his basket, something giving him entertainment. Joanna padded across the room and took the children from their baskets, bringing them to bed with her and tucked them into the plump pillows and fine blankets and coverlets. Nara drifted off to sleep with a thumb in her mouth but Leof was happy to kick and wriggle, occasionally laughing. Finally, he settled down when Joanna sang a lullaby and then she too fell asleep but was stirred awake when she felt a breeze. Someone must have left a window open. In this weather? She'd have to speak with one of the servants about that. The rain would surely soak the floor. Peering out from under the blankets, Joanna stifled a scream when she saw the three men standing at the foot of the bed.

"Who are you?" she demanded.

They didn't speak, nor move.

"What do you want?"

Slowly a light like a lamp or a candle started to surround each of them, and then soft, warm flames encircled their heads. They were singing, or rather, chanting, and it was soothing. It was a dream, surely.

Joanna fell back to sleep and didn't wake until the bells rang for *Matins.*

Brother Prior greeted her when she entered the church.

"Peace be with you, Brother," Joanna greeted after receiving his blessing. "I wonder if you would be kind enough to give the knights guarding the Abbot's Lodging something to break their fast?" she asked.

"Knights?" he asked.

"Yes, my husband sent three knights to guard the lodging."

"Surely it wasn't a dream?" the Abbot asked kindly.

"Why would you suggest that?" Joanna responded, frowning. "The weather last night was foul, and they are no doubt soaked to the skin for standing guard and watching over us, indeed the whole of the abbey."

"My lady,"

"Brother Prior, it is charity I ask, nothing more," Joanna said, turning to go.

"There were no soldiers in the close, and certainly not at the Abbot's house, my lady."

Returning to the Lodge, Joanna stopped and felt her chest go cold from fear. Outside the door was the sack of food and jug of brandywine, untouched.

✠

THE ASCALON BANNER and cross were on the table, the lily sitting in a vase. Beside them were the sword, lantern and alabaster jar. Joanna saw them immediately when she arrived at the Abbot's Lodging. The women looked up, smiling in greeting and Nara started to fret when she saw her mother, sucking noisily on her lips and leaning towards her out of Miriyam's arms.

"Where did those come from?" Joanna wanted to know, gesturing.

"I thought you brought them, my lady," Margaret said. "Anna, did you?"

"I don't know what they are, to say the truth," Anna replied as she shifted Leof to the other breast. "Perhaps Miriyam knows?"

"Not I," said Miriyam, shrugging.

"There were three knights yesterday evening when we came back from the church," Joanna now said as she approached the table. Hesitantly, she touched the banner and felt the familiar, smooth cloth and the silkiness of the embroidered design and lettering. The cross was cold and smooth to the touch as a gemstone would be. The lily was fragrant and fresh as if newly plucked from a garden. "They brought them as gifts from George."

"No one was outside when I rose this morning," Margaret said. "Perhaps they went back to the Ascalon camp."

"Perhaps," Joanna murmured doubtfully. During the day, however, she watched every man that entered and left the abbey or watched the people in the high street of Grasmere, looking for the knights. She sank into a fitful sleep that night worrying that they may have been King John's spies come to take her hostage and her dreams were of the day not so long ago, when she was stolen from the convent at Towyn, bound and gagged to be carried off on horseback with the bells of the convent sounding the alarm as it burned to the ground. The landscape she rode through was dark and frightening with hellish creatures following her alongside the road. She remembered them from Grasmere and Eskeleth: the decaying knight in the market square at Grasmere, the specters in Kentmere Wood, the Goliath, the Archangel and finally, the Dragon. Each charged her horse and made it rear up, but Joanna managed to hold on despite the ropes and chains binding her. One by one they were vanquished, all but the Archangel, who took flight and became a cloud on a moonless night, following her as the king's men took her hostage to a place and time she wanted to forget. The ringing of the abbey bell changed, as she traveled and now sounded like a trumpet.

The plaintive note roused Joanna into a state of panic, waking as the trumpet blast kept sounding, carried through the air by the wind and above the constant thrum of rain pouring over the abbey and Grasmere. She sat up, listening. There it was again. The wail of a call to arms.

"My lady! What is it?" Rhosyn asked as Joanna appeared past the bed curtains, reaching for her clothes.

"A battle is ready to be met."

"God help us! Are the King and Eustace going to attack?"

"If I'm not mistaken, it is Earl George marching on Skelwith."

They went to one of the upstairs windows and glanced out. The townspeople were clamoring at the gates of the abbey while the brothers stood at the bar pressing to keep the portal closed. "This is wrong! There is enough room in the abbey close for all of Grasmere. Find the Prior and bring him to me," Joanna instructed.

"But if it is Earl George's army that comes, why would everyone seek sanctuary?"

"It is not George they fear, but the army that will meet them," Joanna said as they hurried downstairs. "It's no surprise what they would do to Grasmere and her people. That army will sack and pillage rather than fight honorably."

"I go, mistress, and in good time,"

"Not that way," Joanna said and took Rhosyn by the hand, leading to the audience chamber, where she pushed the stone by the hearth and opened the door into the secret passage. "This way! Make sure no one sees you enter the church by this passage."

"Aye, my lady!" Rhosyn said. The door to the secret passage rattled and banged shut.

The trumpets were louder now as the army marched on Skelwith. Margaret and Miriyam came in with the children. "Take them into the church! It isn't safe here," Joanna snapped. "Go now!" Again, the secret passage was opened.

"What about you, my lady?" Margaret asked.

"I can look after myself," Joanna said. After the women and children disappeared into the stairwell at which end was a faint glow of candlelight, Joanna wondered just how she would do it with the frightened crowd outside and an army ready to attack.

CHAPTER 26

I AM DYING; I am falling to hell. This is my harrowing.

The brightness of the light was blinding, yet mesmerizing. George couldn't look away from the shades of saffron, of poppy red, of molten gold that continually washed over him in waves.

This is the water of death, not of life.

He was calm as the waves continued, ebbing and flowing around him, impervious to heat that would have killed him, had he been alive.

I am alive. This is a new life.

The heat was nothing like he'd experienced before. Excruciating yet soothing. Around him were the shadows of trees and familiar buildings. There was 'The Hiding Place,' the sanctuary of his childhood, the great tree with its branches reaching to God like Job crying out in supplication and in anger. The town of Grasmere, once a village and now a thriving town thanks to Will Longleate's administration. The trade in wool and lumber had been good for Ascalon. Here was also the abbey, his grandsire's foundation and the stepping stone for his father, now Bishop of Carlisle. Their shadows drifted by like boats on the mere.

The Abbey!

Joanna and our children were safe. They must be safe.

Another shadow. This time the shape of a warhorse. No, not a warhorse but a lizard with an immense neck and tail. It moved slowly and then lumbered, then it was swift, coming at him.

No, I've been through this.

George reached for his shield and sword and marveled that they hadn't melted in the heat. In fact, they were as cool to the touch as if on an autumn morning. With these in hand, he adjusted his footing and stood ready for the dragon to attack again, for surely this must be what it is.

But why?

He'd been promised no more contests.

The sound. Oh God, that horrible, frightening sound! It was so loud that it made everything vibrate and ground to shake like the advance of war horses. Worse, could it be the beast from his final contest in the pavilion at Eskeleth? The dark shape materializing as the smoke cleared and the flames died confirmed it could be: the long neck, the spiked tail, the body as large as a knarr and wide, the wings like sails. Just as George gripped his sword and placed himself at an angle with steady footing to meet the certain approach of the dragon, the combination of fire and sound was like an explosion and he was thrown into the air. When he landed and opened his eyes, he was on his back and dirt and blood were raining down upon him and other knights outside the walls of Skelwith.

"My lord! My lord of Grasmere!"

Richard Day of Oxen Fell was crouched over him, patting arms and legs to make sure George was whole. Moments later, Geoffrey Cole of Winster slid to a halt on his knees in the smoldering grass, pitching his sword to the ground as he helped Richard drag George to his feet.

"Was it ours, or theirs?" George gasped, looking about.

"Theirs, my lord," Geoffrey answered.

"Jesu Maria, you'd think with the tales of his ability at warfare, the King could at least hit a target!" George said.

"We should praise God he didn't."

"He's done some damage – but not much."

There was a chunk of the outer bailey wall missing as if something had taken a bite out of the stone. Bodies were draped over it and piled beneath it. George thought of the beast he'd fought at Eskeleth. It was a mouth swallowing its kill.

When the smoke cleared George gave thanks that the great keep and Ravenglass Tower were still whole. He'd instructed his army to leave them alone. and thankfully John had not set fire to either. The great stone walls of the bailey would be easier to repair once the castle was his again.

"Look out!" someone shouted and looking up the men saw another missile of pitch and fire aiming for them. George threw himself behind a tuft of hillock and raised his shield. Again, the fire, heat and thunderous sound together with the screams of the wounded and dying.

"Fall back! Retreat! Fall back!" George screamed at his men while fire and pitch continued to find their marks on knights and footmen alike. The survivors escaped to the high ground above the castle where beyond The Hiding Place was a wood. Well into the protection of the trees, George gave the command to halt and threw himself against an oak, weary and discouraged.

"How many are we?" he asked Geoffrey.

"Still too early to book the dead and make an accounting of who is still with us; the men are still coming."

Nodding, George said, "Once we're all gathered, we'll go to Rowantree Crag."

"It was a good strategy," Geoffrey said.

"No it wasn't," said George. He closed his eyes and prayed for sleep to take him. Three days wasted. It would have been better if they'd held the army at Keld.

As George drifted into slumber he found himself riding up this very hill to The Hiding Place, the rallying point for the Ascalon armies.

Dismounting, George surveyed the familiar landscape and looked south to where the forest called Little Skelwith obscured his borderlands. If worse came to worse, the army could retreat here. Small wood that it was, it was as dangerous as the great Andresweald in the southeast of England. Men were known to go into Little Skelwith and not return, either lost or killed by wild boars or wolves. Knowing this, George still gave the order for the greater part of the army to camp and hold there.

He settled against the tree as he had done on so many occasions before in his life, both good and bad times. On this day George removed the dagger from his belt and started to dig in the soft dirt at the foot of the tree until he found a leather pouch and pulled it up. Wet and stinking of loam and earth, George wiped it carefully to reveal the Ascalon family's seal and his initials - GA - then opened it and let its contents roll into his palm.

The large medal of the Archangel Michael was unchanged after nearly fifteen years buried in this hiding place.

And now, nearly fifteen years later, George understood why he hid it and why his Father had gone away so secretively to return a changed man and left all to George, including this struggle.

He pulled the cord out from under his brigadine and first kissed the cross hanging from it, and then slipped the medal behind it. George was tucking them back under the layers of protective clothing and his shirt to have them lie against his skin when Osprey rode up, shortly followed by Richildis and her escort. George got to his feet and assumed a defensive stance as they ranged around the tree.

"My lord," Richildis greeted, and then looked around, a frown etched on her brow. But then, George thought, when didn't she frown? Those lines would be drawn on her white skin for all eternity.

"The armies have gathered in Little Skelwith," George said without preamble, gesturing with his dagger to the wood. "Our left flank waits over here, and the right, here. The vanguard is just beyond the first line of trees."

Richildis dismounted and walked towards the wood and back, the metal plates and mail of her surcote catching the sun and throwing sparks onto the ground, the hem dragging in the mud and making ruts like rows in a farmer's field. "And what will you do, My Lord, if John's army has engines and throws missiles and fire into that wood?"

"It would never happen," George scoffed. "The range is too far."

"Isn't that what you told your men at Constantinople?"

"That is the past, my lady."

"So it is. But it is something to think about. You wouldn't want the past to repeat itself, would you?"

"I can do without the lack of confidence, Richildis," said George, sheathing the dagger and crossing his arms defensively.

"But you do have the same misgiving."

He did, but he wouldn't admit it to her, especially her.

"We will follow our plans discussed yesternight," George answered. "You will keep your promise?"

"As I have said I will," she answered.

But she was right, George remembered now as he looked around at his tired men gathering around the oak where he sat. John's mangonels and trebuchets didn't have the range to reach the wood but give them six hours to a day and the King's men could wheel them into place.

"Your battle plan, George?" Richildis asked as she came from the wood. She wore that smug look of superiority and knew that every man was looking at her, desiring her, even begrimed with blood and gore like the rest of the soldiers.

"I'm thinking," George said.

"Aren't we fortunate?" she answered.

CHAPTER 27

MAYBE IT WAS *a good plan*, George thought as he sat alone on the steps of the preaching cross outside the church of Saint Freyswide in the village of Rowan below the crag. To admit to himself that he was never a battle commander was an easy thing; to admit the same to his men and Richildis was definitely not.

How much easier it had been to battle a dragon.

George sighed loudly and disturbed a crow foraging in the grass. It cawed angrily and then followed George as he went into the church, hopping delicately as it continued to voice its disapproval.

An afternoon service was underway, and George stood at the back and in the shadows not wishing to identify himself in case one of John's spies or supporters happened to be in the nave. A young priest of no more than twenty-five stood at the lectern reading the lesson in a powerful, energetic voice as if telling a story and not offering the daily lesson:

> . . . *die autem septimo diluculo consurgentes circumierunt urbem sicut dispositum erat septies cumque septimo circuitu clangerent bucinis sacerdotes dixit Iosue ad omnem Israhel vociferamini tradidit enim vobis Dominus civitatem.*

"And at the seventh time, when the priests had blown the trumpets, Joshua said to the people, 'Shout! For the Lord has given you the city,'" George whispered to himself. An idea came to him just then and George laughed aloud, making heads turn and the priest to stop in his recitation of the lesson. He apologized and dropped a coin in the poor box on his way out, the coin hitting metal and ringing loudly.

As loudly as trumpets.

On his way back to camp, George slowed to give the horse its head, to let it pick its way carefully past the fall and on the path to the top of the crag where the Ascalon army was encamped. Twice he stopped so that the horse could enjoy the tender green shoots that grew at the foot of the rocks and he could stretch his legs. Being that high up gave him an opportunity to look south to the red sandstone buildings of Skelwith Castle, his sights on the main tower - the donjon - where undoubtedly Petronelle, Roger, and Adam were being held.

"It's a better plan."

George hadn't heard the footsteps, but the voice startled him. Leaping to his feet, he reached for his sword and was face to face with a cloaked man. By the cut of the cloak and hood, his boots and what he could see of the jupon underneath, he was someone of means. George pushed the tip of the sword none-too-gently into the thick woolen cloak and jupon.

"And how would you know?" George asked. "The king's man, are you?"

"That would depend on the king, my lord. I think we have the same king in mind. Put away your sword. I mean you no harm."

"That's as you say."

"Would this remove your doubt?"

The man reached inside his cloak and pulling his closed fist out, extended it to George, opening the hand to reveal what looked like an iridescent flower petal the length of his thumb, an oval of ivory, pale blue, mauve and pink. Upon closer inspection, it was one of the magical dragon scales.

"March only three times around Skelwith's walls. That will lead you to victory. Have no fear, George Ascalon. You have my protection," the man said and touched George's breast where the cross and medal hung. The touch was warm. When George looked up from where his hand lay, the man's face was transfigured with an incredible light the colors of the scale.

The clouds that had been forming took the shape of wings behind the man. A hand still on George's breast, he dissolved into the afternoon sunlight.

"Call the captains, and find the Lady Richildis," George told a sentry when he arrived back at camp. When all were assembled in his tent, George wasted no time in giving orders. Only Richildis and Osprey seemed unaffected by what was said.

"What will it profit us to expose the army like this?" Geoffrey Cole asked.

"We will have the castle back."

Richildis took the cup of wine in George's hand when everyone else left. She drank and offered the cup back and when he didn't take it but stared silently at her, she placed it on the map of Grasmere and Skelwith.

"And where do you want me tomorrow at dawn?" she asked.

"With me in the vanguard," he answered, moving away from her. He busied himself with clearing off things from his cot and summoning servants and ignored Richildis as she took a tour of the space, picking up books, weapons, and clothing in turn. "We make an early start tomorrow, Richildis. You should be in your own tent and abed."

"In good time. Will you come to the church and pray with me? We will ask for the Christ's protection and help tomorrow."

"I've said my prayers. I prayed that you will keep your promise. Good night, Lady. We'll see each other in the morning."

They exchanged hateful, cold, looks before she curtseyed and left the tent. The whisper of her hems on the earth as she walked away sounded like the footsteps of a dragon. George poured more wine into his cup and drank, and then poured again and drank.

✠

THE TRUMPETS BLASTED a long note and then a shorter one, silent for thirty paces and a long note, then a short note.

The plan of Skelwith Castle was like others in England: a motte and bailey layout. Skelwith had two baileys with the central tower and keep protected by two walls. This was the inner ward. The larger ward stood before it in the shape of the number eight. Here stood the stables and barracks with the armory and several domestic buildings. The wall walk facing the outer ward was taller than the others and was pocked with arrow slits, lancets, and platforms. It was on this wall walk John and his captains had assembled to look for the approaching army when they first heard the trumpets. Below them, the Ascalon army, rather than range itself in battle formation was continuing to march. March around the entire perimeter of Skelwith rather than attack. Their action bewildered the captains, who looked to the King.

"What are those whoresons doing?" John squealed.

For the second time the Ascalon army marched Skelwith's perimeter and for the second time their shields went up to protect them from the oil and arrows showered down from the walls and towers.

"*Fire!*" John screamed.

Cauldrons, some overflowing with oil and some with pitch, were moved into place and men tipped them over. Almost immediately the shields were up, each of them glowing strangely as if reflecting moonlight. But it was the middle of the day and the skies had been overcast since the siege began that morning.

Oil and pitch failed to hit their marks and the trumpets blast a long note and then another, silent for thirty paces and a long note and another.

"It's witchcraft, that's what it is!" John hissed. "By God, I'll burn every last one of them to a man when we've captured them!"

Below, George rode at the head of the vanguard with Richildis and a herald, the silver falcon of Ascalon leading. "Shields up!" George ordered as he saw another round of oil and pitch falling from the walls. Richildis raised a hand and whispered "*Crist amddiffyn ni a Ascalon.* Christ protect us and Ascalon - *Christus defendat et Ascalone et Gaza.*" The shields glowed silver again, the light rippling back through the ranks as the army marched. Trumpets calling drowned out the sound of the oil and pitch hitting the ground.

Once more, George thought as he passed the northern gate, which marked the starting point of the march. He looked back and caught the attention of Geoffrey and Richard, who both nodded and shouted orders to their men. Swords were drawn, pikes and seaxes positioned for combat. Archers knocked arrows. Knights bent low in the saddle with shields and weapons at the ready.

Upon reaching the drawbridge at the southern perimeter, the ground started to quake, and the walls shook. Richildis raised a hand and repeated her prayer "*Crist amddiffyn ni a Ascalon.* Christ protect us and Ascalon - *Christus defendat et Ascalone et Gaza! Christus defendat et Ascalone et Gaza!*" The quaking was stronger, and stones started to fall from the great bailey walls. Again she prayed but in a shout and it seemed as if the entire ground would break apart. The army was unaffected by this. King John's men, however, fell from the walls.

"Now! *Now!*" George screamed.

Men came from the back of the ranks with ladders and shoved them up against the walls. Once in place, they were scaled just as quickly. George was at the fore and easily climbed, for there was no one to block their advance. As soon as he reached the top and leaped over the crenellations, he led his men down into the greater bailey where John's men waited.

Automatically, George raised his sword and brought it down on the shoulder of a man coming at him, then shoved the blade into his stomach, knowing where to inflict wounds between the metal plates in the brigadine. He fell and died. George stepped over him to greet the next man, who carried an ax. He ducked as the ax swung over his scalp, and jabbed at the man's knees. The fellow was quick, though, and cantered like a pony to one side, swinging again. George felt the drops of blood as they fell from the blade, the fragments of muscle and bone from someone else's body. He reached up under the mail shirt and dug into the groin area. Moments later another opponent was dead.

The Ascalon army was surging over the walls now, following George as he murdered his way towards the gatehouse of the inner bailey where they came headlong into royal soldiers trying to hold Ascalon back as they tried to assemble and place small siege engines, such as hand-held ballistae and onagers. A small catapult stood at the wall of the bailey leading into the castle. Several of the foot soldiers were rolling barrels and jars of pitch and rush behind the engineers, stacking them haphazardly as men tried to load the catapult while soldiers fought and died around them.

"Stop them!" George yelled. He waved forward his archers coming in now and held his shield over his head as the arrows whistled above him. It was safer to stay on the ground now, and George started to crawl towards the catapult. He felt something like the rush of wind, then smelled sulfur, felt the heat and heard the deadly whistle of a projectile. It exploded against the great bailey outer curtain and blew to pieces the Ascalon soldiers trying to scale the wall. George guessed it was a miscalculation and not a planned attack. In order to attack the army outside the castle, the catapult would have to be moved out further into the yard, perhaps to the very edge and at the walls, in order to strike and hit its mark. The royal army would have to work quickly and soon, for outside the Ascalon engineers were rolling catapults into place at the marks set the night before by George and his captains.

George managed to crawl up to the catapult and with the help of his men knocked out the supports and attacked as the machine crashed to the ground, its ordinance exploding and lighting men, both Ascalon and royal, afire. This distraction gave George the opportunity to reach the greater gatehouse over the moat.

Outside the Ascalon army was loading its siege engines to send jars of Greek Fire over the walls. Caught in the crossfire, George pushed desperately towards the gatehouse. Around him, missiles were exploding and killing men and beasts. A royal archer ran from the stairwell and knocked an arrow, taking aim. He was dead before the weapon was loosed, for George hurled a mace and caught him in the chest. "Stay with me!" George shouted at his guard trying to push their way into the gatehouse around the royal soldiers now snaking down the stairs from the crenellations. "Watch out! Move away!" one of his men screamed. Boiling pitch was falling from the murder holes above them and the thick, sticky, substance was lit by flame-tipped arrows. George rolled into a corner by the entrance, cutting men down as they approached. He screamed at his men to hold their ground and keep moving forward, but the men who had formed a guard around him were gone and George was alone.

He was in the gatehouse and could see the stairs to the donjon where he was certain his sister, Roger, and Adam were being held, and the scores of soldiers coming at him. At least he'd gotten this far.

George screamed the order to retreat.

CHAPTER 28

FIGHTING HIS WAY out of the wards, dodging missiles and arrows, blocking deadly blows of swords and axes, and back to his camp, was so much easier than his arrival; the king's engineers had blown holes into the walls and it was only a matter of climbing over bodies and rubble to escape. George stood at the gap and waved his men out while he cut down the enemy as they approached. He ducked behind the shields of dead men and slabs of masonry whenever an arrow came at him, or someone fired a bolt from a crossbow. It was only when he saw the ball of fire as large as the sun flying at him that George decided it was time to go. Once again he was hurled through the air by an explosion.

I am dying; I am falling into hell. This is my harrowing.

The brightness of the light was blinding, yet mesmerizing. George couldn't look away from the shades of saffron, of poppy red, of molten gold that continually washed over him in waves.

This is death, not life.

He was calm as the waves continued, ebbing and flowing around him, impervious to heat that would have killed him, had he been alive.

I am alive. I have a new life with my countess and children. I will live to spite everyone.

When he landed, he was on his back and dirt and blood were raining down upon him and the remainder of the Ascalon army outside Skelwith's walls.

"My lord! My lord of Grasmere!"

Richard Day of Oxen Fell was crouched over him, patting arms and legs to make sure George was whole. Moments later, Geoffrey Cole of Winster slid to a halt on his knees in the smoldering grass, pitching his sword to the ground as he helped Richard drag George to his feet.

"That was a foolhardy venture," George groused, looking around for his sword and shield. "Just because it worked for Joshua. . ."

Richard Day said nothing has he handed over George's sword and shield, not remarking that they still glowed a moon-colored silvery blue so many hours after they'd marched around the castle as if they were the walls of Jericho. He'd heard the men grumbling about witchcraft and the ways of the ancient people, how the beautiful lady Richildis was nothing more than a sorceress who should be burned at the stake. That didn't bother him as much as having to bring it to George's attention – as if he already didn't know.

They were seated in George's tent in the camp they'd pitched in Skelwith Wood. George was having his battle wounds looked to by a physic while he read the list of Ascalon dead.

"I know what is said about the lady," George remarked. He turned his face so that the gash above his left eye could be washed with wine. "She used to practice what some would call witchcraft, but it was nothing more than magic like that of the people in England before Saint Augustine brought Christianity to our shores."

"How do you explain the earthquakes today? Why weren't we injured?" Day asked.

"'*Crist amddiffyn ni a Ascalon.* Christ protect us and Ascalon - *Christus defendat et Ascalone et Gaza.*' It was a prayer to Jesus Christ. Surely you know that faith can move mountains. Why not walls?"

"My lord, I am afraid that if you give the lady Richildis such freedom, the men will desert or worse. They will go to the King."

George winced from the stinging over his eye as more wine was applied, and offered a lopsided smile from the uninjured side of his face, saying, "I will take what you've said to heart, Richard. I would not imperil the souls of so many good men. Now. Let me tell you what I want to do next."

✠

KING JOHN AND his captains laughed and clinked goblets together to celebrate the retreat of George Ascalon's army. The royal banners and coat of arms decorated Skelwith's great hall and a feast was spread. Sitting quietly at the high table were Petronelle, Roger, and the dowager countess, Maud. Elinor sat apart from them at John's right, enjoying her role as *chatelaine*.

"Countess Petronelle!" John called out. "Lady! I am in the mood to do something clever," he said, looking around at his guests. "What say you to being invested Countess of Grasmere tomorrow morning?"

Elinor's head shot up at hearing this and would have spoken but for John's staying hand.

"Your grace honors me and my family," Petronelle said. "But for all I know, my brother is still alive and still the earl."

"Your brother is an attainted traitor. Be glad I do not extend the courtesy to you, Petronelle."

"I am right glad."

"Good! Good. Tomorrow then."

"May I ask a boon of you, King John?" Petronelle asked now.

"While I am still in the mood."

"Release our friend Adam Middleton of Gawthorp. He is no threat to the Crown and upon my life, I will be surety against his loyalty to you," Petronelle said.

Cups were held in mid-air and choice bits of roasted fowl and beef waited to reach lips as people waited for John's response. The king took a drink from his goblet and thumped the heavy gold cup down on the cloth.

"Done, Lady. I would not refuse such a beautiful woman a small request. What about you, Earl Roger Mowbray? You've been unusually silent."

"You told me to keep quiet," Roger answered and signed for a pot boy to bring more wine.

"I like a man who learns quickly. Too bad young earl George hasn't."

Roger nodded and drank again, glaring at Petronelle.

"What is it?" she whispered to him when the musicians struck a tune and the King and Elinor rose to lead off the dance.

"I don't think Adam considers his life worth that of your brother's."

"You're wrong. George will understand my actions."

"After you've been invested, do you think it ends there?" Roger asked, reaching for the cup Petronelle was pulling away from him. "He'll keep making bargains that won't be kept."

"I will repudiate this bargain as soon as I know George is alive and walks into this hall!" Petronelle declared.

"As you say," Roger answered with a shrug.

John kept his word to Petronelle.

The following day, no sooner had the service of Matins ended than he called his barons to Skelwith's chapel and summoned the priest to prepare for Petronelle's investiture. The King looked about at the barons and courtiers with a smug smile, pleased with himself. Elinor wasn't smiling.

"Your grace!" Elinor called to him as he was heading to his apartments to change into something more regal for the ceremony. John turned and smiled, kissing Elinor's hand and then her lips.

"What does my lady require, as if I didn't know already?"

"You lied to me," Elinor said quietly but with menace.

"So?"

"Grasmere was to be mine!"

"Elinor, you know how it is; alliances change and I need security here in the north."

"I would give you that."

"You turned on Ascalon. How do I know you wouldn't turn on your king?" John said. He raked her up and down with a leer. "Change your dress, love. You'll want to look your best."

She was left standing in the passageway of the great tower.

Enough was enough. She'd been betrayed by George. Left to suffer a barren marriage with Will, and used by the King. Elinor followed John out the passageway.

"My king!" she shouted but he didn't stop. He paused only for a second to look over his shoulder and smirk but kept going. "Why is it so difficult to keep your word? You won't be safe. She'll betray you! She has the northern witch's blood in her veins and will use the dark magic against you!"

John now stopped and twisted around, hands outspread in supplication or frustration.

"What would you have me do?"

"Something remarkable. Keep your word. How many times did you promise me the earldom? How many?"

"Ellie, Ellie! What's whispered in bed is just that. Whispers."

Elinor ripped the brooch from John's cloak and the sharp point grazed his left cheek below his eye when she lunged at him. Shrieking in pain, he pulled the edge of his cape to the wound and ordered the guards to take her. Their hands were on Elinor and wrenching her away when the stairwell shook as if by an earthquake, the sound of missiles pounding the tower walls and then a blast of trumpets drowned out the King's orders and screams for vengeance. Elinor wrestled free and escaped with her life as a fire pot flew through the window, scattering mortar, debris, flesh, and blood.

CHAPTER 29

"IT'S YOUR HOME! Your own castle!" Richard Day shouted at George over the din of troops shouting and rushing at the crumbling walls.

"It can be repaired," George shouted back. "Reload!"

Oil pots and sacks of debris and rotting animal flesh were loaded into the catapult ropes and once set, George gave the order. He shielded his eyes from the sun and watched as the missiles sailed unobstructed overhead and slammed into Skelwith's walls. More cheers went up as they hit their marks.

"Stand ready!" one of the captains screamed, pointing with sword toward the advance of royal soldiers streaming from the greater ward and down the hill towards the army drawing up ranks with what few soldiers it had left. The royals managed to skirt around the spikes and caltrops thrown up and down to slow their advance. The knights charging forward, their number formidable, were thrown from their horses as the animals rode over the caltrops and screamed in pain, slaughtered by pikes and swords. Knights pulled from the saddle were taken and murdered quickly, some taken for ransom when their identities were revealed.

George signaled his vanguard to attack and began what he hoped would be the last stand for either the king or himself.

Christ behind me, Christ before me, Christ above me, Christ below me, he whispered the old prayer. One of the royals recognized him and shouted to his companions in arms and they rushed, cutting men and horses down as they tried to reach George. His ransom or death would be the making of the champion in this match. Before they could reach him, however, the Ascalon war engines were at work again and launched missiles and bolts.

The smoke and fire threw up ash and made it impossible to see or gauge direction. George dropped to a knee as if wounded when a soldier ran towards him and just as he was within striking distance, George ran him through. He rolled out of the way as the man fell. Again he feigned injury and caught another soldier on his sword as if spearing trout in a stream. Behind him, the Ascalon army managed to hold its lines and move forward while fending off attacks.

Christ behind me, Christ before me, Christ above me, Christ below me, he prayed again.

"Why would Christ favor Ascalon over Plantagenet?" said a knight at George's right and blocking would have been a murderous blow.

"I've never thought about that, to say the truth," George gasped as he prepared for another attack and assault. "Why? Why do you ask?"

"Surely these royal soldiers fighting at the orders of the king are as worthy of Christ's love as you and me."

George recognized the voice and went cold, turning to look at the man. The face was handsome and bathed in light so blinding white that it was both painful and frightening to look upon him. The warmth George felt was coming from him and not the fires smoldering in spots on the approach to the drawbridge over the dry moat.

"Prove victorious, George Ascalon of Grasmere, and you will have favor. Surely there is no one on earth so righteous, even you, as to do good without ever sinning!"

"I know you, Michael!"

"You have the right of it. How will you lead your army to victory?" the archangel asked. "How will you show yourself better than the man who calls himself a king?"

George blocked the sword thrust of a knight that aimed at Michael. With a circular maneuver, he unarmed the man and tripped him up, pinning the knight to the ground with a mailed boot. He pressed the tip of his sword none-too-gently between the knight's pauldrons and breastplate, touching the rings of his mail shirt. A good quick lunge and the sword would bring death.

"By showing mercy," George said. To the knight he said, "Go back to the king, sir, and tell him that

Ascalon will not yield until he acknowledges my wife as heiress to Merioneth and I as earl of Grasmere and heir to Ascalon. If he does not yield, I am not afraid to bring this castle to the ground. Go now. Do as I bid."

The knight flailed about like a turtle on its back, trying to rise against the weight of his armor. George sighed impatiently and extended his hand, pulling the man to his feet. He grabbed the knight's sword at the same time and shoved him off in the direction of the castle.

"He might have killed me," said George to the archangel.

"He knew better. Your quality is known, and your word holds its weight more than that of the man who calls himself king."

"If you say so,"

"My Lord?"

George turned to his right and standing in the place of the archangel was Richard Day and several of his captains.

"A spy came from the castle – the man we sent yestereve. The king is starting to panic, he says."

"Is he?" George said with a smirk. He nodded and wiped the blood and grime from his face, squinted in the sunlight to see the damage his catapults and other siege engines were doing to the walls and towers. The donjon, called the Great Tower, was pocked by missile strikes, but there was little more than that. A few places, such as the walls directly under arrow slits and windows, suffered enough damage that the interiors were visible. He'd start on the repairs tomorrow, God willing.

"Reload!" George shouted and watched as Richard, Geoffrey, and others loaded the baskets and adjusted counterweights, nodded as another round of missiles struck and shook the walls of Skelwith Castle.

✠

ELINOR MANAGED TO climb the stairs to the Lady Tower while George's army assaulted the castle. John's men had abandoned their pursuit of her and were now trying to defend the King. The guards were absent from the passage leading to Joanna's suite of rooms where Petronelle and Roger were being kept. She tried the door and found it latched, locked tight. Looking about, she found a small ax dropped by one of the guards when they probably fled and she used it to pound on the wood but all it did was make indentations and splinter the oak finish.

"Lady Petronelle!" Elinor shouted. "Earl Roger! Open the door if you can!"

Again, Elinor banged on the door as another of George's missiles hit the tower directly and she was thrown down the stairs. When she came to, the passageway and stairwell were foggy with the dust of crumbling stones. There were uneven ribbons of sunlight falling through the damaged walls. Several of the stairs were gone and left a chasm. Struggling to stand and hampered by her skirts, Elinor pushed against a stair to gain her footing and screamed in pain. Her right arm was covered in blood and her hand was useless.

"Elinor?"

She looked up and saw Petronelle and Roger on the other side of the chasm.

"How?" Elinor gasped, clutching her arm, "How did you get out?"

"What does it matter?" Roger said as he carefully picked his way down to her. "It looks as if the door was blown off."

"The King is going to kill me,"

"Take my hand, Elinor," Roger said, reaching towards her.

"I tried to kill him. He made a promise to me," Elinor started to sob.

"Elinor, never mind that. Take my hand."

"I tried to kill the King! How much better would England be if he was dead!"

"Elinor, stop talking and take my hand, damn you, Woman!"

Elinor started to laugh, and she tried to hug herself to stop trembling. "Do you know what? I came here to kill you, but it seems that George will do my job for me. I believe if there is one more strike, the tower will surely fall and we'll die. George will kill his beloved sister."

"Shut up, you cow!" Petronelle shouted. "Do what Roger says and take his hand! We have to get out of here!"

Roger leaned down across the intact and broken stairs across the chasm and managed to take Elinor's uninjured forearm. She struggled as he pulled her up and just when she was suspended over the gap, she wrestled free and hurled herself down into the hole that was spewing up ash and smoke from fires like the mouth of Hell.

CHAPTER 30

"THERE'S NOTHING WE can do. She's dead."

Petronelle nodded absently as she stared at the place where Elinor had been and then moved to one side to allow Roger a safe ascent. They stepped carefully over the stairs and broken flooring to a section of the passageway that looked sound.

"That leads to the Great Tower and donjon," Petronelle said, pointing down a debris-riddled stairway to the south. "I don't think anyone is guarding the stairs now, do you?"

"No, you don't lead. Let me. Just point me in the right direction," Roger said as he gently pulled her back.

"She's going to Hell if she isn't there already," Petronelle said as she lifted her skirts and followed her husband down, running her hand along the walls for stability and direction. Fortunately, George stopped the siege engines and now from the sound of it, the Ascalon army was in the castle. That would give Petronelle and Roger freedom. Who would be concerned about hostages when their own lives were at risk in battle?

They would need weapons, Petronelle thought as Roger led her towards the vaulted passage into the great hall behind the screen. The donjon had been spared and the King was using it for a staging area.

People and dogs were running, shouting, barking, in various stages of readiness for defense of the castle. The king, however, was nowhere to be seen.

"We should go to the prison cells. They're under the barracks, am I right?" Roger whispered as they paused in a dark corner behind the screen.

"This way," Petronelle answered. She pointed to a buttery and pantry that on any other day would have had the attention of the household, but today were all but deserted.

"Find the lady Petronelle! If she hasn't been killed by her bastard brother, bring her to me now!"

The king was shouting orders and the scrape and clang of metal on stone meant that soldiers were hurrying off. It was time to go and quickly. Grabbing Petronelle's hand, Roger sprinted to the buttery and stopped only to look for another way out of the room. There it was – a door leading out to the inner ward.

It was easy once outside. Chaos had taken over and no one paid any attention the couple hurrying away from the donjon and to the barracks, where, beneath the ground, the prison cells were ranged in catacombs. They were courtiers trying to escape like everyone else.

"Holy Mother, please let him be alive and unharmed!" Petronelle prayed aloud. Roger pulled a sword out of the clenched hand of a dead soldier lying with others outside the barracks.

"George's aim is good," Roger commented, looking around. It seemed the only buildings in the ward that were still whole were the chapel and great tower. The barracks was missing a wall and door.

Roger took Petronelle's hand and led her into the pile of rubble.

Iron bars destroyed and mangled by fire poked out like shoots of grass from debris spattered with blood and gore.

"I don't think he's alive!" Petronelle wailed after an hour's futile search.

Then she heard a sound, like a mewling kitten or a babe, that grew in age and strength. "Shh!" Petronelle gripped Roger's arm to prevent him from moving more stones. "Listen! It's coming from near the back; one of the back cells!"

They climbed up and over debris, over bodies, following the calls for help until they were right over it. Both Petronelle and Roger looked about frantically.

"Petra? Over here!"

It was Adam. Roger and Petronelle found him half-buried under what had been a cell wall. Together they managed to shift the broken stone and pull him out in a quarter-hour's time, hurrying when they heard the king's soldiers, voices in French and Languedoc.

"Thank the saints and angels!" Petronelle cried, embracing him. Adam groaned in pain and shook his head when Petronelle backed away, alarmed.

"My side hurts, but that is all," Adam said. He wiped the dirt from his face with a dirtier hand and squinted in the light coming down from cracks in the remaining walls and the entrance, looking to Roger.

"Where are George and Joanna? The babies? Are they safe?" he asked.

"All we know for certain is that George's siege engines are doing this harm," said Roger. "Can you stand? We're going to make our way to George's camp. I think it's beyond the curtain wall. Come on then,"

"He can't walk, Roger!" said Petronelle after they'd cleared the barracks and were making their way to the southern postern gate when Adam collapsed. They dragged him none-too-gently to the shelter and security of a fletcher's shed near one of the perimeter towers when a handful of soldiers entered the yard. "We can carry him if we had a length of sackcloth."

"No time for that, my darling girl," Roger grunted and he hefted the boy over a shoulder as if he was a sack full of apples.

Adam groaned in pain as he was jogged over the uneven ground and bounced on Roger's shoulder. Petronelle hitched her dress and surcote hems into her girdle to free her legs for running and ran alongside Roger. It was then she saw the blood soaking Adam's shirt and hose, and would have called out for Roger to stop a moment but for the royal knights and footmen barring any escape.

"My Lord, that is not your way out," said a captain. "Put him down and come by; we'll show you."

"You'll not harm the Countess?" Roger demanded. "She's got no quarrel with you. Neither does the boy."

He gently lowered Adam to the ground and waited for the soldiers' next move. One of them made ready to stop Petronelle as she knelt by Adam, but the captain held him back.

"We'll keep our word," the captain ordered. "One of you, help carry the boy."

"He won't be coming," Petronelle spoke up. "The boy is dead."

"One less hostage for the King," the captain said. He held out a hand for Petronelle and she took it, surprised by how gentle he was. He released her and then stepped back to bow, saying nothing as Roger took her hand. With another gesture, the captain pointed towards the donjon and great tower.

CHAPTER 31

JOHN'S SMILE WAS victorious and smug as he nodded to his captain and watched as Roger and Petronelle were pushed forward and then to their knees before him.

"Wasn't there a third conspirator?" John asked, looking around at his councilors.

"Dead of his wounds. Ascalon's killed him. What was it? You found him in one of the prison cells?" the captain said, looking to Roger and Petronelle for confirmation. Both nodded and Petronelle raised a hand to wipe the tears from her face. John now tut-tutted and came closer, bending down before her.

"Was he dear to you, my lady? This little boy of Gawthorp?"

She nodded.

"Well, my lady?"

"Yes, your grace. As good a squire and gentleman as they come."

"A squire, eh?" John looked at Roger. "Or your lady wife's lover."

"A good youth. That is all, though it be much," Petronelle said, glaring at him. "He was with Earl George during the trials at Eskeleth."

"So an enemy of the crown, then! He's lucky George did my work for me."

John lowered his head to make eye contact with Petronelle and when she refused, he raised her chin violently so that she cried out.

"Do you want to become Countess of Grasmere, Lady Petronelle? It is your right," John said.

"I've changed my mind. My brother is Earl. I am Lady of Osterle, Kenning, and Myrce. I am content with that."

"It is my will that you are Countess."

"I've changed my mind. I have no desire for it, sire."

"What if I were to tempt you?" John purred. "Just a little? Did you know that Elinor Longleate wanted the honor? I know she hated you. Wouldn't you want to spoil things for her?"

"She wouldn't care now, my lord. She's dead."

John looked up at his councilors and then at Petronelle, saying, "What happened? Does anyone know?"

"She fell to her death when the stairs gave way beneath her," Roger said.

"Or maybe she was pushed?" John started to laugh and then patted Petronelle's cheek. "Well, no matter; she was of use only for a little while. God, but she was tiresome in her demands."

"She was your only ally in Grasmere," Roger said.

"No; I have the lady Petronelle, don't I?"

"No."

John looked at Petronelle and saw that she now stared at him and the hatred was evident. He pushed himself to his feet. He then pushed the toe of his boot towards her knee.

"What was that?"

"I said, no."

"Come, come, my lady. You will have the benefit of the crown's protection and friendship. It is little to ask of you."

"I said, no!"

John kicked her now and if Roger hadn't tripped him, would have continued. The guards rushed to take both in their custody while John scrambled up from the floor and wiped the blood from his mouth. Now he struck Roger with a ham-handed fist and then Petronelle. He pummeled her while Roger was held back to watch, the guards and the king deaf to their screams.

"We will help you make up your mind, Petronelle Ascalon!" John growled and snapped his fingers at the guards, following as the prisoners were led away.

✠

"THERE'S SOMEONE ON the wall walk!"

George looked where Geoffrey pointed and first saw a purple cloak flapping in the wind, then the unmistakable glint of the gold of a crown. He gave the order to the engineers to stop and then ordered the archers and foot soldiers to stand down.

John stood alone with arms outstretched. Looking at him posturing in his fine clothes and crown, George thought, *how easy would it be to kill him.*

"Someone! A crossbow, a bow, anything!" George called to his men. Moments later an arbalest was at his feet and he was pulling on the windlass. Hefting the weapon to his shoulder, George positioned himself for a shot.

As much as he hated the man, as many hated him, regicide was not something he wanted to have as his legacy. The men around him relaxed when he dropped the weapon and turned to his captains. "Come with me," George said to Geoffrey and Richard, and they walked closer to Skelwith's battered walls.

"Your grace!" George shouted up. "I'm sorry to have ruined your stay in my castle, on my land."

"You have a beautiful home; or at least, you did. The weather's not been kind, either," John said. "I would have loved to hunt in your forests."

"There was no reason you couldn't; after all, I hold license to hunt and forest by your good grace, and that of your father and brother before you."

"True."

"Shall we talk of rights now?"

"By all means, Ascalon."

"I beg your leave to enter the castle, Your Grace, so that we may parley and come to terms. Shall we meet in the inner bailey on the donjon steps?" George asked, pointing at the drawbridge.

"Come unarmed, then."

"You'll give me safe conduct?"

"By all means!"

George waited a moment, staring up at the man grinning down at him. "Safe conduct, then."

"Didn't I just say?"

"Call off your guards."

John waved at the soldiers around him and when they retreated, George and his men walked slowly, cautiously, waiting as windlasses and pullies went to work creaking and groaning, over the lowered drawbridge and into the greater ward and then picking their way into the inner ward where the king's household knights formed two columns leading up to the donjon stairs. George acknowledged them with a nod and they in turned bowed as one. It was some time before the King appeared at the entrance to the donjon and George waited before the King invited him to approach. He knelt a safe distance away.

"I thank you for agreeing to discuss terms, Your Grace," George said when he was given leave to rise.

"New demands, I hope. Let's not quarrel over the rights to Merioneth for your countess. We've had this discussion. Your wife is a traitor, as are you."

"I am wrongfully accused of murder. I had nothing to do with your son Warennes' death."

"My son? What do you mean?" John laughed.

"Come, My Lord, Abbot Warennes was your mirror image, and he had your fine appreciation for books and learning."

"So? What's that to me?"

"The gossip of courtiers and churchmen doesn't offend you?"

"Why should it? I'm King. It should bother you."

"I had nothing to do with his death. I was wrongfully accused of murder."

"Liar!"

"There is a man whose allegiance is not to you but to a man who seeks only to enrich himself by stealing from the crown and those barons who are loyal to you. He is Eustace des Jumieges. Ask the Bishop of Eden; he'll say the same. Ah! Wait, no. He murdered the

Bishop and your godson. A dead bishop can't speak on my behalf."

"True. And who else could? The Archbishops of York or Canterbury?"

"Why wouldn't they? They owe nothing to the man or me, but they speak for righteousness and justice as men of God."

"There's the Bishop of Carlisle, too."

"My father would bring twenty knights and more if asked."

"My condolences, Earl George. The Bishop of Carlisle is dead. Killed by Eustace des Jumieges at my request."

The men around George watched him for a reaction. His face was ashen and he looked as if the wind had been knocked out of him. His right hand was shaking and it squeezed the pommel of his sword, open and close, open and close. He took a step back and Richard Day moved as if to catch him if he fell. George was steady on his feet, however, and did draw his sword to a chorus of gasps and protests. The sword was pitched into the soft earth.

"I never wanted a quarrel with you!" George shouted at John. "I came home seeking a quiet life. I was fortunate to find my wife and discovered how our lives intersect and how perfectly matched we are including our petitions to our King! You have given me no choice, my lord—"

"Bring twenty men to speak for you, Ascalon; it won't change my mind. There is too much evidence against you. You've conspired against the crown more than once on behalf of your wife, and I know that you went to Prince Dafydd to ask his help in taking Skelwith. Much good it did you!"

"All I have to do is give the order and the catapults and trebuchets will start their work again. This time they'll have a better aim." George said.

"My lord!" Geoffrey gasped.

"Think of what you're doing," Richard joined in.

George waved them off. "Your grace, my grandsires have always served England and they were honored by the King in their times for that service. We have always been loyal until the crown saw fit to take without cause and persecute those who have only done what was right for their vassals and freeholders."

"Do you mean me, George?" John hissed.

"I mean those who speak and act on your behalf. Like those who accused me of killing a man only to take what is mine and rob my son of his birthright, of taking my wife's dower rights and inheritance, and call it the King's will!"

"No man would dare,"

"They do."

"Then they will answer for their crimes."

"Do I have your word, my king, that you will absolve me of this heinous crime and give me leave to keep Skelwith and Grasmere? I want nothing more."

It was some time before John spoke. The banners snapping in the wind whipping up dark clouds that were gathering along the horizon, the ringing of metal on bridles as horses grew restless with the coming storm, the creak of the siege engines, trebuchets and catapults, as they were buffeted, filled the silence as George and his men waited.

"Give me leave to think on it, George," John said finally.

"Do I have your word?"

"I said, give me leave to think!"

"Let us call a truce, a cease-fire, while you think."

John offered what George knew might be a disingenuous smile.

"Done. You have it."

✠

FOR THE FIRST time in weeks, the countryside around Skelwith was silent, save for the creak and groan of carts en route to the market at Little Langdale, or the bells of sheep and cattle as they were herded to folds and barns, the gentle ringing of church bells that marked the hours. George shifted on his cot and watched the rain outside the tent and the shadows of the men walking back and forth between sputtering fires and their tents. His soldiers were growing impatient, for the King was taking his time coming to a decision.

He drifted off to sleep again as night fell and church bells started to call the faithful to the Vespers office. This was when he thought most about Joanna and the children. How old were they now? Six months, almost seven? They'd be sitting up and playing, trying to capture attention and smile. Leof, he remembered, looked the most like his mother, and Nara was like himself and Petronelle. What he'd give now to hold them and their mother, to live quietly at Skelwith.

He would have to wait for that, being at the King's mercy.

"Good evening, my lord,"

Richildis entered the tent and offered a curtsey, waited for an invitation to be seated. George sat up and waved towards the stool near the fire pit in the middle of the tent.

"Something to drink, Richildis?" he asked, pushing himself off the cot.

She took the cup offered and drank, then kicked aside the muddy hems of her cotte, surcote, and cloak to move her toes closer to the fire, so close that George worried that she would catch, but just as he was about to give a warning, Richildis moved back and looked up, smiling.

"Well, sir! I think you've done well in spite of everything."

"How so?"

"You've made the King think and worry. Other barons would have given up by now. And you with a sister and brother-in-law hostage, a wife and children safe in an abbey. But for how long?"

"I can always count on your unswerving loyalty and support, Richildis Wulfstandattir."

"Do you want someone to give you aye and nod no matter the consequence?" Richildis asked. "I think not. I've come to say that you know me and you do not know the King. He won't keep his word, no matter what it is."

"That's no surprise to me."

"He'll offer terms tomorrow morning. You must be ready. I will help you this once more. You will also know what you must do. It will come of a sudden."

Richildis put down her cup and as she rose, she smoothed the fabric of her cotte over her waist and hips. George watched uneasily as she approached and was alarmed when she rose on tiptoe and kissed him full on the mouth. Instinctively, he closed his eyes and tasted her lips – sweet, full, and warm. When he opened them, the Lady in Blue with the Crown of Silver stars was smiling at him.

"The peace of the Lord be always with you," she said, and backed slowly out of the tent until she was gone, a silvery-blue mist that was dispersed when Osprey entered with Richard and Geoffrey.

"George, we have a message from the King," Osprey greeted.

"What news?" George asked, his voice barely a whisper as his heart continued to beat faster and his breathing difficult.

"We meet at dusk in the great hall of the donjon."

CHAPTER 32

MISTS ROSE UP from the damp ground as George finished arming and left the command tent, his captains and grandfather joining as they came from their tents. An escort of six knights surrounded him as he walked the path cleared for them by soldiers the night before. Broken siege engines and the detritus of war piled up on either side of the path, the last of the sun shining in puddles that reflected the white, puffy clouds that replaced the heavy storm clouds of yesterday and the image disturbed by boots. George entered the great hall alone; his men ordered to stand down and wait without. With heart pounding and a sweat starting on his face and hands, he walked toward the screen where his chair of state stood on its plinth. His approached scared a cat that hissed and jumped from the feasting table crowded with maps and the remnants of a meal and a war council. George stopped, waiting for the echo of his footsteps to die before he called out, "John! I am here! You promised me safe conduct! I'm waiting!"

By the time those echoes faded John appeared from behind the screen.

"What a strange man you are, George Ascalon," the King greeted, flicking his hand at them to rise. "You're not like my other barons. You keep your word."

"God give you peace this day, your grace," George said. "May I be able to say the same of you when our parley is ended."

"What? That I am not like your other Kings?" John laughed.

"I have but one King - that which resides at the right hand of God in the Kingdom of Heaven."

"And what am I?"

"A poor substitute for Him, but one I am compelled to honor nevertheless."

"You say well, George; politic enough to save your neck."

"I am here. What is your decision?"

"I've forgotten why it is we've risen so early from our beds," John replied in exasperation.

"I asked for your clemency and the titles, rights, and lands given to me by my grandsires; left to me by my father, who until late was Bishop of Carlisle at your request."

"That."

John shifted impatiently and tapped his fingers on the arm of George's throne, staring off into the distance, and then looking around as if surprised to find himself where he was. Finally he threw up his hands.

"Earl George, you've put me in a difficult place. There's nothing more I'd rather do than give you what you want, but if I do that, barons who are more ambitious than you and with greater affinities will start making demands. We are at an impasse."

"I have no choice then. Either meet me in battle, or I will start the trebuchets and catapults," George answered. His voice was calm but he clenched his fists to hold off the anger and trembling.

"If you keep pounding away at the castle you'll leave me with nothing, George."

"It is my castle!" George shouted. "It is my land, my title!"

"I tell you what," John said, and snapped his fingers to someone behind him. "Agree to my terms, and we shall be generous."

George choked on the scream in his throat and thought he'd be sick when Petronelle and Maud were brought into the hall.

From their stance and ragged appearance it was apparent they'd both been abused. His sister's dress was in shreds and stained with blood at the waist and below; Maud was no better, though she held her chin high and looked as dignified as one could with eyes nearly swollen shut from a beating and her lips and cheeks swollen and bleeding. Petronelle kept her head down. Visible were patches on her scalp where she'd been pulled by the hair and beaten. She looked worse than her mother, her face almost unrecognizable.

Maud raised her head just a little, or as much as she was able and George saw an imploring, yet disappointed gaze from one moment to the next. Then he remembered.

The letter. *She had sent him a letter.*

And he had ignored it.

George now met her gaze and felt the tears sting. She tried to nod and looked away. She understood.

"The ladies of Grasmere were not as cooperative as you, Earl George," John said.

"Take me!" George screamed at John. "Leave them alone!" Two of John's guards took George and held him back, pinioning his arms.

"Good to know you've come to your senses," John said. "But on second thought, if you're not Earl of Grasmere, that would mean your sister is the Countess, and who's to say she wouldn't rebel? I couldn't have that."

The King snapped his fingers and a man came from the shadows. One at a time he tossed the heads of Adam and Roger at George so that each rolled to a halt at his feet. Roger's dead, clouded, eyes stared back at him. Adam's face was frozen for all time in agony and fear. He thought first of Lady Middleton now left with a single boy at home. How long before John came for him?

And Roger. His friend and companion at arms. His kinsman now. George looked to Petronelle, who still kept her head down, blood dripping from her wounds to the pavement. He wondered if she could even see what had been done to her lover and husband. Had she watched the execution? This thought, and the horrific vision of what she and Maud suffered now brought George to the edge.

"Not even William the Bastard was as cruel a monster," George growled at John. "What will you do when there is nothing and no one left on this island, John Lackland? You'll be content, no doubt, living in an empty manor or castle with your books. All you'll have left is your books. Who will be left to govern over? To till the land and strike iron on the forge? Who will protect you, John Lackland? The people will go to ground in the greenwood and plot their revenge and happily watch you drawn and quartered when you're caught off guard. A king bleeds and can suffer like any other man!"

Now he lunged at John but was held back. The King smiled, assured that his actions had the effect he wanted; George's foolhardy threats and rage had no effect on John, however, and now he raised a hand and gestured with his fingers in a graceful movement better suited for a court feast.

The henchman now came forward and stood behind the women. George felt the grip tighten on his arms and one of the guards grabbed his head and turned it forwards. When the glint of a knife showed in the dim light, George tried to look away but he was forced to watch as the henchman quickly, quietly, and ruthless efficiency, sliced a dagger across each of the ladies' throats and they slumped, then toppled forward, like half-full sacks of grain where they stood. They were soon encircled by pools of blood that crept out like tentacles. George fought against his captors and continued to threaten and scream invectives, while John stood a safe distance away, arms folded across his chest and smiling. Finally John stepped from the plinth and approached George by an arm's length.

"Be quiet now and leave. Continue, and I can go to Abbey next," John said. He glanced at the guards. "Take him outside beyond the walls. Do him no harm; I'm sure he's had enough for one day. One can't be too sure about tomorrow, though." As soon as George was gone, John sat in the Grasmere throne behind him and sighed contently. A servant came forward with a tray of wafers and wine.

"A good day's work," John said to the boy.

✠

THE DRAWBRIDGE SHUDDERED and shook as the windlasses stopped their grinding. George glanced behind him and saw a sliver of light from the edge of the bridge planks. Soldiers lighting the lamps. He shook his head, thinking, how often does one light the candles and torches in a tomb?

As he retraced his steps to the command tent in camp, the men stood silently, waiting. Geoffrey, Richard, and Osprey met him at the river bank that threaded its way into the wood.

Without greeting or preamble, George said quietly, "My sister, her mother, her husband and young Adam are all dead. My father, too, is dead. Executed by the King or on his orders. This is what we expected, wasn't it?" He turned to Osprey, who was trying to control anger and grief and embraced him tightly, saying, "Our dead will have honorable burials and then we will attack," he said. "It's what the King expects."

"God save you, Earl George of Grasmere!"

"Long life and favor be yours!"

"May the Blessed Mother be with you and your countess! Your children!"

"We will avenge them! We will stand with you!"

The men's shouts followed George as he walked back to the command tent. Richildis was waiting outside and she fell to her knees as he approached.

"They're all dead," George said before she asked.

"It should not have happened, my Lord!" she whispered. She was pale and trembling. He took her aside, saying, "Whatever you must do, Lady, do it, and quickly."

"I will. It should not have happened."

"Yes, you said,"

For a moment George forgot his grief and remembered a moment with Joanna not long after they met. He wanted to grab a horse and ride to Grasmere to the Abbey where he prayed Joanna and the children and her women were safe and in the protection of the Benedictine community.

"Earl George?"

Richildis was looking at him, concerned. He shook his head and entered the tent.

The squires jumped to their feet and hastened to bring wine and food, which George rejected silently, waving them away. Once alone, George fell to his knees and wept.

"No good, no use! No good," he sobbed repeatedly.

He was oblivious to his surroundings. Outside clouds gathered and the wind picked up, ominous signs of a new storm ready to break. His army was retreating back into the forest and the rattle and creak of the siege engines being wheeled to cover, the shouts and orders, were drowned by his own screams as he vented a terrible grief.

"Not since that night in Constantinople has your heart been so rent,"

"Leave me, Grandfather!"

"George, do you think their memories will be served by your self-pity?"

"Leave me!"

"Stand and be a man. Your fight is far from over. Come now, stand!"

"I said, leave me!"

"You knew the moment you camped in the forest that this would happen. What else would John Lackland do? Now prove yourself a better man than the King of England. There is still hope!"

"Get out!"

He curled himself into a ball and lay on the straw mat of his tent, shivering from both the cold and raw emotion. The new footsteps and the drag of the tent flap told him his servants found the courage to return. George felt the warmth of a blanket across his shoulders and slowly his body relaxed, and he started to give way to sleep his body and mind craved. The watery waves of light that splashed across his plane of vision each evening before he fell to sleep crept up. It was golden light, but not that which one would use to find their way in darkness. His old nurse told him it was a plague of the eyes that could not be cured save by herbs found in the mountains of Wales and by prayer. As he had done in childhood and during the long journey to and from the Levant when he took Crusade, he found the words to the *Trisagion*, an ancient prayer from the East: Ἅγιε Θεέ, Ἅγιε καὶ Παντοδύναμε, Ἅγιε Ἀθάνατε, λυπήσου μας.

*Agie Thee, Agie kai Pantodyname, Agie Athanate,
lypēsou mas.*

Holy God,
Holy and Mighty,
Holy Immortal One,
Have mercy upon us.

The words fell from his lips with the rhythm of his
heartbeat until at last he knew he had slipped into the
strange realm of dreams.

The tantalizing scent of exotic spices made him
look west on the quay of Constantinople where he
found himself.

It was a quiet morning; surely market day by the
number of people coming and going and the bright
canopies over booths and stalls blocking out an
already burning sun. A little boy beckoned to him
from a fruitmonger's stall. He held out a pomegranate
half, the bitter ivory skin bleeding ruby-colored juice.

"*Geuse! Den echeis dokimasei kati tetoio, engleze!*
Taste! You've tasted nothing like this, Englishman!"

George obliged the boy and bit into the fruit.
They both laughed as the juice ran down George's
chin and drops fell on the linen shirt beneath his
open robe.

"The fruit of the tree of knowledge," said a richly-
dressed gentleman in silks and embroideries matching
the color of the fruit. He had sidled up and ran his
fingers over the pomegranates, lovingly caressed them
as if they were a lover's breasts. Indeed, George
watched in fascination when the globes began to glow
with flickering candle flames and pulsate like living
hearts.

The gentleman cut another pomegranate and pressed the half into George's hand. It was scorching, and it seared George's skin, but stayed his hand and kept the gentleman's gaze. "Prove victorious, George Ascalon of Grasmere, and you will have favor. Surely there is no one on earth so righteous, even you, as to do good without ever sinning," said the man and he bowed away, leaving the Ascalon cross in George's hand.

Now, as in other times and dreams, the world around him began to swirl like mist and George felt himself floating with angels. They were moving towards a column of fire that spun with different shapes and colors of flame. As George approached, he panicked and started to fall. The angels surrounding him did nothing to help and he knew he was going to die in the fires of Hell, for that was certainly what this was before him.

Then he woke screaming and soaked with sweat and tears.

"Better now, George?"

George dragged a sleeve across his eyes and nodded, used the bench beside the cot to pull himself to his feet. He turned, expecting to find Osprey behind him and was face to face with the Archangel. With him was the Lady and two gentlemen in scarlet and white robes of Byzantine nobility, their garments encrusted with gold thread and polished jewels in the shape of Greek crosses. All four bowed in greeting.

"Revenge is the Lord's," said one of the gentlemen. "Ask, and you will have it."

"God does not hate; man hates!" George hissed.

"Prove it."

His sword Ascalon was presented by one of the men. George was afraid to take it, for the blade glowed warmly with saffron, then rose, then gold light. The crossguard and pommel were repaired, and the words etched into the fuller were legible and glowed sapphire:

> Η νύχτα είναι μακριά, η μέρα πλησιάζει. Ας αφήσουμε στη συνέχεια τα έργα του σκότους και να θέσει στην πανοπλία του φωτός

"The night is far gone; the day is near. Let us then lay aside the works of darkness and put on the armor of light; let us live honorably as in the day," the Archangel read as he ran a finger over the letters. He then turned to George and smiled. "You of all men know that to claim victory does not always mean death, but a new life. Take the sword."

George took the sword that had been his since the age of sixteen, had seen battle and now felt as if it had been molded to his hand and made for him and not his father.

Ascalon was his.

CHAPTER 33

"WHAT IN GOD'S holy name is *that???*"

John, seated at dinner with his men and ladies of the court, grabbed the silver-wrought goblet in front of his trencher to keep it from tumbling and spilling wine into the roasted boar and gravy before him. Again, the donjon shook, and torches flickered in their sconces.

"Someone, you!" John snapped at a knight standing behind him. "Go and see what it is!"

The man bowed and hurried away, returning moments later with several of the garrison, who were bloodied and dusty as if they'd been in battle.

"Ascalon is attacking again, my lord!" the knight said breathlessly as he dropped to a knee.

"What?" John squealed. "It's past eight and dark as midnight out!"

"He started just as the bells rang for Vespers," one of the garrison said.

"Is there some importance in that?" John sneered.

"It's said Ascalon is a very pious man,"

The crash and pounding of missiles against the donjon walls and towers drowned the exclamations of fear and anger from John's guests. John threw down his towel and gestured to his captains, who followed him out. The guests were left to fend for themselves and they ran in every direction, some shrieking when another bombast or missile struck and shook the castle buildings like an earthquake.

"Your grace, I wouldn't go up there," warned one of the captains as John made for the inner ward's wall walk.

"Do you think that fool is stupid enough to murder his king?" John asked, laughing nervously.

No one bothered to reply.

Outside the night was dark save the pots of fire and the torches lighting the Ascalon camp. From where John had a clear view of George's soldiers as they scurried back and forth carrying out orders, loaded the trebuchets and catapults, wound windlasses on crossbows and arbalests, knocked arrows to bows and Welsh longbows.

"I heard rumors that Ascalon went mad in Constantinople," one captain murmured to another, avoiding the King, who turned, interested.

"He's destroying his own castle; not hard to cipher the truth of that," said John, and then, "Lights! Let Ascalon know I'm here."

As soon as John was surrounded by torchbearers, shouts went up from the army below and the bombardment paused.

John summoned a herald, who, after consultation with the King, grabbed a white towel one of the captains still had from the banquet table and waved it.

"Ascalon!" the herald shouted. "Why do you destroy all you have left? The King will grant you clemency if you cease your warfare and retreat."

Moments later, George's herald came into the light, carrying his own white flag. "And where would the Earl of Grasmere retreat?" he asked.

"He's no longer the Earl of Grasmere!" John screamed, rushing at the broken wall of the inner ward.

"He is; by right of name and birth, as well you know! Your father, the great King Henry, and his forebearers, all confirmed this! Even to the time of William of Normandy!"

"They are dead and I am not. I am king!" John screamed back. "What I say is what is law. Ascalon, you'll be fortunate to leave Cumbria with your skin because if I catch you, I'll take every inch from your body and when I'm done, I'll start on your wife!"

Down in the camp, George observed this parley quietly. The Ascalon herald glanced at him and he nodded, stepping back into the shadows to stand with Osprey and Richildis.

"My king!" the herald shouted. "It is you who must retreat. Go back to London. Leave the north of England. You have barons to hold it for you. You have their loyalty. Ascalon only wants what is Ascalon's right: Grasmere. Grant this, and he will live in quiet and give you hospitality when next you visit Cumbria."

There was a pause while John conferred with councilors who had joined him on the wall walk. Their shadows danced against the stones of the castle as the torch flames began to waver and flicker in a wind starting up.

"What of Merioneth? What of your illegal marriage to the heiress Joanna ferch Rhodri? Renounce her and you shall have all that you want. Joanna will be returned to her kinsmen in Gwynedd or Merioneth or whatever cave the Welsh princes hide in now."

"No!" George shouted back.

That was all. He summoned the herald back into the command tent and gave the army the order to fall back away from the castle walls. Siege engines were pushed away.

The quiet that followed was shattered by the laughter and exclamations of the King's men when they realized they had won.

"Now is the time," George said to Richildis.

From around his neck, George took the Ascalon Cross and cupped it in his hands. A priest now joined them and together Richildis and the priest whispered:

> O Lord God, the strength of my salvation,
> you have covered my head in the day of battle.
> "Do not grant the desires of the wicked, O
> Lord, nor let their evil plans prosper . . .
> surely, the righteous will give thanks to your
> Name, and the upright shall continue in your
> sight.

Now George clasped their hands in his and said, "Lord God, give me the joy of your saving help again and sustain me with your bountiful Spirit! Glory to the Father, and to the Son, and to the Holy Spirit: as it was in the beginning, is now, and will be forever. Amen!"

The cross was held up and started to glow, flames dancing within it. Suddenly a ray of golden light shot out like a quarrel from a crossbow and there were three angels surrounding it. The light struck one of John's captains and the man fell. John and the others around him jumped back, waiting, but the man wasn't dead. He had been turned to stone. The three angels circled the castle ramparts and the fields and meadows below as one by one the King's men were struck until only John was left. His army had been turned to blocks of stone, scattered throughout the environs.

Finally, the walls of the castle shook and started to crumble.

"Retreat!" John screamed at Eustace, who followed the King into the castle donjon.

"Did you see them? Did you see?" John cried as he paced the great hall. "How in God's name did Ascalon make this magic and trickery?"

"My lord, we have to go. We have to go now!" Eustace said.

"Go straight to Grasmere to the Abbey," John ordered. I'll meet you there."

The Ascalon army waited at the perimeter of the castle, certain that the King would eventually leave. The rays of light continued to bombard the walls and the angels flew courses around it, singing *alleluias* and sounding trumpets.

Standing beside George, Richildis was quiet and watched the spectacle. The soldiers and knights were kneeling and praying and some wept. She touched George's arm to get his attention and he started, surprised.

"Lady, you have kept your word," George said, smiling, and kissed her hand.

"Do you think, Earl George, that there will be a room for me in the house of God? Jesus of Nazareth said as much."

"I have no doubt of that."

"Good. It is done well. It is how I had hoped," Richildis said and stepped away from him, drawing up her hood so that for a moment George remembered the lady in the common room of the inn. His recounting of that meeting was on his lips when Richildis offered a radiant smile as a mist enveloped her. When it cleared, she had taken on the appearance of The Lady with the Crown of Stars. Still smiling, she nodded farewell and faded into another mist.

"Once more I will help you. Fear not!" she whispered.

She was gone.

"My lord! My lord, you must come now!"

One of George's scouts was shouting and pointing. "He's fled—he's all that's left save Eustace des Jumieges and his men. They're riding to Grasmere!" the scout gasped in broken sentences.

Orders now spread for the army to break camp as quickly as possible and follow George to Grasmere.

✠

THE MARKET WAS burning, as were the church and guild hall. Shops and houses were looted and the goods not taken strewn every which way to soak up blood and gore on the ground. The townspeople not slaughtered by Eustace's men made their way to the abbey and pounded on the gates, demanding sanctuary. Inside in the forecourt, brothers leaned all their weight against the oak and iron gates and shouted at one another to stand fast. There were only so many the abbey could house. At least a hundred townspeople had managed to get in and they were now sitting in groups in the nave of the abbey church, doing their best to stay calm, and calm those who were frightened or hysterical. Brothers of the community and women ministered to the wounded and dying set on pallets and cloaks in front of the altar.

Joanna came from the Abbot's Lodging when she heard the bells, screaming, and shouts, and did her best to hide anxiety when she saw George's vassals and the leading citizens of Grasmere huddled in the choir and nave looking dazed and fearful. These were the nobility of Cumbria who always showed themselves assured and proud and now they were frightened, wounded, and no different from the dairymaids, bakers and blacksmiths they sat with, waiting for the end. Most tried to stand and offer respect with a bow or a nod of the head, as Joanna walked past but she bade them stay where they were and crossed the nave to where the Prior knelt over a gravely wounded lady and was giving instructions to a monk trying to administer a posset to ease her pain.

"My lady!" the Prior exclaimed when he saw Joanna and scrambled to his feet.

"Nay, Prior. I would not take you from your holy work," she said.

"You're not safe here, Lady Joanna. The King's army—"

"Yes, I know."

Their conversation was interrupted by the explosion at the doors into the cloisters and the charge of soldiers into the nave. Brothers and citizens trying to stop their entrance were cut down. One of Eustace's captains followed his butchers in and seemed to pause for affect at the nave crossing, looking about to make sure all saw him and then slowly he raised a gloved hand and pointed at Joanna.

"Run, my lady!"

"Get you away!"

"Stop her!" the captain shouted when more people encouraged her and blocked his way. Joanna dodged around people to escape through the sacristy and then out into the infirmary gardens. The captain was on her heels. Joanna hitched up her skirts and jumped over the cloister parapet and tramped through patches of rosemary, lavender and wort, running through the physic's shed and knocking down pots and pans, jars of herbs and a cauldron still bubbling with a fragrant posset to avoid him. The brothers were quick to follow, thinking her a mischief maker and their joining the chase only helped Joanna. She managed to reach the night stairs only to have the captain tug at her skirts to trip her up. Joanna grabbed on to the rope along the wall for support and fought against him. The more he tugged at the heavy fabrics the more she fought, when he twisted the skirt into a rope and thought to make her fall, Joanna was within distance to strike. She kicked him in the chest and the surprise, if not the force, knocked him down the stairs head first. The sword he'd been carrying fell nearby and Joanna grabbed it. She paused only a second to make sure he was unconscious or dead. He didn't move; it was one or the other.

"Thanks be to Saint Michael!" she whispered as she raced through an ambulatory outside the church and into the secret staircase, into the Abbot's Lodgings.

The women screamed when Joanna appeared suddenly and slammed the door shut and barred it.

"It's as bad as you could imagine," Joanna gasped, leaning on the door to catch her breath.

"Where do we go?" Margaret asked.

"We make our way to George's camp if we can," Joanna said to Margaret.

"But how? The town is sacked and it won't be long before they come to the abbey!"

"Give me leave to think a moment," Joanna said and gave her a quick hug.

"I beg you, Lady, let's not stay here longer than we have to!" Margaret replied.

"You have it." Joanna went to the window and peered out, keeping out of view. "George must have prevailed against the King for this insult to Grasmere. Yes, we should go. It would be foolish to stay here and wait for George."

"We can strap the babes to our backs and leave everything else here," Anna the Nurse spoke up.

"Yes; that way we'll travel more quickly," Joanna answered and froze when she heard a death scream. Outside the noise of the pillaging and rape in Grasmere grew louder and more violent. Would there be a chance at all to escape? And if so, how would they leave?

"Lady Joanna!" Miriyam called. She was at the window and was gesturing excitedly. Joanna joined her and looked down to where the girl was pointing. She saw brothers and townspeople run to and fro, looking for places to hide from the army they were sure was coming. Thus far the Abbey had been spared, not considering the captain and his men. None of the other soldiers in Eustace's guard followed them. Looking down at the walled entrance, she saw why. The three mysterious guards had returned and held aloft magnificent lanterns that lit the yard with pale silver light that encircled the entire building and the immediate environs. No one went near them. In fact, it was as if something protected the house, for whenever someone approached, they backed away, crossing themselves, and then ran for their lives.

"Get the children," Joanna said. "Now is the time to leave."

✠

ONE OF THE knights walked before Joanna and the other two walked behind with Margaret, Rhosyn, Anna, and Miriyam before them. They held their lanterns high and despite the pandemonium gripping the abbey and town, the party passed unmolested from the abbey to the street.

The journey through Grasmere, Joanna surmised as she clutched the captain's sword, would be treacherous, she was certain of that. As they walked through the ruined market square and past several looted houses and shops, the knights began to chant.

Veni, Sancte Spiritus,
et emitte caelitus
lucis tuae radium.
Veni, pater pauperum,
veni, dator munerum,
veni, lumen cordium.
Consolator optime,
dulcis hospes animae,
dulce refrigerium.

People fell away and to their knees, crossing themselves as if Joanna's party was a procession on a holy day. They passed through the town and it wasn't until they reached the mere that horsemen approached. Riding at the fore was Eustace. He yanked on the reins and drew his sword, raising it as the first knight continued to walk solemnly and chant the prayer.

"By order of the King, you are commanded to stay where you are!" Eustace shouted over their chanting, but as he shouted the chanting increased in volume. Now Joanna and the women joined the knights in their song.

"You will stop!" Eustace screamed; "You are commanded to stop! By order of the King!"

Eustace bounded out of the saddle and landed, crouched in place like a cat, then he ran at the knight who just as suddenly threw off his cloak and exposed the mighty wings of an archangel shimmering ivory, pink, blue and gold in the moon and lamplight. Eustace gawked at it and raised his sword nevertheless. His thrust was parried and before he could attack, the other guards also threw off their cloaks and stood ready for battle. Joanna stepped back several paces, shaking with fear, and huddled with her women, crouching low to protect the children who were now wailing.

Eustace's men dismounted and came at the angels screaming oaths and one at a time they were thrown into the air and were vaporized, each dissolving into a mist that floated away. Eustace, however, was spared, continued to fight and it seemed to Joanna that the archangel was letting him take the advantage for they fought equally, and neither was losing stamina as blows rang, the swords meeting sounding like church bells calling the hour. Indeed, the people Grasmere came from hiding to watch the spectacle; in the midst of the battle were Joanna, her women, and children, protected by a pale blue light.

Some of the spectators fell to their knees and crossed themselves, some wept, as the girl called Miriyam was suddenly enclosed in saffron light. The mesmerizing color faded and there were screams as she rose from the belly of a dragon that had appeared. The girl smiled sweetly as she slowly transformed into a lady wearing a blue gown, mantle, and a crown of stars, her hands resting on Joanna's shoulders.

The ground began to shake and the rumbling of thunder distracted the spectators. It was no heavenly army or stratagem, however, but the approach of George Ascalon and his vanguard.

Eustace, distracted by the cheering of the townspeople, looked to where everyone was pointing – the torchlight and shadowed men and horses as they rode forward - and when he looked back, Joanna struck.

As she thrust her sword into his chest with all her might, the archangels dissolved into golden, silver, and sapphire mists. She screamed as she struggled to remove the sword and then threw it into the mere. Eustace received a deadly blow to the chest. He swayed drunkenly and then fell, first to his knees and then face forward into the mere. The splash of the body hitting the water sent rings out that rippled on the shore followed by a ribbon of blood to stain the mud and dissipated. While spectators gaped incredulously first at Joanna and then the body bobbing gently in the mere, John, the King of England, escaped their notice as he galloped through Grasmere and took the road south.

Heaving for breath, Joanna looked up at the lady standing before them. "I did think I knew you!" she said. "So I did! Miriyam, you are a holy woman."

"I am who I am," the lady answered.

"Thank you!"

"Accept this kiss of peace, and know that all will be well, Joanna Ascalon!"

Joanna received her benediction and then turned when she heard her name. George had broken away from his vanguard and dismounted and strode towards her.

"My lady wife!" he called. "Once again you cheat me out of a battle."

"I assure you, George, that contest was mine, for I know that God owed me revenge. Don't you think?"

"Well fought," he answered as he embraced Joanna and drew her even closer for a kiss.

The children started to fret and George gathered both into his arms. He walked with Joanna to the edge of the crowd, which cheered and started chanting his name and Joanna's. Summoning for quiet he said, "My friends, you've seen what I've done to my own land and castle. For that, I ask your pardon and God's. What has happened here cannot be undone, but I offer you this: follow me to Eskeleth where we will build a new home and new land free of King John's tyranny. Wulfstan of Eskeleth has promised me the lordship or Arkengarthdale in return for the favor I did him in vanquishing darkness and evil, and I cannot do other than accept. I do it in gratitude for the help his daughter gave us on the field and to honor her, for she turned to God and Christ and she, I know, has been received into their loving arms for her sacrifice. What do you say?"

Again, the crowd chanted their names, George and

Joanna, and continued until the sun came up.

✠

"MY LORD! They come!"

Wulfstan and looked out at the seemingly endless line of people, horses, and wagons on the southern road. He looked for the banners of his son and smiled broadly when he saw them in the middle of the pilgrims. Gone were the symbols of his ancestors. The new banners proclaimed 'ASCALON' in gold and jewels with George and Joanna standing beneath an apple tree clasping hands, the ancient cross of

Ascalon and the sword on either side of them. As they approached, the people sang the hymn, *Vene Spiritu Sanctu.* They stopped at the gates and parted as George and Joanna rode forward. The captain of sentries came from the gatehouse and bowed in greeting.

"Welcome, my lord Ascalon," he said.

"Grasmere asks your hospitality," said George, gesturing behind him.

"You have it!" Wulfstan called down from the wall.

Looking up, George broke into a great smile and waited for Wulfstan to come down. The crowd burst into applause and cheering when George and Wulfstan embraced and George knelt before him.

"I present to you your high and mighty lord of Eskeleth and Arkengarthdale, George Ascalon!" Wulfstan proclaimed.

More cheers and shouts went up, this time from the people of Eskeleth who lined the streets of the town all the way to the Golden Tower. As soon as the last pilgrim from Grasmere passed through the gates, they were closed and, a rainbow of many colors wrapped itself around Arkengarthdale. If one were to look up on the roof of the great tower, three great archangels circled the castle throughout the rest of the day and just as the sun set and made the walls of the tower shimmer gold, pink, and pale blue, they lighted on the stones, and gradually turned to the finest marble while the Lady in Blue with the Crown of Stars sang a hymn. As soon as the last rays of light faded, she disappeared into the heavens.

From their vantage points, the archangels looked out over the vale, each holding a sword, each protecting the realm of Ascalon and her people.

THE END

ACKNOWLEDGMENTS

Once again I've written a story during a bleak moment in my life, a story that tells of faith lost and regained.

I couldn't very well end *Armor of Light* as I'd written it; leave George riding off and Joanna wondering what would happen.

Now you know what happened to the puppy.

And Elinor.

And Richildis.

My thanks to Joyce and Damby Editorial Services for the editing, encouragement, and proofreading. Special thanks to Jason Brown, my beta reader, who read *Armor of Light* and asked to read the draft of *Ascalon*. He gave me some wonderful ideas, as did Joyce and I incorporated their suggestions into the final draft.

To all who waited patiently over the past four years for this book, which had a lot of starts and stops, and stalls, thank you.

ABOUT THE AUTHOR

ELLEN L. EKSTROM is a native of the San Francisco Bay Area and was educated locally. She holds a bachelor's degree in theological studies and her area of concentration is Christian Mythos, also known as church history, with a sub-specialty in Christian Social Ethics, for both of which she took honors in seminary. Ellen has been fascinated by all things medieval since childhood and is now studying Late Anglo-Saxon England.

The genres Ellen prefers are fantasy/historical and literary fiction. Occasionally she delves into matters of the modern heart. Just as a painter has many subjects to bring to a canvas, Ellen believes that there are many stories to tell and to limit oneself to a niche isn't the way she lives or writes.

Ms. Ekstrom's growing library of work includes *The Legacy, Armor of Light, What She Wished For...a Cautionary Tale (formerly titled A Knight on Horseback),* The *Midwinter Sonata* Series, which includes the companion novels *Tallis' Third Tune* and *Scarborough,* the first of the *Cheshire Tales, St. Edmund Wood* and the faery tale, *The Shopgirl of Flowergate.*

Coming soon: the third book in the *Midwinter Sonata* series, *The Shambles; Swannsaeld,* a story set in England on the eve of the Battle of Hastings, and *The Sometime Queen,* the second of the *Cheshire Tales,* set in the fictional village of Knowstone.

www.ingramcontent.com/pod-product-compliance
Lightning Source LLC
Chambersburg PA
CBHW031419240626
47154CB00001B/113